SPARK

USA Today and International Bestselling Author

Lauren Rowe

Published by SoCoRo Publishing

Cover design Shannon Passmore of **Shanoff Designs**

To Chloe.

Thank you for your beautiful heart, genius mind, endless love, and sharp wit. Thank you for being an incredible storyteller in your own right. You amaze me. Thank you, thank you, for being the first person to read this book. I love you more than words could possibly say. As your mother, it's only right and undeniable: I love you more.

1

KENDRICK

Chicago
Twelve years ago

"Let's make a pact about this Rufus guy," my big brother, Kai, says from across the basement. As he speaks, he's bent over, meticulously hooking up an amp, which means Savage and I are free to exchange a look.

I didn't lie to my brother for kicks, by the way. I just knew telling him the keyboardist coming to audition for our fledgling band any minute now is a dude who plays linebacker for my new school's football team was the only way he'd keep an open mind.

After Kai's band at his hipster music college downtown fell apart following his breakup with the lead singer, he's now got it stuck in his head *our* band isn't going to have any girls in it, which I personally think is stupid. Kai is three years older than Savage and me and in his first year of music school, though, so the band is kind of his baby at the moment. At least, according to Kai. If you ask me, with Savage being front and center and so fucking talented and charismatic—there's no doubt he could become a superstar on his own, unlike Kai or me—I personally feel like Savage, not Kai, should call the shots. At least, as to whether a female keyboardist should be allowed to audition for us tonight.

Granted, Savage couldn't run a band if his life depended on it. He's flighty. Never on time. And when he finally makes it to wherever he's going, he's easily distracted and totally lacking in motivation, despite his insane, God-given star quality. But still, the fact remains I'm irritated my big brother thinks he can act like a dictator, and I know Savage feels the same way. Hence, me lying to Kai about the identity of the keyboardist coming to audition for us tonight. Not for Kai. For us.

"I'm just saying," Kai replies, his attention still focused on the cords and wires he's connecting for our imminent jam session with Rufus, "we should all agree this dude has to be a perfect fit—and I'm talking musically and personality-wise— or else he's a no-go. We don't need a keyboardist. I know you want one, Savage—"

"So do I."

"—but why set ourselves up to split the money four ways, instead of three, if—"

"What money, Kai?" I blurt, cracking up at my brother's ridiculousness, while Savage's chuckles shake the couch cushion next to me. Fugitive Summer, as we've recently decided to call ourselves, hasn't played anywhere but this dank basement in our apartment building. We haven't even posted any of our rough demos online, either. And yet, some- how, Kai's utterly convinced that with Adrian Savage as the face and voice of our band, we're headed for worldwide fame and fortune.

It's real pie-in-the-sky stuff, regardless. But even more so because we all know I'll drop the band like a hot potato when I get the football scholarship I'm gunning for. Come to think of it, though, Kai probably thinks he'll easily replace me on drums, once I've handled my best friend for him and gotten him invested in the band. And you know what? He's probably right about that.

Kai straightens up from the work he's been doing. "The gigs will pour in once we get the right musicians in place and dial in our sound. And from there, the money will come. That's why we have to do everything right at the beginning: because soon we're going to have more gigs and money than we know what to do with."

Savage is the one to crack up first this time. "No disrespect, man, but we sound like every other garage band." That's why he keeps pushing for a keyboardist—so we can fill out our sound with all kinds of cool stuff that can't be created on the classic combo of guitar-bass-drums.

"I can do amazing things on Pro Tools," Kai insists.

"Yeah, for the recordings," Savage shoots back. "But you're the one who keeps saying we have to be able to play our songs live because nobody buys music anymore and streaming doesn't pay shit."

"You do say that a lot," I agree.

"Stop kissing his ass, Kendrick," Kai grits out, glaring at me with dark, intense eyes. Kai takes after our late father with his brown hair and eyes, while I take after our mother with sandy hair and light eyes. It's why nobody thinks we're brothers when they first meet us. Not to mention, because Kai's broody and closed-off by nature, and I feel like life is too short not to enjoy the ride.

"He's not kissing my ass," Savage spits back angrily. "He's being truthful, for the greater good of the band." He shifts on the couch, gearing up for whatever he's about to say next. "If nothing else, we need someone who can sing harmonies behind me. You sing like a bag of cats, and KC can't harmonize for shit. No offense, KC. You know I love your voice."

"No offense taken." It's a basic fact: I can't harmonize for shit. I've been working on it during runs at football practice and in the shower, but improvement has been pretty slow.

"So, if we're adding someone to sing harmonies," Savage continues, "let's also make sure they play an instrument none of us can play. Ideally, someone who'd contribute some fresh songwriting ideas, too."

"Well, that's a tall order," Kai says with a scoff. "Someone who sings harmonies, plays keys, and writes kickass songs—*and* wants to be in a band, instead of being a solo singer-songwriter? Guys, I'm the only one going to music school, remember? And I'm telling you—"

"Here we go again." Savage rolls his eyes.

"—that the kind of musician you're talking about would never want to play *behind* you, Savage. They're going to want to be front and center, if not solo. And we don't want anybody who sees our band as a stepping stone. We all have to be completely committed to Fugitive Summer."

Kai's eyes meet mine, and I flash him a warning—one that says *tread carefully, Kai Cook.* If I've told him once, I've told him a thousand times. If he pushes too hard on the "our band is life" bullshit, Savage is going to walk, whether I'm in the band or not.

"But I mean, obviously, I'm open to trying to find someone like that," Kai says quickly. "Hence tonight's audition."

"Gee, thanks," Savage says sarcastically.

Kai looks at me. "This Rufus guy can harmonize?"

"Like a beast," I lie without hesitation. Truly, it's amazing how easily falsehoods keep tripping off my tongue, all in the name of making sure my brother gives Ruby a fair shake. In reality, I have no idea if she can carry a tune, let alone sing harmonies, let alone sing them "like a beast," any more than I know if she can play more than simple "Chopsticks" on her keyboard.

The only things I know for sure about Ruby and her musicianship are the few tidbits she's mentioned during natural conversation. She was assigned as my lab partner in chemistry after I started at St. Francis Academy on a football scholarship a month ago. Since then, she's mentioned she's been playing piano since grade school and that she performed a song she wrote in our school talent show last year. That's it. That's all I know. But since I was looking for any excuse to spend time with her outside of school, and I'm way too shy to actually ask her out, I leaped at the chance to kill two birds with one stone: getting my best friend the new musician he keeps asking for, while also creating the perfect environment for my crush to get to know me beyond the sadly too-brief interactions we have in class on Tuesdays and Thursdays.

Ruby sits with her band of cool, edgy misfits at lunch, unfortunately. The goths. The theater kids. The weirdos. The insanely smart kids furiously working on homework at all times. It's an interesting blend. And I sit with my teammates, clear on the other side of the cafeteria, covertly peeking at her and trying to figure out a way to get her to notice me. At my old school, girls were always falling all over me. And, actually, I guess that's true at this one, too. But not the right girls. Or girl, rather. Not Ruby. And I can't figure out how to change that.

A sharp knock makes all three of us look toward the door of the basement. I lurch up from the couch, butterflies ravaging my belly. But Kai is already walking over there.

"I'll get it!" I call out. "Hang on, Kai!"

I'm too late.

By the time I've reached my brother, he's already opened the door and discovered Ruby standing in the doorframe next to someone totally unexpected: my new teammate. A linebacker. Titus. Aw, fuck. Is Ruby dating a football player? Before now, I'd convinced myself she never looks at me twice because football players and athletes aren't weird and/or cool enough to be her thing. But if she's dating Titus, so much for that theory. Also, if she's got a boyfriend at all, whoever he is, so much for me dating her. Fuck my life.

"Hey, Rufus," Kai says warmly, his greeting directed at Titus. "Thanks for coming, man."

Titus places his large palm on his chest. "Titus. I hope it's okay I tagged along. I didn't want my sister coming all the way out here by herself."

Sister.

Connolly.

Holy shit. Titus *Connolly*. I can't believe I didn't put two and two together over the past month. In my defense, however, it's not too unusual a last name at a school filled with Irish Catholics. Also, Ruby and Titus are in the same grade, and they look nothing alike—Titus is a big, scruffy football player and Ruby's a cute little pixie with purple hair—so the possibility of them being siblings never even crossed my mind.

I nudge Kai out of my way and say, a bit too loudly, "I'd have done the same thing, if I had a sister. Come on in, guys. Thanks for making the trip from Evanston, especially on a school night."

"No worries, I finished all my chem homework on the train," Ruby chirps brightly as she and her brother enter the basement.

"Shit. That's due tomorrow?"

Ruby chuckles, and her cute little freckled nose scrunches up. "No, on Friday. I was working ahead."

"Of course you were," Titus says playfully.

"You might want to try it sometime," Ruby quips. "You know, in case football doesn't work out as a career."

Man, she's so freaking cute. Besides her freckled, button nose, she's got huge, dark eyes framed by dark lashes, plush lips that pull my attention like a goddamned magnet every time she's within ten feet of me, and a personality that instantly draws me in. And it's not just me. Everyone loves Ruby. I figured that out on day one at my new school.

Ruby's not my usual type, based on the kinds of girls I've been kissing since sixth grade. I mean, yes, personality-wise, she's everything I always go for: smart, sweet, funny, confident. But I guess with me playing football all these years, I've always gravitated toward ... well, cheerleader types, for lack of a better description. No one edgy and cool like Ruby. Not girls who don't give a flying fuck that I'm good at football. But I guess that's what makes my crush on Ruby stick, even when she doesn't seem interested: the fact that I'm feeling all these crazy butterflies for someone who's a first for me. A total departure.

Kai's not talking. Rather, he's glaring at me as I lead Ruby and Titus into the room. So, I quickly fill the awkward silence as best I can.

"Savage, this is Ruby Connolly and, apparently, her big brother, Titus."

"We're twins, actually," Ruby says.

"I'm still her big brother, though."

"Shut up, T."

Titus snickers. "I was born three minutes before her."

"And he thinks that entitles him to boss me around for the rest of our lives." Ruby adds an eye roll for emphasis.

"Titus and I play football together."

"And we're lab partners in chem," Ruby adds, motioning between herself and me.

Savage welcomes our guests with enthusiasm, while Kai continues to hang back, not even trying to hide his disdain.

"Savage lives down the hall from Kai and me," I explain to the Connolly twins. "Kai's my big brother."

"Who plays what?" Ruby asks.

Kai finally deigns to speak. "I play bass. But I can also play guitar in a pinch. And Savage sings lead vocals and plays guitar."

"Very cool."

"Kai's also amazing with production and sound stuff, too. He's the one who sets up our sound system for practices."

"A man of many talents." With that, Ruby flashes my big brother a beaming smile I've never witnessed before—one that would have turned me into a goddamned puddle on the floor, if only she'd directed it at me. When Kai only shrugs like he doesn't give a shit what Ruby thinks, or how beaming her smile might be, she blushes, droops, and shifts her attention to Savage. "Is Savage your actual name?"

"Yeah, my last name. My first name is Adrian, but everyone calls me Savage."

Ruby smiles brightly again, her blush still lingering. "Savage, it is."

Savage motions to Ruby and Titus. "I wouldn't have guessed you two are twins."

"People always say that," Ruby agrees with a chuckle. "But I don't understand why."

Everyone laughs. Everyone, except Kai. And it's totally noticeable.

Titus says, "Our mom always says I must have stolen most of Ruby's nutrients in the womb."

"Although we were in totally different amniotic sacs," Ruby chimes in, "so that's not possible."

Awkard silence ensues for a beat.

"So, yeah," Ruby adds, fidgeting. My god, she's adorable. I've never seen her nervous before. Normally, she's a queen bee. The most confident person in any room. We have to wear uniforms to school, but with her purple hair, and even more so with her uniquely sparkling personality, Ruby always comes off like she doesn't give a flying fuck what anyone thinks about her. And yet, apparently, she's acutely aware she's not winning over Kai for some reason, and the effect on her is obvious: she desperately wants to. Fuck my life.

"Hey, can I talk to you in the stairwell for a minute?" Kai says, breaking the awkward silence. Unfortunately, he's talking to me.

"It's a school night," I reply lamely. "And they came all the way from Evanston, so let's not waste any valuable time." I jerk my chin toward the long, keyboard-shaped duffel bag in Ruby's hand. "There's an amp for you right there, Ruby." I point to the space between Kai's bass and my drumkit. "Do you need any help setting up?"

"Nope, I'm good. Thanks for the amp. I have one, but it was nice not to have to lug it on the train." She flashes my brother another beaming smile—yet another that would have melted me, if aimed my way. "Did you set up the amp for me, Kai?" When Kai grunts, she thanks him. But he's already walking away.

Titus asks, "So, is it cool if I sit on the couch and watch, or should I step outside?"

"Sit," I say quickly, cutting off whatever Kai might be inclined to say. "We're just having fun here." I look at Ruby. "It's more of a jam session than an audition. Just have fun with it, okay?"

"Okay," she squeaks out. But it's easy to see she's a ball of nerves.

"Do you sing, Ruby?" Savage asks. "We could use some backing vocals, if you—"

"I love singing back-ups!" Ruby gushes enthusiastically.

"Awesome." Savage looks at Kai. "Set her up with your extra mic."

Kai frowns. "It's upstairs."

"That's okay," Ruby chirps. "I brought one, just in case."

It's the final straw for Kai—a bridge too far. "KC," he snaps sharply, his hard gaze cutting into me. "Stairwell. *Now.*"

———

"A keyboardist named Rufus who's a linebacker on your football team?" Kai hisses at me the second the metal door to the basement closes behind us and we're alone in the cold stairwell. "That was an awfully specific series of lies, Kendrick."

I throw up my hands. "You wouldn't give Ruby a chance otherwise."

Kai doesn't have a thing against women, generally speaking. How could he, when we were raised by a kickass, widowed mother and her kickass, widowed mother? But in the context of our fledgling band, Kai's been adamant: no girls allowed. Why? So we never repeat what recently happened when his ex-girlfriend, Courtney, broke up with him and took their entire band with her.

"Are you into this chick?" Kai asks, his dark eyes laser-focused. "Is that why you asked her to come here—to try to get into her pants?"

I gasp like that's the craziest, most insulting thing I've heard. "Don't be an asshole," I spit back piously. "I asked Ruby to come here because she's insanely talented. Because I'm trying to give my best friend in the world, who's also the most talented person in our band—sorry, Kai, but it's true—everything he wants. And fuck you for suggesting otherwise." I don't know when I suddenly became such a convincing liar, but I guess it's true what they say: necessity is the mother of invention.

"Sorry," Kai mutters. Apparently, my passionate speech

has convinced him. At least it's dispelled the notion that I invited Ruby here because I've got a crush on her. Which I do. And I did. "But, come on," Kai continues. "We all agreed no girls in the band for good reason. Why risk a Fleetwood Mac situation?"

I roll my eyes. "First of all, *you* decided no girls in the band, like a fucking dictator. Savage and I had nothing to do with that. And second of all, if you mention Fleetwood Mac as a cautionary tale one more time, I'm gonna grab your amp cord and strangle you with it. For fuck's sake, they're one of the most successful bands of all time, Kai."

"Yeah, they've sold a shit-ton of records, but being in the band was messy and toxic. That's my point. They had to break up because of the personal chaos, and we don't want that." When I laugh in my big brother's face, simply because he's being over the top about this, he takes a deep breath and assumes a fake-calm tone. "It's a good thing she's not even remotely close to your type," he says slowly, "or I'd never believe you're not crushing on her."

"This again? Kai, for fuck's sake—"

"Calm down. I believe you. I know you never go for girls like her. Actually, she's much more my type than yours." He snickers. "Frankly, if anyone needs to remember the cautionary tale of Fleetwood Mac here, it's probably me."

Fuck.

Fuck.

FUCK.

How did I not see this coming, when it's now so clear to me I was playing with fire by inviting Ruby here? Other than her age, Ruby's exactly my big brother's type. And I overlooked that fact because I was so tunnel-visioned on my own feelings for her. In my defense, though, personality-wise, Ruby is way too nice and bubbly for Kai. A total miss. And thanks to our mother, Kai knows better than to even think about messing with someone Ruby's age.

"Are you trying to get strangled? I warned you about saying the name of that band again. Also, she's sixteen, remember?"

"I know that, dumbass. I'm not saying I'd actually go for her. Just saying I believe you."

"Thank you." *I think?*

Kai bites his lip. "I guess it doesn't hurt that Ruby's super pretty. Music is a visual medium these days. The more eye candy in a band, the better."

Super pretty? Eye candy?

Hearing Kai, a notorious ladies' man, describing my secret crush like that definitely isn't my favorite thing. In fact, those words have set my teeth on edge.

"Okay, I'll give her a chance," Kai declares on an exhale. "But if she sucks, I'm sending her packing after one song. I don't care how far she lugged her gear—"

"Fine. One song. As long as you give her a fair shake."

"I said I would. Stop nagging me about it."

"I will when you stop acting like a dick who deserves to be nagged."

With a roll of his eyes, Kai swings open the metal door, and it's back into the basement we go. But only two steps into the room, we're surprised to find Titus slaying a nasty riff on Savage's guitar, while Savage looks on like he's witnessing Titus turning water into wine.

Kai and I look at each other in disbelief. Savage never lets anyone touch his most prized possession: the second-hand electric guitar he bagged groceries for a year to be able to afford.

When Titus sees my brother and me, he abruptly stops playing and looks sheepish. "We were just messing around till you got back."

"He's incredible, guys!" Savage blurts excitedly. "Holy shit, Titus! Play something else."

"He's a great singer, too," Ruby offers proudly. She's now standing behind her keyboard, patiently awaiting her chance to dazzle us.

"Not as good as you, though," Titus replies.

"Wait, you *both* play and sing?" Savage asks.

"We grew up playing with our parents," Ruby explains, like it's no big deal. "They were in a band in college. Our mom's a music teacher now."

Savage looks thoroughly energized. Indeed, the dude is physically hopping from foot to foot with excitement. "Can you both sing harmonies?"

Both Ruby and Titus confirm as much. But they do it casually, like it's nothing. Which means they both must be pretty good, because only people for whom harmonies come naturally think it's nothing.

"We're not looking for a second guitarist," Kai interjects. "Savage plays guitar."

"Like I said, I was just fooling around till you got back," Titus says evenly as he heads to the couch, his stiff body language a mixture of "fuck this guy" and "I'm not gonna say what I'm thinking so I don't blow this for my sister."

For a longish moment, a thick silence hangs in the air. To fill it, I stride toward my drumkit, which prompts everyone else to start getting settled with their instruments, too. Finally, when it seems like we're all set and ready to roll, I shoot an encouraging smile at Ruby. "Are you ready?"

"Sure," she chirps. "Which of your songs would you like to start with?"

My eyebrows ride up. "You learned more than one of them?"

"I learned all of them."

"All *four*?" When I sent Ruby our rough demos—the only

four Fugitive Summer songs currently in existence—I only meant for her to learn one. And I'm positive I told her that.

"Take your pick," I manage to say. "Whichever one you're most excited to play."

"Okay, can we start with 'Little Demons,' then? I love that one. I mean, I love all your songs. But that one really spoke to me."

I shoot Savage a pointed grin. *Damn, she's good.* "Little Demons" is Kai's favorite of our four songs. Not surprisingly, since he's the one who wrote the lion's share of it.

"Sounds good," Savage says smoothly. "Count us off, KC."

I pause and clear my mind, getting the tempo in my head, and when I've got it, I click my sticks together at the right pace, counting us off. A moment later, we launch into the song … for the very first time, with four musicians instead of three.

———

"That was as good as sex," Savage declares as he leans back onto the tattered, discarded couch we dragged into the basement a few months ago. Ruby and Titus, our band's two newest members, just left, following a three-hour jam session that blew all our minds and quite possibly changed all our lives forever.

Right out of the gate on "Little Demons," Ruby was a star. Everything she added to the tune was perfect—stuff that immediately made the song so much better. Fuller. Catchier. In particular, the subtle counter-melody lick she played to complement Kai's bassline in the first verse was out of this world. Pure gold. And it only got better from there.

For instance, when we reached the first chorus and Ruby switched to a meandering synth riff that made the song feel kind of celestial and other-worldly—a touch demonic, you might even say—and all while singing pitch-perfect backing harmonies behind Savage's kickass lead vocals, that was it. We all knew. We'd found our keyboardist. Even Kai started exchanging nods and electrified expressions with Savage and me at that point.

At Savage's insistence, Titus got up to play Savage's guitar on our second song, which then gave Savage the freedom to move around while singing, like the future rockstar he is. And I'll be damned, by the end of that second song with all five of us playing, and Titus and Ruby supplying some perfect backing harmonies, a five-member band was born.

"That was *better* than most sex," Kai retorts, one-upping Savage's prior comment. "If I had to choose making music like that every day of my life but at the cost of only ever getting myself off with my hand, I'd do it. It was just that good."

"Well, let's not get too crazy," Savage mutters. "That was awesome, but better than sex? Nothing is better than sex."

"Making great music is better than sex."

"No."

"And sex is amazing. That's my whole point." Kai whacks my leg. "Would you hurry up and fuck somebody already, so you can weigh in on this argument?"

"I'm saving myself for marriage." It's my usual joke—the thing I say to deflect attention whenever the subject of my virginity comes up. Of course, they know I'm not actually waiting for marriage or anything else in particular to do the deed for the first time. So far, I just haven't had the opportunity to take things past kissing and making out. It certainly doesn't help that I've switched schools midway through my high school career, and that I'm now attending a school that's a long train ride away, making hanging out difficult. But, hey, I'm only sixteen. Almost every guy I know, other than Savage, is still a virgin, too. Hell, Kai didn't lose his virginity till he got to college and met Courtney.

"Speaking of sex," Kai says. "Let's talk about the elephant

in the room. Ruby's off-limits, guys. We all agree to that, right?"

"I don't think we need to make an actual rule about that," Savage says. "Let's just play it by ear."

My heart stops. I haven't told Savage about my crush on Ruby, but he knows me well, so I'm guessing he's at least wondering. Did Savage leave the door open about Ruby for my sake . . . *or for his*?

"You can't mess with Ruby, Savage," Kai says sternly.

"Why are you saying that to me, when Kendrick's sitting there looking like a golden god?"

"Because she's not his type. But you? You don't have a type. As long as a girl's hot, she's an option."

Fuck. Shit. *Did Kai just imply Ruby is hot?*

"That's fair," Savage concedes.

"So, respect the off-limits designation, motherfucker."

"I don't like being told what to do, though. If I'm feeling it with Ruby, then I'll do something about it, no matter what you say."

"Savage, fucking hell."

"*However*, you'll be happy to know I'm presently not feeling it and don't anticipate that changing anytime soon." Savage winks at me, all but confirming he's managed to sniff out my crush far better than my big brother. "I agree she's hot, though," he adds, still looking at me. Probably, for a reaction. When I don't give him one, he adds, "In a cute, pixie-fairy sort of way."

"So, why aren't you interested in her then?" Kai asks, looking suspicious.

I hold my breath, praying Savage won't say something stupid like, *Because I can tell Kendrick's into her.*

"She's too sweet for me," Savage replies, and I exhale in relief. "You know I like my women a little bit mean."

We all laugh. It's true. He does.

"Okay, can we all agree, then?" Kai asks. "Ruby's off-limits."

"I didn't say that," Savage counters. "I said I've personally got zero interest in her. But if one of you wanted to go for it with her, that'd be fine with me. Why make stupid rules when this band is supposed to be about having fun?" He shoots me the tiniest of smirks.

Kai's not having it. "If anyone messes with Ruby and it goes sideways—which it would, because young love never lasts—then we'd lose two players, not one. The band wouldn't survive that, guys. Definitely not worth it, no matter how cute she is."

Savage and I look at each other. Who's Kai trying to convince with that? Savage or himself?

Kai cracks open one of the cheap beers a neighbor bought for us on the sly. "Also, let's not overlook the fact that Ruby's jailbait, on top of everything else. At least, for me. Even if I was tempted, which I'm not, I couldn't do that. Certainly not with her corn-fed brother in the band, too. Did you see the arms on that dude? Holy fuck. Titus's guns were bigger than Kendrick's!"

I'm reeling. All the words Kai's been saying are the right ones. Reassuring, on paper. But the fact that my brother feels the need to say them at all? This increasingly feels like a "lady doth protest too much" situation, like I've been hearing about in English class lately.

"You okay?" Savage asks, batting my leg. "You're awfully quiet."

I force a smile. "Just tired. Three hours of banging on drums after a rough football practice will do that to a guy."

"You killed it tonight. You're so fucking talented, KC." He returns to Kai. "You should apologize to him for being such a dick about Ruby. That wasn't cool, man."

To my shock, Kai doesn't flinch or flip Savage off. On the

contrary, he jumps right in with the requested apology. "Yeah, sorry, KC. I was a dick. Turns out, you were right. Ruby's incredible."

Incredible.

Eye candy.

Pretty.

Cute.

Hot.

The hits just keep on coming.

"Titus is pretty damned incredible, too," Savage says, unaware that I'm spiraling next to him on the tattered couch.

"But Ruby was definitely the secret sauce," Kai mutters.

"Yeah, she was the spark that lit the fuse that caused the explosion," Savage agrees.

Spark.

Fuse.

Explosion.

Those are exactly the things I felt when I first met Ruby. The second I saw her, my palms went clammy and my heart skipped a beat. I swear to god, a swarm of butterflies attacked my stomach, just like they talk about in cheesy movies.

"Now that we've got the right musicians in place," Kai says, "the sky's the limit for us, guys. I can feel it."

"Fuck yeah, it is," Savage says, with far more enthusiasm than I've ever heard from him in relation to the band. "Hey, toss me one of those beers, man. We're celebrating."

Kai grabs beers and throws one to Savage, as requested, and then to me, even though I never drink during football season. Fuck it. I crack open mine and guzzle the whole thing in one gulp. My body is normally my temple until the season is over, but tonight, I'm making an exception. Because tonight? Fuck me, it was pretty damned clear the girl I've been crushing on, the girl who's the spark that lit a fuse inside me and caused an explosion, felt that exact same kind of a spark tonight. *For my brother.*

"Slow down, KC," Kai says. "We're gonna have a toast."

"Here's my toast." I let out a long, loud burp, making the guys laugh.

"Cheers to that," Savage says, still chuckling.

"Actually, you know what?" I blurt, suddenly determined to keep Ruby away from Kai. "I agree with you. I think we should all treat Ruby like a sister, the same way she's a sister to Titus. Our whole band will be an all-for-one-one-for-all kind of a thing."

Savage furrows his brow. "You really want it that way?"

"I do."

"Good call, KC," Kai says. "From this moment on, we're all Ruby's brothers, not just Titus. That's the only way this is ever going to work out."

Savage trains his dark gaze on me for a long moment. And when I don't give him anything to work with, because I can't without giving myself away, he shrugs and says, "As long as it's *Kendrick* Cook telling me what to do, and not *Kai* Cook, then count me in."

We raise our beers to seal the deal. Although mine is empty, unlike theirs. Is that the equivalent of crossed fingers? Probably not. More likely, I think I've just managed to keep my best friend and big brother from making a play for the girl I'm crushing on . . . while simultaneously decimating my own slim chances with her as a result.

2

KENDRICK

Present Day
12:33 am
New York City

T*hump, thump, thump.*
　　"Yes, yes, yes!"
　　　　I open my eyes, yanked from a dream, and spit out, "Fucking hell." I was having a sex dream, I think. A good one, based on the boner that's currently poking at my briefs. But maybe not. Maybe I'm confusing the sounds wafting through the shared wall with Kai and whatever I was dreaming about.

Thump, thump, thump.

"Oh, God, Kai! Yes!"

Jesus. Are the walls of this hotel made of cardboard, or is my big brother's fuck buddy for the night the loudest groupie in the history of sex, drugs, and rock 'n' roll?

As the offending sounds persist, I glare at the clock on the nightstand. I don't judge my brother or anyone else if they want to have sex with a rando. Before Savage fell ass over feet for his blonde popstar of a wife, Laila, he made a goddamned sport of doing exactly that, and I never once judged him. Well, maybe once or twice. But not too much, when I've certainly played "horny rockstar" more than a few times. Especially during our first tour. I admit I was a bit unhinged.

But, anyway, me not judging my big brother for rhythmically thumping a woman into our shared wall doesn't mean I'm not pissed at him for waking me up from my first dead sleep in a long while. Kai knows we're sharing a wall tonight; he saw me entering the door next to his earlier, when we got our room assignments. And he also knows I've been uncharacteristically battling insomnia for the past two months. Not to mention, it's now, officially, my twenty-eighth birthday. So, knowing all that, why wouldn't Kai think to at least shove his hand over his new friend's mouth to muffle her sounds while he rails her?

With a sigh, I reach for my phone on the nightstand, figuring I'll scroll for a bit, but when I see my lyrics journal sitting next to it, I grab that, instead. Throughout my recent sleepless nights, I've been scratching out little snippets of lyrics here and there, to pass the time. I'm not one of the lyricists in our band—that would be Savage or Ruby. Sometimes, Kai. But you never know what might inspire someone else, so we all keep notes and share them when it's time for our next songwriting session.

Journal and pen in hand, I flip to the next open page and begin to write:

Lying awake, my body staging a coup

It's as far as I get before my phone pings on the nightstand. When I grab it, I've got a new text:

> Ruby: Happy 28th birthday, my darling! Titus and I are in the hotel bar downstairs, enjoying cocktails, so if you see this, come and let Mr. Rivers buy you something ridiculously expensive to celebrate the glorious day of your birth!

I chuckle to myself. Whenever we're on tour, our label, River Records, founded by Reed Rivers, picks up the tab for our band's food and drinks, no matter the cost. So, of course, we all exploit that policy to the hilt.

> Me: Hey, cutie. I'll be right down.

> Ruby: WAHOO!

I throw my journal onto the bed and start throwing on clothes. Truth be told, if Ruby's boyfriend, Cooper, were still tagging along with her on the tour like he's been doing for the past two months, I'd probably pretend not to have seen her text till morning. I used to like Cooper a lot, before he started dating Ruby about three months ago. But watching him . . .

I pause what I'm doing, slammed with an idea for some lyrics.

My heart crashing, I grab my journal and pen off the bed, sit on the edge of the mattress, find the spot where I left off a moment ago, and begin furiously scribbling my thoughts down, as fast as my hand can write them. For the next several minutes, the words barrel out of me, like I'm in a trance. Like it's not me writing them at all. Like I'm simply channeling them from someone or somewhere else.

Finally, the words stop flowing. The inspiration has passed.

I glance down at the journal and discover my rushed, chaotic, urgent handwriting is covering *two* full pages—both the left and right sides of the opened book. Not only that, I've written an entire song, which never happens to me. Verse, chorus, verse, chorus, bridge, chorus. What the fuck? I've heard Savage and Ruby talk about lyrics coming to them in a trance like that, but it's never happened to me. I can't wait to tell them about this!

Feeling giddy, I read my words back . . . and quickly realize, no, I can't tell Savage or Ruby or anyone else about this. Ever. Or they'll think this flush of words is about Ruby—and that it reflects my actual, current thoughts and feelings about her.

I mean, sure, there are some seeds of truth here, probably. Some long-buried ones. But I've mixed them with fantasy. What ifs. And I can't afford for anyone, least of all her, to read this and think it's some kind of naked confessional.

Maybe I should rip the pages out and destroy them. Just in case. But then again, I'm awfully proud of this. I've never written this long a song or lyrics in my life.

No, it's too risky. I should definitely destroy it.

It occurs to me the piece deserves to have a title, even if it's ultimately going into the trashcan. So, I quickly scribble the first word that pops into my head—"Spark"—at the top of the left page.

Ping.

I look at my phone. Another text from Ruby.

Ruby: I'm waiiiiiiiiiting, my darling! Titus is cranky and wants to go to bed. Are you coming, Birthday Boy? Don't make me drink alone!

Me: Coming now, cutie!

Hot damn. I never get Ruby all to myself these days. But with Cooper finally gone and Titus wanting to go to bed, it sounds like I'll have my cute little bestie all to myself down there. Excited, I leap up, finish getting dressed, grab my White Sox hoodie and my keycard, and barrel out the door with an extra skip in my step.

3

KENDRICK

I peck Ruby's cheek in greeting, as always, and slide onto the vacant stool next to her.

"Hey, bestie," she says. "Happy birthday. Twenty-eight is a biggie."

"No, it's not."

"It is to me."

Like me, Ruby looks like she rolled out of bed to come down here. She's dressed in soft, comfy clothes—sweats and an oversized sweater that hides her rocking little body and the Greek mythology–inspired tattoo on her shoulder.

I look around. "Did Titus already go upstairs?"

Ruby nods. Her long, pink hair is tied into two messy space buns. "The second he found out you were coming down here, and I wouldn't be alone in a bar in New York City—gasp!—he went back upstairs."

"I'm insulted he didn't stick around long enough to wish me happy birthday, at least."

"I'm pretty sure he got a text from Stephanie. He loves you, babe. But he loves FaceTime sex with Stephanie more."

"Can't say I blame him. I'd pick FaceTime sex over birthday drinks with me, too."

Ruby scoffs. "If that's what you wanted, you could have all the FaceTime sex in the world." She frowns. "I texted you just in case, but I was hoping you'd be fast asleep. You seemed really tired after the show."

"I fell asleep pretty quickly this time—right after we got back. But . . . some noisy people in the hallway woke me up." After everything that went down between Kai and Ruby years ago, I'm not going to tell her the truth. True, what happened between those two is ancient history by now. But, still, why rub salt in whatever Kai-inflicted wounds Ruby might still have, even if they're mostly scarred over by now?

"People in hotels can be so damned rude," Ruby mutters.

"It's okay. One more week, and I'll be sleeping like a baby in my own bed."

"Another full week is a long time to be sleep deprived. Especially after so many months."

"It's only been a couple months. Before that, I was okay."

Ruby thinks about that. "When did college football season start? About two months ago, right?"

"Something like that."

Wanting to change the subject, I signal to the bartender, and he comes over with a smile on his rugged face.

"Hey there. What can I—" His face lights up. "Wait, aren't you the drummer from Fugitive Summer? You're awesome, man! One of the best out there."

"I agree," Ruby says, pinching my arm. "Although I'd say he's *the* best."

The guy blushes. "Oh, yeah. Definitely."

"She's messing with you. She's our keyboardist."

The bartender looks sheepish. "I'm sorry. I only knew his face because my sister is obsessed with *Sing Your Heart Out*, and I watch it with her."

"No worries," Ruby says. "I thought Kendrick was incredible on that show, too."

"Your other bandmate, too. Savage?" He looks around excitedly. "Is he here?"

"No, not in the bar," Ruby says. "Sorry."

The guy grabs his phone and excitedly asks for a selfie with us, which we happily give him.

"Drinks are on me tonight," he says. "What can I get you?"

"Another one of these for me," Ruby says, raising her empty glass. "And for the birthday boy . . . A double pour of your most expensive scotch. Neat." She looks at me to confirm.

"You know me well."

"But don't comp us," Ruby says. "Our label pays for everything when we're on tour. In fact, go ahead and charge everything to my room—1653—and give yourself a two-hundred-percent tip, courtesy of Reed Rivers."

"Wow, thanks so much."

The bartender saunters away, but not before flashing an extremely flirtatious smile at Ruby.

The second he's out of earshot, I whisper in a sultry, teasing tone, "I'm in room 1653, *big boy*. Come up and see me."

Ruby snorts and rolls her eyes. "You're delusional."

"I'm repeating it exactly how you said it."

"Not even close."

"Are you fighting the urge to step out on Cooper with a hot hotel bartender? Because if so, that's probably not the best sign for your relationship."

"You're sex-starved and horny these days, so you're seeing what you want to see."

"You can't deny he's exactly your type, babe." It's the truth. Like Ruby's current boyfriend, Cooper, and also Ruby's favorite boyfriend in college, Ryder, that guy is a tall, tattooed, dark-haired, mysterious type with lean muscles and a resting "fuck you" face. In fact, everything about him screams, *I'd make a horrible boyfriend.* Which means he's right up Ruby's alley.

"You're so dumb," Ruby says.

"You gave him your room number, dude."

"*For the drinks.*"

"You never do that, though. You always give Titus's."

"Kendrick, your gaydar is terrible."

"What?" I look over at the guy. "*No.*"

"Yes. Babe, he was hitting on *you.* Not me."

"You think?"

"One thousand percent. That's why I felt comfortable giving him my room number. Because if he ever came up, it'd only be to beg me for yours."

We both crack up, and a moment later, the bartender appears with our drinks. We chat briefly with the guy—and I'll be damned, now that Ruby's mentioned it, it seems probable he's flirting with me.

Finally, the guy walks away and Ruby lifts her glass to me. "Happy twenty-eighth, my darling. I love you so damned much, Kendrick Cook."

"I love you, too. Thank you."

We clink and drink.

"So, what's new?" I ask. "We're so rarely alone these days. Someone's always around. Everything good with Cooper? Are you missing him since he had to leave?"

Ruby twists her mouth. "No, I don't miss him at all. Cooper left because I broke up with him."

Well, hot fucking damn. Happy birthday to me. "Oh, wow. Are you okay?"

"I'm great. Cooper? Not so much. He keeps texting me, begging me to take him back." She scowls. "But no thanks. I'm done."

I'm so fucking relieved. Despite the outward armor Ruby wears—her dyed hair, piercings, and tattoos—she's a tenderhearted person who bends over backwards for the people she cares about. And unfortunately, our buddy Cooper was taking a whole lot more from Ruby than he was giving. That was my impression, anyway. Did he pursue her solely because her band was more successful than his? I don't think that. But it certainly didn't hurt, from his perspective. Even beyond that, he didn't treat her right as a boyfriend. He didn't listen to her the way she deserved to be listened to. Didn't get her sense of humor the way those closest to her do. Combine that with the fact that he can be a whiny little bitch with a short temper and a victim complex, and what you get is a guy whose mere existence on our tour has been driving me up the wall for the past two months.

"Why didn't you tell me about the breakup?"

"I didn't feel like talking about it."

"Have you told Titus yet?"

Ruby nods. "A couple days ago."

"And?"

"He told me not to settle for a guy who doesn't deserve me, ever again."

"Amen." I nod decisively. "Words to live by."

"From now on, if it's not amazing, I don't want it."

"Atta girl." I raise my glass. "To amazingness or nothing at all."

We clink and drink.

"Are you signing onto this life philosophy as well?" Ruby asks. "Or did you only drink to that for *me*?"

"I drank to it for both of us. I'm the only one of the two of us who's been single this whole tour, remember? I've been living the 'amazing or nothing' life for a while now."

"Yeah, and it's killing you slowly."

I scoff. "Not at all."

"This is the first time you haven't fallen into something hot and heavy with a tour girlfriend, and it's also the first tour you've experienced persistent, chronic insomnia. Do the math, babe."

I roll my eyes. "One has nothing to do with the other. And I've never had a tour girlfriend. I'm clear up front, it's always a tour *fling*."

"How gallant of you."

"And this isn't the first time I haven't gotten together with anyone on the road. I was a rockstar cliché during our first tour as openers, remember?"

"Sweetheart, it's burned into my brain like witnessing roadkill too close."

I laugh. "You're one to talk. You've had some meaningless fun here and there over the years, too. We all have."

"Yeah, but I've always been more discreet about it than any of you. Is it more nature or nurture for men to enter dick-swinging contests, do you think?"

"Little bit of both, I'm sure."

She sips her drink and pauses like she's gearing up to say something.

"What?" I ask.

She purses her lips. "Do you think that quarterback doing so well is the main reason for your insomnia? It started right around the time he started making national news."

She's talking about the star quarterback from the college I dropped out of after my knee injury—a guy who's been tearing it up so much this season, everyone's saying he's a front-runner to win the Heisman. What she hasn't clocked, however, is that Cooper joined the tour about two months ago, too—and he immediately started annoying the fuck out of me to the point where I can't stop thinking about him and how much I can't stand him whenever I try to fall asleep. But since I don't feel like I should admit that to Ruby, I reply, "Yeah, that's probably it."

"It's either that or no tour girlfriend. Sorry, fling. Those are the only two things that are different this tour. I don't believe in coincidences, sweetheart."

"Maybe."

"When you were banging Tracy during the last one, did you sleep like a baby every night?"

I cringe. "Why bring Tracy up?"

"Why not?"

"It's my birthday. You know it didn't end well, and I feel bad about that."

"Sorry."

During our last tour, I fell into a tour relationship, as one does, with our tour manager at the time, Tracy. And I swear, I made my intentions with her clear out of the gate. I'm not ready to settle down. Not looking for anything serious. I'm going to be really busy when we get home to LA. Blah, blah, blah. She said that was perfect because she wasn't looking for a relationship, either.

But then, I'll be damned, on the last night of the tour, Tracy told me she'd fallen deeply, madly in love with me. And when I told her I didn't feel the same way and didn't want to continue the relationship, she didn't take it well. In fact, she said some things that made me realize I'd kind of been a dick without meaning to be. I couldn't help the way I felt, but I kind of knew she was falling for me and I looked the other way.

"You were dating Finn when I got with Tracy, and he wasn't exactly someone to write home about."

Ruby pulls a face. "What does Finn have to do with anything?"

"I'm just saying."

"Saying what?"

"That people sometimes get with people they later regret."

"I don't regret Finn. He was nice. And fun. A total cutie pie."

"Oh."

"Was it deep and meaningful? No. Was he long-term boyfriend material? No. But not everything has to be serious. Honestly, after three months of Cooper love-bombing me and talking about me having his babies, a meaningless fling is the only thing that sounds even remotely attractive to me right now." She sips her drink. "Speaking of Tracy, Titus said you've been a monk this whole tour because nobody's caught your eye, but I said it's because Tracy's made you once bitten, twice shy. Who's right?"

"It's nice to know you and Titus gossip about me behind my back."

"We gossip about everyone. If it makes you feel any better, we've been gossiping about Kai the most lately. It used to be Savage. But ever since he got married, there's nothing juicy to say about him anymore. He's kind of boring these days."

"In the best possible way."

"Right?" She grins. "I'm so happy for him."

"I've never seen him happier." That's saying a lot for a guy who's known Savage since age twelve.

Ruby rolls her eyes. "Kai, on the other hand? My god. Is your brother going through a quarter-life crisis or what?"

Does it bother Ruby, whenever she finds out Kai's fucked yet another rando in another city, or has she long since gotten over her heartbreak about the way he rejected her years ago? For years, I've been dying to ask Ruby her side of that story, but I've been too afraid it might crush me.

"So, why no tour fling this time?" Ruby pushes, running a fingertip over a drop of moisture on the bar. "Seems to me you're avoiding the question."

"Why are you so obsessed with my sex life?"

"I just want to know who's right about you—Titus or me?"

"You make it sound like I can 'pick' women like picking

apples off a tree. It doesn't work that way. It's got to be a two-way street."

"You still haven't answered my question."

I finish my drink. "Maybe I'm just sick of the grind. Sick of trying to get to know new people. Sick to death of small talk."

"Gah. Me, too."

"Maybe it's got less to do with Tracy and more to do with me realizing she had a point. I'm emotionally unavailable and not a good bet in relationships, even though I *seem* like I am."

"You definitely seem like classic boyfriend material, on the outside. But in reality, you're kind of a fuckboy. Like Kai."

"What? No, I'm not. Not at all."

"Okay, not exactly like Kai. Not as overtly, because you're a serial monogamist rather than a hook-up artist, like him. But, still, you don't give your truest self to anyone, any more than Kai does. Or like Savage used to do, before Laila. You always hold back."

She's not wrong. But if Ruby's guidepost is that I don't act like I do with her around anyone I'm dating, then that's not something I'll ever be able to change, because I'll never have this same kind of deep trust and friendship with anyone else. Would I like to find someone like Ruby to date? Yes. But the truth is she's one of a kind.

"I shouldn't talk, though," Ruby mumbles. "Everything I just accused you of doing, I do too. Every. Fucking. Time." She sighs. "That's why I went against my instincts and started dating Cooper in the first place. I was so sick of trying to get to know someone new, and so sick of watching myself self-sabotage, I figured, hey, maybe dating someone who's already a good friend would turn out differently. Well, guess what? It didn't. In fact, it was even worse. A colossal mistake. One I'll never, ever repeat."

My heart stops. "I dunno. I don't think this one bad experience with Cooper should make you set such a hard and fast rule."

"Kendrick, trust me. It's the worst. Things get way too intense, way too fast." She sets down her glass. "See, the problem is, you're already friends to start with, so when you add in the sex, they think they can skip all the early phases of a romantic relationship and zoom straight to 'baby, we're end game.'" She shudders. "But, no, you can't do that. At least, *I* can't. I need *time.* I need space. It's like, give me a minute, please." She picks up her glass again and sips her drink. "I mean, Cooper was fine as a friend, but the second we slept together, he got all jealous and possessive. It was like, one day, he was chill and fun, and the next, simply because he'd had his dick inside me, briefly—the boy has lots of talents, but sexual endurance isn't one of them—he suddenly felt like he owned me." She snorts. "All of a sudden, he started professing his 'undying love' to me. Telling me he'd always secretly loved me, since the first minute he'd laid eyes on me—way back when his band opened for us. I mean, excuse me? What kind of douchebag only *pretends* to be good friends with a woman because he's secretly hoping to figure out a way to fuck her? It's so classic. So obvious. But I didn't see it at all."

I feel like barfing, so I nod vaguely, mumble something incoherent that hopefully sounds like agreement with her comments, and flag down the bartender by wildly flinging my arm into the air.

"Another round," I blurt when the guy comes over to take our order.

"Sure thing. Hey, are you from Chicago?"

I'm still feeling dazed and confused, not to mention tongue-tied and nauseated, from Ruby's speech about Cooper, so I stare at the bartender blankly, hoping he'll explain how he figured that out. Did he google me while he was over there? If so, I'm never going to hear the end of it from Ruby, since she already thinks my inability to pick up on this guy flirting with me is the funniest thing in the world.

The guy points at my sweatshirt. And when I look down and see the White Sox emblem on my chest, everything makes sense.

"Oh. Yeah." I look back up. "I'm from the South Side. Born and raised."

"Right on. I'm from Bridgeport. Go, Sox."

"Hell yeah." I fist-bump the guy and then point my chin at Ruby. "She's from Evanston."

"Ah, so you're a Cubs fan, then?" He flashes me a knowing look about Ruby's hometown suburb that's right outside the city limits of Chicago. It's not a foolproof formula, but generally speaking, White Sox fans tend to be blue collar and from the South Side, like Kai, Savage, and me—and this guy, apparently. Cubs fans like Ruby's family tend to be yuppies and rich folks from areas like the North Side and the 'burbs.

"My family has always loved the Cubbies," Ruby confirms. "But personally, I don't give two shits about sports."

The guy acknowledges Ruby's comment with a chuckle, but a second later, his smile is trained back on me. "You look like you play sports."

"Nope. Drumming is my only sport."

Ruby touches my hand. She knows what happened to end my football dreams well enough to know I don't want to talk about it with this guy or anyone else.

"Awesome. Okay, well, I'll get those drinks started for you."

"Thanks."

As the bartender leaves, Ruby says, "Wouldn't it be amazing if there was a fast-forward button that would let us to jump straight to the part where someone already knows us well, so we wouldn't have to sit through all the small talk to get there?"

"Sign me up."

"But also, they wouldn't think knowing you well before sex means that sex suddenly turns everything into an instant happily ever after? What's the rush, dude? Why so serious? Some of us are young and not at all ready to settle down, you know? Je-zus."

When she looks at me for a reply, I mutter, "Yup. Gimme that button. Sounds amazing to me."

Ruby gasps. "You're ready to settle down?"

I don't know how she got that from my body language. Because, no, I'm not ready for that. Not at all. "No. Why did you say that?"

"Because you looked like you were lying."

I shrug. "I don't know. If I met the right person, I'd maybe be ready to settle down. But I'm also sick to death of dating total strangers, so I don't see how that'll ever happen."

Ruby ponders that. "Well, on your quest to find The One, don't bother dating a friend. At least, in my experience, it's a terrible idea."

"So, what then? You're saying I'm gonna die alone?"

Ruby giggles. "No. You're irresistible. You'll meet the right person." She pauses. "But if you don't, you'll never be alone, my darling. I'll be right there with you, holding strong." She raises her empty glass. "Amazing or nothing."

I clink her empty with mine. "Amazing or nothing."

The bartender arrives with our next round. And this time, he takes the hint and skedaddles quickly.

"Cheers," Ruby says, clinking my new glass with hers.

"Cheers."

"How's your knee, by the way? Has it been bothering you from last night's rain?"

"It's fine." I reflexively place a palm on my knee.

"Could your knee be affecting your sleep?"

"The knee is fine. I've just been having trouble turning off my brain for some reason."

"So it really must be that you're horny and sex-starved, and that quarterback stole your dream. I mean, who wouldn't have insomnia under those circumstances?"

Ruby's the smartest person I know, so I'm surprised she keeps overlooking the obvious. Cooper. He's the first boyfriend Ruby's ever invited to join our tour, and I really, *really* didn't like having him around. I didn't like watching the possessive way he treated Ruby. Didn't like watching him sitting around writing songs with her for his band to use. Didn't like his penchant for PDA. And on and on.

I scoff. "I don't have trouble sleeping at home, even when I'm sex-starved and horny."

"But at home, you're in your own comfy bed and strangers aren't shouting in the hallway outside your room. Plus, your schedule isn't crazy, and you're probably not drinking like a fish, like you do on tour."

"God, I hope not."

"Don't you dare turn into C-Bomb on me."

"I'm in no danger of that." Ruby is of the opinion that our good friend, Caleb "C-Bomb" Baumgarten, the iconic drummer of Red Card Riot, should be in rehab and anger management counseling.

"What have you tried so far to combat it?"

With a sigh, I list off everything: guided meditations, weed gummies, melatonin, booze, and a heating pad applied to various strategic places on my anatomy.

"Hmm," Ruby says, tapping her chin. "What else could it be, then?"

I clear my throat. "It's got to be the quarterback. It's definitely not the lack of sex, because I beat off every night, which is basically the same thing as sex to my body and brain."

Ruby scoffs. "Beating off isn't nearly as calming as sex with another human. For men, anyway."

My eyebrows ride up. "You're implying it's something different for women?"

Ruby snorts. "Ask any woman, at least those who have sex with men, and she'll tell you getting busy with a vibrator is way, way better than sex with any man. At least, in terms of her orgasm count."

I'm appalled. "Is that how it is for you?"

"Of course." She looks at me like I'm dumb. "Babe, if we needed all men to band together to save the world by harnessing screams of ecstasy, like an X-rated version of the monsters in *Monsters, Inc.*, we'd all be doomed."

I crack up. "That's not true."

"I'm not trying to offend you, my darling, but unless your dick vibrates, has multiple speeds and options, and doesn't come with any emotional baggage, clinginess, anger management issues, emotional unavailability, and/or jealous rages, you're not going to get the job done better than any woman's battery-operated-boyfriend. In my case, his name is Bruno, and he literally never fails me, unlike every boyfriend I've ever had."

"Bruno?" I ask with a laugh.

"He's my longest relationship."

This bombshell makes me want to offer Ruby my services to prove her wrong. But since I can't do that, I pick up my drink and say, in the most casual tone I can muster, "I think I'd give Bruno a run for his money, honestly."

"I'm sure you would." She pats my hand. "For a mortal man. But we're off topic again. Your insomnia. What about therapy? Maybe that will help you deal with the quarterback who's stolen your dream."

"He's not torturing me. He merely annoys me."

"Okay, well, it seems to me he's thrown you into some sort

of an existential crisis. For the past couple months, you've seemed agitated and stressed, and that's so unlike you."

Yeah, I wonder why. "I think it's just one of those things, babe. Let's drop it."

Ruby taps her chin. "What if it's more about the lack of human contact than the lack of sex itself? You slept in a tiny bed with Kai for years as a kid, right? After your dad died?"

Thanks to our countless conversations over the years, Ruby knows, after our dad died, when I was four and Kai was seven, we had to cram into one small bed together for years, when our grandma and grandpa came to live with us to help our grieving mother.

"It's an interesting theory."

That's all Ruby needs to leap into action. She throws back the rest of her drink and hops off her stool. "Come on, birthday boy! I think we've found the answer!" She extends her hand. "I'm going to cuddle you to sleep!"

I don't move. "What?" I'm equal parts elated and terrified about this idea. For one thing, there's a risk I could pop a boner against Ruby's leg if she cuddles me too close. But then again, what are the odds of that happening after so many years of genuine friendship? Maybe, at this point, my brain has convinced itself she's truly like a sister to me, rendering my body incapable of having that kind of a physical reaction to her closeness.

Ruby's certainly fallen asleep against my shoulder a thousand times in buses and on planes, and my dick always remains limp. Plus, the girl rides my back every goddamned time she has a drop of alcohol, and that's never been a problem for me.

On the other hand, I've never gotten into an actual bed with Ruby. Especially not when we're all alone.

My mind racing, I ask, "What if one of our bandmates sees you coming out of my room at the crack of dawn?"

"You think I'd leave at the crack of dawn?" She snorts. "Sir, I need my beauty sleep."

"They might think something's going on between us."

Ruby scoffs so loudly, the sound not only hurts my ears, it hurts my feelings. "Nobody would ever think that. They all know you're my best friend—like a brother to me. Now, stop acting like a weirdo and come on. I'm excited to test my theory about this."

Still, I remain frozen. "Have you ever slept in the same bed as Titus?"

"Lots of times. At our grandma's, we always had to do that, and it wasn't weird in the slightest."

"As adults, though? Have you ever cuddled Titus in a bed, as an adult?"

Ruby scowls. "Well, no. But so what? If Titus was suffering from chronic insomnia, and I had the brilliant idea that cuddling him might cure the problem, I'd do it in a heartbeat. Why not? Only a pervert would have a problem with that. So, come on, the only way to prove you're not a pervert is to come with me."

I chuckle. "That was brilliant logic, even for you."

"Thank you. I thought so."

Fuck it. Sighing, I take Ruby's hand and rise from my stool. "Okay, cutie. Cure me. Save me. Through any means necessary."

4
RUBY

"Thanks for trying to solve my Insomnia Rubik's Cube, Ruby Duby," Kendrick says as we step into the hotel elevator. I'm riding his back, piggyback-style, so he's got to be the one to press the button for our floor.

"Cuddling with you is going to be a special kind of torture," I deadpan. "But that's the kind of friend I am. I'm a saint."

"No, you're a gem."

It's what Kendrick always calls me. His gem of a best friend.

"If it turns out your theory is wrong," Kendrick says, "feel free to ditch my sleepless ass and go to your own room after fifteen minutes. No sense both of us lying awake in the dark."

"Pfft. I can sleep anywhere. You know me."

The elevator doors open, and we begin trekking down the long hallway toward Kendrick's room, with me still on his broad back. Before we reach our destination, a door ahead of us opens and a dark-haired woman emerges, her backside facing us.

"I had so much fun, Kai."

"Me, too," Kai's groggy voice replies from inside the room. "Take care now."

"Call me, okay?"

"If I can."

After blowing a kiss into the room, the woman steps out and pivots, letting the door shut behind her, and that's when it's plain to see she's floating on air.

Quickly, Kendrick stops in front of a random door and pretends to be looking for his key as she passes. And the second she's gone, he gallops past Kai's room and toward his own with me on his back and both of us laughing like hyenas.

Inside the room, I slide off Kendrick's back and buckle over with laughter as he imitates his brother's comment: *if I can.* Soon, we're falling onto his bed and belly laughing like a couple of goofballs.

Still chuckling, I turn onto my side and take in Kendrick's handsome face. He's mere inches from me, and he looks as drunk as I feel. "She looked really happy. Hopefully, having whatever she thinks is good sex and a fun story to tell her friends will soften the blow when he never calls."

"Ye of little faith. Maybe Kai's a changed man. Maybe it was love at first sight for both of them."

I snort. "That doesn't exist. Especially not for Kai Cook."

"Sure, it does."

"For *Kai*?"

"For anyone."

"Have you experienced it?"

Kendrick pauses a weirdly long time, his cheeks flushed. Finally, he says, "No. Not personally. But I believe it exists."

I swat at him. "You're such a romantic." I flop onto my back and sigh. "Why has your brother been acting like such a douchebag this tour? Did his breakup fuck him up that badly? He's acting like pre-Laila Savage." Kendrick doesn't reply, so I look over at him. "What's wrong? Aw, is your sweet, tender heart sympathizing with your brother or with the girl he fucked and won't ever call again?" Kendrick looks like he's biting his tongue, so I push on his arm. "Spit it out."

"Spit what out?"

"Whatever's making you look sad."

"I'm not sad. I'm just . . ." Kendrick drags his teeth across his lower lip. "Was it hard on you seeing that girl come out of Kai's room?"

I snort. "Yes, it was torture." I laugh, thinking he'll join me. But he doesn't. Not even a little bit. I sit up. "Why would it be hard for me to see that? Was it hard for *you*? What does that even mean?"

"I just . . ." He sits up, matching my position, and runs a hand through his hair. "Actually, never mind. I shouldn't have said that. Fuck, I must be really drunk."

"Why shouldn't you have said it?" I pause, waiting for an explanation. When it doesn't come, I poke his muscular bicep. "What the fuck is going on with you? Kendrick, spill."

"Come on, Ruby. I'm sure you don't want to talk about this."

"About *what*?"

"You know . . . What happened between you and Kai."

I stare at him blankly, having a hard time processing his words.

"Way back when," he adds, like that will clarify things for me. But I'm still confused.

Does Kendrick know about that thing that happened between his brother and me, despite Kai making me promise on my life I'd never to say a word about it, ever? If so, that can only mean that Kai himself must have told Kendrick. Which would then mean my long-ago promise is now null and void. At least, that's my interpretation of our binding agreement.

It suddenly occurs to me that if Kai told his brother that story accurately, then there'd be no reason for Kendrick to think, even for a minute, that I'd have a hard time seeing his brother with some fuck buddy. Am I deeply confused because I'm shitfaced? I definitely drank too much down at the bar. "Did Kai tell you something about him and me?"

Kendrick nods.

"Did it involve something that happened at my twentieth birthday party?"

Kendrick's nostrils flare, as he subtly nods again. "I promised him I'd never breathe a word about it, though."

My heart is thumping. "Why did he make you promise that? What was Kai worried about—his bruised ego or Titus kicking his fuckboy ass?"

Kendrick furrows his brow. "*His* bruised ego? No, he wanted to protect *you* and *your* bruised ego."

"Huh?"

"Kai wanted to protect you from embarrassment. Not that you have anything to feel embarrassed about, of course. You were young, and what you felt was perfectly natural. But—"

"Kendrick, I don't know what Kai told you happened between us, but I'm beginning to think he told you the story in reverse." Adrenaline is flashing through me. "Because I assure you, if anyone had a bruised ego that night, it was Kai. Not me."

Kendrick's lips part in surprise, and suddenly, despite the haze of my drunken stupor, I'm positive Kai has slandered me. Lied, lied, lied, like the motherfucking snake he is.

"Kendrick, tell me right now what fucked-up story Kai told you, in detail, or I'm going to march right down to his room and—"

"No, don't do that! I promised him I wouldn't say a word to you."

"Well, you did, and I have a feeling your brother lied through his teeth. So, you'd better start talking."

"Fuck."

Kendrick's Adam's apple bobs. But that's the full extent of his response. So, I grip the White Sox emblem on his hoodie and hiss, "If you don't tell me everything that weasel of a brother told you, right fucking now, I'll . . ." I pause to think of the worst thing I could possibly do, in Kendrick's eyes. And when it comes, I smile broadly. "I'll sob. All over you. I'll cry and cry, buckets of tears, with snot and everything, till you have no choice but to tell me."

"Come on, Ruby. You're not fighting fair here."

"Boo-hoo-hoo. Wracking, heart-wrenching sobs, because you wouldn't come to my aid when I needed you most."

"Can we forget I said anything, please? I promised Kai I'd never—"

"Well, it sucks to be you, then, because I promised him the same thing after he begged me not to say anything to anyone, ever. But now, it sounds like Kai has used my silence against me, to secretly slander me, which means all bets are off, motherfucker."

"Ruby, please. I promised."

"Too bad. You're going to tell me what I want to know, or I'm not only going to Kai's room, and I'm not only going to sob all over you till you're covered in my snot and tears, but I'm going to Titus's room first to tell him and ask him to beat the truth out of your brother."

Kendrick palms his forehead. "There's no need to involve your henchman, okay? That's exactly what Kai wanted to avoid."

"I bet he did." I look at my watch. "You've got exactly ten seconds to make your decision. Nine. Eight."

"Okay, okay!" Kendrick exhales loudly. "Jesus Christ, you're scary."

"Four. Three. Two."

"I don't know too many details, okay? Kai just told me the gist of what happened."

"What did he say?"

"That you, you know, asked him to go upstairs at your twentieth birthday party. To . . . sleep with you. And he turned you down."

My heart explodes in my chest. "Motherfucker! Kendrick, *I* turned *him* down! Kai asked me to go upstairs, and I said, 'Dude, I think of you like a brother!'"

Kendrick's jaw drops. "No fucking way."

"I swear."

He's floored. "Could you have misinterpreted what he said? Could there have been a misunderstanding?"

"Absolutely not. That boy pulled me aside during my party and told me he'd felt an 'attraction' to me from day one, but—"

"What?"

"—because of my age, and the band, and blah, blah, blah, he felt compelled to ignore it and pretend it didn't exist."

"Motherfucker!"

"He was like, 'But, hey, now that we're both adults and it looks like the band is falling apart, anyway. . .' This was when you were still off being a football god, and the band was dying a slow death without you. So anyway, he goes, 'We're both adults now, and the band is on life support, and, oh, ha, ha, I had a super-hot sex dream about you the other night, so—"

"What?" Kendrick bellows, even louder than before.

"'—I'm curious to see if the real thing would be as hot as my sex dream.'"

"I feel sick."

"That's how I felt! Kai was like, 'So, what do you say, Ruby? You wanna go upstairs and do something crazy and have meaningless sex with me?'"

"Kai swore *you* said that to *him*!"

"Lies!"

"Not only that, but Kai also said you confessed to being in love with him."

"In love with him?" I scream. "Oh, hell no."

"Actually, he said you confessed to being 'desperately' in love with him."

"What the serious fuck?" I shove Kendrick's broad shoulder. "And you believed him? This whole time, you've been thinking that I was 'desperately in love' with your idiot douchebag brother?"

"He's exactly your type, Ruby."

"No, he's not. He's an idiot."

"When you get to know him, yes. But why would I doubt his story when all your boyfriends have been exactly like him, and you looked at Kai like you were extremely interested the first time you met him."

"I did not."

"You did, Ruby."

"Oh my fucking god. Kai hit on me and lied to you about it for years, but I'm supposed to defend myself for the way I supposedly looked at him, back when I was a sixteen-year-old virgin who'd never been kissed?"

"What?"

"*What* what?"

"What about Dexter Brenner? You kissed him, didn't you?"

"Dexter Brenner is gay, Kendrick."

"Oh. I thought . . ."

"Jesus, your gaydar is the fucking worst. Now, *focus*." I grab his chin. His eyes are half-mast from all the booze we drank downstairs. "Tell me what you said to Kai, right after he'd told you all those horrendous lies about me."

"I think I was pretty much speechless."

"Don't you dare lie to me."

"I'm not. I swear."

"When did Kai tell you this bullshit story? And why?"

"It happened right after I dropped out of school and came back home. After I rejoined the band. I could tell something was off between you two at practices, so I asked Kai what happened while I was gone. He denied anything was weird, but I kept insisting it was, until finally—"

"Why didn't you just ask me?"

Kendrick pauses. "I don't know. I wanted to hear it from Kai, I guess. And once I did, asking you about it was out of the question, since he made me promise not to talk to you about it. Why would I want to, anyway? I didn't want to embarrass you, Ruby. That was the last thing I wanted."

I shake my head. "I can't believe, for all these years, you've been thinking I threw myself at your fuckboy brother after declaring myself 'desperately in love' with him."

Kendrick shrugs. "I mean, women have always chased Kai. I know you think he's an idiot because you know him well, but women who don't know him think he's irresistible. I've seen it my whole life. Kai's a chick magnet. Not as much as Savage, but who is?"

Hearing Savage's name makes me realize something. "You've told Savage this bullshit story, I presume?"

"Of course not. I told you, I promised Kai not to say a word to anyone."

"But you did, anyway, didn't you? Don't lie to me, KC." I squeeze Kendrick's face between my fingers and thumb and stare him down. "Kendrick Alan Cook. Tell me the truth."

"Fuck." He sighs. "Fine. Yes. I told Savage. But I didn't tell anybody else, I swear."

I grunt in frustration and release him. "Why the hell did you do that?"

"Because I tell Savage everything. You know that. He's my boo."

"*I'm* your boo!"

"But he's my *first* boo. And he didn't tell anyone, and neither did I, except for him, so it's fine."

I can't help chuckling, despite my anger. "Sweetheart, your math ain't mathing. You telling Savage means two-fifths of our band has believed Kai's bullshit story for five long years. That's forty percent of the band."

"Oh."

"And if you take Kai out of the equation, and me, too, then that's a full sixty-six percent of our band believing Kai's horrible slander about me."

"I didn't think of it like that."

I swat his shoulder. "I'm so mad at you for believing Kai all this time."

"I couldn't fathom he'd lie to me about something like this."

"Babe, I know you never would, but the world is filled with men, like Kai, who'd lie to save face without a second thought."

Kendrick exhales. "I'm sorry."

"Sorry's not going to fix it. Come on." I pat his thigh. "It's time for an emergency band meeting."

"Now?" He looks at his watch. "It's almost four."

"I don't care. If I wake anyone up, they can sleep on the plane."

"But what about testing your theory about my insomnia?"

I pull a face. "Seriously?"

He shrugs. "I mean, it seems like an intriguing idea. I'm definitely curious if it'll work."

"Jesus Christ, KC. Get your priorities straight, dude. Your brother has slandered me!" I grab his hand and yank on him. "And I'm not willing to wait another second to clear my goddamned name!"

5
RUBY

After a bit of a crankiness and confusion at his door, our groggy-eyed front man, Savage, his dark hair askew, steps back from the doorframe and lets all four of his sleepy-eyed bandmates into his massive suite. With Savage's popstar wife, Laila, traveling with him—not as our opener this time, but simply for pleasure—and thanks to Mr. and Mrs. Savage having more money than God, due to their multi-year judging contract on *Sing Your Heart Out*, Savage has been booking insanely expensive suites for him and the missus throughout our entire tour, while the rest of us peons settle for the standard rooms supplied by our label.

Yawning, we all shuffle toward the various seating options in the large sitting room.

As he flops into an armchair, Savage murmurs, "Happy birthday, KC. Is this a dare?" He's referring to *Birthday Truth or Dare*, the game that's become a tradition for our band on every member's birthday.

"Nope," I interject. "Thanks to Kai, I've been forced to call an emergency band meeting."

Savage scowls at Kai. "What'd you do?"

Kai leans back in a chair. "Fuck if I know. I was minding my own business in my room when Ruby and her two goons here showed up at my door, talking about all three of them beating the shit out of me if I didn't voluntarily come with them."

Savage looks at me. "What'd he do?"

Before I get a word out, Laila emerges from a bedroom in silk pajamas, her blonde hair in a ponytail and her gorgeous face etched with confusion. "Is it already time to go to the airport?"

"Not yet, babe," Savage says. "Go back to sleep. Ruby called an emergency band meeting for reasons yet unknown. All we know is it's because of something Kai did."

"Sorry to wake you," I say. "Your room is the only one big enough for all of us to sit and talk."

Laila yawns and flops onto her husband's lap. "Is it okay if I stay? This sounds juicy."

"I'd love for you to stay. When a certain lying sack of shit tries to gaslight me about his slander of me, I'm sure I'll appreciate having another woman here for support." I glare at Kai for emphasis, and he rolls his eyes.

"I have no idea what you're talking about," Kai says.

"I'm talking about the bald-faced lies you told Kendrick about what happened between you and me at my twentieth birthday party."

Everyone except Kendrick, who already knows the purpose of this meeting, looks wide-eyed and highly intrigued.

"Hello?" I shout at Kai. "What about that, Kai? Do you deny lying about that to Kendrick or not?"

"You'd better start talking," Titus says to Kai. "What really happened, and what did you *say* happened?"

When Kai says nothing, I address the group with my arms crossed over my chest. "Kai hit on me at my birthday party. That's what happened. And then he went and told Kendrick the exact opposite happened—that *I* hit on *him*." I scoff. "As if."

"As if?" Kai says indignantly, speaking for the first time during this inquisition. "Careful, Ruby. You know there's more to this story than what happened at your birthday party. Honestly, given what happened years before that, I'm shocked you're bringing this up with the whole band rather than coming to talk to me about it in private. That would have saved you a whole lot of embarrassment."

"I have nothing to feel embarrassed about! I was sixteen and stupid, and I barely knew you. What was your excuse, all those years later?"

Kai shoots daggers at his brother. "I told you that stuff in confidence, KC. What the fuck?"

"This isn't Kendrick's fault," I yell, as Kendrick mumbles something in defense of himself. "It's yours and nobody else's."

"You tried to fuck my sister?" Titus booms. "Even though you've always said she's like a sister to you?" He looks at Savage and Kendrick. "He's always said that, right?"

Kendrick and Savage confirm that's true.

"Has everybody tried to fuck my sister behind my back, or just Kai?"

"Just Kai," Savage says with a yawn.

"Fucking hell, Kai," Titus says, his face the color of a beet.

"Would you calm the fuck down?" Kai says, leaning back into his armchair. "This is being blown way out of proportion. I promise you, when you hear the full context of *why* I did what I did—"

"So you don't deny it, then?" I interject. "You don't deny hitting on me, and then turning around and telling Kendrick the exact opposite story?"

"I don't deny it, no. But context is everything."

"Liar!"

"Look, I had to tell Kendrick something, okay? When he came back from school, he was totally depressed and not himself. We all saw it. He wasn't good. And he was all over me about the band feeling weird. The vibe being off. Especially between you and me. He wouldn't let it go. But he was feeling so down in the dumps, I didn't feel like I could pile on and tell him the truth. So, I switched things around to make it go down a bit easier for him."

"What are you talking about?" Kendrick asks, taking the words right out of my mouth.

Kai exhales. "You don't know this, Ruby, but the three of us agreed, from day one, that you were off-limits, okay? Our honorary sister. So, I didn't want Kendrick to be pissed at me for being a hypocrite and breaking that longstanding agreement."

It's a lightbulb moment for me.

Is that the reason Kendrick's never once shown romantic interest in me? Or would he have ignored that stupid agreement, regardless, if he'd been genuinely interested? I mean, Savage has never shown interest in me, either, and that boy definitely would have broken their agreement if that's what he'd wanted to do.

"So, let me get this straight," I say to Kai. "You were scared of your brother finding out you're a hypocrite, by your own admission, so you opted to tell a horrendous lie about me hitting on you, instead?"

Kai rolls his eyes. "I told a little white lie. One that was actually based in reality, if you think about it."

"Ha!"

"Ruby, you know what I'm talking about."

"I assure you, I don't."

Kai glares at me, like he thinks I'm lying, but I shrug, letting him know whatever he's thinking about is a mystery to me.

His eyes narrowed, Kai says, "You've forced my hand, Ruby. I've never told this story to anyone, because, contrary to what you think, I've never wanted to embarrass you. But now that you've opened Pandora's Box—"

"Oh, *I'm* the one who did that?"

"I feel like I've got to tell it to defend myself. Unless, of course, you'd like to do the honors."

"I already know you lied to Kendrick about all that prior stuff, too, Kai. Kendrick told me. So, let's get everything out in the open."

"I didn't tell Kendrick a single lie about that part. The only lie I told was about your birthday party."

"Not true. You told Kendrick I professed my desperate, undying love for you."

"Because you did."

"*What*? Are you delusional?"

Kai's expression is smug and immovable. "Wow, look who's lying now."

I gasp. "I was never in love with you. Let alone desperately."

"Yes, you were."

"I had a teeny-tiny crush on you—an older guy who seemed mysterious and knowledgeable about music—for a nano-second, back when I was a sixteen-year-old virgin with zero experience with boys. And you knew that, so you lured me to admit my crush on you—"

"Lured you?"

"Yes, because you loved the ego boost of it all. I assure you, though, once I got to know you the tiniest bit, I quickly realized my so-called crush on you was stupid and not even about you as a person. That I'd sooner kiss a maggot-covered pile of shit than kiss you!"

Everyone chuckles. Everyone except, Kai, who's looking damned furious at this point.

"You're so full of shit," Kai grits out, and everyone in the room shifts their gaze to him, like we're watching a ping pong match. "We both know after I turned you down in that stairwell—"

"You didn't turn me down."

"—you never stopped giving me puppy-dog eyes from across every room."

"What? After our conversation in the stairwell, I was so embarrassed I'd said anything to you, I could barely look at you, let alone give you 'puppy-dog eyes.' And you didn't turn me down, Kai. Quite the opposite. You intentionally kept me hanging, because you wanted to keep me as an option for a later time. Like, maybe, I don't know, my twentieth birthday, perhaps?"

Kai adamantly denies it, and I insist I'm right, with both of us shouting until, finally, Titus intervenes and screams, even more loudly, for both of us to shut the fuck up. When a charged silence ensues, Titus looks between both of us, his chest heaving.

"Ruby, you have the floor first," Titus commands. "Tell us what happened in that stairwell, from your point of view. And, Kai, keep your mouth shut."

I take a deep breath. "Thank you, T. Okay, so this was maybe a month after we'd joined the band. After practice one night, Kai went out into the stairwell to smoke, while the rest of you party animals stayed behind to drink beer. I followed Kai into the stairwell, because, yes, I had a little crush on him, and I was hoping to flirt with him a little bit and see if maybe he'd show any signs of interest." I roll my eyes at my embarrassing admission. "Well, we got to chatting out there, and, suddenly, with nobody else around, Kai started being super flirty with me. Like, it was really obvious, you guys."

"Bullshit," Kai murmurs.

"Let her speak," Kendrick says, his large palm raised. "You'll get your chance."

"She was *sixteen*," Kai insists. "I knew better than to flirt with her."

"No, you didn't," Titus pipes in. "You always looked at her like a hungry lion. Right from the start."

"I did not."

"You sure as fuck did. Honestly, you were my only reservation when we agreed to join the band. But I knew how excited Ruby was, and also that she'd kill me if I tried to ruin things for her by telling her to watch out for you. So, I kept my mouth shut while vowing to keep an eagle eye on you."

"Lovely," Kai says. "It's great to know you've been pretending to like me for twelve fucking years."

"Only for two, at the very beginning. I started genuinely liking you after that, against my will."

Both men can't help but smile at that, along with the rest of the band.

"I still don't like you for my sister, to be clear," Titus says. "Fuck no. You're an emotionally stunted, fuckboy menace. You're no better for her than Cooper."

In a flash, the entire band starts grumbling about Cooper and how annoying it was to have him on the tour and how frustrating it was to watch all our public displays of affection.

"Okay, I get it, guys," I say, cutting everyone off. "I have a defective picker. I admit that. Sorry he was so annoying."

"So annoying," Savage grumbles.

"Ugh, I hated him," Titus adds.

"Seriously, though, what was up with all that PDA?" Kai says with a grimace. "Every time I turned around, that fucker was swallowing your face, dude." He pulls a face like he's smelling rancid milk.

"You don't get to join in on this hate-fest," I hiss at Kai.

"You're not my brother, like everyone else, so you've lost the privilege of scolding me for my bad taste in men."

"Just saying."

"Well, don't." The group is looking at me, pointedly, so I add, "Yes, I admit the PDA was over the top. Trust me, I felt smothered and icked out, too, okay? Hence, he's now gone."

Everyone applauds and cheers.

"Cooper felt insecure, so he was, you know, 'claiming' me in front of the world. I was stupid to go along with it as long as I did." I sigh. "Listen, I didn't call an emergency band meeting to talk about my icky relationship with Cooper. He was a mistake, and I should have said no when he asked to travel with me on tour. Now, back to Kai and his bald-faced, inexcusable lies."

"I didn't lie," Kai insists. "At least, not about the stairwell."

"Are you done telling your side of that story?" Kendrick asks me.

"No. There's more. Kai was brazenly flirting with me, like I said, and because I was an inexperienced moron whose defective picker had already started forming, I felt stupidly excited about that. And that's when Kai asked me if I had a boyfriend at school."

Everyone collectively gasps and looks at Kai accusingly, and I know that little nugget has instantly swayed them. Because, seriously, what nineteen-year-old boy asks a sixteen-year-old girl in a stairwell if she has a boyfriend, unless he's flirting with her?

"I told him, no, I didn't have a boyfriend. And, no, I'd never had a boyfriend at all, actually. And he goes, 'Do you have a crush on someone, though? Maybe at school . . . or from somewhere . . . else?'"

Everyone gasps again and glares with even more gusto at Kai. Once again, they're reading through the lines, every bit as much as I did all those years ago.

"She's making me sound like a creeper," Kai mutters. "But I was just making small talk."

Everyone pounces on him, letting him know he's full of shit. But it's Kendrick who defends my honor the most vehemently, telling his big brother to shut the fuck up till it's his turn to speak.

"Thank you, sir," I say primly to Kendrick. To the group, I continue my story. "So, silly girl that I was, I mustered the courage to tell Kai I didn't have a crush on anyone at school. Winky winky. But, yes, there might have been someone outside of school I'd been crushing on. Winky winky." I look around at the group. "And Kai lit up, you guys. Obviously, he understood what I meant, even though I didn't have the courage to say the rest explicitly."

"Most human communication is nonverbal," Laila offers, her index finger raised.

"It sure is. And trust me, the nonverbal communication in that moment was crystal clear: I tacitly admitted my little crush on Kai, and he was *super* stoked to hear it."

Kai mumbles something under his breath that ends with the phrase "such bullshit," and everyone tells him to shut the fuck up, once again.

"What did Kai say when you revealed you had a crush on *someone*?" Laila asks, leaning forward. And I swear, I can practically see a big ol' tub of buttered popcorn in her lap.

Performing my best Kai Cook impression, I reply, "'Wow, Ruby. Whoever he is, he's a lucky guy. If, by some chance, he's someone in our band, however, now wouldn't be the right time for either of you to act on those feelings. Not with you being sixteen and the band just now getting off the ground.'"

"That's not what I said!" Kai shouts.

"Yes, it is!" I shout back. "Word for word."

"You're delusional."

"No, you are. Not to mention, an egomaniac." I address the faces staring at me. "But guess what Kai didn't say to me. 'Hey, Ruby, if your crush happens to be *me*, I'm sorry, but I'm not into you as more than a friend.' And you know why he didn't say that? Because, like I said, he fully intended to string me along and keep me as an option for later."

"That tracks," Titus says, as Kai grumbles, once again. "Considering the fucker tried to get into your pants only a few years later."

"Oh, I'm a fucker now?" Kai retorts, shaking his head. "Guys, even in Ruby's self-serving, untrue version of events, I turned her down. So, who cares what I said to her years later, when I was drunk, and she was a grown-ass woman? By then, she wasn't even close to a sixteen-year-old virgin anymore, so—"

"Oh, you're slut-shaming me now?" I shriek, as Kendrick, Titus, and Laila all shout something similar in my defense.

"That's not what I meant, and you know it," Kai shouts. "Would everyone please calm the fuck down? Jesus."

I waggle my finger at Kai, feeling like I'm physically vibrating with indignation. "If you want to slut-shame some-one, then do it to yourself, you fucking dickhead. You're the one who's been banging randos all tour, not me."

"I wasn't slut-shaming you, Ruby! I meant you were an adult by then, and you'd gotten yourself plenty of experience."

"*Plenty*? There you go again!"

"You're being hyper-sensitive. Jesus Christ. I don't care if you want to fuck an entire football team, okay? I truly don't give a shit. I just meant, in the full context of everything, me getting stupid-drunk at your birthday party, right after a bad breakup, and then suggesting we go upstairs to fuck for the fun of it wasn't a capital offense. Was it my proudest moment? No. But it wasn't as fucked up as you're making it sound."

"What about the sex dream you'd had about her?" Kendrick interjects. "Ruby said you told her you'd had one about her, when you hit on her."

Kai shrugs, looking remarkably unbothered. "I've always had all kinds of weird sex dreams. I used to have them all the time about my geometry teacher, too, and she was a literal grandma."

Everyone in the room, including me, cracks up at the revelation. But that's Kai for you. He's always been one hell of a horny motherfucker.

"Guys, I did something stupid. I admit that. But look at it from my point of view. One, Ruby's objectively hot. That's a fact. Two, I knew she'd always been desperately in love with me—"

"I had a teeny-tiny crush on you for all of five weeks!"

"It's my turn to talk now. You've had your chance." With blazing eyes, Kai returns to the group. "From my personal point of view, I truly thought Ruby'd always been desperately in love with me, based on several nonverbal communications." He ticks off on his fingers. "Three, whatever girlfriend had just broken up with me, and I was feeling low about that, and Ruby being Ruby, she was probably being extra nice to me that night to make me feel better about myself."

"No good deed goes unpunished," I murmur.

"And five, or six, or whatever number I'm on, I was shit-faced at the time, and that impaired my judgment and made me suggest something I shouldn't have—something I would have regretted in the morning, if she'd been stupid enough to say yes to me."

"As if."

"And that's it. End of story."

Everyone looks extremely persuaded by that little speech. And that pisses me off, since I did *nothing* to give Kai the impression that I was in love with him, let alone desperately. And certainly not for years and years, since age motherfucking sixteen.

"Not every crush blooms into deep feelings," I sputter. "In fact, it's usually the opposite. You look back and can't believe you ever had that crush in the first place. Look at Kendrick and his fleeting crush on Laila, for example. I'm sure, when he looks back on that . . ." I trail off when I realize Kendrick looks mortified. Shellshocked. *Furious.*

Shit. I think I've just done something unthinkable: I've thrown my best friend under the bus to save myself.

"It's okay, Kendrick," Laila says quickly, apparently reading his body language. "I've always known about your tiny crush on me."

"I told her back then, during the tour," Savage explains. "It's nothing to feel embarrassed about."

"We all knew about it," Titus adds.

My heart is hammering. Kendrick is glaring at me in a way he's never done before—the same way he sometimes glares at Kai, after Kai's fucked up. Man, he's furious with me.

Kendrick grits out, "My crush wasn't about you, specifically, Laila. Sorry. You were a placeholder."

"I know that, KC."

"Everyone in the band was dating someone at the time, or at least crushing hard on someone, and I just wanted to feel that way, too."

I pull a face. Well, that's not true. As I recall, I was the only person even remotely involved with anyone at the time—with Finn. Everyone else was extremely single.

"You don't need to explain," Laila says gently. "I've had plenty of crushes that went nowhere and weren't even about the actual person. Like I said, you've got nothing to feel embarrassed about."

When Kendrick shoots daggers at me again, I look at Savage and blurt, "You're not upset with your best friend for having a tiny crush on your future wife, right? Because you know that happened before you and Laila got even together, and his feelings weren't real."

"Of course, I'm not upset," Savage says calmly. "I actually tried to push them together at one point, before I realized my own feelings for her."

"I was so pissed at you for that," Laila says, swatting her husband's shoulder, and they both crack up.

"And, of course," I continue, "nobody here thinks Kendrick still feels that way about Laila. Not for a minute. And that's my entire point. My schoolgirl crush on Kai was ancient history in a matter of weeks, the same as Kendrick's crush on Laila. Which means Kai's version of events is absolutely ridiculous." I look at Kendrick with raised eyebrows, nonverbally begging for forgiveness, and his blazing eyes and tight features make it clear my comment not only didn't dig me out of the hole with him, it dug the hole even deeper.

After exhaling loudly, Kendrick says, "Okay, guys. Here's the deal. It's my birthday, so we're gonna play a round of *Birthday Truth or Dare*. Except in my game, truth is the only option."

Everyone expresses shock and disagreement. Ever since the Cook brothers and Savage started this birthday tradition, it's dare that's been the only possible option.

"Come on, KC. Leave *Birthday Truth or Dare* for your birthday party in Vancouver," Kai says, yawning. "We're all tired."

With an angry glare directed at Kai, Kendrick forges ahead like he didn't hear a word out of his brother's mouth. "Kai, when Ruby joined the band, did you or did you not declare her off-limits for all of us because you secretly wanted her yourself?"

Kai scoffs. "No, but even if I did, I'm pretty sure there's a statute of limitations on that crime."

"Is that a no that morphed into a yes?"

"It's an 'I don't think so, but if I did, who gives a shit at this point?'"

"I do."

"So do I," Titus interjects.

"Why?"

"Because I don't like liars," Titus supplies.

"Same here," Kendrick says.

"Would you two put your pitchforks away?" Kai shouts. He looks at Kendrick. "I didn't have some big master plan to seduce Ruby from day one, if that's what you're getting at. People are complicated. *I'm* complicated. And horny. And as I've said, Ruby is objectively hot. Who knows what I was thinking back then? Whatever it was, I've stopped thinking it now, I assure you. The same way Ruby's earliest feelings for me, whether they were a crush or something much more—"

"They weren't."

"—are long gone now."

Another silence ensues as we all process that logic. Unfortunately, I think Kai's scored big points with that one. Damn.

"I knew this would happen," Kai grumbles. "I told you guys from the start we'd have a Fleetwood Mac situation on our hands, and here it is."

"Would you shut the fuck up about Fleetwood Mac?" Kendrick booms.

"I haven't mentioned them in a decade."

"Yeah, and I told you never to mention them to me again, or I'd kick your ass."

"Strangle me with my amp cord, actually," Kai says with a laugh. "Those were your exact words. I've never forgotten them."

Laila clears her throat. "Sorry if I'm dumb, but didn't Fleetwood Mac sell, like, some huge, record-breaking number of albums?"

"Thank you!" Kendrick bellows, making all of us crack up. "Kai always brings them up as a cautionary tale: as proof co-ed bands can't avoid getting blown up by romantic entanglements."

Titus scoffs. "If that's his point, there are better bands to bring up. The White Stripes, for instance."

"Now, *that's* a cautionary tale," Kendrick says. "Take notes, Kai."

"ABBA's a good one, too," Laila offers.

"What about No Doubt?" Savage contributes, which launches the group into talking about Gwen Stefani and her bass player, and the hit songs they got out of their breakup.

When that conversation runs its course, Kai exhales loudly and says, "So, are we done here? I'm fucked out and want to go to bed."

Kendrick shakes his head. "Not till you apologize to Ruby."

"For what?"

"For telling lies about her, dumbass."

"I've explained all that."

"Explanations aren't apologies. You were a dick to her. It's time to own that and say you're sorry."

When Kai hesitates, the entire room screams at him to do it, once and for all, if only to get us all some sleep before it's time to head to the airport.

"*Fine,*" Kai yells in a huff. He looks at me, his eyes blazing. "Ruby, I'm sorry. I was a dick. I shouldn't have said what I did to you. And I shouldn't have said what I did to Kendrick. Now, can I please go to bed?"

I cross my arms. "That wasn't the least bit sincere."

Kai scoffs. "Too bad. It's all you get."

"Dick."

"You're overreacting, and you know it."

Before I reply, all our phones simultaneously beep. When we look, there's a text from our tour manager, Caden, in the group chat:

Caden: Wakey wakey, folks! It's airport time!

6

KENDRICK

I'm the first person to step foot onto our private plane for the six-hour flight to Vancouver, so I plop myself down in one of the coveted rows with only two seats, hoping Ruby will grab the one next to mine.

It's possible Ruby will avoid me like the plague out of guilt for the stunt she pulled this morning. But knowing her, I think it's more likely she'll confront what she did head on and beg for my forgiveness. Which I'll give her. But not before making her squirm a tiny bit.

In her defense, it was only when Ruby drew the comparison between my ridiculous, fleeting crush on Laila back in the day and hers on Kai that I truly understood how dead as a doornail her feelings for my big brother must have become. But even so, I'm going to make her grovel at least a little bit. I've never once had the upper hand like this with Ruby. Usually, she's coming at me, rightfully so, for something stupid I said or did. So now, I'm going to milk my present state of moral superiority. But only for the duration of this six-hour flight. Probably not even that long, if she starts pulling any of her highly effective mind-control strategies on me. The girl is good. But, still, I'm determined not to fold too quickly.

Our tour manager, Caden, and his trusty assistant enter the plane as I'm getting settled into my seat. Not surprisingly, they head toward the back cabin together, probably to go over whatever details and logistics are coming up on our busy schedule.

After that, Kai shuffles on looking like a sleep-deprived, annoyed hot mess. And after him, there's a trio of high-level staffers.

When my brother locks eyes with me, he motions to the empty seat next to me, and I shake my head.

Whatever, his expression says as he flops down into a seat several rows away.

When our eyes met in the van on the drive to the airport, I flipped him off with both hands, and Kai returned the gesture. But apparently, he's ready to make nice now. Me, not so much. He doesn't realize this, of course, but the lies he flippantly told me about Ruby quite possibly changed the trajectory of my life.

Maybe Ruby never would have been interested in me romantically, but I guess I'll never know. Why not? Because it's too late now. Because we're best friends and she's never shown interest in me, anyway. And oh yeah, mere hours ago, she literally told me she'll never date another guy who started out as a friend.

But what if Kai had never told me those lies? What if I came back home after dropping out of college, and I finally mustered the courage to spill my guts to Ruby, like I'd been planning? What if I'd told her how I felt about her back then— how I've always felt? But no. I returned and found out Ruby had been "desperately in love" with Kai since age sixteen. That, in fact, she'd felt so strongly about him, she'd even begged him to fuck her on her twentieth birthday, which Kai had declined to do.

Ruby.

She's boarded the plane now, and she's heading down the aisle behind Titus, her pink hair piled on top of her head and her sexy tattoo on full display, thanks to the shoulder-baring tank top she's sporting underneath a pair of oversized denim overalls.

Ruby usually sits next to me or Titus on longer flights like this one. So, it's anyone's guess if she'll pick me or her brother this time. I'm hoping me, since she often says she prefers sleeping on my shoulder the most because Titus always falls asleep, too, and then he gets all wonky in his seat.

When Ruby's dark gaze lands on me, she smiles cautiously, as if to say, *Do you forgive me?* When I don't return her smile, her shoulders droop. She says something to Titus, which I think is something like "Let's take that row there," so, fuck it, I motion to her to come over to me, instead.

At my beckoning, Ruby's beautiful face lights up. She says something else to Titus, and with her backpack slung over her shoulder, bounces down the aisle to me.

"Hey, bestie. Does that mean you're okay with me sitting here with you?"

I shrug. "Suit yourself." It's as nonchalant a tone as I've ever used with Ruby. But since I'm hoping to get my first-ever grovel from her, I feel like I've got no other choice.

Ruby seems unfazed by my cold tone as she plops herself down next to me and begins pulling all her usual shit out of her big backpack. An iPad and charger. A packet of almonds. Some lip gloss and moisturizer. And so on.

"Are you still mad at me?" she asks, keeping her eyes on her task.

"Yes."

She gasps and stops what she's doing. "Still?"

"It's been an hour, Ruby."

"I know. I can't believe you've managed to stay mad at me for that long. Wow. That's a long time to stay mad at someone as sweet and lovable as me, who's also regretful and repentant about what she did."

I try not to crack a smile. Goddamn Ruby. If this is the direction her grovel is going to go, I'm going to crumble like a cookie in record speed.

"Are you furious with me? Or just mad?"

"Furious is too strong a word."

"Mad, then? That's still a really strong emotion, if you think about."

Fuck. She's batting her lashes, and I can feel the corners of my mouth itching to trend upward. "I'd say I'm more annoyed than anything, at this point."

"Progress!"

"But I'm very, *very* annoyed with you, Ruby. As precariously close to being mad as a person can get."

"And rightly so. I behaved like a monster by bringing up your crush to save myself. I can't believe I did that. What was I thinking?"

"God only knows."

She stops what she's doing and fixes her dark, soulful eyes on mine. "Seriously, KC. I'm deeply sorry for what I did. I'm a horrible friend. When I felt like I was drowning in stormy seas, I used my very best friend in the world as a flotation device. Because that's me. Selfish and despicable to my core." She shakes her head. "In my panic not to drown, I didn't think twice to climb aboard your big, broad, strong back and—"

"Flattery will get you nowhere."

"It's not flattery. Your back is strong. And so I climbed it, and—" She pounds her closed fist violently into her open palm and grimaces dramatically. "Then I shoved your sweet, innocent, saintly face underwater, to save myself, causing you to go down, down, down, all the way to Davey Jones's locker."

I don't want to do it, but I can't help chuckling at her little passion play.

Ruby flashes me an adorably apologetic look. "Will you ever be able to forgive me, my darling bestie, or will my monstrous behavior shatter our friendship forever?"

"It's been sixty minutes, Ruby. And I never get to be mad at you."

"I thought you were only annoyed." She pinches my forearm. "Think about it, my darling. Wouldn't it be so much more fun if we joined forces against Kai as our common enemy? Why waste another valuable minute longer than necessary being annoyed with me, when Public Enemy Number One is sitting right up there, and we could talk shit about him the whole flight together, if only you'd forgive and forget and accept my heartfelt apology now."

"What shit-talking would we do, even if I forgave you now? We both know you're going to fall asleep right after they feed us."

"No, this one time, I'd force myself to stay awake the whole flight and shit-talk Kai all the way to Vancouver, if I knew that was the price of your forgiveness."

"My forgiveness doesn't have a price tag. I just need some time to process. What you did was shitty, Ruby."

"I know. I'm sorry."

She juts out her lower lip and hangs her head, and I swear, every cell in my body yearns to take her in my arms and kiss her pouty mouth.

"If I were you," Ruby says, "I'd tell me to get the fuck out of my airspace and go sit with Titus because you can't stand to even look at me."

I snort. "That tactic isn't gonna work on me, babe."

Ruby bats her eyelashes. "What tactic?"

"Making your *mea culpa* so over the top, I feel compelled to reassure you that what you did wasn't that bad."

Ruby snickers. "You know all my best tricks."

"And I'm ready for all of them. You can sit here next to me, if you want. In fact, that's what I want, as part of your penance. But just so you know, I'm not going to forgive you for a while."

Ruby's eyes go wide. "For how long?"

"I guess you'll have to wait and see."

"Will you still be mad at me after we get to Vancouver?"

"Maybe."

"Kendrick!"

"At least till we land. The rest is a wait-and-see kind of thing."

"Kendrick Cook! Vancouver is six hours from now. I won't survive anything beyond that." She bats my shoulder. "You're entitled to be annoyed with me, but don't be *cruel*."

Goddamn her. How does she do this? I'm smiling from ear to ear, against my will. "Well, maybe next time you'll think twice before throwing me under a double-decker bus to save your own embarrassed ass."

"I will. I promise." She pinches my shoulder. "Will you still be my pillow for the flight, even if you're annoyed with me?"

"Nope."

Ruby gasps. "Cruel."

"There have to be consequences for your bad behavior, Miss Connolly, or you'll never correct it in the future."

"The punishment has to fit the crime, though. Not being my pillow is the equivalent of sentencing me to death for a misdemeanor."

"You really think what you did was a misdemeanor?"

"We were all there when you saw Laila at Reed's party and called dibs, Kendrick. It's not like it was some kind of state secret you were interested in her."

Yeah, and only a half-hour before that happened, I had to watch Ruby in an extremely flirtatious conversation with Finn, one of the many musicians at Reed's party, which then led to Finn pulling me aside to ask if Ruby was seeing anyone. In that moment, I was once again reminded of the fact that Ruby is, always has been, and always will be a non-starter for me. Because she wanted my brother over me. Finn over me. Cooper over me. Hell, anyone and everyone over me.

The pilot's voice erupts over the speaker with an announcement: the doors have closed and we're heading to the runway. But when he's done giving us his spiel, Ruby pokes my forearm and asks, "At least admit you're more annoyed with Kai than me. Give me that if nothing else."

I roll my eyes. "Fine. Yes."

Ruby fist-pumps the air. "Progress, again!"

I lean into her, like I'm telling a juicy secret. "When I made eye contact with Kai during the drive to the airport, I double flipped him off in your honor."

She purrs and pats my shoulder. "You're my knight in shining armor."

"I try."

She snorts. "Rightly so, since I'm your BFF, and Kai's only your stupid big brother."

"What he did was dumb, but it wasn't malicious."

Ruby agrees. "But, still, let's let him suffer a bit longer."

We start looking for a show to watch together, but when the flight attendant comes by with food and drinks, we ditch that idea and dig in.

"It's a bummer we didn't get to test my theory about your insomnia," Ruby says, chomping on her food. "If you've forgiven me by the time we get to our hotel in Vancouver, we can try then."

I'd kill or die to make that happen. But still, I reply calmly, "I'm too annoyed with you to make any firm future plans."

Ruby rolls her eyes before pointing at my tray. "Are you gonna eat that second piece of toast? It looks awfully lonely over there."

"Go for it."

"Thanks, bestie."

I watch her scarf down my toast with gusto, and I can't help grinning at her adorableness.

"What?" Ruby asks when she catches me staring at her. She pats her chin. "Do I have jam all over on my face?"

"I'm amused at how much you like plane food."

"It's the best. Do you have any butter? I'm all out."

I hand her the butter, and she opens it with enthusiasm.

"Being a horrible friend works up an appetite," she says, making me chuckle against my will.

"I wouldn't know."

"No, you wouldn't. Because you're the best friend, ever, and I'm a monster. The worst friend in the history of the world."

"Not the worst. Close, but not quite."

"Gotcha."

"Shit. I just reassured you, didn't I?"

"Oldest trick in the book, my darling."

After a bit more conversation, we finish our meals and a flight attendant takes our trays away. With a yawn, Ruby pulls out her phone and connects to the plane's Wi-Fi. It's what she always does before hunkering down to sleep on a long flight: she catches up with her parents, just in case things go badly while she's fast asleep. It's a morbid approach to flying, if you ask me, but Ruby says it's the only reason she can fall asleep so easily: because she knows she's said what needs to be said to her loved ones as her last conscious act.

"Oh, fuck," Ruby says, looking down at her phone. "Crap."

"What's wrong?"

"I just got a text from my building manager. A pipe broke

above my unit and three others, and they all got water damage."

"Shit. How bad is it?"

"He doesn't know yet. He says not to worry, it'll be covered by insurance, and he's got a crew already there assessing the damage and figuring out what needs to be done." She looks up, frowning. "He says there's a good chance I might need to be out of my place for as long as a week after we get back."

I don't hesitate. "You can stay with me."

She bites her lip, like she didn't hear my offer. "Stephanie's coming to stay with Titus when we get back."

"Like I said, stay with me."

"I don't want to cramp your style. It's only a week. I'll stay in a hotel."

"But you're sick to death of hotels."

"I'll survive."

"Ruby, I've got no style for you to cramp. I'm single, remember?"

"Yeah, single and ready to mingle. You always date like a maniac when we first get home. And this time, I'm sure you'll go balls to walls, considering how horny you must be."

"We're talking about one week. I can survive that long. I've come this far, haven't I?"

Ruby considers it briefly but eventually shakes her head. "You've only got one bed. I'll ask Savage and Laila."

"They're all the way out in Malibu, though. Aren't you going to be doing some songwriting sessions for some of Reed's newbies when we get back?"

Reed's studio is right down the street from my place. It's Ruby's biggest dream—writing songs for other artists. The bigger the better. So, to his credit, our label owner has invited Ruby to sit in on some writing sessions with some of his up-and-coming artists at his studio in North Hollywood.

"We could test out your theory about my insomnia during

that week," I add, when she looks like she's seriously considering saying yes to me. "Come on, Ruby. I'm genuinely curious to see if you're right."

Ruby flashes me a side-eye. "You said you don't get insomnia when you're home."

"Did I? Oh. Well, that probably won't be true with that quarterback still all over the news." My heart feels like a herd of wild horses stampeding in my chest. In this moment, I'll say whatever it takes to get Ruby to stay with me, in my bed, for one glorious week.

Ruby nods slowly, like that makes sense to her. "Thanks for the offer. I'll think about it and let you know once I have more information." With a big yawn, she tugs on the shoulder of my T-shirt. "Now, will you please forgive me for my sins and be my pillow? I'm sleepy and contrite."

I laugh. "What happened to you staying awake to shit-talk Kai all the way to Vancouver, as the price of forgiveness?"

"Oh. Yeah. I did say that, didn't I?" She yawns. "God, he's such a dick. Your turn now."

I crack up. "It's okay, monster. You've worn me down."

Ruby flashes me an adorable smile. "Does that mean we're besties again?"

"Besties again." It pains me to call her that, even though I genuinely cherish our friendship. But the thing is I love this girl too much not to have her in my life, one way or another. For a long time now, when it comes to Ruby, I've been resigned to take what I can get.

As Ruby snuggles up against my shoulder, I kiss the top of her head. "Sweet dreams, Ruby Duby."

"Use my head as a pillow, if you start to feel sleepy."

"I won't, but thanks." Unfortunately, I never sleep on airplanes. That's not a recent thing. My whole life, I haven't been able to get my body to relax enough to sleep when my brain knows I'm hurtling through space at three hundred miles per hour in a metal container. And it certainly doesn't help watching Ruby texting her loved ones her final goodbyes.

"Don't forget to wipe my drool, as needed," she murmurs.

"I make no promises about that."

Ruby yawns. "Sorry for using you as a flotation device, my love. I promise I'll never pull that kind of bullshit again."

"You'd better not."

With her head still resting on my shoulder, she holds up her pinky, and I link mine in hers. But the truth is, even though I've been talking a good game, I'd let Ruby use me as a flotation device any time she needed. Even in shark-infested waters. In fact, if I saw this girl of mine drowning, I'd jump in and try to save her without a thought to my own safety, even in the face of great whites circling. So, really, I can't blame her for using me to save herself this morning when, in reality, I'd demand she swap my life for hers if the opportunity arose.

"I forgive you," I whisper into her hair. I close my eyes and inhale the scent of her shampoo. *And I love you.*

"Now I really will have sweet dreams," Ruby whispers.

It's the last thing she says before her breathing turns rhythmic, making it clear she's fallen fast asleep against my shoulder. As usual. And once again, like always, I love every second of Ruby's body pressed against mine. Albeit, not in the precise way it'd be, in a perfect world.

7
KENDRICK

Turbulence jostles me awake, and I'm yanked out of a dream.

A sex dream.

About Ruby.

I look around, feeling disoriented, and remember I'm still on the plane to Vancouver, sitting next to the woman who was sucking me off in my dream.

I fell asleep? That's a first. And so was that dream. At least, that was the first time in a long while. Thanks, Kai. I've probably got you to thank for planting the idea of a sex dream about Ruby into my subconscious brain.

An uncomfortable ache between my legs commands my attention. When I look down, sure enough, I've got a raging, straining boner poking up behind my soft sweats—one Ruby will surely notice, if that turbulence woke her up, too. I cover my tent pole with my hand, just in case, and then sigh with relief when it's apparent Ruby is still dead to the world.

Taking care not to wake her, I tilt her slack body away from me, slide out of my seat, and head toward the back of the plane. A few minutes later, after exiting the bathroom, I notice

Savage and Laila hunkered together watching a show and head over to say hi. Also, to make sure they're both genuinely unbothered by Ruby reminding everyone about my embarrassing early crush on Laila.

"Hey," I say, resting a forearm on the back of an empty seat in front of them.

After they both greet me warmly, Savage asks, "Did you forgive Ruby yet?"

"Yeah. I let her sweat it for a bit, though."

The three of us chuckle.

"What about you and Kai?" Savage asks.

"No forgiveness yet."

"Good," Laila says with a laugh. "Let him suffer till at least Vancouver."

"Agreed." I shift my arm on the seat. "So, listen, I just want to double-check we're cool. You know, because of what Ruby said."

They both simultaneously wave at the air.

"That's old news, KC," Savage says, as Laila says something similar.

"Just wanted to be sure. Thanks." I bite my lip and shift my position again, wrangling my thoughts. I don't think that's why I came over here, after all. I think maybe there was something else motivating me. "Hey, would you two do me a favor? If Ruby asks to crash at your place for a week when we get back, could you make up some reason why she can't?" I explain the text Ruby got from her building manager and the fact that she didn't leap at the chance to crash at my place, even though it's way more conveniently located to Reed's studio in North Hollywood. "She said she doesn't want to cramp my style," I say. "I've only got the one bed, and she's convinced I'm going to be fucking half of LA in it when we get back."

"Sounds about right," Savage says with a snicker.

"Not true."

"KC, you always date like crazy when we first get back from tour. You settle down after that, but it's definitely your pattern."

Laila's been looking at me suspiciously this whole time. With narrowed eyes, she says, "So, if I understand your motivations here, you want us to turn Ruby away—"

"If she asks, yeah."

"So she says yes to staying with you."

"Right."

"For no other reason than it'd be more convenient . . . for *her*?"

"I told her it wouldn't be a bother. That it might even be fun. But she's being too polite about supposedly inconveniencing me."

Savage and Laila look at each other, and it feels like they're having a lengthy, nonverbal conversation about me.

"What?" I finally ask.

"Are you sure *her* convenience is the only reason you want Ruby to stay with you?" Laila asks slowly, her perfect eyebrow arched.

"Well, I mean, I also think we'd have a good time. I rarely get to hang out with Ruby, just her and me, these days. We used to do that all the time when she was at Northwestern, right after I dropped out of school. I'd come visit her on weekends and sleep on the floor of her dorm room. But these days, it's a rarity."

Again, my best friend and his wife have an entire conversation without speaking.

"What?" I ask again, this time with a bit more oomph. "Whatever those looks mean, I'd appreciate you looping me in on it."

"Why do you think you're jonesing to spend more one-on-one time with Ruby?" Laila asks coyly.

"Because we're almost always in big groups on tour, and when we get home, we don't tend to hang out as much. Not sure why."

"No?" Laila asks innocently.

"He's not sure why," Savage deadpans to Laila, making her chuckle.

"I'm gathering you both think *you* know why?"

"We definitely have a theory," Laila concedes.

"Well, don't leave me in suspense."

When Laila motions to Savage to explain, he says, "Speaking for myself, I think it's because Ruby usually starts dating someone when we get back, and you—"

"Yeah, both of us get super busy, whenever we're home," I supply. But I say it at the same time Savage finishes his sentence with, "—can't stand seeing Ruby with someone else."

My jaw drops. "What's that supposed to mean?"

"Tell me this, Kendrick," Laila says. "How did it make you feel to find out Ruby's never been 'desperately in love' with Kai, like you've been thinking for so long? Was that a neutral fact for you to learn, or did it cause you to have some kind of emotional reaction?"

"Of course it wasn't neutral. I was pissed at my brother for telling me lies. That wasn't cool."

"But was it also a relief for you to find that out? Did it make you feel like a weight had been lifted off you?"

"Yeah. Sure. Because now I don't have to walk on eggshells, worrying I'm rubbing salt in Ruby's teenage wounds every time Kai's name comes up."

Laila looks at her husband and snickers.

I roll my eyes. "What are you not saying?"

Laila smiles. "You want to know what I said to Savage when he first told me what you'd told him about Ruby supposedly being secretly in love with Kai?"

"You're such a fucking blabbermouth, Adrian Savage."

"She's my *wife*."

Laila's smile broadens. "I said, 'Wow, I would have bet any amount of money on that exact same story being true about Ruby and Kendrick, not Ruby and Kai."

My heart stops. "W-what made you think that?"

Laila stares at me for a long moment, like she's expecting me to answer my own question. But since I don't know what the fuck she's expecting me to say, I simply wait for her to speak again with bated breath.

"Just a feeling, I guess," Laila finally says, with a shake of her long, blonde hair.

My heart is crashing against my sternum now. "Did Ruby say something to make you think that way?"

Laila shakes her head. "No, it just seems to me, from being around you two, that you have insane chemistry together. A million times more so than she's got with Kai. Or anyone else, for that matter."

My spirit sinks. "Yeah, that's because Ruby thinks of me as her best friend."

"You don't think of Ruby the same way?"

My cheeks feel hot. "No, I do. She's one of my best friends. Savage and Kai, too."

Laila looks skeptical. So does Savage. Which is weird, because I've never once told him about my feelings for Ruby.

"Have you ever felt anything but friendship for her?" Laila asks.

Panicking, I turn and look around, making sure nobody can overhear this conversation. When the coast is clear, I return to Laila and whisper, "I mean, I might have had a small crush on her when I first met her. But those feelings are long gone now that we've been such close friends for so many years."

Savage and Laila exchange another look. One that makes Laila return to me with a wicked smile.

"I just had a brilliant idea," she says. "Right before we boarded, I got an email from Nadine, requesting my top three choices for guest mentors this season." She's talking about Nadine Collins, the executive producer of the reality TV singing juggernaut that pays Laila and Savage a king's ransom to appear as judges. "What if I put Ruby as my number-one request?"

"Holy shit, Laila. That'd be a dream come true for her. Please, yes. She deserves so much more credit and recognition than she gets in the industry." The very thought of Ruby getting an opportunity like this makes me feel like my heart is beating out of my chest.

"I couldn't agree more," Laila says. "Which is why I thought of it." She smiles mischievously. "Not to mention, it'd give you and Ruby more time to hang out together after we get back." She's referring to the fact that I'm already booked to appear as Savage's guest mentor this season.

"Thank you, Laila. Ruby's gonna lose her shit when she finds out about this."

"Don't tell her yet. It's not a sure thing I can make it happen, since she's not a big name yet. But I promise to do my best to convince Nadine to give her a shot."

I'm not a big name, either. I'm just a drummer in a band. Not even a vocalist. But during Savage's first season on the show, he demanded me as his guest mentor as one of his deal-breakers. And since the ratings that season broke records, no thanks to me, Savage didn't have any trouble getting the green light for my return.

"Well, thanks for even thinking of her," I say. "Fingers crossed."

The pilot's voice blares, announcing we've started our

descent into Vancouver, so I say my goodbyes and ask them to keep me posted.

"Will do," Laila says. "And keep *us* posted if you happen to think of any other reason you want Ruby staying at your place, besides her convenience and wanting to hang out with your BFF for a week."

When Savage snickers, I flash both of them a look that says, "Mind your business," before heading down the aisle to return to my seat. When I get there, I discover Ruby's awake, though groggy and rubbing her eyes.

"Hey, cutie," I whisper as I slide past her into my chair.

"Hey, hot stuff. Are we landing?"

"Almost. Sorry if I woke you. I had to use the bathroom."

"The pilot woke me up." She yawns so big, I can see her tonsils. "Did you sleep?"

"No. But you know I never sleep on planes."

"Damn. You're so sleep-deprived lately, I thought there was a chance."

"I thought so, too. But no such luck."

I'm not normally a liar. In fact, I pride myself on my integrity. But sometimes, little white lies are justifiable, when they do no harm and serve a greater purpose. In this case, the greater purpose being the fact that Ruby mentioned she'd take a nap with me at our hotel if I didn't happen to catch any ZZ's during our flight.

To be honest, I don't fully understand the weird cocktail of emotions that erupted inside me when I found out Kai and Ruby were never a thing, right after finding out Ruby had finally kicked Cooper to the curb. All I know is I'm feeling a near-maniacal need to spend as much quality time with her, one-on-one, as possible. Even better if I get to do that while lying in a bed with her, even if it's only for Ruby to test her silly theory.

8

RUBY

I'm freshly showered, wearing soft clothes that feel as cozy as pajamas.

After we received our latest round of room assignments here in Vancouver, Kendrick and I parted ways to freshen up in our respective rooms. And now, about thirty minutes later, I'm headed to Kendrick's pad, determined to cuddle that sweet insomniac to the best sleep of his life.

I'm no sleep specialist, obviously, but it's my strong suspicion Kendrick could use some extra TLC to help combat his quarter-life crisis. Also, selfishly, I sleep better on Kendrick's shoulder than on any actual pillow, so I feel like this "sleep therapy" idea of mine is a win-win.

I reach Kendrick's door and double-check the room number, since it's all a blur at this point, and when I've confirmed I'm in the right place, I knock ever so lightly, just in case Kendrick's asleep in there by some miracle. Unfortunately for Kendrick, he opens the door, dressed in sweats, his sandy hair damp from his shower and the scents of aftershave and toothpaste wafting off him.

"Hey, cutie," he says.

"Hey, hot stuff. Are you excited to take the best damned nap of your life?"

Kendrick chuckles. "So excited." He widens the door, and I step inside the room. Not surprisingly, it's tidy and neat, as all Kendrick's living spaces are, whereas my new hotel room down the hall already looks like a bomb went off inside it.

Kendrick claps his palms together. "So, how do you want to do this?"

"What do you mean? We'll lie down and cuddle, and hopefully you'll be snoozing in record time."

"Maybe some chatting first, to help me relax?"

"There's no need to wine and dine me, babe. This isn't a date. This is sleep therapy."

Kendrick flushes. "No, yeah."

"I'm kidding."

He rubs the back of his neck. "Honestly, this is a little weird for me."

"I just slept on your shoulder on the plane for hours. It's no different than that."

"Isn't it, though? I always slept on the floor in your dorm room, rather than in the bed with you, for a reason."

"Yeah, because my bed was the size of a stick of gum. If it had been bigger, I would have gladly scootched over to make room for you." I was also dating Ryder at the time, and I'm sure sleeping in a tiny bed with a hunk like Kendrick wouldn't have gone over well with him, no matter how much I explained that Kendrick and I were best friends. But there's no need to mention that to Kendrick now, since he never particularly liked Ryder. Especially on the heels of my breakup with Cooper, I'm not in the mood to remind him of yet another example of my defective picker.

I take off my shoes and leap onto the bed. But when Kendrick doesn't join me, when he stands frozen and staring at me like I'm covered in plutonium, I pat the mattress and say, "Come on, hot stuff. Stop making this weird."

"I'm not *making* it weird. It's just weird. And maybe don't call me hot stuff when I'm about to get into bed with you."

I roll my eyes. "This is no weirder than you sleeping in a bed with Kai for years. Come on."

With a twist of his lips, Kendrick exhales and slowly lies down next to me on top of the comforter. "Probably good we're not getting into the bed," he mutters. "Since it's just a nap."

"Yeah, I agree, since they'll be coming to get us for sound check in a few hours, it's probably best if we don't get too comfy. Now, close your eyes, take a few deep breaths, and try to clear your mind."

"Why do I feel like you're getting ready to give me a prostate exam?"

I giggle. "If I thought shoving my hand up your ass would get you out of your head long enough to fall sleep, I'd do it in a heartbeat."

A deep rumble of a chuckle escapes Kendrick's throat. "This is your idea of getting me in the mindset to *sleep*? With one eye open, maybe."

We both laugh. But when our laughter dies down, I turn onto my side, prop myself up on my elbow, and use my free hand to stroke his face. "Stop fighting sleep. Close your eyes. Take deep breaths." He follows my instructions, and his broad chest expands and contracts with his breathing. "Good," I purr softly. "Clear your mind."

As he continues breathing deeply, I brush my fingertips over his cheeks and forehead, and then gently through his hair, and it's plain to see he's soaking up my touch like dry sponge dunked into a bucket of water. As Kendrick relaxes under my fingers, I let my eyes drift down his muscular body. To the large hand that's now resting idly on his powerful thigh. Suddenly, the sight of that hand provokes a long-ago memory: the sight of Kendrick's big hand caressing his then-girlfriend's soft cheek as he made love to her, enthusiastically, on a raggedy couch in the front room of his student apartment.

I shake my head, trying to banish the unwelcome vision, but it's no use. Suddenly, I'm just shy of nineteen again. Standing on the doorstep of Kendrick's student apartment. Getting an unintended eyeful through a crack in his blinds. I'm feeling the same rush of emotions as I did back then: heart-break and rejection. Also, foolishness and embarrassment, since I knew I had zero right to feel either of those emotions.

It was a surprise to me, when I realized my feelings for Kendrick had morphed. I'd never expected to ache for him the way I did, after we both left for our respective colleges. I figured I'd miss him, of course. By then, we'd seen each other virtually every day for two years. But I thought I'd be busy with my new life, and meeting new people, and so would Kendrick. I figured we'd drift apart, despite our assurances to keep in touch, and that would be that. But as it turned out, when I got to Northwestern, I ached like was missing a limb—a limb called Kendrick Cook. And with each passing day at my new school, the ache only got worse and worse, despite all the new people—and boys—I was meeting.

And so, after Kendrick invited me to come visit him "some-time" in a text exchange, I made the fateful decision to take a four-hour train ride to his college for his birthday. My mission? To find out if Kendrick had even the slightest interest in exploring something physical with me. If so, I planned to jump right in and ask him to take my virginity that very night.

Best-laid plans.

Rather than making Kendrick my first, as hoped, I got an unwitting eyeful of Kendrick's naked, muscular backside, as he passionately kissed and made love to a beautiful blonde on a couch, his hips gyrating enthusiastically and his palm placed tenderly on her cheek.

I don't even remember how I got back to the train station after seeing that. All I remember is sobbing on the train ride back to school, even though I knew I had no right to feel that way. How can a person grieve the loss of something that was never theirs to begin with, right? But that's how I felt, so I cried my eyes out and resolved never to tell another living soul about what I'd stupidly done.

When I got back to my dorm, my first-year roommate was shocked to see me so soon.

"I thought you went to visit Kendrick," she said.

"I got the dates screwed up," I lied. "Kendrick wasn't there. He had an away game this week."

Thankfully, she accepted my story and never asked any follow-up questions, since she didn't know me well enough to detect that I was brazenly lying. Which means, to this day, nobody in the world knows the truth.

To add insult to injury, Kendrick brought that gorgeous blonde home during Christmas break that year and introduced her around as his girlfriend.

Florence. That was her name. I didn't like her.

I'd tried to like her, but it was obvious she only liked Kendrick the Football Star, not Kendrick the Goofball Sweetheart, and I didn't like that. But since it was none of my business, and he obviously liked her a lot, I went back to school and hooked up with a boy in my dorm. Ryder. And acted like that unfortunate incident on Kendrick's doorstep never happened.

My phone vibrates on the mattress, drawing my attention to a text from my good friend, Miranda Baumgarten, who works in PR for River Records.

Miranda: I've got some bad news, babe. Just found out APM is releasing a surprise single, and you're not going to like it. It's dropping at 6:00 Pacific time, but I'm sending it to you now so you can get your game face on in case anyone asks you about it, which I'm sure they will. So sorry, love.

"APM" is Cooper's band, Alexa Play Music; and the link supplied by Miranda is for a song called, "Don't Call Me." So, naturally, I'm figuring it must be about our breakup. Bastard. If so, this could be bad. Cooper isn't the kind of guy to hold back in his lyrics, and he didn't take our breakup well.

My stomach churning with anxiety, I glance at Kendrick next to me on the bed and discover he's fast asleep. Shoot. I don't have my earbuds with me, so I dart into the bathroom with my phone.

After closing the door, I put the toilet lid down and take a seat. And with a shaking hand, click on the link.

There's a short musical intro to kick things off, during which I tell myself not to panic; it won't be that bad. But when Cooper begins to sing, it's instantly clear this song is going to rip me a new one:

"Don't Call Me"

The Stones got Ruby Tuesday
I got some hell to pay
My only goal is letting you know
I don't want you anymore, anyway

You told me you loved me,
And I believed

So why is he starring
In your sex dreams?

Bye bye, baby
See ya, adieu
Don't call me, won't call you
Ooooh
I'm done feeling sapphire blue

The Stones got Ruby Tuesday
Gimme diamonds, emeralds, jade
Any gem that's not you, don't care who
As long as she's not red
As long as I'm not seeing red
Cuz now I'm seeing red

Bye bye, baby
See ya, adieu
Don't call me, won't call you
Don't call me, won't call you
Don't call me, won't call you
Ooooh
I'm done feeling sapphire blue

"He's like a brother to me."
That's what you said, remember?
Remember?
If that's true, Ruby Tuesday:
Why do ya wanna fuck your brother?

Bye bye, baby
See ya, adieu
Don't call me, won't call you
Don't call me, won't call you
Oooooh
Won't see you around
Don't wish you the best
Your loss, not mine
Take you out with the trash
This hasn't been "nice"
Curse your name at night
Won't catch you on the flipside
You said his name twice!

When regret comes
Makes you wish you stayed
Don't call me babe,
Don't call me to beg
I don't want you anymore anyway
No!
Don't call me, won't call you
Don't call me, won't call you
Don't call me, won't call you
Oooh
Gonna get me somebody new

As Cooper's song reaches its final notes and chords, I scream bloody murder, feeling like I'm going to explode from homicidal rage. In a fury, I fling open the bathroom door and discover Kendrick sitting up, bleary-eyed and panicky.

"What happened?" he gasps out, clutching his broad chest. "Are you okay?"

"I need to commit a murder," I choke out, my voice raspy and tight as I march to him on the bed. "A grisly one. And I need your help figuring out how I'm gonna get away with it."

[To listen to "Don't Call Me" by Alexa Play Music go here - https://laurenrowebooks.com/pages/spark-dont-call-me]

9
KENDRICK

As I listen to Cooper's cocky voice blaring from Ruby's phone, my blood feels like it's simmering to a rolling boil. Mostly, I feel fiercely protective of Ruby and pissed at Cooper for unfairly dragging her. But also, if I'm being honest, even as those emotions overtake my body, my brain is furiously trying to process and analyze some of his most eye-popping lyrics.

Why do you want to fuck your brother?

What did he mean when he wrote that? More precisely, *who* did he mean? Did he write it about the same guy supposedly starring in Ruby's sex dreams? Seems like they're one and the same person, but you never know when it comes to songwriting. People write untrue, fantastical, and hyperbolic shit into their songs all the time, for all kinds of reasons. Hell, some of the best, most memorable lyrics only make it into songs because two words rhymed. Is that the case here? Did Cooper write the lyric "you said his name twice," simply because the prior line ended in "nice"?

"I'm gonna kill him," Ruby murmurs, yanking me from my thoughts. She's sitting next to me on the edge of the bed, her phone placed between us on the mattress, and Cooper is now launching into his final chorus.

With a little whimper, she leans her forehead against my shoulder, and I wrap her in a warm hug. But quickly, my thoughts spiral again. Assuming the guy in the song is based on a real person, there are only three possible options for his identity: Kai, Savage, or me. We're the only three guys in the world who are "like a brother" to Ruby.

But which one of us is the guy?

As the song reaches its final chords and notes, my brain furiously weighs the respective likelihoods of those three options:

Kai.

If Savage passed along Kai's false narrative about Ruby to Cooper, either when Cooper's band opened for us two years ago, or more recently when Cooper was traveling with us as Ruby's boyfriend, then this option simply can't be ignored. To put it mildly, Savage isn't a steel trap when he drinks, and that's especially true when he's got juicy gossip burning a hole in his pocket.

Did Savage let that little tidbit rip during a night of drinking with Cooper? If so, Cooper would have thought Ruby had some longstanding romantic history with Kai, dating all the way back to her teenage years, which then might have made Cooper jealous of Kai. Maybe even enough to write a song about him? I must admit, it's not a terrible theory. But it all depends on Savage opening his big mouth and spilling that bullshit story.

And then there's Savage.

Door Number Two.

He's less likely, I think. The only way he'd make sense is if those lyrics were a songwriting device, rather than a factual retelling, because Ruby's never had a singular romantic impulse toward Savage, and vice versa. It certainly would be a genius-level marketing strategy for Cooper to hint at some lurid past between Ruby and our world-famous, global thirst-trap of a front man. But still, at the end of the day, that doesn't seem like something hotheaded Cooper would do. It's hard to believe he'd sing *that* passionately about a scenario fabricated out of whole cloth. One possibly designed to sell records.

Which brings me to me.

Door Number Three.

Did Cooper write those shocking lyrics . . . about me?

If he did, the marketing strategy theory doesn't hold water. My celebrity status got a major boost after my appearance on *Sing Your Heart Out* a couple seasons ago, but still, I'm not famous enough for Cooper to include me in a song just for publicity. No, if those lyrics are about me, then he wrote them out of real jealousy. So, that begs the question: does Cooper feel jealous of me? And if he does, is his reason rooted in paranoia and delusion, or some facts I'm clueless about? Like, maybe, I dunno, Ruby having sex dreams about me and saying my name twice?

"I can't believe he's attacking me like this, for the whole world to hear," Ruby mutters and sniffles into my chest as I hold her tight.

"He's an asshole," I murmur, rubbing her back. "I'm so sorry, Ruby."

Ruby cries in my arms for several minutes as I do my best to comfort her. But finally, she leans out of my embrace, wipes her eyes, and says, "I knew he took the breakup badly, but I never thought he'd do this."

"Give him a call. Beg him not to release the song."

Ruby scoffs. "The song is literally called 'Don't Call Me,' Kendrick."

"Call him anyway. What do you have to lose?"

"My dignity and self-respect?" She shakes her head. "I refuse to give him the satisfaction." She leans her head against my shoulder again. "It's a moot point, anyway. He blocked my number."

"Call him on my phone, then. Or I'll call him and—"

"Absolutely not." She sits up straight. "You can't call him about this or anything else, or you'll only make things worse for me."

"Why? Cooper's always liked me."

"No, Cooper secretly hates you."

I laugh. "Why?"

"Jealousy. You're everything he wishes he could be."

Jealousy. The word stops my heart. That sure feels like a point in favor of door number three. "Good," I mutter. "Because I secretly hate him, too."

Ruby giggles, despite the tears still raining down her pretty cheeks.

"You could call Reed and ask him to pull the song."

"He'd never do that for me."

"You never know. You're one of his favorites. Everyone knows that." It's true. Ever since Reed came to that fateful gig in Chicago and signed our band on the spot, he's always had a soft spot for our adorable keyboardist. It's never been anything weird or sexual. Nothing inappropriate. More like a big brother vibe, thanks to the way Ruby always manages to provoke smiles and laughter from him like nobody else.

"Reed won't care about my feelings if it means screwing himself out of a hit song."

She's probably right about that. The Prick, as we all call Reed, is all about the Benjamins. His nickname definitely didn't come out of nowhere. "What do you have to lose?" I ask, even though I'm now feeling less confident about my idea. "The Prick seems fractionally less like a prick since he got married. Georgina's cast some kind of happy spell on him, I think."

Ruby twists her plush lips. "Yeah, he does seem a tiny sliver nicer these days."

"Right? And if appealing to Reed's new softer side doesn't work out, then you can always threaten to sue him, River Records, and Cooper's band for defamation and emotional distress."

Ruby presses her lips together. "I doubt Reed would take a legal threat from little ol' me too seriously, sweetheart."

"Why not at least try? Even if your chances of convincing him are slim, they're not zero."

Ruby processes that. "I'd probably have a better chance at convincing Reed than Cooper."

"I agree."

"Although that's not saying much." With a long, dejected sigh, she grabs her phone and places the call. And a moment later, she straightens up and says, "Yes, hi, Owen." That's a good sign. Owen is Reed's longtime, trusty personal assistant, and he adores Ruby even more than his powerful boss.

After pausing for Owen to speak, Ruby says, "Unfortunately, not great. I just heard Cooper's new song. Mm hmm. So, I called to talk to Reed about it." She pauses. "Owen, I don't care if he's brokering world peace. This is my life we're talking about, my reputation, and I—" Ruby pauses again, and a second later she exhales, shoots me an excited smile, and replies to Owen, "Thank you so much, O. You're the best."

I squeeze Ruby's shoulder, and she flashes me a heart-melting smile.

"Put it on speakerphone," I whisper, and she immediately grants my request.

A few seconds later, Reed says, "Hey, Ruby Tuesday. I'm assuming you're not a fan of Cooper's new song?"

"Don't release it, Reed. I'm begging you."

Reed audibly shrugs. "Cooper's an artist. He's entitled to express himself in his art."

Ruby scoffs. "That song isn't art. It's slander."

Reed chuckles. "Slander? My goodness."

"Don't mock me. It's slander, Reed."

"I disagree. In fact, if the tables were turned and Cooper called me because you'd written a breakup song about him, maybe one called 'Flying the Coop' or something, I'd tell him the same thing I just told you: Ruby's an artist. She's entitled to express herself in her art."

"Except I'd never write a mean-spirited, whiny little bitch-fest of a temper tantrum and try to pass it off as a song. And, please, let's not pretend you give a flying fuck about art, okay? Music is nothing but a money-making venture to you. Period."

"That's categorically false," Reed retorts, sounds surprisingly indignant. "I genuinely care about putting great music into the world. And I *also* expect that music to make me a shit-ton of money. The two things can co-exist, Ruby Tuesday."

"Stop calling me that. Cooper's so-called art slanders me, so I need you to pull the plug on it, right fucking now."

Reed chuckles. "Explain this slander thing to me. I'm genuinely baffled."

"What's to explain? The motherfucker literally says my name, repeatedly, in a song that trashes me. How is it *not* slander?"

"He doesn't say 'Ruby Connolly.' He says, 'Ruby Tuesday.' That's a term of art in the world of music."

"It's my name, Reed."

"No. Ruby Tuesday is a phrase that's so legendary, it's transcendent. Poetic. For all we know, he's singing about a woman called Sheila. Or a man named Bob. Or maybe someone who doesn't exist at all."

"Everyone knows Cooper was recently dating Ruby from Fugitive Summer. Don't bullshit me."

"*Everyone*? Maybe your short relationship with Cooper is a known fact in your tiny corner of the world, but casual fans of both your bands wouldn't know either of your names, let alone that you dated."

Ruby looks at me, like she's losing confidence, so I gently squeeze her forearm and nod encouragingly.

"Even if 'casual music fans' of our bands don't know about Cooper and me, they'll find out soon enough after this stupid song drops, and everyone starts googling to figure out the lyrics. I hard-launched him while he traveled with me for two months, Reed. There are photos of us holding hands and kissing, all over the internet now."

I grimace. There sure are. Because Cooper is an insecure little prick who couldn't keep his hands off Ruby, especially when cameras and other people were around.

"You should want people to connect the dots and figure out you're Ruby Tuesday," Reed says calmly. "Because that will help make the song a smash hit, which is in everyone's best interests—yours, Cooper's, and mine."

"How do you figure? Why on earth would I ever want a slanderous, misogynistic breakup song about me to become a smash hit?"

"Because there's no such thing as bad publicity. A rising tide floats all boats."

Ruby looks at me for encouragement again, and I give it to her.

"I didn't want to have to do this, Reed, but you've left me no choice. If you don't pull the plug on this song, I'll be forced to sue you, River Records, Cooper, and his band for defamation and emotional distress and whatever else my lawyer can figure out."

A small snickering noise wafts from the phone, one that sounds like Reed stifling a much bigger reaction. "Ruby, if you follow through with that threat, you'd only fuck yourself over."

"No, I'd fuck over you, Cooper, and your label. It'd be like an anti-slander, vengeful gang bang."

I can practically hear Reed's smile over the phone line. "Ruby, think. If you filed a lawsuit claiming the song slanders you, then you'd have to explicitly admit that 'Ruby Tuesday' is you. That's how slander works."

Ruby's jaw drops. "Oh."

"Lawsuits are publicly filed. Anyone can read them. Do you really want to admit, in writing, for the whole world to see, that you're 'Ruby Tuesday?'"

Tears prick Ruby's eyes, and I stroke her arm.

"At the moment," Reed continues, "that song is subject to interpretation. And I assure you it'll stay that way, because I've firmly instructed Cooper not to publicly confirm his muse. Will people speculate? God, I hope so, because speculation and theorizing will only help the song go viral. But unless *you* confirm you're Ruby Tuesday, nobody will ever know for sure."

Ruby hangs her head and wipes her eyes, so I rub her back to console her.

"This conversation is a moot point, anyway," Reed says. "The song has already gone out to all our distributors. Even if I wanted to stop it, which I don't, it's too late."

"You could still do it, if you wanted to," Ruby squeaks out, her shoulders slumped.

"Maybe," he concedes. "I guess we'll never know."

When Ruby lifts her head, full-blown tears are streaming down her cheeks. "You're not concerned about the Rolling Stones coming after you?"

"For what?"

She wipes her face with the back of her hand. "For Cooper using 'Ruby Tuesday' in his song."

Reed *tsks*. "Song titles aren't subject to copyright or trade-mark protection. All song titles, even ones as famous as 'Ruby

Tuesday,' are fair game. Ever heard of a restaurant called Ruby Tuesdays? Case in point."

Ruby lets out a long, defeated exhale. "Reed, please. I never consented to Cooper airing our dirty laundry like this."

My breathing halts. *Dirty laundry?* That sure seems like an admission that Cooper's lyrics, at least some of them, are based in truth. That's interesting, to say the least.

"It's going to be okay, sweetheart," Reed says softly. "Trust me."

"Don't tell me to trust you when you're releasing a song that defames me."

"This song will turn out to be a great thing for you. A blessing in disguise. Mark my words."

Ruby sniffles. Apparently, she's now resigned to her fate. "How do you figure?"

"Write a song in response to Cooper's, and it'll make more money than God."

Ruby wipes her eyes. "I'd sooner write a song about a fly sitting on a pile of dogshit."

I can't help chuckling along with Reed. Not only about Ruby's word choice, but out of relief that Ruby's definitely not planning to let Cooper grovel his way back into her good graces. I was already assuming that, given her reaction to his song. But it's nice to get verbal confirmation.

"Is that Kendrick?" Reed asks at the sound of my laughter.

"Hey, Reed."

"Hi, KC. I'm glad you're there with her. Give our little pixie dream girl a squeeze for me, would you? Tell her everything's going to be all right in the end."

"Don't try to gaslight me," Ruby snaps.

"I'm not. I genuinely believe you'll thank me one day. So, listen, if you're not going to write a response to Cooper's song, then will you at least sit down and write me a motherfucking sequel to 'Hate Sex High,' like I keep asking for?"

"There's no such thing as a sequel to that song," Ruby says. "Savage wrote it during a uniquely honest moment that can't be duplicated. And you want to know why? Because he's an actual *artist,* unlike Cooper. Because he wrote that song to express his honest feelings, not to give the head of our record label a made-to-order song."

Reed chuckles. "All right, Ruby Tuesday. Have it your way. It was great talking to you, my dear, but I need to take another call now."

"Tell Georgina hello for me. Tell her I'm sorry she's married to a man who's incapable of empathy and compassion."

Reed laughs. "Will do. But only if you do me a favor in return. When it turns out I'm right about this—"

"That will never happen."

"Yes, it will. I don't know what form it'll take. All I know is this song will bring you some opportunity and/or financial gain that's not presently visible on the horizon. And when that happens, whatever form it takes, I want you to shoot me a text that says, 'You were right, Reed. Cooper's song was a blessing in disguise. Thank you so much for not pulling it.'"

"I'd rather die than send you a text like that."

"That's all the more reason it's going to delight me when it comes."

10

KENDRICK

Three days later

This is one hell of a twenty-eighth birthday party.

It's also the wrap party for our tour, thank God, which probably explains why everyone is letting loose to the extreme. Ruby, especially, has been whooping it up tonight. Surely she's trying to give herself some fun—and alcohol-induced amnesia about the insane success of Cooper's song these past three days—even more so than she's celebrating her bestie's twenty-eight trips around the sun. Either way, Ruby's boisterous energy has whipped up everyone here, and the night has been all the more fun and rowdier because of her.

We're in Savage and Laila's massive suite, and it's packed to the gills tonight with dancing, laughing, chatting people. In addition to all my bandmates, the spacious room is filled with all our staffers and most crew members, a few of their plus-ones, and a smattering of celebrities and their guests. With

Savage and Laila enjoying A-list status these days, every famous face with access to a private jet, or who already happened to be shooting a project in Vancouver, seems to be here. It's kind of wild, honestly. The kid practicing his drums in that basement in the South Side wouldn't have believed the guest list if he'd been shown this scene in a crystal ball.

We're about three hours in, so I'm honestly pretty drunk. Presently, I'm sipping on a double whiskey neat while chatting with a pretty actress who's shooting season three of a hit show on a streaming platform—a show I've binged with Ruby, actually.

Speaking of Ruby Tuesday, she's currently dancing like a maniac with her gaggle of friends from the staff and crew to her favorite pop song. And, man, she's a sight to see. Thoroughly entertaining. Funny. Sexy. While trying to squeeze upcoming plot points out of the actress I've been chatting with, I can't keep my eyes from constantly drifting to her. She's on fire out there.

The current tune blaring through the party is Aloha Carmichael's iconic, girl-power anthem, "Pretty Girl," and Ruby and her friends, led by Ruby, are doing the famous choreography from the music video. Watching her now brings to mind a vision of her dancing and singing along to this same song with all her high school friends at our senior prom, back when the song was a new release. Man, I was in love with her back then. Desperately. And she had no idea.

Ruby being Ruby, she went to prom with a group of girlfriends rather than trifling with Jake Silva, the football player who'd shocked her—and me—by coming out of the woodwork to ask her to be his date. I wanted to go with friends, honestly, so I could dance with Ruby and her friends all night. But, really, with Ruby.

But since Titus and all my other teammates were taking dates—apparently, that's what the cool kids and athletes did at St. Francis Academy—I bowed to expectation and asked Celeste Matthews, the head cheerleader, to the dance. I wasn't particularly feeling anything for Celeste, but several of her friends were already going with some of mine, so it made sense. Once we got to the dance, however, I spent the whole night covertly watching Ruby dancing, much the same way I'm watching her now.

"So, anyhoo," the actress says, temporarily drawing my eyes from Ruby on the dance floor. "It was a lot of work to learn how to use a sword properly and convincingly, but it's also been rewarding to hear everyone saying I got it so right, you know?"

My drunk brain registers it's my turn to speak now. "Cool. What's your favorite and least favorite things about doing the show?"

"Oh my gosh. That's such a great question. Let's see."

As she launches into her reply, I return my gaze to Ruby, just in time to see her performing the famous ending dance moves with flair. As Ruby and her friends whoop and celebrate, a new song begins, and they all start screaming and jumping around. It's none other than Fugitive Summer's biggest hit yet—the song we released a few years ago that changed all our lives forever: "Hate Sex High."

"Excuse me," I blurt, cutting off the actress mid-sentence. "Sorry, it's our tradition. I have to dance to this song with my band." It's not a lie. But it feels like one, since I would have said anything at this point to disentangle myself from that flirty actress and join Ruby on the dance floor.

As I make my way toward the makeshift dance floor, I lock eyes with our tour manager, Caden, our DJ across the room. I salute him in thanks, and he winks and returns the gesture. And a moment later, when I reach Ruby, I take her hands in mine, and we jump around like two kangaroos on meth. A few seconds after that, our three other bandmates, plus Laila,

arrive and join our huddle, and the six of us start dancing like
there's no tomorrow, even before Savage's voice starts singing
on the track. But of course, when Savage starts singing on the
recording, all six of us sing along with him at the top of our
lungs:

> *Saw you with him at the show*
> *I didn't like it*
> *I played it cold to your face*
> *But I was on fire*
> *He said you were his all along*
> *And I didn't like it*
> *Turns out I'd imagined it all*
> *Went back and punched a hole in the wall*

> *You're falling (falling) falling (falling) falling in hate with me*
> *I'm feeling (feeling) feeling (feeling) something I don't want to feel*
> *You're falling (falling) falling (falling) falling in hate with me*
> *I'm feeling (feeling) feeling (feeling) something I don't want to feel*

> *La la la la la la la . . . Laila, Laila*
> *La la la la la la la . . . Laila, Laila*

At this point in the song, when Savage on the recording
sings his wife's name at the end of those la-las, every person in
the party, not only the six of us huddled together in celebra-
tion, screams those "Lailas," emphatically. It's a worldwide
inside joke at this point, thanks to Savage publicly, and not-

so-convincingly, denying the song was ever about Laila Fitzgerald at the time. "I don't know what you're talking about," Savage said at the time in an interview. "I'm singing nothing but *la la*, throughout the entire song."

Of course, his lie became an internet sensation the second Savage and Laila came out as a couple, and even more so after the pair became husband and wife—all of which only propelled the song into the stratosphere further. Now, singing "Laila" on those parts, very loudly, is something of a world-wide custom.

During the bridge, Ruby tugs on me the way she always does when she wants to ride on my back, so I lean down and let her hop aboard, and then gallop around like a pony, while she whoops and sings.

When the final chorus heads our way, I let Ruby down, and we huddle with our other band members again for the dura-tion of the song, including loudly speaking along with Savage on the recording, his now-famous, spoken dig at Laila during the outro: "Did *he* make you come three times? Yeah, didn't think so."

When the song ends, we hug as a group, and everyone wishes me a happy birthday and congratulates each other on a tour well done. Immediately, a new song starts—Red Card Riot's smash-hit, signature song, "Shaynee," and Ruby grips my hands and starts screaming the iconic chorus, "Shayneeeee!," along with me and everyone else in the room. This one isn't a dance tune, per se. It's a wailing song about heartbreak with a catchy chorus you can't help singing along to—but thanks to its crashing beat and singalong, gut-wrenching chorus, it's one of those tunes that gets a party cranked up once everyone is inebriated enough to join in on the singalong without holding back.

Midway through the second verse, Savage taps my shoulder and motions for me to come with him toward a bedroom in the back. When I look at him, like, *Now?* he nods and shouts above the music, "I need to talk to you in private!"

Well, fuck. This can't be good. In a flash, my drunken brain goes straight to my upcoming stint on *Sing Your Heart Out*. The show begins shooting right after we get back from tour. Is Savage pulling me aside to break the news that the show's cancelled me for a bigger name?

Savage motions to Laila, who joins our trek to the back bedroom. Maybe this is good news, after all? Like, maybe news about Ruby being approved as Laila's guest mentor this season?

We reach the room, and Savage closes the door to muffle the blaring music.

"What's up?" I ask.

"Eli texted me," Savage says. "Your phone is off. He told me to find you and ask you an urgent question, because he needs your answer right away." Eli is our manager. Which means this must be something work-related.

"Am I being dropped as your guest mentor?" I ask before Savage gets his next words out. The producers of the show are notoriously fickle and scheming, as they connive to achieve maximum ratings for the show. In fact, as Eli explained it to me, the standard guest mentor contract includes a loophole clause giving producers the right to cancel any guest mentor at the last minute, as long as they do it before the dog-and-pony-show press conference that announces the upcoming season's full cast.

"No, they still want you," Savage says. "Now more than ever, thanks to Cooper's song breaking the internet. Eli said they're seriously considering Ruby, too."

"Really? That's awesome." *What does Cooper's song have to do with it?*

"But first, the producers want assurances from you.

Confirmation you're willing to play along with a certain story-line they'd want for Ruby that would involve you."

I scowl. "What's the storyline?"

Laila says, "The whole world knows Ruby is 'Ruby Tues-day,' and mostly everyone thinks *you're* the 'brother' she wants to fuck from the song. The producers see all the buzz, and they're excited about the possibilities."

My eyebrows ride up. "People think I'm the brother guy—not you or Kai?"

"Everyone thinks he's you, KC."

"Well, no, I'd say over half the internet thinks he's you," Laila interjects. "Second place is Kai. Savage is a distant third."

"It's so insulting," Savage quips.

I don't know whether to smile or scowl at the revelation that I'm the world's front-runner, so I work hard to keep my face neutral. "So, what's the storyline? A romance between us?" That's what they required of Savage and Laila their first season. In fact, that's their origin story as a couple: the show required them to fake a passionate relationship as a prerequi-site to them both getting signed for the judging gig. So, it stands to reason the producers are reaching into their old bag of tricks.

Savage shrugs. "You'll have to ask Eli for specifics. He said something about them wanting to make sure you and Ruby wouldn't publicly deny her being Ruby Tuesday and you being the guy in the song. You know, leaving everything open to speculation, at least. But who knows."

I shrug. "I'd be willing to do whatever it takes to get Ruby onto the show. I know for a fact this would be a dream come true for her. Life changing." I pull my phone out of my pocket. "I'll text Eli now and let him know—"

"No, not yet," Savage says. "There's something else." He looks at Laila and grimaces before returning to me. "Cooper. Eli said they've confirmed him as a guest mentor this season."

"What the fuck? Seriously?" I look at Laila, frowning. "I thought you were the only judge without a guest mentor confirmed."

"I was, which is why I asked for Ruby. They initially said no about her, by the way. They said she's not a big enough name yet. But then, Cooper's song came out and took the internet by storm, and since they already had you, they decided to bump the guest mentor lined up for Jon and replace him with Cooper."

"Poor Ruby," I murmur. "Talk about an impossible choice to make. Saying yes to her dream opportunity and working alongside Cooper or turning it down and getting the biggest case of FOMO ever."

"I know," Laila says. "It sucks."

I rough a palm down my face. "So, are they gunning for a love triangle storyline here, then? Is that what's really going on?"

"Eli seems to think so," Savage says. "But for now, I guess they're being pretty vague about their intentions. First things first, they want to know if you'll play ball. If not, they're not going to make an offer to Ruby."

"Like I said, I'll do whatever Ruby wants. The question is whether Ruby will want to do the show with Cooper. Honestly, I don't know. The past few days have been pretty rough on her." I turn on my phone, and a bunch of texts and missed calls from Eli pop up. "I'll let Eli know I'm in Ruby's corner, no matter what."

"He figured you'd say that," Savage says as I tap out the message. "But he just needed to know for sure before he replied to the producers. Apparently, time is short for his response."

As I'm still typing out a message to Eli, Laila says, "So, Kendrick. Have you talked to Ruby about Cooper's song yet?"

"Yeah. I was there when she heard it for the first time. She's furious about it."

"No, I mean, have you talked to her about the lyrics? Does she know if the guy in the song is you?"

My heart is thumping. "We haven't talked about any of that stuff. Ruby was sobbing when she first heard it, and I haven't wanted to upset her again or dignify Cooper's lyrics by asking too many questions."

"You haven't asked her if you're the 'brother' she wants to fuck?" Savage blurts, his face awash in disbelief.

"I can't ask her that. If I did, she'd think *I* think those lyrics are about me."

"Well, don't you?" Savage asks. "I sure as hell do."

My heart stops. He does? Does everyone in the band think that way, too? Does Titus?

"Who knows?" I babble, sweating bullets. "For all we know, they're totally fabricated. Or maybe the guy in the song is a mash-up of you, me, and Kai. You know how songwriting is."

"Maybe," Savage concedes. "But it seems most likely they're real and about you."

"I'd say so," Laila chimes in.

"Why do you both think that?"

They look at each other and shrug, like I've asked, "Why do you think the sky is blue?"

"Who else would they be about?" Laila asks. "I mean, if you want proof, I think Ruby being a 'gem' in the song is a nod you. You're the one who always calls her that. A gem."

"And I'm sure Cooper noticed," Savage adds. "Both back when he opened for us and during his stint as tagalong boyfriend."

Laila adds, "We think he's giving you the middle finger by repeatedly calling her that in the song."

"You think so? Seems to me, Ruby being a gem is low-hanging fruit in terms of a metaphor. It's not like I'm some poetic genius for coming up with that."

"But you're the only one in the band who ever calls her that," Savage shoots back. "The only one, KC."

He's not wrong about that. Suddenly, Ruby's comment to Reed pops into my head: the one about Cooper's song airing their "dirty laundry." And my heart rate increases, yet again.

I shift my weight. "Even if Cooper's lyrics are true from his perspective, they'd still only be *his* version of the truth. Not Ruby's. I don't want to ask her about what Cooper might have meant and make her think I'm anything less than completely in her corner."

Savage scoffs. "You've got far more willpower in this situation than I ever could."

"Yeah, well, willpower isn't what you're known for, brother."

We all laugh. Savage is nothing if not impulsive.

"All I'm saying," Savage says, "is that it's an objective fact Cooper's song is about *someone* who's like a brother to Ruby. And that someone, if you ask me—"

"And most internet sleuths," Laila interjects.

"Is you."

I bite the inside of my cheek. Am I fervently hoping they're right about this? Fuck yes. But I don't want to admit that to anyone, not even Savage and Laila. Unfortunately, I know for a fact Ruby's never felt that way about me, and I'm only willing to embarrass myself so much.

I take a deep breath and address Savage. "Hey, have you ever told Cooper what Kai told me about him and Ruby? You know, about Ruby supposedly being 'desperately in love' with Kai since the very beginning?"

"No."

"Are you sure about that, Savage? Think."

"I'm positive I didn't say a single word about that to Cooper or anyone else in the entire world."

Laila raises her index finger. "You told me."

"Except Laila."

I roll my eyes. "Could you have said something to Cooper while you were shitfaced? We all know you're the opposite of tight-lipped when you drink."

"Why are you asking me this?"

"I'm just trying to get inside Cooper's head. If you told him, maybe that would make it more likely Cooper's lyrics are about Kai."

Savage shakes his head. "They're about you, KC. I'd bet anything."

Laila nods her head in agreement and says, "The only question is whether those lyrics are the rantings of a jilted ex-boyfriend or factual."

We all contemplate that for a moment. But before anyone speaks, my phone buzzes with a text.

"It's Eli," I report. "He says the producers have the information from me, and they'll make their decision about Ruby by tomorrow morning. He says we shouldn't tell Ruby about this yet, in case the offer doesn't come in."

We all agree to keep our mouths shut, and I let Eli know as much in a reply text.

That task completed, Savage claps his hand to my shoulder. "Okay, birthday boy. Let's get you back out there for a game of *Birthday Truth or Dare*."

He's no sooner gotten the words out, however, than a new song begins blaring in the adjacent party: none other than Cooper's viral, smash-hit single that's been tearing up the charts and wreaking havoc with Ruby's nervous system for the past three days.

"Who the fuck put this on?" I roar, marching toward the

door of the bedroom. "Whoever did this is about to get a beat-down from me!"

———

"Turn that shit off!" I shout as I barrel toward Rex the Soundman. All night long, our tour manager, Caden, has been manning the iPad that's been cranking out party tunes. But now, it's Rex the Soundman who's standing in Caden's former spot with a smug expression on his face and his phone trained directly on Ruby on the dance floor. Plainly, he's hoping to capture her reaction in a video. Will he post it? Send it to Cooper? Fuck. I suddenly remember: Rex is close friends with Cooper, dating back to when his band opened for us.

As I cut through the party, on my way to beat the shit out of Rex—or at least, to scream in his face that he's a massive asshole and this will be his last tour with us—Ruby races toward me, looking frantic. I don't blame her. This party was supposed to be a safe space for her after the past few days chewed her up and spit her out. Doesn't this motherfucker realize Ruby's one-fifth of the reason for his paycheck?

Ruby is shouting something as she gets closer to me, something that's getting swallowed by the loud music. But I don't need to hear her to understand her body language. She wants me to make Rex stop playing this goddamned song—probably, to make him stop shooting his video, too—through any means necessary. And that's exactly what I'm going to do.

Before I've reached Rex, Ruby cuts me off at the pass. And when she's close enough for me to hear what she's saying, it's not what I'm expecting.

"Stop!" she screams. "KC, no! Your reaction is confirming the song is about *me*!"

Shit.

That didn't occur to me before now. But I think she's right: I've just handed Rex a viral video on a silver platter. Fuck.

"Kiss me!" Ruby screams above the music, right before she double-fists the front of my T-shirt and pulls my lips to hers.

When our lips collide, my drunken brain can't make heads or tails of what's happening for a second, but my body sure can. Instinctually, I slide my arm around Ruby's back, pull her closer, and kiss the hell out of her, like I'm a soldier returning home from war. The result, at least for me, is fireworks.

As my tongue swirls with Ruby's, my entire body explodes with elation, love, and lust. Euphoria that the kiss I've waited so long to experience is finally here—and it's better than my wildest dreams. And best of all? Ruby's unmistakably returning my kiss, her body making it clear she's every bit as—

The song abruptly cuts off, right before it reaches its now-infamous line: "Why do you want to fuck your brother?" Apparently, someone got to the iPad and turned it off in the nick of time. And suddenly, it's like a spell has been broken.

With our blaring soundtrack no longer goading us on, we're suddenly surrounded by nothing but whoops and cheers, all of which are mingling with the loud thumping of my heartbeat in my ears.

Reality sets in again.

Abruptly, Ruby breaks free of my lips and lurches back, like she's been zapped by an electric fence.

Flustered, I open my mouth to confess that kiss was better than my wildest fantasies about it—fantasies I've been having since age sixteen. But, thankfully, Ruby speaks first.

"That was perfect," she whispers with a snicker. "Now, drag me out of here like you're taking me somewhere to fuck me." She grabs my hand and shouts, loud enough for everyone at the party to hear, including Rex, "Come on, baby! I can't wait to give you your birthday present in private!"

. . .

[To listen to "Hate Sex High" in full go here - https://
laurenrowebooks.com/pages/hate-sex-high-music]

11

KENDRICK

"Guys, hold up!"

It's Titus, shouting down the length of the hallway after Ruby and I barreled out of the party. Ruby's riding on my back. She immediately hopped aboard, like she always does, when moving from one drinking location to the next. It was a tad demoralizing—confirmation that nothing's changed between us, despite that amazing kiss. For her, anyway.

As I come to a stop with Ruby on my back, Titus shouts, "Seriously, guys, don't do this." When I turn around, he adds, "You're both shitfaced and might regret it in the morning."

Ruby scoffs, and her breath flutters against my ear. "Are you serious? T, we kissed for Rex's camera. He's obviously going to send that video to Cooper, and I knew kissing Kendrick would give him the biggest possible 'fuck you.' Thankfully, Kendrick knew to play along." When Titus looks skeptical, Ruby adds, "It's like Dad always says: 'If they're running you out of town, get out front and make it look like a parade.' So, that's what I did."

Titus narrows his eyes. "That kiss looked awfully real, Ruby."

"What would have been the point, otherwise?" She pokes my shoulder. "Tell him, KC."

"Yup. All for show," I choke out, barely able to command my tongue. I feel deflated, confused, and embarrassed. My brain understood the situation, I think, when Ruby first planted her lips on mine. I saw the camera. I knew Cooper's song was blaring. I mean, I didn't fully get her logic, but I knew something was up. Something she'd explain later. But then, somewhere along the line, my body convinced my brain Ruby was kissing me for real—that she was feeling every kilowatt of electricity in that moment that I felt. I was such an idiot.

Titus says something I don't catch, because my mind has been racing and spiraling. But Ruby's reply to her brother draws me back.

"You honestly think if I was truly kissing my best friend, for real, for the first time, I'd do it in front of you and the rest of the band? Not to mention, in front of everyone at the party, and possibly the whole world, if I'm right and Rex is going to post that video?"

Well, there it is.

Drunk or not, I was most definitely a fool.

"Come back to the party," Titus says, motioning toward the door behind him.

"We can't," Ruby says. "We made it seem like we were running off to hook up. If we come back now, everyone will think Kendrick jizzed in his pants before we ever got to his room." Ruby snickers at the idea, but the scenario doesn't seem that far-fetched to me. It's never happened to me, thank God, but after twelve years of pining over and fantasizing about this girl, I wouldn't call it out of the question if Ruby ever kissed me for real and gave me the green light for more.

"Kendrick, come on. We haven't even played *Birthday Truth or Dare* yet."

"We played the other night at the emergency band meeting."

Titus scoffs. "That one question didn't count. And we never play with Truth as an option, anyway."

Why is Titus pushing so hard for us to come back into the party? Is he, like Savage and Laila, convinced I'm the 'like a brother' guy in Cooper's song? If so, my kiss with Ruby surely added fuel to that fire.

"Right, KC?" Ruby asks, jerking me from my thoughts.

Clearly, I missed something when I zoned out. "Huh?"

"You've been out of good ideas for birthday dares for a while now."

"Oh. Yeah. Definitely." I rap the side of my head with my knuckles. "Can you hear that echo? There's nothing inside there."

Ruby squeals with laughter and squeezes my neck. After kissing the side of my head, she says to her brother, "Are you done interrogating us now? Because I want to go to Kendrick's room, have a nightcap from the minibar, and help him fall asleep."

"Help him what?"

Ruby explains the whole insomnia thing to him, as well as her theory. "I told him we'd test it out days ago, but then Cooper's song came out, and I got distracted and fell down on the job."

Titus doesn't look convinced. In fact, he looks downright cynical.

"Now, go back to the party," Ruby says to her brother with a shooing motion of her hand. "And tell our bandmates the deal about that kiss, okay?" She giggles. "Man, I wish I could be a fly on the wall when Cooper sees it. He's going to lose his mind to find out I've moved on from him so fast—and with his nemesis, of all people."

Nemesis? The word feels like a record scratch to my brain. *I'm Cooper's nemesis*? That seems like a pretty strong characterization, even if he secretly dislikes me.

Titus exhales. "She's shitfaced, KC. You realize that, right, brother?"

"I am, too."

"I'm saying don't do anything she might regret. Not when she's shitfaced. Okay?"

"What the fuck is your deal?" Ruby yells. "We've both been shitfaced together a million-billion times, and you didn't feel the need to give us this speech any of those times."

"Yeah, well, if you'd kissed right before taking off together any of those times, I certainly would have."

Ruby flaps her lips together. "It was a fake kiss, dude. Are you not listening to me at all?" With that, she bats my shoulder. "Come on, horsey. Giddyup! Let's ditch this wet blanket and keep the party rolling!"

Titus sighs. "Goodnight, guys. Happy birthday, KC."

"You, too. I mean, thanks. Sorry if we confused you."

"The only thing that's confusing to me is this conversation." With that, Titus swings open the door to the party and disappears.

"Weirdo," Ruby mutters.

"What did he mean by that?"

"By what?"

"That our conversation was confusing to him."

"Who knows and who cares?" Ruby says with a wave of her hand. "Now, giddyup! I'm thirsty!"

I adjust her on my back and grip her thighs firmly, the same way I always do at times like this. Except, if I'm being honest, the touch of her bare thighs against my palms feels different now. More loaded. Thanks to that kiss. Just this fast, I already know it was The Kiss That Changed Everything, and I'm not sure I'll ever be able to go back.

"My room or yours?" I manage to choke out.

"Yours. Mine's a mess. Plus, when we get to the sleep therapy portion of the birthday party, I want you feeling as comfy as possible."

"What's my room number?"

Giggling, Ruby tells it to me, and off we trot down the carpeted hallway, with her singing "Tiptoe Through the Tulips," at the top of her lungs.

"Why did you say I'm Cooper's nemesis?" I ask midway through her song.

"I already told you: Cooper's always been crazy-jealous of you."

"Yeah, but nemesis seems like a more intense word than someone you're merely *jealous* of."

Ruby snorts. "Okay, well, Cooper was jealous of you, even before I started dating him. But once we started dating, his jealousy became more like an obsession. He was convinced I wanted to break up with him and get with you."

My breathing hitches. Lyrics flood me. *Why do you want to fuck your brother? Why is he starring in your sex dreams? You said his name twice.*

"W-why would Cooper think that?" Fuck it. I can still taste Ruby on my lips and tongue. Like a drug, the sensation is making me reckless, apparently.

"Because he's a simpleton who can't fathom a woman being close friends with a hot guy." She exhales. "Come on, birthday boy. Open the door. I need another drink."

"But I mean, do you know of any objective reason, other than Cooper's own insecurities, why he'd think that way?"

Ruby grunts. "Who knows what goes on inside the mind of

an insecure, jealous ex-boyfriend? Your guess is as good as mine."

My mind hurtles back to Ruby's comment about Cooper airing their dirty laundry a couple days ago. Is there something she's holding back?

"Open the door already," Ruby says with a pinch to my neck.

I let Ruby slide off my back, fish my key out of my pocket, and unlock the door; and the minute Ruby enters my room, she takes a running, flying leap onto my bed, like she's belly flopping into a summer lake.

I laugh at her silliness. At first. But all it takes is one glimpse of her inner thigh as her skirt rides up, as she lands and bounces, and I'm dangerously close to popping a boner. What's wrong with me? One kiss, and I'm suddenly incapable of being around her?

I stride to the minibar, telling myself to get ahold of myself. "It's an embarrassment of riches in here," I report, after opening the fridge. At Ruby's request, I list off every beverage option in front of me, expecting her to cut me off at some point with her selection. But she doesn't make a peep. Did she pass out while I was droning on?

I turn around to face her and discover Ruby's slowly flipping the pages of my lyrics notebook, which is laid out before her on the bed.

For a split second, the sight doesn't concern me. During countless writing sessions, Ruby's perused the pages of my journal, and vice versa. But, suddenly, just as she stops on a page and her eyes go wide, a thought pings my brain.

Spark.

Shit.

Did I tear those two pages out in New York like I was intending to do? Or did I get distracted? In a flash, I hurl myself across the small room and snatch the journal off the bed, causing Ruby to yelp in surprise.

"Hey!" she shouts. "Give it back. I just started reading something juicy." When I shake my head, Ruby waggles her eyebrows and says, "Come on. I just saw a two-pager called 'Spank,' you naughty boy, and I'm dying to know what that's all about."

12

RUBY

When I land on Kendrick's bed following my flying leap through the air, something hard bonks my belly. With a frown, I reach underneath me and discover the assailant is Kendrick's lyrics notebook. I've read it countless times, but not recently. Not since our last songwriting session as a band, before the tour started. Feeling excited to see what he's added to it, I start flipping pages toward the back of the book.

"It's an embarrassment of riches in here," Kendrick says, peering into the minifridge.

"What are my options?" I ask, as I flip another page. Kendrick isn't normally a big contributor of lyrics in our band. Kai, Savage, and I write those, while Kendrick and Titus contribute riffs and musical ideas. But still, on occasion, Kendrick supplies some little snippet of a lyric or the seedling of an idea that knocks everyone's socks off. Or at least, inspires someone else to run with it.

As Kendrick is still listing my beverage options, I flip a new page and land on something that instantly makes me tune out his voice: a two-page set of lyrics, written in urgent, messy handwriting. I've never seen Kendrick write this many lyrics all at once, and I'm genuinely shocked.

My eyes drift to the top of the left-hand page—to the title. Kendrick's handwriting is always hard to decipher for me. But here, it's even harder than usual, which suggests these words must have poured out of his brain in a torrent his hand could barely keep up with.

"Skank." That appears to be the title at the top of the page. But then again, I've never heard Kendrick use that word in my life. No, wait. "*Spank.*" Yeah, I think that's it. Is spank a word Kendrick uses often? No, but I've definitely heard him calling masturbation "spanking the monkey," so this song title makes a lot more sense.

I lower my eyes to the first line of Kendrick's lyrics, eager to begin reading; but unfortunately, the rushed, jagged script is as hard to decipher as the title. Slowly, however, I'm able to make out the beginning line:

Lying awake, my body staging a coup
Can't have—

All of a sudden, before I can read another word, Kendrick yanks the journal away from me. "Hey!" I shout, looking up at him. "Give it back. I just started reading something juicy." When he shakes his head, I purr, "Come on. I just saw a two-pager called 'Spank,' you naughty boy, and I'm dying to know what *that's* all about."

Kendrick blushes. "There's some personal stuff in here."

I cock my head. "In your lyrics journal?" That's new. "Is 'Spank' the personal thing you don't want me seeing, you naughty, horny boy?" When he says nothing, I snicker and ask, "Is it about spanking your monkey or spanking someone's ass?" When he doesn't reply again, I reposition myself on the bed and sit up. "Look, there's nothing to be embarrassed about, okay? I've let you read some of my most honest and vulnerable lyrics. I won't judge you. I promise."

"It's not that it's honest or vulnerable. It's just stupid. It was a creative writing exercise. A 'what if.' There's nothing true or honest about it. Not a single thing."

That only makes me want to read it, all the more. Especially because Kendrick always lets me and everyone else in the band read everything in his lyrics notebook, no matter what it is, and we all do the same for him. That's our way. Our songwriting process. So, why is he acting so weird now?

"All the more reason to let me read it," I insist. But when he doesn't budge, I add, "I didn't realize you'd started writing personal stuff, or I never would have opened it without your permission. I'm sorry."

Kendrick sighs. "It was dumb of me to put something personal in here. I had insomnia one night, so I opened my notebook, and, all of a sudden, words just started pouring out of me, like I was in a trance."

"Isn't that the best? I love it when that happens."

"It was a first for me. Super weird. Cool, though."

"Put that down and come lie down with me. Let's get you some good sleep."

Kendrick motions to the fridge. "What about the cocktails?"

"The moment's passed. Let's crash."

Kendrick looks at me suspiciously. "In your room, then."

"You don't trust me?"

"No."

I laugh. He's a smart man. Obviously, I want to respect Kendrick's surprising request for privacy. But also, everything about Kendrick's body language is making me rabidly curious to read those damned words. *Spank.* My god, that's a sexy title. Is it filled with graphic, sexual confessions about how he likes to spank a woman's ass while fucking her? I'm dying to know. *Especially after that kiss.* Just thinking about it is causing every nerve ending in my body to zip and zap, the same way it did when Kendrick deepened our kiss. Holy fuck, that was hot.

"Ruby?" Kendrick says, jolting me back to the present. He motions toward the bathroom. "I'm gonna pee, grab my pajamas and a toothbrush, and then we'll go. Okay?"

Dang it. Sounds like I'm not going to get the chance to satisfy my curiosity tonight. "Okay, yeah. Whatever will make you feel most relaxed and comfortable for your sleep therapy, birthday boy, that's what we'll do."

13
RUBY

We're in my room now.

Kendrick's in bed in his pajamas, with his teeth brushed and his face washed, while I finish up in the bathroom. In truth, I finished up my nighttime routine a few minutes ago, but I'm stalling, hoping to drag this out long enough to find Kendrick already fast asleep by the time I slide into bed next to him.

It's not that I don't want to be in a bed next to an awake Kendrick Cook. It's that I do. Too much. Thanks to that damned kiss.

It was all for show, when I pulled his lips to mine. But when he joined in on my performance so convincingly, my body reacted in a way that felt extremely real. And now, I can't deny I'm feeling curious. Tempted to do it again. Except for the fact that I'm not willing to make a move on a drunk man. Or to get rejected by said drunk man. Or to *not* get rejected, only to wind up ruining my closest friendship because we're both regretful in the morning.

Looking at myself in the mirror, I point emphatically at my reflection and mouth *"No, Ruby,"* before shuffling out of the bathroom. When I get into the bedroom, Kendrick's on his back in bed. One languid, muscular arm is bent and slid under his head. One muscular leg is peeking out of the covers.

"Hey, cutie," he says with a grin.

"Hey, hot stuff," I reply. But this time, calling him that feels loaded somehow. Like I'm flirting with him. So, I quickly whisper, "Happy birthday."

I flip off the overhead light, since the lamp next to Kendrick is on, and slide underneath the covers on my side.

"That was the best birthday party ever," he says. "Thanks for making it so fun."

"I didn't do anything. Savage and Laila planned the whole thing." Are his eyes flickering from my eyes to my lips, or am I imagining that?

"You were the life of the party, though," he says. "You got everybody going."

Okay, Kendrick's gaze definitely flickered to my lips that time. "I needed to let loose."

"How are you feeling now?"

"So much better. Drunk, though."

"Yeah, me, too." Kendrick drags his teeth over his lips, drawing my gaze. Would he return my kiss the same way he pretended to do back then, if I leaned in and kissed him now? Or this time, with no camera pointed at us and no reason to pretend, would he jerk back and say, "I'm sorry, I don't feel that way about you, Ruby." God, that would be mortifying.

"Sorry if I made you leave earlier than you wanted to," I say softly. We're both lying on our sides now, face to face.

"I was looking for an excuse to leave, anyway."

I chuckle. "Liar. You were just getting started. Like Titus said, you didn't even get to play *Birthday Truth or Dare*."

"Like you said, I'm all out of good ideas for dares, anyway." His Adam's apple bobs. "But I guess, I mean, if you insist on me getting to play, we could do it now."

My heart rate increases. The boy wrote lyrics for a song called "Spank," and now he wants to play one-on-one *Truth or Dare*? Color me intrigued.

"Okay, sure," I say, trying to sound unbothered and nonchalant.

He licks his lips. "Tell me the truth, Ruby. Am I the guy in Cooper's song?"

Well, fuck. That's not what I expected.

Unfortunately, the honest answer to that question is yes. In fact, I can't even count the number of times Cooper brought up Kendrick throughout our short relationship, in exactly the same ways he brought up the guy in the song. Indeed, our final fight was mostly to do with his jealousy about Kendrick.

"Come on, Ruby Duby," Kendrick coos, cutting the thick silence. "It's my birthday. You have to answer truthfully."

I exhale. "I think it's possible, considering how jealous he's always been of you."

"Did he ever tell you *why* he was so jealous of me, in particular?"

"He couldn't understand our close friendship. But I'm not inside Cooper's head. Who knows what he was thinking?" I do. I know exactly what Cooper was thinking, because everything he accused me of during our relationship made it into that damned song. "I certainly never gave him any reason to be jealous of you, if that's what you're asking me."

Kendrick twists his mouth, but he doesn't say a word. Can he sense I'm not telling him the full truth? But how could I tell him about the time Cooper accused me of having a sex dream about Kendrick, when I genuinely don't vividly remember the dream myself, so I can't confidently confirm or deny the accusation? For all I know, I was moaning "Kendrick" loudly in my sleep because I was dreaming of him giving me a slice of delicious chocolate cake. Or hell, maybe I wasn't moaning "Kendrick" at all, like Cooper insisted. Who knows? I'm certainly not going to take Cooper's word for it that I did that. Repeatedly. And I'm not going to pass along Cooper's possibly baseless accusations to Kendrick.

"What about the other lyrics?" Kendrick asks. "The sex dreams and 'you said his name twice?' Do you think those lines are about me, too?"

Jesus. "How many questions do you get in a one-on-one game of *Birthday Truth or Dare*?"

"Unlimited."

"No way. You don't get unlimited dares when we play. You only get one per player. It should be the same with truth."

Kendrick smiles. "Dares take more energy to execute, though."

"I'm too tired for more." I fake a yawn. "Let's stop and go to sleep."

"Just answer that last question."

"I forget what it was."

"Do you think the other lines were about me, too? The sex dreams and saying his name twice."

"I have no idea." It's not the truth, but there's no way I'm going to admit Cooper accused me of everything in his song. "Can I ask you a question, even though it's not my birthday?"

Kendrick touches my hair. "Ask me anything. I'm an open book."

I snort. "Says the man who literally snatched away an open book from me."

I giggle at my own cleverness, and Kendrick cracks up, too.

"That's actually an amazing segue to my question. What's 'Spank' about?"

"Here we go."

"I know I can't read it, but can you tell me the gist?" He doesn't respond, so I add, "Just tell me if it's about spanking the monkey or spanking an ass. Tell me that, and then I'll drop it." I probably shouldn't be steering this intimate conversation in bed to anything sexual—even a sexual song or poem. But I can't resist.

Kendrick smiles. "It's about both. Spanking my monkey while fantasizing about spanking a woman's ass."

I gasp. "Kendrick Cook, you naughty boy."

He grins. "'Spank' is all about the primal urge to have dirty, raw sex."

"It sounds like the perfect starting point for a sequel to 'Hate Sex High.'"

"They're not proper lyrics, though."

"The rest of us could whip them into shape. Seriously, the title alone would make it a hit."

"How much of it did you read?"

"Just the title and the first line. But just that bit had me frothing at the mouth to read the rest." I pause to remember the scrawled words on the page. "'Lying awake, my body staging a coup.' That's about your insomnia?"

He nods slowly, his eyes wide.

"What's the next line?" I whisper.

Kendrick exhales. "Nope."

"Come on, KC. Please?"

"You said you'd drop it, Ruby."

"I will. Just tell me this. Were you lying awake, spanking your monkey, and your body was staging a coup because you were so horny? Is that what that line meant?"

He smirks. "What else? I was horny as fuck, jerking myself off and thinking about how much I wanted to fuck someone. Spank someone. Anyone. I mean, that part was honest. But the rest was just a creative writing exercise. No basis in fact whatsoever."

"I don't get why you're so embarrassed to show it to me. Everyone masturbates and gets horny and lonely. And everyone fantasizes about spanking an ass or getting their ass spanked, as the case may be."

"I'm not ashamed to jerk off or get horny. I just don't have any desire to share something I wrote about my hottest sexual fantasies."

"Oh my gosh. Your hottest . . . ? Kendrick Cook, you have to let me read it."

"Nope."

The image of Kendrick making love to that blonde on that couch all those years ago pops into my head again. My god, Kendrick was going to town on that woman, but with his palm tenderly cupping her cheek. For years afterwards, that was my hottest sexual fantasy. Until, of course, I managed to exorcise the image from my head and genuinely accept the fact that Kendrick and I would never be anything but best friends.

The thought jolts me back to reality. The fact that Kendrick has never thought of me as anything but his close friend. Like a sister. And one fake kiss didn't change that for him. *I'm* the only one who went to visit the other one at their school, unannounced, because I was hoping the weekend might lead to me losing my virginity. Kendrick never did that. Or even thought about that. Only me.

I reach out and touch his hair. "Okay, I'll drop it."

"Thank you." He yawns, which makes me yawn.

"You're sleepy?" I whisper.

"Yeah. You?"

I nod. "Try to sleep. Close your eyes, and I'll stroke your face and hair. That worked last time, before I woke you up screaming about Cooper's song."

Kendrick makes a sympathetic face.

"It's okay. I feel much better about that. Cooper is dead to me now. I don't give a fuck."

"Good. Don't let him ruin anything for you, okay? He's not worth it."

I exhale. "Okay."

"Promise?"

"Promise."

"Good girl."

Shit. Good girl. That was smoking hot.

"Don't let him win," Kendrick murmurs, closing his eyes.

"I won't," I whisper. "Now, take deep breaths. You're going to have an amazing, restful sleep."

Kendrick smiles with his eyes closed. "You know what? I think you might actually be right about that."

14
RUBY

Titus and I are lying in a flower garden together. Oh, it's the garden at our grandma's house. But we're not kids, which is weird, since she passed away when I was twelve. We're grown adults. The present versions of ourselves.

Even weirder, Titus is spooning me in the garden. Softly kissing my neck. His arm around me feels kind of nice, actually. Comforting and sweet. Not sure about the kissing thing, though. That feels a little incest-y.

Without notice, I feel the unmistakable sensation of a hard-on poking my ass cheek, and I'm pretty sure about that one: it's most definitely incest-y.

Screaming, I scramble away from Titus' erection and out of his embrace, and wind up falling off the edge of a cliff.

Thud.

"Gah." When I open my eyes, I'm on the floor in my hotel room, crumpled in a heap right next to the side of the bed. The heavy blinds are drawn, keeping the room in sleep-inducing darkness, but there are narrow slivers of sunlight peeking through the edges of the window covering.

"Ruby?" Kendrick croaks out. "Are you okay?" He sits up and our eyes meet. His golden hair is a rat's nest. His face is etched with concern, the whites of his eyes a telltale shade of "partied too hard last night" red.

"I, uh, had a nightmare. I'm okay."

"You screamed like you got stabbed."

"I dreamed a snake chased me off a cliff." It's not a complete lie. The hard snake poking my ass cheek most definitely made me scamper.

I stand up with a soft groan, prompting Kendrick to stretch and yawn—at which point, I notice an unmistakable tent pole poking up from underneath the flimsy top sheet covering his lap.

Apparently, I'm not subtle about staring at Kendrick's crotch, because he quickly looks down and covers his eye-popping bulge with his hands.

"It's not . . . ," he begins. "I wake up every morning like this, pretty much. It's not specific to—"

"No, yeah. I've got a brother, remember? I know all about boys and morning wood." It occurs to me that dream with Titus must have felt so real because Kendrick was spooning me in real life and kissing my neck. And Kendrick was . . . . Oh my god. Did my brain incorporate all those physical sensation from real life into my dream?

I check my phone on the nightstand. "Holy shit. My phone's blowing up."

Kendrick's got his phone in hand now, too. "So is mine." We both start swiping and discover the same thing: Our kiss from last night has gone viral. In fact, it's breaking a certain corner of the internet.

My heart racing, I crawl onto the bed next to Kendrick, and we watch different versions of the same video on his phone, all of them featuring last night's kiss. In some of the clips, the original audio of the moment is used, and Cooper's godawful song is blaring in the background. In others, people have posted the video with new audio overlaid: the precise moment in the song where Cooper sings, "*Why do you want to fuck your brother?*"

"Looks like they've decided I'm the guy in the song," Kendrick says with a nervous laugh.

I rub my forehead, feeling out of sorts. I remember kissing Kendrick last night, of course, but I was so drunk, I don't remember the details of it—the physical sensations of the kiss. Mostly, I remember seeing Rex's phone trained on me and wanting to take control of the narrative. Frankly, that's the overriding memory I've got from that shocking moment. But somewhere in there, if only briefly, I'm pretty sure I also remember thinking, "This is one hell of a kiss."

"I'm sorry, Kendrick," I murmur.

"For what?"

"For kissing you without your consent. For dragging you into this without consulting you first."

Kendrick chuckles. "I was more than happy to be of service. And how could you have asked me? You had to make a game-time decision, and that's what you did."

He swipes, and we watch another version of the same video, this one featuring a talking head influencer who walks the viewer through the "tea" about the supposed "love triangle" between Cooper, Kendrick, and me.

"I'm sure Cooper's seen it by now," Kendrick says. "Your plan worked like a charm."

I snicker. "The kiss is Cooper's worst nightmare. I guarantee you, he's now convinced I was secretly screwing you behind his back the whole time."

Kendrick smirks. "Good. Let him think that." His phone buzzes, and he looks down. "Eli wants you to call him. He says you're not replying to any of his texts or calls, and he needs to talk to you urgently."

"Shit. Do you think he's upset about the viral video for some reason?"

"I highly doubt it."

"He's never needed to talk to me urgently before. I hope it's not bad news."

"Only one way to find out, babe."

"Will you call him and explain the video for me, just in case? I have to pee. Tell him I'll be right out."

Before he responds, I hurtle into the bathroom to do my thing. And by the time I come out, Kendrick has Eli on speakerphone, and it seems pretty clear Eli's not in any kind of distress.

"She's here," Kendrick announces.

"Hey, Eli."

"Hey, Ruby Duby. I've got some great news for you that comes with some not-so-great news. On balance, though, I think you'll feel it's a great opportunity." He pauses for dramatic effect. "Ruby, *Sing Your Heart Out* wants you to be Laila's guest mentor this season."

My heart stops. "What? Oh my gosh, Eli!"

"Congratulations, sweetheart. You deserve this."

I squeal and hug Kendrick sitting next to me . . . until I remember there's some not-so-great news that's coming next. "So, what's the catch?"

Eli exhales loudly. "Cooper. They've already confirmed him as a guest mentor this season."

"No."

"Yeah, sorry. They bumped whoever they had lined up for Jon Stapleton to offer him the gig. Also, brace yourself; they're giving APM a performance slot in the finale."

"Fuck. To perform 'Don't Call Me?'"

"What else?"

"Fuck, fuck, fuck. So, if I do this, I'd have to interact with him on Mentor Day?"

"Yep, and at the press conference, too. And at the finale. You might even have to sit there, watching APM perform, while they grab close-up reaction shots of you and Kendrick."

"Of me and Kendrick? What does that mean?"

"They're hoping for a love triangle storyline. Especially now that you've gifted them with a viral kiss."

"Fuck!" I shout. "Can you please ask them to let me on a different season?"

"Nope. It's now or never, baby. They're salivating over the idea of having the trifecta, all at once, at this specific moment in time, while 'Don't Call Me' is riding high on the charts and that viral kiss is making the rounds."

"Shit."

"I could tell them you're not willing to overtly help their storyline along. I think they'd agree to you simply not actively thwarting it, since the storyline kind of writes itself at this point. Fair warning, though, I'm sure they'll do their damnedest in the edit to make you three look like the second coming of *Twilight*."

I look at Kendrick. "What do you think?"

"I don't give a flying fuck if Cooper's there. I can ignore him. I wouldn't want him to ruin this chance for you, Ruby. But if it wouldn't be fun for you with him there, then don't do it. It's totally up to you, babe."

"If you're willing to play up your new romantic relationship, I'm sure I could negotiate bonuses for both of you," Eli offers.

"We don't have a romantic relationship to play up," I insist. "That kiss was fake, Eli. Someone played the song while recording me to get my reaction, so we seized the opportunity to send a giant fuck-you to Cooper."

"Oh. Huh. I thought . . . Okay, well, the producers don't care if it was real or fake. All they care about is ratings and what storylines they can sell to their audience."

"They did the same thing to Savage and Laila during their first season," Kendrick says to me. "They made them pretend to be madly in love."

"And those two hated each other at the time," Eli adds with a laugh. "So, at least you two have the advantage of genuinely loving each other already."

I smile at Kendrick. "Okay, let's do it. I'm in."

Both men whoop and congratulate me.

"As long as I've got Kendrick there with me," I add, "I'm sure I'll have the time of my life."

"Fantastic!" Eli says with a clap. "I'll call them now with the great news and try to negotiate that bonus option, too."

"Wait," I say. "There's a condition to my yes. I want a performance slot in the finale for Fugitive Summer, the same length as the one APM is getting. And I want us to go on after them, or else my answer is no."

Eli snickers. "You're going to write a response song, huh?"

"No. That would only confirm I'm 'Ruby Tuesday.'"

Eli scoffs. "Hate to break it to you, kid, but if you go on the internet for all of two seconds, you'll find out—"

"The whole world knows I'm her. Yes, I know. But people assuming that is different than me and my band expressly confirming it. I refuse to give Cooper more clout than I've already given him."

"Amen," Kendrick murmurs.

"Then why do you want to perform right after?"

"Because I want them teasing and hyping up the world premiere of Fugitive Summer's brand-new song throughout the whole damned finale. That's going to make everyone and their mother think we're going to perform a diss track of some kind, so they'll all tune in with bated breath."

Eli laughs. "You're a genius."

"And with that many eyeballs on us, whatever new song we debut will smash it."

"Absolutely. It'll go to number one that night. And as long as the song is catchy enough to go the distance, you'll have a massive hit on your hands. Great thinking, Ruby. I love it."

I wink at Kendrick. "And the best part is, when we don't, that'll be an even bigger diss than any song about him could have been."

We all cackle with glee.

"You're so smart," Kendrick says, beaming a smile at me. "You're actually kind of scary." Clearly, he means this as high praise.

Eli says, "For what it's worth, I'd strongly advise you to include at least one line in the new song that could be interpreted as a 'fuck you' to Cooper, even if it's a stretch. Do that, and the song will go ten-times diamond."

"I'll think about it," I say, as Kendrick waggles his eyebrows at the suggestion. "But first things first, get us that performance slot. Tell them if they won't do that, my answer is no."

"I'm sure they'll agree. I honestly predict they'll go batshit crazy for this idea."

"Just tell them it'll be a new single that we're in the midst of writing now. No specifics, okay?"

"Gotcha."

Kendrick clears his throat. "Hey, Eli, do you think the producers might want Ruby and me to live together, like they required of Savage and Laila their first season?"

"Nah. That made sense for Savage and Laila because they were judges. With two guest mentors, I doubt they'll want to pay all the extra expenses to make that happen. I'm sure they'll be thrilled with you two looking cozy at the press conference, and then again during Mentor Day and at the finale."

Kendrick exhales. "Okay. Cool." He presses his lips together. "That's a relief."

"I'm guessing I'll have an answer for you within an hour. Don't tell anyone about this yet. Wait for the deal to be finalized."

"Can I tell Savage and Laila, so I can thank them? We're all headed to the airport in a few minutes."

"Yeah, you can tell them, since they've already signed an NDA with the show."

"What about Titus? I swear he won't say a word."

Eli chuckles. "Tell the whole band, Ruby Duby. That's fine. But that's it."

We say our goodbyes, and Kendrick disconnects the call.

"Thank God you're going to be there with me," I say to Kendrick on a sigh. "With Cooper there, I doubt I would have said yes, if not for you."

Kendrick smiles and bites his lip. For a moment, his eyes drift to my mouth. Ever so briefly. Or maybe I'm imagining that. "I'm gonna head to my room to shower and pack before they come get us for the airport."

"I need to do all that, too. Thank you again for everything."

"Anything for you, Ruby. Always."

He slides out of bed and saunters toward the door. But as he opens it, Titus is standing in the doorframe, his fist raised like he's about to knock.

"Oh!" Kendrick blurts, as both men take surprised steps backwards.

"I know what this looks like," Kendrick says quickly. "But nothing happened last night between Ruby and me. We crashed right after we got here."

"Okay," Titus says. But his raised eyebrow makes the word sound more like he's saying, "Bullshit."

"It's true," I say. "Not that it'd be any of your business, either way."

"I never said it's my business. All I said was I didn't want you two doing something shitfaced you wouldn't have done sober."

I vaguely remember Titus saying something like that, now that I think about it. But last night is kind of a blur for me, thanks to the copious amounts of booze and weed in my system. The only two things I remember with perfect clarity from last night, now that I think about it, are the following: one, I definitely kissed Kendrick last night, as a 'fuck you' to Cooper, and, two, somewhere in there, while my lips were still connected with Kendrick's, I thought: *This is the best kiss of my life.* Sadly, I don't remember the physical sensations that prompted that shocking thought. Honestly, I don't remember what it felt like to kiss Kendrick at all. But now that I'm remembering I had that surprising thought, I can't deny I'm deeply curious to kiss Kendrick again—while sober the next time—to try to find out exactly what prompted it.

15
KENDRICK

"It's official!" Ruby shouts, looking down at her phone. "They accepted my demands. I'm going to be Laila's mentor!"

I high-five her and whoop. "Congratulations, sweetheart!"

We're sitting together on the airplane to LA, so Ruby tilts her screen toward me to show me Eli's exciting text.

"The press conference announcing the cast is so soon after we get back," Ruby says, referring to the timeline contained in Eli's text.

"Yeah, they always do it the night before the season starts taping."

As Ruby taps out a reply, it occurs to me this is a good opportunity to try to persuade her to stay at my place while they're doing repairs at her condo.

"So, have you figured out where you're going to stay? You know, while they're making those repairs on your place?"

"A hotel. It's only a week."

"Don't do that. Stay with me." I wiggle my eyebrows. "Your fake boyfriend."

"They're not requiring us to live together. I don't want to inconvenience you."

"Would you stop with that? It'll be fun. Like when I used to visit you on weekends at school. We'd also save the world by carpooling to the press conference together."

"Well, that's true. I certainly wouldn't want to be a bad global citizen."

I smile. "It's settled, then."

"Only if you're sure I won't cramp your style."

"Ruby, I'm not Kai or Savage before Laila. Like I keep telling you, I've got no style for you to cramp."

Ruby giggles, and I feel a rush of adrenaline to be able to make fun of Kai without worrying I'm rubbing salt in an old wound. For so long, I've avoided all mention of Kai's sexcapades, thinking I was saving Ruby from memories of her rejection at Kai's hands. But now, it's like all the guard rails between us are down. The eggshells I've been tiptoeing around for so long, vanished.

"Now that you're supposedly my beloved girlfriend," I say, "I couldn't date anyone in LA, even if I wanted to." *Which I don't.* On the contrary, after The Kiss That Changed Everything, I can no longer deny Ruby's the only person I want to kiss on Planet Earth.

"Okay, I'll stay," Ruby says. "Thank you. But after the press conference, if my place isn't ready, I'll get a hotel or stay with Savage and Laila."

"Don't do that. I'd be insulted."

Ruby blushes. "Hopefully, it won't take that long, and it'll be a moot point."

"I've got fingers crossed for you." I nudge her. "So, are you going to text Reed and tell him about the show?"

"I'm sure he already knows. Nothing this big happens to one of his artists without him knowing about it."

"No, I mean, are you going to text him to admit Cooper's song has turned out to be a blessing in disguise, like he said?"

Ruby scoffs. "I think I'll wait to see how the show pans out first." She pops out of her seat. "I'm going to tell my brother the good news and thank Laila and Savage. You want to come?"

"No, I think I'll chill for a bit. Maybe chat with Kai. Would you be cool with me telling him the good news and declaring an end to the Cold War?" Ever since the emergency band meeting the other day, I've been giving Kai the cold shoulder, in solidarity with Ruby. But I feel like the time has finally come to bury the hatchet.

"Sure. I'm so happy right now, I can't muster the energy to hold a single grudge. Not even against stupid Kai." With a cute little squeal, Ruby musses my hair and bounds off to her brother a few rows back.

I wait a few minutes to peek behind me again, and when I do, Ruby has finished talking with her brother, and she's now at the back of the plane, chatting enthusiastically with Savage and Laila. With the coast clear, I unbuckle my seatbelt, slide into the aisle, and head not to Kai, but two rows back to Titus.

"Hey, man. Can I sit for a second?" I take the seat next to him. "So, about last night. I want to talk to you about that."

"It didn't go down nearly as platonically as you two said? I figured as much."

"No, no. I swear nothing happened. I'd never make a move on anyone who's shitfaced, Titus."

"But if Ruby had been sober, that would have been a different story?"

Shit. Is that what I just admitted? "No. That's not what I meant."

Titus grins. "It's okay, Kendrick. Like I said, I just didn't want you two getting together for the first time drunk. Other than that, you can do your thing, if that's what you want to do." His next words, he murmurs under his breath. "And it seems to me you do . . ."

My eyebrows ride up. My brain feels like it's scrambling. I think that means Titus is giving me his blessing to date his sister? It's a moot point, anyway, since Ruby's not interested in me like that. But still, I can't deny it's pretty cool to find out Titus would be cool with it. Especially because, during our emergency band meeting the other day, he didn't have quite the same reaction to Kai making a move on his sister.

"That's . . . Wow," I stammer. I pause, gathering my courage, and finally ask the thing I'm dying to know. "Has Ruby ever expressed interest in me to you? As more than a friend? Or was your comment about me making a move only . . . hypothetical?"

Titus grins. "It was hypothetical. Sorry to disappoint you, man." Well, that's pretty damned clear: Titus knows I'm into his sister. And not only as friends. How long has he known that?

My head is spinning. In a short space of time, I've let the cat out of the bag with Savage and Laila, and now it kind of feels like I've done the same thing with Titus. And you know what? The sky isn't falling. The band isn't crumbling. In fact, it feels like all three are totally rooting us on.

My heart thumping, I peek toward Savage and Laila at the back of the plane and discover my best friend is now sitting alone, and Ruby and Laila are nowhere to be seen. Probably chatting with our tour manager, Caden, in the next compartment.

It's the perfect opportunity for me to pick Savage's brain in private, so I beeline over to him. When Ruby stays at my place this coming week, it'll be the perfect opportunity to make her see me in a new light—as more than a friend. But *how*? Normally, I'm pretty good with women. No, I'm awesome, actually. But when it comes to Ruby, I don't trust myself to get it right without some help. I'm too close to the situation. Too invested.

But Savage? He's not only far more detached and clear-headed than me, he also happens to be one of the world's foremost former fuckboys. True, he hasn't plied his trade in several years now, ever since meeting Laila, but I have to assume seduction is like riding a bike. So, hell yeah, I'm going to use this opportunity to come clean and seek his expert counsel.

————

"Hey, Savage, can I get some advice from you?"

Savage looks up from the movie he's watching on his iPad. "What's up?"

I slide into the empty seat recently vacated by Laila.

"What I'm about to tell you is highly confidential. You can't even tell Laila."

Savage's dark eyebrows cinch together. "Okay."

"Promise me, Savage. I mean it this time. If you're going to tell her, I can't tell you this."

He twists his mouth. "I mean, realistically, I'll probably tell Laila, without meaning to do it. But I swear to God, nobody else. And I'll make sure Laila doesn't tell anyone. She's super trustworthy, KC, unlike me."

I can't help laughing.

"I don't want to keep secrets from her," Savage adds earnestly. "She's my *wife*."

I pat his shoulder. "Okay. That's good enough for me. But you have to make sure she understands she can't tell anyone, especially not Ruby. This is life or death for me, Savage. Promise me that, on your life."

"I promise on my life. What's going on? You're scaring me."

I take a deep breath. "I'm totally obsessed with Ruby, man. Sexually, I mean. Romantically. In every conceivable way, actually. And if I don't take things to the next level with her soon, I'm pretty sure I'm going to physically die."

Savage looks deeply amused. "So, Laila was right. That kiss was for real?"

I run a tortured hand over my face. "No. Well, yes, for me. But not for Ruby, unfortunately. She thinks I was brilliantly playing along to help her mess with Cooper."

"Shit."

"What did Laila say?"

"That you two left the party after that kiss to fuck for the first time."

I shudder. "God, I wish. Sadly, no."

"How long have you been feeling this way?"

I pretend to think about it, but I'm only doing a bit. "I think, uh, hmm, since . . . the instant I met her."

"What?"

"Remember how Kai accused me of inviting her to audition because I had a crush on her? He was right. I hadn't even heard her play yet."

Savage throws his head back and belly laughs. "What the fuck, KC? Why didn't you tell me?"

"I don't know."

"I had a feeling you were into her that first night. But then you kept denying it and swearing you only wanted to help the band, so I eventually took your word for it. And then you two became such close besties, I figured . . . Damn, KC."

"I know. It's been torture. I mean, the friendship has been real. But I've loved that girl for as long as I can remember."

He shakes his head. "Jesus, Kendrick. I'm sorry."

"When I dropped out of school, I was determined to come back home and finally tell her the truth. But that's when Kai told me she'd been desperately in love with him from day one, and not only that, she'd asked him to have sex with her at her birthday party, so . . ."

"Fucking Kai."

"When that domino fell the other night, combined with her ditching Cooper, I started to feel this crazy electricity, Savage. Add in my kiss with her, and I can't go back to the way things were. I have to have her, Savage. There's no other option for me now."

"Hell yeah. Get your girl."

"It's tricky, though. Ruby's never felt anything but friendship for me. Not once in twelve years. So, the last thing I want to do is get rejected and mess up one of my closest friendships."

"Yeah. No pressure, but the band would never be the same again."

"Fuck the band. Sorry, but all I care about is figuring out how to make Ruby want me the same way I want her, without messing up our friendship. The band is secondary to that mission now."

"I get it. If me having Laila meant I'd fuck up the band, then the band would get fucked."

I exhale. "Thank you for understanding. I want Ruby. Period. But I don't know how to make it happen. We've got too much history. If she was even capable of wanting me the way I want her, wouldn't she have shown signs by now?"

"Maybe the stars have never been aligned, like they are now. Also, I wouldn't count yourself out completely. My guess is Cooper's lyrics—and the jealousy that inspired them—didn't come out of nowhere."

My heart races. "God, I hope you're right about that, because I've got the perfect window of opportunity when we get back. She finally agreed to stay at my place for a week while her condo is getting repaired."

"That's perfect. She'll be sleeping in your bed, right?"

"Yeah, I've only got the one bedroom." I don't need to explain further. Savage knows I've converted my other two bedrooms into a gym and a recording studio. I continue, "If I can't make it happen while Ruby's sleeping next to me for a whole week, maybe I'll have to accept she really does see me like a brother, the same way she sees Titus."

"No, KC. Failure isn't an option, like you said. But also like you said, after twelve years of friendship, you have to be strategic here. You can't be too aggressive with her, or she's going to wonder what the hell you're doing."

"I agree."

"You have to make Ruby come to you. Seduce her in a way that makes *her* want to seduce *you*."

"Awesome. Yes. This is exactly why I came to you. I need all your fuckboy wisdom."

He laughs. "You can do this. I know you can. But I think one week to pull this off is bit of a tight squeeze, honestly. Two would be much better. A slam dunk."

"Well, no shit, Sherlock, two weeks would be better than one. But my hands are tied; her building manager said the work on her place will only take a week."

Savage pulls a face. "So, call the building manager and bribe him to say he found some mold or something, and the work will take a week or two longer than expected. Easy peasy."

For a moment, I'm stunned into silence with my jaw hanging open. Finally, I manage, "I couldn't possibly do that."

"Why not?"

"Savage, you just made a big deal about how you never keep secrets from Laila."

"Because she's my wife. Before that, while I was seducing her, I kept a shit-ton of secrets from her, and she did the same thing to me. And do you know why? Because seduction inherently requires manipulation. Seduction is war. And when it works, that's the end of the war—the moment when both players lay down their swords and start a whole new game: the actual relationship, which requires full honesty."

I stare at him in disbelief. "I don't even know how to respond to that."

He shrugs. "It's how it works. Believe me or don't. It's up to you."

"I just want Ruby, Savage. But I don't want to manipulate her like that. Help me. Tell me what to do."

"Well, I can tell you what *not* to do. The exact same thing you've been doing for twelve fucking years. You can't do that and expect to get a different result. Ya feel me? That's the very definition of insanity."

I pull a face that concedes he's got a point. But what I say is, "What do you suggest I do, then? Specifically. Other than bribing her building manager, because I'm not going to do that."

"I think you should."

"I'm not doing it."

"How about I do it for you? That way, you'll have plausible deniability."

"Never say 'plausible deniability' in my presence again. You sound like a psychopath when you say that, man."

Savage laughs, while I lean my head back and exhale.

"Just tell me what to do to get a different result than the one I've gotten for the past twelve years."

He exhales. "It's pretty simple, really. You have to make things feel sexually charged between you. Show her some skin, every chance you get. Work out shirtless. Come out of the bathroom after a shower, wet and wearing nothing but a towel. Show her the merchandise, man. Remind her you're Kendrick fucking Cook. Show her why every other woman on the planet wants you."

"That's not going to work."

"Kendrick, have you seen yourself?"

"Dude, Ruby's seen me. A million times. She's been looking at me for twelve years, including countless times half-naked in a bathing suit."

"It'll be different when she's staying with you. When it's just you and her, and she's sleeping in your bed every night." He winks. "Make things feel sexual, whenever you can, and when you show her some skin, it'll hit different for her. I guarantee it. Especially if you touch her a lot, too. You know, brush hair out of her eyes. Scoot past her in the kitchen and make contact when you do. Oh, and talk about sex with her, however you can squeeze it into conversation. Do all that, and she'll eventually give you an obvious green light. I promise you. And when she does that, you need to be ready to go for it without hesitation. Without over-thinking it. Just go for it. Seize the moment when she serves it up to you."

My heart is racing. "This could work."

"I know it will."

"Add to the list, I'll pretend to have insomnia every night, so she'll cuddle me." I explain the whole thing about Ruby's theory, and Savage agrees it's a fantastic addition to the overall plan.

"I have to play it really cool with her, though," I say. "After her breakup with Cooper, she made a huge thing about never wanting to date a friend, ever again. Actually, she made a thing about not wanting a relationship, period. Only a fling."

"Now, see, that's some great intel. When Ruby gives you that green light, let her know it's got to be a fling. A 'best-friends-with-benefits fling.'"

"I want more than that, though."

"I know. But trust me, that's all you can offer her. Tell her it's gonna be like a tour fling: it ends when she moves out of your place. But then, during the fling, you're gonna give her so many amazing orgasms, while still being the bestie she loves so much, that she'll be the one who asks to keep things going for real."

"You're a genius."

"I know."

"I really think this could work."

"It will. The key is, you've got to go through Ruby's 'meaningless fling' door, so she doesn't feel like getting down with you is such a major life decision. You can't make her feel like she's got to take a huge leap of faith to have sex with you—a leap that might fuck up her closest friendship forever. Hell, no. 'This is nothing but fun, Ruby! A fling. And everything will go back to normal after you move out!' That's how you're gonna play it, man. And she's gonna eat it up." He waggles his eyebrows. "She'll be in love with you in two weeks or less."

I frown. "I've only got a week, like I said."

Savage shrugs. "I mean, that could work. Just saying, after twelve years of friendship, that's a tight squeeze. But, hey, if anyone can do it in a week, you can."

"Hell yeah. I'm a man on a mission, baby. Failure isn't an option."

"Atta boy." Savage fist-bumps me. "You've got this, brother."

"Thanks for the strategy sesh. I feel confident now."

Laila appears in the aisle, and Savage and I immediately shut up and smile.

"Hey, KC," Laila says. "Do you want to sit here for the rest of the flight? I'd be happy to grab my stuff and—"

"No, I'll go back to sitting with Ruby. We were just shooting the shit." I slide out and Laila slides in. "Good talking to you, Savage."

"You, too, KC." He winks.

I start walking back to Ruby. But then I remember I wanted to talk to my brother to let bygones be bygones. Kai might very well have changed the trajectory of my relationship with Ruby, but he didn't do it on purpose. Plus, now that I've got my plan in place, I'm choosing to believe everything happens for a reason. As it should. That when Ruby finally falls in love with me this week, her love will arrive right on time.

16

RUBY

"I didn't know you like having flowers in your house," I say, gesturing to the spray of orange tulips on Kendrick's kitchen counter. I've just entered his living room with my suitcase, after parting ways with him for a few hours after the airport to check on the status of my place and grab a few things.

"I got them for you. To welcome you here." He smiles at my shocked reaction. "It's no big deal. I always get my mom her favorite flowers, too, whenever she comes to visit me."

"That's so sweet. How did you know tulips are my favorites?" I don't think I've ever mentioned that to him.

"On tour once, when you were feeling homesick, you stopped at a flower stand and bought yourself a huge bouquet of them for your hotel room."

"I did? Which tour was that?"

"Our very first."

"As openers?" I'm flabbergasted Kendrick remembers a meaningless detail like that, let alone from so long ago, especially when I don't remember it myself.

He smirks. "You also sing 'Tiptoe through the Tulips,'

whenever you get drunk, so tulips were a good bet, regardless."

I giggle. "That's one of the first songs my mom taught me on piano. Her mom taught it to her."

"I know. You told me."

Again, I'm surprised he remembers that detail. "What's your mom's favorite flower?"

"Hmm?"

"What do you get your mom, when she comes to visit?"

"Oh. Uh. Hmm. What's the flower that smells really good?"

"Lilies, maybe?"

"Yep. That's it. Lilies."

Kendrick's doorbell rings, and he looks toward the door with a look of surprise on his handsome face. "Nobody knows I'm back yet."

"It's probably the air mattress I ordered." I hold up my phone, displaying the delivery notification that just popped onto its screen.

"Why'd you order that? My bed is plenty big enough for both of us."

"Staying here with you is one thing. Staying here *and* sleeping in your bed, when we both know you've been dying to get home and sleep like a baby in your own bed, is a bridge too far."

"Ruby, I slept like a baby with you last night, remember? You saved me from insomnia."

"You said you don't get insomnia when you're home."

"I did? Well, I mean, normally that's true. But with that damned quarterback out there, who knows?"

"Okay, well, if you need some sleep therapy from me, you'll know where to find me. But we should still set up the air mattress."

We argue about it, until finally Kendrick says, "At least set the damned thing up next to my bed. That's the only place with enough space for it. My other two bedrooms are filled with workout gear and recording equipment."

"I really don't want to invade your privacy."

"It'll be fun—like old times."

I return his wistful smile. "I always loved our little slumber parties."

"Me, too. Those were some really happy times for me."

"Minus the part where you had crippling depression about your lifelong dreams being crushed."

Kendrick snorts. "Yeah, that part sucked. But the rest was awesome."

We share a chuckle.

"So, it's settled, then?" he asks. "You'll set up camp in my room?"

"If you insist." I bat my eyelashes. "Now, would you be my hero and carry my air mattress into your bedroom for me? I think the box will be too heavy for me to pick up."

———

"Oh my gosh, Kendrick. More tulips?"

We're in his bedroom now. He's putting down the large box containing my new air mattress, while I roll my suitcase into the room behind him—and, immediately, I'm flabbergasted by yet another, even bigger, bouquet of gorgeous, orange blooms. This one on his dresser.

"I just wanted you to feel at home," he says casually. Is he blushing?

"Well, in that case, maybe you should have messed up the place a bit. You're much neater than I'll ever be."

I'm expecting Kendrick to chuckle, but he doesn't. He actually seems a bit stiff and nervous. He clears his throat and gestures to my suitcase. "I cleared out the top two drawers of my dresser for you." Next, he motions to a walk-in closet. "And there's half a rack in there for you, too."

"That's more than enough room. Thank you. I didn't bring much, since I'm only staying for a week, and I can do laundry."

We consider the placement of the air mattress and ultimately decide to set it up alongside Kendrick's bed to maximize our ability to chat at night, like we used to do in my dorm room. And with that decision made, Kendrick gets to work, while I begin unpacking my suitcase.

It's Kendrick who finishes his task first.

"I think I'll get in a quick workout," he says. "While you finish unpacking and getting settled. Cool?"

"Of course. And there's no need to make it quick. Live your life, babe, like I'm not even here."

"Well, what would be the point in that, when I'm so excited you're here?" There's that blush again. "I normally work out shirtless, by the way. I get super sweaty, so that cuts down on laundry. Okay with you?"

"Why wouldn't it be? I've seen you shirtless a million times, KC."

"I know, I just want you feeling comfortable in close quarters with me." Without further ado, he slowly peels off his T-shirt, and, suddenly, at the sight of Kendrick's bare torso mere feet away from me, I don't feel quite as nonchalant about his half-nakedness, as I claimed a moment ago. Indeed, standing here now, I'm feeling the unmistakable sensation of physical arousal at the sight of him. What's wrong with me?

I wrench my eyes off Kendrick's smooth, bare muscles and take a deep breath, feeling deeply annoyed with myself. I've been to countless hotel pools with this man. Sat in countless hot tubs and on sandy beaches around the world with him, too. He's shuffled past me, shirtless, on tour buses, on his way to the bathroom or the fridge in the back. And not once, on any of those occasions, did my body react to Kendrick's body the way it's reacting now. Is it that drunken kiss I can barely remember that's wreaking havoc with me? I don't consciously remember the details of it, true, but perhaps my subconscious remembers it all too well—and now, it's goading me on to do it again . . . .

"Let me know if you need anything, cutie."

"Do your thing, hot stuff." My chest tightens. With his shirt off, while standing in his bedroom mere feet away from me, right next to his bed, and with that big palm of his is resting on his cut abs, which draws my attention to them, everything feels heated and charged. Indeed, I'm feeling weird tingles I shouldn't be feeling.

"Okay, well," Kendrick says. "Lemme know if you need anything." With that, he strides out of the room, leaving me to gawk at his graceful, muscular backside in motion as he goes —which, damn it, then provokes fleeting visions of that very same backside in a different kind of motion. Namely, gyrating on top of a blonde on a couch.

A thudding sound from the next room jolts me from my memory. It's the sound of heavy weights thudding to the ground.

I shake off the long-ago, illicit images in my head and return to my suitcase. After a bit, I get to a small, purple bag— one that's filled with all my nighttime stuff, like birth control pills, migraine meds, lip balm, earbuds, and my vibrator, Bruno. Obviously, I'll need to wait for Kendrick to be out of his house to use Bruno while I'm staying here. But whenever those rare opportunities arise, I'm sure I'll want to have him, and the rest of this stuff, close by, rather than stowed away in the dresser.

I stride toward the nightstand to put the bag away. But before I reach my destination, I remember Bruno probably needs to be charged. I sit on the edge of the bed and pull Bruno out. When I flip his switch, I get nothing. He's dead as a doornail. I put him down next to me and rummage around in the bag, quickly finding his charging cord.

After a quick scan for outlets, I notice a lamp on Kendrick's nightstand that seems to be plugged in behind the furniture, so I formulate the plan to plug in Bruno back there, while discreetly placing him on the floor behind the nightstand. But first, I open the drawer of the nightstand, intending to stow my little purple bag.

Whoa. Inside, there's a variety of interesting items: condoms, lube, and soft handcuffs—the kind people use during kinky sex. All of it makes my eyebrows ride up and my heart rate increase. But none of it more so than the most exciting item in the drawer: Kendrick's lyrics notebook.

My heart thrumming, I peek at the empty doorframe of Kendrick's bedroom. And when the coast is clear, I drop everything in my hands onto the bed next to Bruno, take the journal out of the drawer, and quickly start flipping pages in search of those raunchy lyrics for "Spank." Granted, it's a violation of Kendrick's privacy for me to be doing this. I know that. But on the other hand, he did tell me to treat this place as my home. And when I'm home, nothing's off limits to me. Okay, yes, I'm playing mental gymnastics here. But the truth is, I simply can't resist.

I can't find it. Did he tear it out?

"You little sneak!"

I look up, and two seconds later, a glistening, sweaty, half-naked Kendrick rips the journal out of my hands, the same way he did in that hotel room in Vancouver. *Damn.*

"Well, I guess that answers that question," I deadpan. "You haven't ripped out the 'Spank' pages."

With the journal in one hand, Kendrick crosses his arms over his bare chest, and his tattooed biceps bulge. "You're a bad girl, Ruby. A very bad girl."

Meow. That was kind of hot, actually. "Such a bad girl," I agree. "What are you going to do about it? Spank me?" I've meant it as a joke. A callback to what he wrote about in his journal. But the blush that overtakes Kendrick's face makes me blush, as well.

"I didn't go looking for your journal, by the way. I opened that drawer looking for a place to . . ." I trail off when I notice Kendrick staring with laser-focus at the hot-pink dildo on the mattress next to me. "Oh. Kendrick, meet Bruno," I quip. "Bruno, this is Kendrick. Finally, my two favorite men meet each other."

Kendrick chuckles. "You were looking for a place to what? Put your massive, pink dildo?"

"Cover your ears, Bruno." I waggle my finger at Kendrick and fake-whisper, "Don't body shame him. He's sensitive about his size and color." As Kendrick chuckles, I pick up my dildo and say, "Bruno, don't feel ashamed. There's nothing shameful about masturbation. Or being big and pink. You do a valuable service, when you do me." I snicker. "Or, rather, as the famed lyricist Kendrick Cook calls it, when you spank my monkey."

"You're obsessed."

"I am. There's no denying it. But the fact that I happened upon your journal, by chance, when I was innocently looking for a place to put some things, feels like a sign from the universe that you should let me read it. Don't you agree?"

"I do not."

"Come on, KC. Surely, in my shoes, you would have done the same thing."

"No, I would have respected the privacy of the person who'd said, explicitly, 'Don't look at this.'"

"Well, you'll be happy to know it's a moot point, anyway, because, unfortunately, I didn't find 'Spank' before you barged in here and ruined my fun." I gasp. "Were you spying?" I look around. "Is there a nanny-cam in here? I wouldn't put it past you, with those handcuffs in your nightstand. What's that about, hot stuff?"

"Exactly what you think. And no, I wasn't spying on you. My earbuds died, so I came back for my other pair. Now, stop trying to make a good offense your best defense, and apologize."

"I'm sorry. I had a moment of weakness. I promise it won't happen again."

"Your promises mean nothing to me at this point."

"Smart man. But I really do mean it this time."

"You didn't mean it last time?"

"No, I did. I just couldn't resist."

"I think that's even worse."

"Is it, though?"

He crosses his muscular arms over his bare chest and lets out a tsk. "You really are a monster, aren't you?"

"I am. Who knew? My family, I suppose. But who else?" I pick up Bruno and wave it at him. "Now that you've seen my dildo, and I've seen your kinky little handcuffs, I feel like we've entered a new stage of our friendship, babe. One where it feels perfectly natural for you to let me read your kinky little—"

"No."

I toss my dildo onto the bed in a huff. "Why are you being so stubborn about this? So what, you like to smack an ass on occasion? What could possibly be so shocking that you won't let me read your dirty fantasies?"

"It's not shocking. It's just . . . Personal. Really personal." He shifts his weight. Licks his lips. "Honestly, it's just so fucking hot, I can't believe I wrote it. Since we're only friends, it feels like it would cross a line for me to show it to you."

I open my mouth to speak but close it again. What can I say to refute that, really? If it's that dirty, he's probably right. But do I want that to be right? No. In this moment, every cell in my body wants him to show me what he wrote, anyway. Our friendship be damned.

"Will I show it to the next woman I have sex with?" Kendrick continues. "Hell yeah. Because I'm sure it'll make her super wet and horny."

My eyebrows ride up.

"But, you know, as friends, I think we should draw some boundaries in terms of how graphically we talk about sex and our hottest fantasies. As friends, should we really be talking about the stuff that turns us on the most? I don't think so. You've already found out more about me than I would have told you." He jerks his chin toward his nightstand, presumably referring to those kinky handcuffs, and I swear to God, my clit pulses in reply.

"Um, yeah," I say slowly. "I get what you're saying, in concept. But don't you sometimes talk to your guy friends about sex?"

"Sometimes." He smirks. "But not in graphic detail. And you're not a guy."

"So what? I'm still your friend."

He stares at me, immovable.

"So, does that mean your lyrics are in graphic detail?"

"Very much so. They're as graphic as it gets. Whatever you're imagining, it's that and more. Much more."

My eyes widen. "Really? Jesus, Kendrick. What the fuck is in that thing?" I swear, the more he tells me about it while refusing to tell me about it, the more intrigued and turned on I get.

Kendrick drags his teeth over his lower lip. "Tell the truth. You want to read 'Spank' while using Bruno, don't you?"

I haven't thought about doing that. But now that he's mentioned it, I'm instantly obsessed with the idea. "I mean, I wouldn't say no to doing that. Especially if it'll make you give it to me."

Kendrick's chest heaves. "I might have said yes to helping you out, if you'd been a good girl and respected my boundaries. But as it stands, I can't give it to you, or else you'll never learn your lesson."

"I will, though. Right after you show it to me, I'll learn a valuable lesson, I swear."

Kendrick laughs. "About what?"

"Persistence."

We both laugh.

"Sorry, I can't do it, babe," he says. "You're a monster, and you need to learn." He smirks. "Speaking of monsters . . ." He motions to Bruno on the bed. "Should we agree on a notification system for when you're getting busy with Bruno? A sock on the doorknob, perhaps?"

"That won't be necessary. I'll use him when you're out."

"I wouldn't want to deprive you of a single orgasm, if you suddenly feel the urge to have one."

What's happening? I know his words didn't say it, but it sure feels like Kendrick is tacitly offering to give me orgasms during my stay here. Am I crazy? Am I drunk on all the racy, imagined thoughts I'm having about what might be scribbled on the pages of "Spank?"

Kendrick lays his large palm on his bare abs again, drawing my attention to them, the same as before. "I normally jerk off in bed, but while you're here, I'll do it in the shower. Maybe that strategy would work for you, too. Is Bruno waterproof?"

The image of Kendrick jerking off in the shower flickers across my mind, sending tingles into my panties. "He's waterproof, yes, but I wouldn't be able to do my thing with him in there if I knew you could hear the telltale buzz from out here."

He cocks his head with a smile. "Didn't you just say there's no shame in masturbation?"

"There isn't. But that doesn't mean I can relax enough to

do it when I know someone can overhear me. I'm shy like that. Always have been."

Kendrick jerks his chin at Bruno. "Is he the toy that gets you off better than any man?"

I forgot I told him about that. "Yeah. Not only Bruno, though. His forefathers, too."

"Interesting. And too bad." Based on the wicked smirk on his face, Kendrick clearly believes he could do better. And you know what? Based on the way Kendrick was fucking Florence on that couch, and also based on what Tracy, our former tour manager, said about her time in the sack with this man, I think he might very well be right. I've heard of unicorn men who are better than vibrators. Well, damn, maybe Kendrick Cook is actually one of them.

"I tell you what," I say. "If you let me read 'Spank,' I'll use Bruno in the shower, while you're still home. That way, you could invade my stated boundary, the way I've already invaded yours."

"I'm going to need something far more alluring than that out of you. Like I said, it's my hottest fantasies. I'm extremely vulnerable in those lyrics, Ruby."

"Okay, well, maybe I could show you how I use Bruno—"

"Let's do it."

"—on a guava or some . . . thing. Oh."

"No. Yeah. I meant . . . Not on you. I knew what you meant. On a fruit. Yeah."

We stare at each other for a long moment. Did he just say yes to watching me masturbate with Bruno? Did I imagine that?

His face red, Kendrick clears his throat and holds up the journal. "I'm gonna go hide this atomic bomb somewhere good. Somewhere you'll never find it. And then, I'm gonna finish my workout and make a protein shake."

"Cool."

"You want one?"

"I'd rather poke my eye out. You know I hate those things."

"Just thought I'd ask, out of politeness. You should try it sometime. Being polite, that is."

"I'm polite. Monsters can be very polite."

He laughs.

"Do you have any sandwich stuff? If not, I'd be happy to go to the store."

"I already did, and, yep, I got all your favorite stuff. Stocked the fridge."

"Aw, thanks. I'll make you a sandwich to thank you, if you'd like. How's that for polite?"

"Sounds great."

"We can eat and watch a show."

"Awesome. See you in a bit." He pivots to leave but immediately turns back. "I'll be blaring Red Card Riot's new album in my earbuds for the rest of my workout. For about thirty minutes, I'd say, so I won't be able to hear anything going on around me during that whole time, if you want to have a date with Bruno." With that, he winks and turns to go.

"What happened to those boundaries, dude?" I call out to his back.

"They're overrated, anyway."

"Then show me 'Spank.'"

"Nope. Monsters must be punished." It's the last thing he says before he's out the door. And a few minutes later, I hear the clanging of his weights in the next room once again.

When the sounds in Kendrick's gym seem to be a constant thing, I tiptoe to the bedroom door, quietly close it, grab Bruno and his charging cord, and bring both into the walk-in closet. After closing that door behind me, I find an outlet and plug Bruno in. And then, I proceed to let Bruno have his way with

me, while contemplating all the naughty, raunchy things
Kendrick might have jotted down in that sexy, furious handwriting of his.

17
KENDRICK

Six days later

"Oh, yeah, this is definitely the fit, baby," I murmur to the stylist assigned to me as I gaze at myself in a full-length mirror.

"You have the perfect physique to wear it," she replies, gazing at my reflection alongside me. She launches into a detailed explanation of how and why she thinks this sick outfit suits me and is the perfect choice for today's festivities —the press conference announcing this season's cast of *Sing Your Heart Out*, followed by a raging after-party. All of it happening here at Reed River's sprawling, hilltop mansion in the Hollywood Hills

"When I was Savage's guest mentor two seasons ago, they didn't give me a stylist," I say. "I wore a T-shirt and jeans out of my own closet."

The stylist *tsks*. "Well, this time, Nadine said she wants us pulling out all the stops to make you look like a headliner."

She's referring to the executive producer, a woman who's well known for being a Machiavellian force of nature.

The handler assigned to me for the day—another new thing, since my last appearance on the show—pops her head into the bedroom I've been assigned to use as my dressing room/hiding place, and the moment she sees my flashy duds, she gushes about my appearance.

"Isn't he stunning?" the stylist agrees.

"Stunning. A work of art. Is he ready for hair and makeup?"

"He's all yours."

"Are you doing it in Reed's guest house?" I ask. That's where they did it during my prior season. "If so, I know my way there, so you don't have to take me."

The woman smiles at me in a way that feels like she's calling me a dumbshit. "Yeah, it's over there again. But I have to escort you. Nadine said she doesn't want to risk you bumping into Cooper before the press conference. She wants all on-camera reactions to be 'spontaneous' and 'real.'"

"Okay. Whatever you say." I say my goodbyes and thanks to the stylist, and off I go behind my handler until, eventually, we're heading down a winding path through Reed's spacious backyard that leads to his guest house at the back of his massive estate.

"Well, look at you," a snarky male voice says. When I turn to look, it's Cooper coming up the path from the guest house. Like me, he's dressed to kill. Unlike me, his hair and face are already camera-ready.

"Hey, Cooper," I say flatly. By now, we both know they're going to try to pit us against each other this season. I'm sure Cooper's on board, but fuck him. I'm planning to adopt Ruby's approach and make it clear he's not worth the time or energy to engage with.

"Don't say another word, boys," my handler barks. "Save

whatever you're dying to say to each other for the press conference."

"I'm not dying to say a damned thing," I say nonchalantly.

"Sure, KC," Cooper snaps.

"Stop. Talking," Cooper's handler hisses. "Both of you. Or Nadine's going to kill me."

My handler snaps at her colleague, "Why'd you bring Cooper through here now? Didn't you hear me on the radio? I just said I was escorting KC down the path!"

As the women are squabbling, Cooper sneers and says to me, "You didn't waste any time, getting with her, did you? The second she broke up with me—"

"No!" our handlers shout simultaneously. "No talking. Keep it moving."

Cooper and his handler step aside to allow my handler and me down the path. But as I pass him, Cooper shoots me a look that's so cocky and self-satisfied, I want to punch it off his face.

"I wouldn't smile like that, if I were you," I say. "If I was a guy who couldn't get my ex to the finish line during sex."

"Fuck you," Cooper spits out.

"No, fuck *her*. And when I do, unlike you, I actually get her off."

"No, no, no!" both handlers start screaming at once. Both women physically push and pull at Cooper and me, and in short order, we're both herded off toward our respective destinations once again.

"Didn't APM open for Fugitive Summer a few years ago?" my handler asks. "I thought both bands were close friends."

"We were. But then, we all saw what a clingy little prick Cooper was as a boyfriend to Ruby, and we all started hating his guts."

My handler snickers. "For what it's worth, I'm Team Kendrick, all the way. That's why they assigned me to you."

"Does that mean that other woman is Team Cooper?"

She looks around. "Yes, but she's in the minority. Most of us don't believe for a second what Cooper said about the breakup. We all know he embellished it to make himself look good."

"In his song, you mean?"

"No, besides that, he's telling everyone at the show he broke up with Ruby because she cheated on him. With you."

I scoff. "That's not what happened. Ruby broke up with him, and she never cheated on him."

"I figured. I know a narcissist when I see one. I was married to one." She smirks. "But even if it did happen that way, I certainly wouldn't blame Ruby for doing whatever she had to do to get with you. Nobody would blame her for that."

I don't know what to say to that, so I say nothing, and a moment later, we reach the guest house. Inside, hallelujah, I discover the friendliest of faces: the perfectly symmetrical one that's owned by my lifelong best friend. When I enter the guest house, Savage is sitting in a chair with a hairdresser working on him, looking like he's in good spirits.

"Look at you!" Savage calls out when he sees me bounding toward him. "Hot damn, KC, you're looking fine as wine! Wooh!"

"Same to you, brother. You look like a goddamned rockstar."

"I try."

I take a seat next to him, and we chat for a bit while the hairdresser finishes her work, and my handler scrolls on her phone. But when the work on Savage is completed, and both women have stepped outside to make phone calls, I quickly tell Savage the tea about my exchange with Cooper.

"He's such a dick."

"The worst."

"Have you seen Ruby yet?"

"Not since we drove here together this morning. She texted me she's getting ready in some far-off guest room with Laila."

"Yeah, Laila told me." He arches an eyebrow. "So, how's it been going with Ruby the Roomie? Mission accomplished yet?"

I flap my lips together. "We're still BFFs."

"Fuck."

"On day one, right after Ruby got to my place, things looked really promising, man. In fact, I stupidly thought the mission was going to be accomplished that very night. But then things stalled after that, for reasons I don't understand, and I haven't been able to steer them in the right direction again."

"What the fuck have you been doing every night for almost a week, when she's been lying next to you in bed—singing her lullabies?"

"That's the thing. She hasn't been sleeping next to me. She got herself a goddamned air mattress. So now, it's like we're nineteen again, and she's got a boyfriend, and I'm the depressed bestie who dropped out of college who visits her on weekends and sleeps on her goddamned floor."

"How did you let this happen? What about the insomnia thing? I thought Ruby was going to cuddle you to—"

"She said she'd still help me with that, if needed. But I keep forgetting to fake insomnia because I'm having so much fun talking to her. It feels like old times, man. We talk and talk and never run out of things to say. I mean, that's the good news and the bad news, I guess. We're genuinely having fun together."

Savage grips his newly coiffed hair for emphasis. "Did you not listen to me at all?" he shouts. "I told you to make things sexually charged. I told you to—"

"I did! Savage, I swear, I executed your plan perfectly, on day one. And it was totally working. But then, I don't know, everything just kind of went straight back into the friend zone from there, and that's where it's stayed."

He sighs. "Tell me exactly what you did on day one, when you were cooking with gas. Tell me every fucking thing."

"Dude, I was a Jedi Master. When she first arrived at my place, I had my fridge stocked with all her favorite foods, and I had bouquets of her favorite flowers sitting nice and pretty on my—"

"What the fuck? No, no, no! I asked what did you do to seduce her, ya dumbfuck, not romance her."

"I was getting to that."

"We're not at the romance stage of the plan yet, remember? We're at the seduction phase. The fling-as-endgame phase."

"I know that."

"Obviously not. Kendrick, Ruby likes bad boys she has to chase—a guy who needs fixing and taming. Not a golden retriever on a fucking leash!"

I scowl. "I'm not a golden retriever, and I'm not on a leash."

Savage snorts. "Yes, you are. To both. For Ruby you are, anyway. Now, don't get me wrong, that girl adores that about you. But it's what makes you her *bestie*. If you want her to actually want to *fuck* you, though, then you're going to have to be a Doberman—the same way you are with all the other women you actually fuck. You have to think of Ruby as a tour fling and treat her accordingly."

"I can't do that. I don't even know what that means."

"Yes, you do. You treat tour flings like you don't give a shit about them. At least, compared to the way you treat Ruby."

I scoff. "I love Ruby, Savage. I treat other people differently because I don't love them. Because I can't love anybody but her. You think I haven't tried? I have! To death. But it's not possible, because nobody I've ever been with has even come close to making me feel the way Ruby does."

He looks at me sympathetically. "I get it. I really do, man. But that's all the more reason you need to stick with the plan and make her chase you, not the other way around. Fuck flowers. Fuck stocking the fridge. *Seduce* the girl."

"Giving her flowers and all that was only the first items on my list. You cut me off before I got to the good stuff. Trust me, on day one, I was killing the Doberman game. I was smashing it."

Savage crosses his arms. "Okay, tell me every Doberman-like thing you did."

"Okay, so for context—"

"I don't want context! I want bullet points. Seduction is war, remember? Tell me what weapons you've brought into battle."

"Would you let me talk, for fuck's sake? Jesus." I gather myself. "You know my lyrics journal? Ruby saw it on my hotel bed in Vancouver, right after my birthday party, and she briefly glimpsed this long, crazy-ass song I'd written about her."

"Shit. A love song?"

"Basically, yeah. Thank god, I snatched the book away before she read anything but the title." I smirk. "Which she misread, by the way, thanks to my handwriting." I snicker. "She thinks I wrote a song called 'Spank,' when actually it was called 'Spark.'"

We both burst out laughing.

"And ever since, she's been obsessed with this non-existent song called '*Spank*.' The supposedly filthy, kinky one she's forbidden to read."

"Oooh, this is good."

"She literally begs me to read it, Savage. But I keep telling her no. It's too dirty. Too personal. Not appropriate to share with someone who's merely a friend.'"

Savage is laughing his ass off now. "This is amazing. Dangle those non-existent dirty lyrics like a dick-shaped carrot, baby. Get her simmering in her own juices."

"My thoughts exactly. Well, that and it's better for her to think I've written a dirty song called 'Spank' that she's not allowed to read than to let her read the actual words I wrote about her in a song called 'Spark.'"

"It's not something a Doberman would write, I'm assuming?"

"Definitely not. It's this angsty, pining mess of a confessional, basically."

"Oh, Kendrick."

"Whatever." I wave at the air. "The actual lyrics don't matter. The important thing is that she's been obsessed with what she *thinks* I wrote." I grin. "So, get this. I found my old lyrics notebook from last year and decided to use it as a decoy." I crack up. "I left it in the top drawer of my nightstand for her to find on day one, along with some other stuff to get her motor running: handcuffs, a shit-ton of condoms, and the biggest bottle of lube you've ever seen in your goddamned life."

We both cackle with glee.

"Brilliant!"

"And sure enough, just like I knew she would, the kid went straight to snooping for that damned notebook the second I left the room to work out. She found the fake one I'd left for her in record speed, along with all the rest of the stuff!"

"Nice!"

"And, yes, right before she did that, I took off my shirt in front of her before heading into my workout, like you told me to do. Actually, I peeled that shirt off, like I was starring in *Magic Mike*."

"Atta boy."

"I've gone shirtless so many times around Ruby this past week, she's got to be wondering if I own a shirt at this point." I chuckle. "So, anyway, Ruby found the decoy journal, and then I bounded into the bedroom, right on cue—"

"You were watching her snoop?"

"Of course I was! I had to time it right. So, anyway, I burst in there and snatched it away from her, just in time, like I was freaking out. Except, of course, the lyrics she's obsessed with weren't even in there, since it was my old journal."

Savage cracks up.

"And then, I stood there in front of her, shirtless, going on and on about how hot and dirty the lyrics are, and how I didn't write down my filthiest fantasies for anyone else to read, and I especially can't show those thoughts and feelings to someone I'm not fucking."

"So far, so good."

"It gets even better, Savage. When Ruby found that decoy journal, she was in the middle of unpacking her stuff. When I burst into my bedroom, a sex toy was on the bed!"

"No way."

"Yes! I didn't realize that, at first, not until I was standing right in front of her, chastising her about snooping around for my notebook. But then, holy shit, there it was. This massive, pink dildo-vibrator thing, staring at me."

"Holy fucking shit."

I tell him the whole story, and Savage says he would have thought that sexually charged conversation would have led to us fucking, right then and there. Or at least, that night.

"That's what I thought!" I shout. "Dude, I threw every-thing at her *and* the kitchen sink, when I saw that fucking sex toy. I 'good girled' *and* 'bad girled' her! And it was work-ing, too. Right after that conversation, when I supposedly started working out again with earbuds in, I pressed my ear to the door and heard a buzzing sound coming out of my closet."

"Holy fuck, KC."

"I had to jump into the shower, right then, to whack off, or I was afraid I was going to come in my shorts."

Savage laughs. "How the hell didn't that end in you two fucking? I don't get it."

"I guess that's what happens when two people have been best friends for over a decade. That's a whole lot of history and habits to get past." I shake my head and exhale. "After my shower, we sat down to eat and watch a show together, and I think, somehow, doing that together flipped a switch that reset our friendship. Suddenly, we became Ruby and Kendrick again, the same as always. And I haven't been able to duplicate that energy again, no matter what I do."

"Maybe this is a stupid question, but why not write actual, smutty lyrics for a song called 'Spank' in that decoy journal and let her find it again? Reset the clock, baby. Give yourself a do-over of day one."

"You think I haven't thought of that myself? Dude, I've been trying to write those damned lyrics for six days. But everything I come up with is lame and stupid, compared to what Ruby's thinking it says. I'd rather give her nothing than something that softens her lady boner about the whole thing."

"Something is better than nothing."

"I don't think so. Ruby's a way better lyricist than me, so whatever she's imagining this dirty song says is a thousand times better than anything I could possibly write. Keeping the mystery alive and letting her continue turning herself on with her own imagination is better than letting her read something that falls short of her expectations."

"Yeah, you wouldn't want it to be anti-climactic."

"Literally."

"I could write the dirty song for you."

"No, Savage."

"A dirty song called 'Spank' would be right up my alley. I'm sure I could whip something up in fifteen minutes."

"I can't let you write sexual lyrics intended for Ruby—ones designed to lure her into my bed. That's not only morally wrong; I think that'd legit be a sex crime."

"Yeah, probably."

"No, *definitely.* I'm more than willing to turn myself into a half-naked, dripping wet Doberman to get Ruby to see me as a potential sexual partner, but I'm not going to pretend your sexual thoughts and fantasies are mine."

"Wait, dripping wet? This is new information. When did this little nugget happen?"

"The other day. Ruby was on my couch watching TV, and I waltzed out of my bathroom, dripping wet in nothing but a towel, pretending I needed to grab some shampoo I'd mistakenly left in the kitchen."

"And?"

"She ignored me. Completely. Didn't take her eyes off the TV for a split second."

"What?"

"Now you see what I'm up against. At this point, I'm fairly convinced it's hopeless. A total dead-end. She's just not into me, Savage, and she never will be. That's the only possible conclusion at this point."

"No. No way. I don't even swing that way, and if you waltzed past me, dripping wet and wearing nothing but a towel, I'd be tempted to attack you like a cheetah versus an impala. At the very least, I'd catcall you. What good friend wouldn't at do that?"

"Right? It's the polite thing to do, for fuck's sake! I'm shocked Ruby didn't roast me for walking in front of the TV, half naked, while she was trying to watch."

"That's a fantastic point," Savage agrees, leaning forward

with energy. "The Ruby I know would have said, 'Jesus, KC! I'm trying to watch a show here, and I can't concentrate with all those dripping wet, rippling muscles assaulting my eyeballs!'"

"Yes! That's exactly what Ruby normally would have said to me, in that situation. But nope. Not a word. Not a glance. She gave me no reaction whatsoever."

"This makes zero sense," he whispers. "For years, she's called you 'hot stuff.' And she couldn't be bothered to call you that at the perfect moment?"

"Apparently not."

Savage twists his mouth. "It's unbelievable. And I mean that literally." Suddenly, his face lights up. "What if Ruby did react to you, but she didn't want you to see it? What if her eyeballs popped out of her damned head so much at the sight of you, she tried her best to overcompensate and act like a robot so she wouldn't give herself away? And by playing it that cool, she actually did the opposite?"

My heart leaps in my chest. "You think that's possible?"

"No, I think it's *probable*. In fact, the more I think about it, the more it's the only logical conclusion." Savage smirks. "You've got her, baby. Right where you want her. I'm sure of it."

"Holy shit."

"She's teetering right on the edge. Clinging to the friendship cliff with white knuckles while her body screams at her to let go and jump her bestie's hot-ass bones. I'd bet any amount of money on it. Laila's money, to be clear. But, still, that's a lot of money that's half mine."

I know he's being funny, but I'm too wound up to laugh with him. "If you're right about this, then how do I get her to loosen her grip and stop playing it cool?"

"First of all, you need more time with her staying at your

place. Another week, at least. I know you said no to bribing the building manager, but—"

"I'll do it. What else?"

"You've got the perfect opportunity today, thanks to the show. Don't miss out on what this situation has to offer you, Kendrick."

"I won't."

Savage points at me intensely, like a coach explaining the next play with two seconds left in a game. "No matter what, you have to find a reason to kiss her today, KC. Do it at the press conference. Or better yet, at the party tonight. Or both. You're supposedly her hot and heavy boyfriend for the show, right?"

"Yep."

"So be that guy, at every turn. Don't forget, Cooper's going to be around, watching her like a hawk, which will get Ruby's motor running. So, use all of that as an excuse to kiss the girl and kiss her right."

"I'll do it." Instinctively, I beat my chest with my fist, like a freaking gorilla.

"Listen to me, Kendrick. Focus. This part is crucial. When you kiss her this time, you have to do it like a goddamn Doberman. You hear me? Like a fuckboy who's only interested in a tour fling. Like a guy who wrote a song about her called 'Spank.' You feel me?"

"I feel you."

"Last time, you kissed her like you wanted a wife. This time, you're gonna kiss her like you want to spear her against a wall with the tip of your dick."

I laugh, feeling hopeful and giddy for the first time in days. "This is a savage plan, Savage. You're scary good at this."

"Which is why you need to follow my instructions to a T."

"I will."

He levels me with his dark gaze. "After you kiss her, and it's clear she's totally into it and down to fuck—"

"Oh my god, please."

"Don't you dare pour your heart out to her in that moment."

"I'd never do that."

"Yes, you would. In fact, that's exactly what your natural instincts will tell you to do. 'I've loved you for twelve years, Ruby! It was love at first sight for me, Ruby!' No. Absolutely not. Do you understand me, Kendrick Alan Cook? No. Because that's the precise moment when you're going to pull back and tell her, 'Sorry, babe, I can't do more than a fling with you. A besties-with-benefits fling that will last only as long as you're staying with me.' Ya dig? Make her give you assurances that she can do that. Make her beg for it, man."

"But what if she wants more, in that moment? What if I'd be screwing myself over by limiting—"

"No!" Savage shouts, with so much force I jerk back in my chair. He leans forward sharply, his dark eyes blazing. "Now, you listen to me, you soft-hearted, romantic motherfucker. *I'm* the expert at this bullshit, not you, and I know exactly what I'm doing. You're going to offer her a fling, and nothing more than that, and when she agrees to that and says that's perfect, great, all she wants, too, pretty please, fuck me now, you're going to fuck that woman raw, to within an inch of her life, better than she's ever been fucked before, every day and every night you can buy yourself from bribing her building manager. And you're going to do it all while *also* being the Kendrick she already loves and adores. And by the end of this supposed fling, if you follow my instructions exactly, she'll realize, 'He's the full package! A bestie I also love to fuck. AKA *boyfriend* material.'"

"I'm actually aiming for husband material, but I get your point."

"Baby steps! First things first, promise you won't ask her for anything more than a fling, no matter what. Let her chase you, or the whole plan will fall apart."

"Okay, okay."

"Unlike you, I'm not wearing rose-colored glasses when I look at Ruby. I can see the good *and* the bad. The bad being her horrible taste in men. She likes fuckboys, KC. She likes things to be a bit toxic. Until she doesn't. So be that toxic fuckboy for her, at first, until she realizes she's changed her mind about the fling."

"I understand."

"And don't forget: kiss her today."

"I will."

As Savage fist-bumps me, the door to the guest house opens, and a trio of women enter: the hairdresser/makeup artist from earlier, and the respective handlers assigned to Savage and me.

"Are you ready to get beautified, Mr. Cook?" the hairdresser asks, fluffing my hair with her fingertips.

"Yep. Work your magic on me, Susanna."

"Magic isn't needed with a canvas like this." She grabs a brush. "Unfortunately, we're going to have to do this quickly, though. Nadine said she wants the whole cast assembled in twenty."

18

RUBY

"But are we sure this dress isn't wearing me?" I ask, referring to the bold, sexy designer gown the stylist and Laila convinced me to try on for the imminent press conference. Laila and I are in one of Reed's beautiful guestrooms after getting glammed up by professionals, and I'm feeling equal parts ecstatic and nervous about my sultry appearance. Objectively, I look like a million bucks. Like a model in a magazine. If I saw me, I'd surely lavish myself with compliments. But I'm also unsure about wearing a gown that's this revealing and sensual. I never dress like this. But then again, I've always kind of fantasized about being brave enough to do it. So, maybe now is my perfect chance.

"Ruby, I swear on my love for my baby grand," Laila says. "You've never looked hotter, sexier, or more stunning. You're breathtaking. A smoke show. If I were a cartoon character, my eyes would be telescoping out of my head right now."

"I couldn't agree more," the stylist says. "You're going to break the internet in this dress, especially because nobody's ever seen you like this before."

I feel a jolt of excitement. "Okay, you've convinced me."

"You have to wear it with confidence, though," Laila says, wagging her finger at me like a stern schoolteacher. "Wear it with swagger, babe. Own it."

"I will. Knowing Cooper is seeing me in this dress will give me all the motivation I need to play the part of a *femme fatale*."

The stylist laughs. "Seeing you in that dress will definitely make that boy regret all his life choices."

As we all laugh, my phone pings. I grab it and discover I've got a bummer of a text from my building manager:

> I'm sorry to inform you the construction crew just found evidence of possible mold. They'll need to investigate and undertake all necessary remedial efforts, so we'll need to delay your return to the unit by another week or so. Sorry about this. I'll keep you posted.

"Damn," I mutter.

Laila asks me what's wrong, so I tell her about the text, and both women console me.

"Don't worry," Laila says. "I'm sure Kendrick will be happy to let you continue staying at his place."

"I hate inconveniencing him, though. He's been sweet about it, but I'm sure he's dying to get his life back." I put my phone down. "Laila, would it be possible for me to stay in one of your guest rooms, if Kendrick seems at all stressed when I tell him about this?"

"Shoot. We've got a full house right now, honey. We're packed to the gills with my entire extended family."

"You are? Who's staying with you?"

She rattles off a list of names, and, yup, it definitely sounds like there's no room for me. Not even on her couch.

"I'm surprised everyone came to town to visit while you and Savage have been shooting such long days for the show."

"That's why they all came. Because I told them they'll have the house to themselves while we're at work. It's like a beach vacation for them." Laila points at my phone. "Why don't you text Kendrick and see what he says? I'm sure he'll be thrilled to have you stay for as long as you need."

"He'll *say* that, for sure. But I really don't want him to feel secretly stressed out."

Laila shoots me a look that says, *You're dumb as a box of rocks.* But what she says is, "I guess there's only one way to find out."

I grab my phone and quickly type out the message:

> Me: Bad news. My place is gonna take another week. Are you okay with me staying that whole time? If not, I'm perfectly happy to make other arrangements.

I don't know where Kendrick is currently being held captive in Reed's massive estate, but wherever it is, and whatever he's doing, he replies instantly:

> KC: Stay as long you want, cutie. If there's another delay, no need to even ask me. My home is yours, babe.

After reading Kendrick's sweet reply, I read it to Laila and the stylist, and we all agree he's a total sweetheart. "The best friend, ever," I murmur.

"Arms up, please," Laila's stylist mutters. "I need to sew something down next to your zipper."

Laila dutifully raises her arms and turns around, and the stylist gets to work.

As she's standing like a mannequin across the room, Laila says to me, "I'm sure Kendrick is genuinely over the moon to find out you'll be staying with him longer."

My heart lurches. "Why do you think that? Did he say something?"

She pauses. "No, nothing specific. Just that he's been having lots of fun with you there."

"When did he say that?"

The stylist taps on Laila's shoulder, signaling she's finished with her task, and Laila lowers her arms. "When you and Kendrick arrived here today, I asked him how things have been going this past week with 'Ruby the Roommate,' and he said it's been fun. A blast, actually. That was the word he used."

I try to mute my excitement and speak casually. "It's been just like old times."

"Kendrick didn't need to tell me you're having fun, though. You were both walking on air when you got here, so I figured things have been going well."

"Well, yeah, we're both excited to be on the show—especially together."

"Mm hmm." She sits in an armchair. "It sure seems like you and Kendrick have gotten even closer this week, if that's possible." She smiles. "'Cutie. Babe.' Kendrick sure used a lot of endearments in one short text to you." I look down at my phone—at the text message Kendrick sent me a moment ago. I didn't even realize he'd called me those things, because it's so par for the course with us.

"We've always used endearments. That's not new to this week."

"Mm hm."

Laila looks like a cat with a canary—like she knows something I don't. But before another word is exchanged, there's a knock on the door, and a male voice asks if he can come in. When we say yes, The Man with the Midas Touch himself, Reed Rivers, enters our makeshift dressing room looking every bit like the young billionaire he is.

"Wow, Laila. You look beautiful." His gaze fixes on me. "Who the fuck are you and how'd you get into my house?"

I giggle. "Is that your idea of a compliment—telling me I'm unrecognizable?"

Reed laughs. "I'm sorry." He puts his palms together. "You look stunning, Ruby. That dress is what my mother always used to call 'va-va-voom.'"

Laila laughs. "Ruby's giving 'Nerd in a Nineties Movie Who Takes Off Her Glasses and Lets Down Her Hair and Now Nobody Can Believe She's the Same Person,' don't you think?"

Reed cracks up. "If that was wardrobe's goal, then they've accomplished the mission."

I frown. "I'm not entirely sure if you two are making me feel really good about my current appearance or really bad and self-conscious about the way I normally look."

They both laugh and apologize.

"You're always beautiful, Ruby," Laila says. "It's just fun to see you letting your inner vixen out today. You're going to pop a whole lot of eyeballs, all over the world, and I, for one, can't wait to see it."

"Make that two of us." Reed grins at Laila and me. "Ladies, I've come to escort you to a 'holding tank' downstairs—my game room—in anticipation of the press conference in five minutes."

"Five?" I blurt. "Oh my gosh."

Dutifully, we thank the stylist and follow Reed into the hallway.

"So, Ruby," Reed says as we walk together. "The reason I offered to come get you two is because I wanted to chat with you about Cooper. I just saw him, and he seems pretty wound up about you and Kendrick. So, I wanted to warn you about that before the press conference."

He doesn't need to explain in further detail what he means. We all know Cooper is a tempestuous, emotional person by nature. That's the reason he writes such awesome songs and performs them with such passion. But it's also the reason he was the worst boyfriend ever, after originally being such a seemingly great friend.

"Thanks for looking out for me. But don't worry. With Eli's help, Kendrick and I have already formulated the perfect script for the press conference. And, luckily, Eli said he talked to Cooper's agent, and Cooper's on the same page."

I explain what the three of us have agreed through our agents: not to expressly comment on our personal relationships, including but not limited to none of us confirming the meaning of lyrics or who might have inspired them. Instead, we're going to let what's already out there do the talking for us: Cooper's lyrics, that viral kiss at Kendrick's birthday party, and the various photos of Cooper and me, and then Kendrick and me, that are now being posted and analyzed everywhere, usually alongside Cooper's blaring song, and/or an analysis of his lyrics.

"Strategy and execution are two very different things, though," Reed says. "Be ready to fight back if Cooper comes at you. Don't freeze like a deer in headlights and lose the opportunity to fight fire with fire. I don't want you feeling like you missed your chance to defend yourself."

The hair on my arms stands up. "Do you know something I don't?"

"No, but I know Cooper. If he tries to make you look bad, don't take his shit. I know you're a newbie at all this, so I just want to put it into your head it's okay not to be sweet and polite here. If Cooper pulls out a knife, make sure you pull out a gun."

I crinkle my brow. "Why are you saying this to me? What's going to happen to me in there?" I gasp. "Are you a shill for Nadine right now? Are you trying to get me to go off half-cocked in there for ratings?"

Reed laughs. "Of course not. If anything, Nadine's a shill for me. I run the world, Ruby Duby. Haven't you heard?"

"Yeah, I might have heard a little something about that."

We're all chuckling together as we reach our destination. The door to it, anyway. But rather than opening it, Reed turns to face me, his smile instantly fading.

"I'm saying this stuff because I've been around the block a few times, and I know you haven't. Because I know Cooper, and Nadine, and who knows what side deal she might have struck with him to make him come after you. I want you to be prepared for any possibility. I would have looked after you, regardless, because you and KC are the only members of Fugitive Summer I actually like—"

"I'm right here, Reed," Laila murmurs with a laugh, since he's just implied he doesn't like her husband.

With a wink, Reed continues, "And I promised my sister and Miranda I'd look out for our beloved gem today, and I don't want either of them coming after me if they see you getting steamrolled by Cooper." He's talking about my two close friends, Violet, who happens to be Reed's little sister, and Violet's best friend since forever, Miranda, who works in PR at River Records.

"I appreciate the heads up. But don't worry about me. I'm that bitch, Ruby Tuesday, remember? And I'm dressed to kill." I wink. "I assure you, Mr. Rivers, Ruby Tuesday's not nearly as sweet as she looks."

19

RUBY

"Holy fuck, baby," Savage says, as Laila and I approach him and Kendrick with Reed in tow. "Someone's getting fucked tonight."

Laila laughs. "You look pretty fuckable yourself, my love."

"You're looking stunning, too, Ruby," Savage says. "But I'll let Kendrick—"

"You look gorgeous," Kendrick interjects, cutting off whatever Savage was about to say. "Wow, Ruby. That's quite a dress."

"I'm here, too," Laila deadpans.

"You look beautiful, too," Kendrick says to Laila. But he barely looks at her.

Flushing hot under Kendrick's intense gaze, I run my palms down my barely covered tits. "I was nervous to wear this, but Laila convinced me."

"Thank you, Laila," Kendrick says, sending tingles shooting down my skin.

Reed says hello to the guys, and conversation ensues, but I'm too flustered to take part. For one thing, Kendrick is staring at me like his tongue is dragging on the floor. He's never done that before. And for another, he looks damned hot himself. Like a five-course meal. Almost as hot as when he waltzed past me in a towel the other day.

Lord have mercy, I thought I was going to pass out several times at the sight of Kendrick's bare torso this past week, but never more so than when he was in a towel, dripping wet. I had to force myself to stare at the TV to prevent myself from saying or doing something disastrous for our friendship.

Now, if *Kendrick* were to make a move on me first, would I say yes to that? At this point, I can't deny the truthful answer is yes, our friendship be damned. But *me* making the first move? That's impossible. Totally out of the question.

"Hello, my pretties!" a female voice booms. It's Nadine, and she's dressed to the nines. "You all look gorgeous. Any questions before we begin in exactly five minutes?"

I look around. "Where's Cooper?"

"He's being held in a different room."

Our foursome exchanges a look. One that says, *They're going to milk this love triangle for all its worth.* Too bad for Nadine, however, Kendrick and I have already decided there's no bonus in the world worth playing up a fake relationship and making our personal life part of a soap opera. We're both excited to make the most of this professional opportunity while having fun with each other and our good friends, but we're determined not to say or do anything too helpful to the producers' storyline.

Luckily, from what Eli told us after speaking to Cooper's agent, it seems Cooper feels the same way. We're not friends any longer, Cooper and me. To put it mildly. And God knows, Cooper would love to beat Kendrick in some way. But in terms of the show itself, we're all planning to play it cool and focus on the reason we're here: our shared love of music. At least, that's what Cooper's agent told Eli. Hopefully, that's accurate, and Reed's warning to me earlier wasn't necessary.

———

"Hello, everyone!" the host of the show, Sunshine Vaughn, bellows loudly in the next room, greeting whatever entertainment reporters and influencers are out there to capture this puff-piece of a "press conference."

As a smattering of greetings and whoops rise up in reply, a production assistant whispers to our foursome to wait for our cue. When we reach the designated spot, nerves grip me like a vise, and I let out a long, shaky exhale that immediately prompts Kendrick to grab my hand and give it a good squeeze.

To my surprise, my body jolts at his touch. In a good way. He's never held my hand before. At least, not that I recall. I've ridden his back lots of times. Usually while drunk. I've used his broad shoulder as a pillow. But when I do that, I'm passed out through most of it. I've also linked my arm in his, either when I'm cold and trying to siphon off his body heat or when we're walking with a big group and chatting, and it just feels right. And, of course, most recently, I've lain down next to Kendrick to help him sleep. Stroked his face and hair. Hell, I've even kissed him for a camera. But despite all those times, I can't deny the simple touch of his large, calming hand enfolding mine in a moment of stress is causing my nerve endings to zip and zap while my heart pitter-pats.

"And now, without further ado," Sunshine booms from the next room. "Let's bring in our favorite married couple and reveal the two guest mentors they've selected! Folks, it's the King and Queen of *Sing Your Heart Out*, Mr. and Mrs. Savage— Adrian Savage and his beautiful wife, Laila Fitzgerald!"

Someone opens a door for us, and Savage and Laila float through it, their hands joined, followed by Kendrick and me.

While Savage and Laila hit their mark in front of the crowd for a mini photo shoot, Kendrick and I hang back as instructed

—and through it all, Kendrick maintains that electrifying, yet calming, grip on my hand.

"Great to see you, Savage and Laila!" the host calls out brightly.

Banter ensues, after which the two celebrity judges take chairs facing the crowd, with Laila on the end and Savage three chairs down from her in the middle, so that Kendrick and I can fill in the two empty chairs between them. It's a clever way to make sure Kendrick and I sit together as a couple, while still sitting next to our assigned judges.

"To help guide his team this season," Sunshine says, "Savage has brought back his best friend, the talented and easy-on-the-eyes drummer of Fugitive Summer, Kendrick Cook!"

At rehearsal, Kendrick was told to leave me behind and hit the photo shoot spot first, while I hang back applauding him and awaiting my own introduction. But, perhaps due to my obvious nerves, Kendrick doesn't let go of my hand. Instead, he moves to the directed spot up front, dragging me with him, much to the obvious delight of the crowd.

"Well, goodness, since these two seem to be joined at the hip, I'll introduce them both," Sunshine says playfully. "To help Laila this season, please welcome one of her best friends, the talented musician, songwriter, and vocalist who happens to be in Savage and Kendrick's band, too: *It's Ruby Connolly, everyone!*"

Whoops rise up from the assembled crowd. Either these people have kept up with recent music and/or pop culture news, or they've been given a heads-up about my identity to avoid an embarrassing "Who the fuck is she?" reaction.

Kendrick and I banter with Sunshine, together, before being directed to take our seats.

"Well, I can plainly see you're all eager to ask questions," Sunshine purrs to the crowd. "But before we do that, let's see who's going to be sitting in those last two, empty seats, shall we?"

The crowd applauds. They know one of those chairs will be filled by kind-hearted, longtime judge, Jon Stapleton, a legendary country music star. But who's going to sit next to him and help mentor his team when the time comes? It's anyone's guess, as Sunshine gestures dramatically toward a large wooden door on the opposite side of the massive room.

"Ladies and gentlemen," Sunshine bellows. "Please welcome our beloved teddy bear of a judge, Jon Stapleton!" The large door swings open and the down-home country crooner struts into the room in his signature cowboy boots and Stetson. Jon takes his mark for the mini photo shoot, waving and smiling. But it seems to me, every eyeball is still noticeably trained on that empty doorframe.

There's a long pause, during which time stands still. And then, suddenly, Cooper leaps into view with a shit-eating grin on his face and his fist raised high in the air. Predictably, the place goes bananas, as everyone in the room not only recognizes this cocky, irreverent man of the hour, but they also no doubt connect the dots between him, Kendrick, and me.

"Everyone, give a warm, *Sing Your Heart Out* welcome to the lead singer of Alexa Play Music, the man who's personally responsible for their mega-hit song, 'Don't Call Me'—It's Mr. Cooper Constantino!"

Waving and mugging for the crowd and all the cameras, Cooper joins Jon at the photo shoot spot in the front, where flashbulbs pop and people jockey for the duo's attention. And through it all, I grip Kendrick's hand and exchange "maybe I shouldn't have done this" looks with him.

With the final photo shoot completed, Jon and Cooper assume the remaining chairs, at which point Sunshine launches into some over-the-top comments about the excitement that lies ahead this season. Finally, she asks for questions from the crowd. "But only for our three returning judges, to start with, please."

A Q&A with the judges ensues that feels very much like the appetizer to a much-anticipated main course. But finally, Sunshine opens the spigot on questions for the three guest mentors.

"Cooper! Ruby! Kendrick!" People are shouting all three of our names in a chaotic cacophony, until Sunshine selects someone with a question for Cooper.

"Cooper, does Ruby's presence here confirm she's Ruby Tuesday?"

"I never confirm the meaning of my lyrics," Cooper replies.

That's what I expected him to say, but I don't feel relieved he's stuck with the plan, because he's made his comment with a wicked smirk—one that nonverbally confirms his answer to the question is a resounding yes.

"Is Kendrick the brother Ruby Tuesday wants to bleep?" someone else asks. "I mean, otherwise, it'd be quite a weird coincidence for the three of you to be cast together this season, don't you think?"

"Well, I'm not responsible for casting this show," Cooper says with another mischievous smirk. "And like I said, I don't normally comment on the meaning of my lyrics." He leans forward. "But as a general matter, and not in relation to anything in particular, I don't believe in coincidences." He winks at that, and the crowd explodes with laughter.

"*Motherfucker*," I whisper to Laila sitting next to me.

"What was that, Ruby?" Sunshine asks sweetly. "I didn't catch that."

I force a smile. "I said, 'How lovely.' That's a lovely way to go through life—believing that everything you do, even the hurtful things, are part of some master plan.'"

Another loud reaction rips through the large room, during which I catch Reed's approving eye at the back of the room.

Just this fast, it's now obvious from Cooper's body language that he's not going to stick to the script, exactly like Reed said. Well, guess what? That warning shot let him know I'm ready for him.

A reporter shouts, "Ruby, do *you* believe in coincidences?"

Seems like a softball. "Sometimes. Sometimes not."

"Was it a coincidence you kissed Kendrick passionately in a video while Cooper's song played in the background? Or did you two put that song on specifically—maybe to send Cooper a message?"

I take a deep breath. I'm not ready to go for the jugular yet, since it's still possible Cooper will toe the line. "That video was recorded at Kendrick's birthday party without our knowledge, and the song just so happened to be on. People on the internet assigned meaning to the whole thing, but it was just the song that happened to be playing."

"Well, yeah, we didn't put the song on," Kendrick interjects. "But speaking for myself, I saw someone recording a video and figured he'd post it or send it to Cooper. So, I admit I particularly enjoyed kissing Ruby in that moment, because I knew Cooper would probably see the video and feel like I was flipping him the bird, which I totally was."

As the room explodes, I stare at Kendrick, my mouth parted with surprise. We talked about our game plan, both between ourselves and with Eli, and clearly decided we wouldn't say a word to confirm I'm Ruby Tuesday, even though it's obvious I am. Also, we said we'd let our kiss speak for itself and not expressly confirm our relationship status. So, what's he doing?

"Why on earth would you want to flip off Cooper?" Sunshine asks Kendrick with a bat of her eyelashes.

I glare at Kendrick, warning him not to go off-script again, but he's not meeting my eyes.

"Because Cooper named the girl in his shitty song 'Ruby Tuesday' as clickbait."

"Clickbait?" Sunshine gasps out, like she's aghast at the idea. "Whatever do you mean?"

Kendrick shrugs. "Ruby's in a high-profile band. So, Cooper obviously did whatever he had to do to market his new song." He finally looks at me. "The truth be damned."

I sigh with relief. That wasn't what we planned for him to say, but it was even better.

"I was also pissed at Cooper for dragging me into the conversation about the meaning of his lyrics," Kendrick continues. "My relationship with Ruby, whatever it might be, is nobody's business. So, Cooper inviting the world to speculate about us wasn't cool of him. Clickbait, once again."

The room is atwitter.

"Sounds like there's some bad blood between you and Cooper," Sunshine observes with glee.

"Cooper's not my friend," Kendrick says evenly. "I'll leave it at that."

"The feeling's mutual," Cooper mutters.

"Good," Kendrick says. "Because I don't like being friends with whiny little clout-chasing bitches."

As the room explodes, once again, I rub my forehead. So much for us focusing on our shared love of music. And so much for us not confirming we're the muses for the song.

"Oooh, things are getting a bit heated between these boys," Sunshine purrs. "My goodness, tempers are flaring, aren't they?" She smiles sweetly at Cooper. "Why do you think you two aren't friends, my dear?"

"It's hard to be friends with a guy who pretends to be best friends with your girlfriend so he can steal her at his first opportunity."

In response to Cooper's comment, Kendrick does something that wakes up every hair follicle on my body: he slides his big palm onto my thigh and leaves it there for everyone, including Cooper, to see. In context, the gesture feels like he's saying, "Mine, mine, mine."

"Nobody *stole* me," I choke out, placing my hand on Kendrick's forearm as he continues holding onto my thigh. "I'm a person, not a pack of gum at 7-Eleven. But you know what? Let's be real here. With both of these men sitting here, we can all plainly see one is a man, and the other is a toddler, so I don't think anyone would blame me if I did what Cooper claims. I didn't, by the way. My hand to God. But would you blame me if I did?"

As the crowd loses it, I search for Reed's dark gaze at the back of the room again, and when I find it, he flashes me a wink that says, "Nailed it."

There's some more back-and-forth, during which Cooper seems shell-shocked, and Kendrick seems super-charged. But finally, Sunshine starts wrapping things up by extolling the exciting things to come this season.

"Excuse me," I say, when Sunshine seems like she's wrapping things up. "Sorry, but I don't want this press conference to end without me thanking Kendrick for having my back here and everywhere else." I smile at Kendrick. "Thank you, babe. I didn't have this kind of unwavering support in my prior, extremely brief, relationship, so it means the world to me."

With that, I lean in to kiss Kendrick's cheek, but he turns his head and tenderly kisses my lips. It's a brief smooch—one delivered with a gentle touch of his lips to mine, followed by the smallest hint of his warm tongue. But it rocks my world and makes me want to kiss him again and again. Only more passionately, like at his birthday party. And, for the first time ever, in private.

20

RUBY

"La la la la la . . *Laila! Laila!*"

I'm singing the famous hook from our global hit, "Hate Sex High," alongside my two friends, Laila and Miranda. But I'm not onstage from behind my keyboard, as usual. No, this time, I'm bouncing around joyfully on a packed dance floor, as a group of top-tier, famous musicians, none of them members of my band, bang out this party favorite and make it their own.

It's the raucous after-party at Reed Rivers' house. As he always does when he throws one of his famous parties, he's got a stage set up in the massive main room of his mansion where all the A-list musicians in attendance can climb onstage, at their pleasure, with a random assortment of musicians and perform for the rowdy, mostly inebriated crowd.

As always, the performances tonight have been nothing short of epic. All night long, amazing River Records musicians, whether they're in a band or known as a solo artist, have mixed and matched in random, impossible-to-predict combinations and brought us surprise covers of party favorites. The only rule of Reed's game? Whatever the random group selects to perform, it can't be a song anyone onstage performs in their day job.

Yes, occasionally, I've seen musicians at Reed's parties break this cardinal rule. For instance, when the raucous crowd demands it in no uncertain terms. But normally, what we get is exactly the kind of once-in-a-lifetime performance the partygoers are experiencing now: a breathtaking assemblage of musicians, including the legendary drummer, C-Bomb, of Red Card Riot, brilliantly performing another artist's song.

Currently, the band onstage is barreling toward one of the most famous lines from "Hate Sex High": the one Savage deadpans in a smug, spoken voice: *"You came three times."* And the dance floor is buzzing with anticipation, ready to sing along when Dean Masterson, the lead singer of Red Card Riot, delivers the iconic line. But much to the thrill of the audience rocking out and watching with anticipation, when the time comes, Dean throws it over to C-Bomb, which then causes everyone in the entire party to lose their minds in a whole new way. I mean, come on. *C-Bomb* delivered "You came three times"? Somebody pinch me.

After C-Bomb says the famous words, I high-five Laila, since that line was written about her. I can't even imagine how electrifying it must feel to be the person who inspired a song. A nice one, anyway, unlike what Cooper wrote about me. And then to have that song go on to become a global sensation, an iconic song that will be played at parties for decades to come, now that certain lines from it have reached singalong status. But on top of all that, Laila now gets to hear one of the sexiest, burliest, biggest bad boys in all of music perform the line written for *her,* while her husband can only look on helplessly from wherever he is at this party and watch his wife get aurally fucked by another man? If it were me, I'd need the crash cart.

After high-fiving lucky Laila, I high-five, Miranda, since

she's C-Bomb's little sister, and I can easily see she's *loving* this wickedly fun moment for her big brother. From there, I look around for Savage and Kendrick, since I know they're probably partying together, and I'm dying to see their reactions.

When I locate them, I'm surprised to find them standing at the side of the raised stage. Not surprisingly, both men look thrilled with the performance of our song. But even better than that, at least for me, is the fact that Savage and Kendrick are standing next to two musicians from two other bands, which can only mean one thing in the context of a Reed Rivers party: Our Fugitive Summer boys are waiting in the wings to climb onto that stage to perform some random song that's decidedly not in our band's catalog.

I swat Laila's arm like a maniac and excitedly direct her attention to Kendrick and Savage, and Laila instantly screams and jumps up and down at the sight of them. In a frenzy, we both direct Miranda's attention to the same spot, and our friend immediately shares our over-the-top reaction.

Miranda shouts something to Laila I can't make out, thanks to the loud music, but I'm able to guess the gist of the comment when Laila shouts in reply, "I had no idea!" With a cackle of delight, Laila turns to me and bats my arm. "That man is definitely getting fucked tonight!" When I snicker with her, Laila shocks me by adding: "*And so is Savage!*"

As I gasp at her implication, Laila throws back her head and laughs from the depths of her soul. It's not the first time Laila's dropped a little hint about Kendrick and me getting together. All day long, she's been making suggestive comments like that.

Why? That's the question. Is she merely referring to the fake relationship we play-acted during the press conference? Or is she dead serious—as in, she can tell I've become increasingly Kendrick-curious over the past week? As in, perhaps she sees something I can't see myself about Kendrick's possible sexual interest in me? At this point, I'm fervently hoping that last option is the thing that's been egging her on. But I can't tell for sure, and I've been too afraid to ask.

Till now, that is.

Thanks to liquid courage, perhaps, and maybe also combined with the natural high of all this dancing and singing we're doing, and maybe even thanks to C-Bomb making my panties damp with his delivery of the famous line from our song, I'm suddenly feeling empowered to throw caution to the wind and ask Laila why the hell she's been brazenly shipping Kendrick and me today.

I pull Laila's ear to my mouth. "Why do you keep joking about Kendrick and me getting together? Do you know something I don't?"

Laila opens and closes her mouth, her expression like a kid caught with cookie crumbs all over her lips. But after a beat, Laila taps her ear and makes an "I can't hear you!" face, right before abruptly turning toward the stage to glory in the remainder of the epic performance.

Well, that was interesting. Laila's facial expression practically screamed "Guilty as charged!" So, I don't buy for a second she couldn't hear my question.

Hmm.

I'm deeply tempted to pull on a lock of Laila's famous blonde hair—gently, of course; I'm not *that* a big a monster—and force her to answer me. But then again, the band onstage is reaching their final chorus, which means *someone* on that stage is about to perform Savage's famous, spoken last words of the song: "Did *he* make you come *three* times? *Yeah, didn't think so.*" And I couldn't possibly make Laila miss that historic moment. Heck, I don't want to miss it, either. It's a massively famous line. One I crack up hearing every time we perform the song, even to this day, simply because Savage delivers it with such snark and glee, every single time. Plus, Dean Masterson, the lead singer of Red Card Riot who's singing our song, is one hell of a walking thirst trap. So, whether he's going to speak the line or throw it back to C-Bomb again, I know the moment is going to make my panties wet again, and probably also make every person at this party, gay, straight, queer or otherwise, experience a similar reaction.

The moment is upon us now.

The song is almost there.

But to my surprise and delight, right before the cue comes, Dean Masterson looks to his left, to where Kendrick and Savage are standing with those two other guys, and he shouts into his mic, "Kendrick fucking Cook! Get your hot ass up here and close this shit out for us, KC!"

The scream that involuntarily hurtles from my throat makes the top of my head feel like it's popping off. And when Kendrick immediately answers the call by bounding onto the stage like the athlete he is, my screams, along with those around me, become even louder and more head-popping.

Oh my god. Kendrick is center stage now, in all his swaggy, smiling, muscular glory, pumping his fist and shaking his hot ass to the dirty beat supplied by C-Bomb, while Dean Masterson takes a step back to let Kendrick own the moment.

Dean makes a hand signal to the musicians onstage—the universal symbol for "one more time around"—and off they go, playing the lead-up to Kendrick's cue, one more time, while Kendrick dances around and looks like a golden god up there.

The crowd is going wild with anticipation, not to mention at the sight of Kendrick letting loose. Surely they're all very much appreciating Kendrick's beautiful physique and charisma as he dances around up there at center stage. Especially because it's not something we normally get to see during a show, since he's always sitting behind a drumkit.

Holy shit.

Here we go.

The band has now cycled through the lead-up for a second time. The cue for Kendrick's line is imminent.

But no.

This time, it's Kendrick who makes the "one more time around" signal to the band, which causes the entire crowd to explode even more, especially when Kendrick starts using the extra time to remove some of his pesky clothes while gyrating sexually, like a seasoned male stripper, at center stage.

Off goes Kendrick's jacket first.

And then, the shirt that made his muscles look mouth-watering.

Until, finally, he's standing before the rabid crowd, shirtless, his tattoos and muscles on full display, his smile wide and wicked.

I don't know why normally humble Kendrick chose *this* precise moment to flaunt his jaw-dropping body and become Magic Mike. Is he drunk? Is he doing this to make Cooper, who's around here somewhere, feel insecure about his dad bod? I mean, I personally like dad bods. But Kendrick's body is most definitely the universal standard of beauty. Or is Kendrick just high on life and feeling like a rockstar after that press conference earlier today? Whatever's inspired him to strip off the top half of his clothes, it's very clear I'm not alone in feeling endlessly grateful for it.

Kendrick raises his muscular arms in victory, making the party scream even louder. But then, as he lowers them, his gaze lands on me in the packed crowd. He shoots me a smolder that's so sexual, so intense, so brazen, it instantly turns on the bundle of nerves between my legs, like flipping on a light switch.

Just like that, I feel like I'm physically vibrating with lust for Kendrick Cook. My best friend forever. The boy I've convinced myself couldn't possibly be mine, ever, because he'd never wanted me back, anyway.

Breathing hard, I try to take a mental picture of every detail of Kendrick in this glorious, panty-melting moment, since we all had to check our phones at the door. And as I'm doing that, Kendrick strides to the microphone, clearly getting himself ready to deliver Savage's famous closing line as the band barrels ahead, a third time, toward his cue. Talk about blue balls. After all this edging, I'm sure everyone in this party's got 'em.

As I watch Kendrick in heart-pounding anticipation, he places one of his big palms on the mic and the other flat against his rock-hard abs, and with his blazing blue eyes still trained on me, he leans in and delivers the famous, spoken line we've all been waiting for on the edge of our proverbial seats. Except, to everyone's extreme thrill, Kendrick changes one all-important word.

"Did *Cooper* make you come three times?" Kendrick asks, replacing the word "he" with Cooper's name. Not only that, he delivers the famous line in a far more combative tone than Savage on the recording, which only adds to the delicious electricity of the moment.

With Kendrick's eyes trained on me, I shake my head in reply with enthusiasm, causing the whole party to explode around me. Clearly, they were watching and waiting with bated breath for my reply, and I delivered a home run.

"*Yeah, didn't think so,*" Kendrick replies, delivering the next words of the song, exactly as recorded. But once again, his tone feels far more aggressive than Savage's. Hostile, I'd even say. Indeed, thanks to Kendrick's unique interpretation of the line, his words feel fresh and new, like Kendrick himself, rather than Savage, wrote them specifically about Cooper Constantino and me.

Behind Kendrick, C-Bomb bangs out three crashing beats

on his toms to end the performance, and as that happens, Kendrick's gaze shifts from me to another precise spot in the packed crowd, at which point he raises double middle fingers with a hard, intense scowl aimed at his target.

Holy shit.

I follow Kendrick's gaze to the recipient of that double "fuck you," and not surprisingly, he's delivered his aggressive hand signal to Cooper with his full chest.

In a flash, Cooper hard-charges the stage, heading straight for Kendrick. But since this is a Reed Rivers party, and the place is filled with megastars, security is everywhere. Which means Cooper never gets close enough to the stage to do whatever testosterone-fueled thing his ape brain is directing him to do. On the contrary, in a heartbeat, Cooper is surrounded and escorted off the packed dance floor by three men dressed in black suits, while Kendrick, and all the men onstage with him, laugh and mockingly wave "bye bye" to him below them.

When Cooper's out the door and presumably led somewhere to take a break and simmer down, Kendrick returns to the mic. To the band behind him, he shouts, "Awesome job, guys! C-Bomb, you're going to put me out of a job, man. That was better than my version." As the musicians behind Kendrick variously salute him and wave to the crowd, and then start exiting the stage, Kendrick returns to the mic with a wide smile and shouts to the rabid crowd, "I'm gonna play drums now. Cool with you?"

The crowd cheers wildly, letting him know that's very, very cool with them.

"Get up here, fellas." Kendrick motions to Savage and the two guys next to him at the side of the stage for a quick changing of the guard.

Still shirtless, Kendrick, now sitting at the drumkit, counts off the tempo with four clicks of his sticks, and a second later, all four guys launch into playing yet another iconic hit that doesn't belong to any of them: "Shaynee" by none other than C-Bomb's band, Red Card Riot.

Everyone screams, since it's now clear Kendrick is playing a game of tit-for-tat with the last drummer to sit behind that drumkit. And not only that, he's doing it with one of the most iconic songs in modern music history.

"Shaynee" isn't a dance track like "Hate Sex High," even though it has a danceable, crashing beat. But it doesn't matter, because it's now become one of those songs that's so damned famous and singable, it's a party must.

As I watch Kendrick putting his own unique spin on C-Bomb's well-known drum parts, I'm mesmerized by his talent and the expert movements of his gorgeous body. Not to mention the scowl on his handsome face as he plainly feels the angsty lyrics of Dean Masterson's first verse, currently being delivered by Savage at the front mic.

Whenever I perform with our band, I'm way too busy delivering my own parts to study what Kendrick is doing to my right at the drumkit. But now, getting to watch him performing this tortured banger as a fan, I'm blown away by his expertise, charisma, and musicianship. *Kendrick Cook's a goddamned rockstar.*

I always forget that, since he's been a close friend for so long. Like a brother to me. At least, that's what I always tell myself and anyone else who winks and asks if there's ever been anything more than friendship between us. But standing here now, it's like I'm seeing Kendrick for the first time again. Only this time, as the swaggy, confident, insanely talented twenty-eight-year-old he's become, rather than the sweet, quiet teenager with football dreams who could barely say hello to me twelve years ago.

The song is barreling toward its first chorus now, and everyone on the dance floor is holding their collective breath in anticipation of Savage wailing the titular name of the song, "Shayneeeeee!" with everything he's got. But when the time comes, much to everyone's surprise, Savage changes the world-famous lyric to his wife's name, instead.

"Laaaaaiiiilllaaa!" Savage wails into his mic, sounding every bit as tortured and heartbroken as Dean on the original track. Not surprisingly, every person in the packed party loses it at the name change, but nobody more so than Laila herself, who's standing next to me looking like she's having veritable stroke.

The song progresses, and when the second chorus is imminent, we're all ready for the name change—poised to wail Laila's name along with Savage this time. But of course, the world's favorite unhinged superstar does something unpredictable, this time, calling to Kendrick banging on the drums behind him, "Sing it for them, KC!"

Without missing a beat in his furious, crashing drumming, Kendrick wails from the depths of his very soul, "Rubbbb-byyyyyyyyy!" And again, every partygoer in the building simultaneously loses their shit.

I can't believe Kendrick did that! I feel like I just got shot out of a cannon. Indeed, I'm so swept away and overcome in this moment, I have to grip Laila's arm to keep myself from crumpling to the ground in an orgasmic, feral, lust-drunk heap. Yes, I've played stadiums and arenas with that man and our band. But in this moment, I feel like a groupie. A fangirl. The president of the Kendrick Cook Fan Club. In fact, the way my body's reacting to the sound of my name pouring out of Kendrick's mouth, I might as well be a high schooler at a rock-star meet-and-greet.

Without warning, Laila grabs me by the arm and drags me, rather forcefully, through the packed crowd to the edge of the stage with Miranda in tow; and that's where our trio proceeds to fangirl, scream, and jump around, like we're experiencing a religious rebirth at a Baptist revival. And the best part? Without missing a beat in his playing, Kendrick keeps on staring at me with that same, hot smolder of his, the one that's now causing a specific kind of throbbing and dampness between my legs.

The bridge hits, cueing some famously tricky drum work, and Kendrick rises to the occasion and nails C-Bomb's complex combination with ease and gusto.

Finally, the song reaches its final crashing, heart-wrenching chorus, and I can't help wondering—along with everyone around me, surely—"Who's going to sing the famous chorus this time? *And what name will he sing?* Will it be Kendrick again, singing *my* name?"

Quickly, I get my answer, at least to that last part, when Kendrick yells into his mic, even before the chorus hits, "Peace out, guys!" With that abrupt farewell, he lays down his drum-sticks, lurches from his stool, and leaps off the edge of the stage like a madman, landing right next to me on the dance floor. But since the remaining musicians onstage are pros, they simply carry on with the song, despite losing their drummer to provide the driving beat.

As Kendrick strides toward me, looking like a man possessed, Savage onstage wails the original lyrics of the song for the first time of the performance: "Shayneee!"

Kendrick reaches for me with both arms, his blue eyes blazing, so I wordlessly throw my arms around his neck, rise up onto my tippy toes, and shout, "Kendrick, that was—"

I don't get to finish my sentence. But I'm not complaining. Before I get another word out, Kendrick crushes me into him and urgently smashes his mouth to mine.

Without hesitation, I return his kiss furiously. Like my life depends on it. And Kendrick reacts to my extreme enthusiasm by sliding a greedy hand into my hair and deepening the kiss with near-desperate passion. Even as my body explodes with desire, it occurs to me Cooper's not here to witness this. Which means Kendrick must not be kissing me for show, like he did at his birthday party. That's especially true, since everyone had to check their phones. No, this time, he's most definitely kissing me for real. And I'm right there with him.

As our bodies cleave together and our kiss intensifies, I feel Kendrick's rock-hard bulge pressed against me—and it's a sensation that turns me on even more. He grips my back as his tongue and lips invade and devour, and I'm quickly so aroused, I raise my leg and rest it on his thigh, desperate to feel his hard bulge pressed against a certain spot on my body that's throbbing like crazy.

Looking punch drunk on feral lust and visibly twitching with arousal and adrenaline, Kendrick breaks free of our kiss. With almost maniacal energy, he gestures to the bass player onstage, who throws Kendrick his crumpled clothes in reply, and as the band reaches the very last bars of the song without the benefits of a drummer, Kendrick grips my hand and pulls me toward a hallway on the opposite side of the room from where Cooper was dragged out only a few minutes ago.

21

KENDRICK

As I pull Ruby out of the packed party and into an unfamiliar hallway in Reed's hotel-like home, I'm euphoric. Breathless. Dizzy. Out of my head and experiencing a kind of natural high I've only ever felt playing for tens of thousands of screaming fans. Except this high is even better. Far better. In fact, that kiss with Ruby made me feel so fucking delirious, I almost creamed my pants during the thick of it. Damn. I thought the kiss with Ruby at my birthday party was mind-blowing. But this one blew it out of the water.

Ruby.

Ruby, Ruby, Ruby.

She's the only girl I've ever truly loved. I know that now, without a doubt, and I fully accept it. I'm done trying to deny it or stuff it down. Done playing games. Fuck what Savage told me to do. I know he only wanted to help me, but fuck the games he told me to play with Ruby. The manipulations he convinced me would be necessary to get what I want.

The truth is, I don't want a fling with Ruby. Not even close.

And I don't want to pretend, even for a second, that I do. I love this girl. I've always loved her. And I'm going to tell her that right fucking now. Yes, I also want to fuck Ruby. So badly, my balls hurt. But when I do it for the first time, I want to be able to whisper into her ear, "I love you, baby; I've always loved you." The very thought gives me goosebumps.

My breathing is ragged.

With a gigantic, throbbing hard-on in my designer pants, I yank hastily on a doorknob in the hallway with my free hand, while continuing to grip Ruby's hand with the other, but it's locked. "Fuck!"

"Where are you taking me?" Ruby asks with a sultry giggle as I move on toward the next door. There's no hesitation or wariness in her voice. Only excitement. Eagerness. *Lust.* And thank God for that, because the minute I get her alone, I'm going to open my heart to her. Spill my guts. Leave nothing unsaid.

"I'm taking you anywhere I can lock the door behind us and fuck you," I choke out. "A room with a bed would be a bonus, but that's not required."

At my brazen, no-holds-barred comment, Ruby squeals, sending my balls tightening and my heart racing even more. She didn't say, "Whoa, Kendrick. Slow down." Or, "What the fuck did you just say to me?" Nope, the way Ruby squealed and squeezed my hand in reply made it abundantly clear she's down to fuck—every bit as willing and eager as me to cross that forbidden line of our friendship, once and for all.

I jerk on the next doorknob, and to my relief, the door opens. There's no bed inside the small room, unfortunately, only a washer and dryer. But that'll do for our purposes.

I motion for Ruby to step across the threshold in front of me, but before she takes a single step, a female voice behind us in the hallway shouts my name, loudly, causing us to freeze and turn around.

Fuck me. It's Nadine, scurrying toward us in her sparkling evening gown and heels. Surely, she's intending to scream at me for serenading and kissing Ruby at the party without a single camera in place to capture the sparkling moment for the show. Well, fuck her, if that's what she's followed us here to complain about. The only reason I felt comfortable enough to let loose like I just did, like never before, was precisely because I knew there wasn't a single camera around to capture my unhinged shenanigans.

"That was incredible!" Nadine sings out as she approaches us with a bright smile on her face. "Talk about earning those bonuses! Wow!" She motions to my bare torso. "Kendrick Cook! Good lord! I would have written nudity into your contract, if I'd known you were hiding that kind of perfection." She palms her forehead. "And that kiss! Guys, it was right out of a movie. Heart-melting and ovary-exploding, all at once!"

As she's talking, Ruby and I keep looking at each other in confusion. And when Nadine finally stops talking long enough for us to speak, I ask, "How did we earn bonuses for doing stuff *off*-camera?"

Nadine cackles. "You didn't. We got everything you did on our hidden cameras."

"What?" I blurt. I rough a hand over my face, feeling flabbergasted. I didn't do anything embarrassing in there, I don't think. So, that's not the source of my tight belly and thrumming heart. It's more that I had no idea one of the best moments of my life was being filmed for capitalistic consumerism. Did Ruby know? Was she performing for them the whole time, unlike me? Is this my birthday party, all over again? If so, I won't survive it. I swear, I'll shatter into a million tiny pieces and never recover.

I look at Ruby, terrified to ask the question. But I don't have a choice in the matter. I have to know. "D-did you know?"

Thank God, Ruby shakes her head, her sincerity written all over her beautiful face. Plainly, she's as shocked as I am.

"Well, that's on you for not reading your contracts, then," Nadine says with a sniff. "We always reserve the right to capture video and audio with visible and non-visible recording equipment, at our sole discretion, during any and all show-related events, promotional appearances, and official shooting days. Today is most definitely a promotional appearance for both of you, so you really should have known we'd be capturing every second of it."

Ruby and I look at each other like we can't believe what we're hearing.

"But why hide the cameras?" I ask. "Or at least not tell us about them in advance?"

"Because we've been shooting this show for a very long time, Kendrick, and we know what we're doing." Nadine rolls her eyes. "When people know about cameras, they mug for them. They *perform*. And we wanted to capture people having fun tonight in a way that felt extremely real, spontaneous, and natural." She smirks demonically. "And, boy, did we get what we were after and more. That felt so real, I couldn't have scripted it better myself."

Ruby laughs at Nadine's word salad, but I'm too wound up to join her.

"So, what's the plan for the footage?" I ask.

"We'll use it for marketing, for sure. Probably also put it into a video package shown on Mentor Day." Nadine laughs with glee. "Add that to the press conference, and your almost-fight with Cooper just now—and him getting escorted out of the party—and we'll have more to work with than we could have hoped for in our wildest dreams." She sighs happily. "This is going to be the best season yet. Great job, you two. Seriously. *Bravo*."

"Thanks," I deadpan. "So, is that it, or . . . ?" I motion to my hand clasped with Ruby's, letting Nadine know I'd very much like to return to my original itinerary now, thank you very much, but Nadine's expression makes it clear she doesn't get what I'm saying at all.

"Does Cooper think this is real?" she asks, gesturing to our joined hands. "Or did you all get together after the press conference and—"

"Nadine, I don't know what you're talking about," I grit out. "Maybe Cooper knew about the cameras. Who knows? But we didn't. So, no, we didn't do any of that for you or the show, for Cooper, or for anyone else."

"*Oh*," Nadine says, understanding visibly washing over her. "I'm sorry, guys. Eli told me the viral kiss—"

"Yeah, well, things have changed. So, if you don't mind, I'd like to get back to what I was about to do, before you interrupted us."

For a beat, Nadine's mouth forms into the shape of an "O." But after that, she smiles and says, "Be my guest. Sorry again. I truly didn't realize you two were *actually* . . ." She trails off and her smile turns devilish. "Well, I'll leave you to it, then. Enjoy."

She winks before turning to walk away. But before she takes more than two steps, I call out to her, "Hey, Nadine, there are no hidden cameras in this room, right?" When she meets my gaze, I gesture toward the open door—the laundry room where I'm about to fuck Ruby Connolly and make all my teenage dreams come true.

Nadine smirks. "No, dear. Our cameras are only in the main room of the party and outside on the patio. You're good. Have fun without a care in the world."

"Thanks."

As Nadine walks away, I pull Ruby into the laundry room and quickly lock the door behind us. That exchange has given me the chance to slow down and gather myself, the chance for my brain to take over the wheel from my hard-on and my heart—enough, anyway, to make me realize now isn't the time to spill my guts to Ruby, after all. In fact, now that I'm in complete control of myself again and not caught up in the moment, the kiss, the adrenaline, the feelings, I realize that doing what I was about to do very well might have been catastrophic.

Be a Doberman, I hear Savage saying as I turn around to face Ruby. *Not a golden retriever on a leash. Not the guy who's been in love with this girl for twelve years. You're a fuckboy, Kendrick. A guy looking for a fling, and nothing more.*

"That was crazy," Ruby says, rubbing her forehead. "Did you see Nadine's face when—"

"It's gotta be a fling," I blurt, suddenly breathing hard.

Ruby presses her lips together and her eyebrows ride up.

"A friends-with-benefits fling," I clarify. "I should have made myself clear before kissing you. That's my bad. But that's all this can be, Ruby. A fling."

Ruby bites back a smile, making it clear she likes what she's hearing. "Kind of like one of your *tour* flings, you mean? The 'tour' being however long I'm staying at your place?'"

Well, shit. That went easier than I would have expected. Maybe even easier than I would have hoped, if I'm being honest. "Mm hm." I drop my shirt and jacket onto a nearby chair, barely able to look at her. Suddenly, every piece of me wants to backtrack. To open my mouth and tell her I'm just kidding. That I could never treat her like a simple tour fling when I've loved her for so long. But before I ruin the plan so egregiously, Ruby beats me to the punch.

"I think that's pure genius, KC." She exhales in apparent relief. "I'm so glad we're on the same page about this." She sighs again. "Honestly, after the shit show with Cooper, and especially because I can't do anything to risk our friendship, a fling definitely feels like the right call. But only if we both swear, up and down, crossing that line while I'm staying with you won't change our friendship. Kendrick, we both have to promise everything will go back to normal after the fling is over, or we really shouldn't do this."

22

KENDRICK

Ruby leans her ass against a dryer and flashes me a sultry smile. "You promise you won't hate me after this the way Cooper did? He was a close friend, too. I mean, not nearly as good a friend as you are, of course. But, still, I traded my friendship with him for sex—mediocre sex, at that—and look how that turned out." She rolls her eyes.

My brain feels like it's physically melting. I can't believe Savage was *this* right about everything. About Ruby's reaction. About me needing to be a Doberman at all times. Why did I doubt him? He's always been irresistible to women. Always. But until this moment, a small piece of me doubted him.

I clear my throat. I'm shaking. "Can you do me a favor, please, and not mention Cooper while I'm standing here, hard as a rock for you? Not to mention, I don't appreciate being compared to a guy with the emotional intelligence of a stink bug."

Ruby snickers. "That's fair. Sorry."

I take a deep breath to control my trembling. "I'm not Cooper, Ruby. I assure you, I can handle a fling, the same way you can."

She bites back a smile. "I'm glad to hear it."

I return her sexy smile, my body a riot of greed and desire. *Is this really happening?* I take another deep breath. "Is there anything else you need to chat about before I walk over there and kiss the fucking hell out of you? Don't be shy now. There's no rush."

Ruby's cheeks bloom. "Nope. I think that covers it."

"Are you sure?"

"Yep."

"So, I can come over there and kiss you, then?"

She nods, slowly, her cheeks aflame and her breathing shallow and quick.

"I'm gonna need more than a nod, sweetheart," I say softly. "I'm gonna need a clear and enthusiastic yes out of you, from this moment forward."

Ruby's smile widens. "Fuck yes. How's that for enthusiasm?"

"It's music to my ears."

It's beyond exciting to get confirmation Ruby wants this as badly as I do, even if it's not for the same reasons as me. Plainly, she envisions this as some kind of crazy, temporary detour in our friendship. A footnote to it, rather than the origin story of our happily-ever-after. But, hey, at least, in the short-term, our goals appear to be perfectly aligned. We're both dying to fuck. For now, that's good enough.

With my heart crashing against my sternum, I walk slowly across the laundry room toward Ruby. And when I reach her, she immediately tilts her head back and closes her eyes, inviting me to kiss her. Exhaling slowly, I slide one arm around her waist, pull her close to me, lean down, and press my lips to hers.

After initial contact, my lips open Ruby's and my tongue mingles with hers. And that's it. I'm gone. Experiencing a kind of euphoria that makes my soul feel like it's hurtling into outer space. As my dick hardens to steel, I slide my hand down Ruby's back to her ass, and when she moans her approval, I give her a greedy squeeze that elicits a groan from both of us.

I deepen the kiss, feeling emboldened, and when Ruby reacts with even more overt enthusiasm, I slide my fingers into her hair and kiss her voraciously.

In a flash, the spark of our passion becomes a bonfire. And then, a pyre. A raging forest fire. I can't believe this is happening—this wildest fantasy of mine, the one I've secretly wished for, ached for, and pined for, since age sixteen. So, it's no wonder that I'm already so turned on, I can feel myself dripping with pre-cum inside my briefs.

As our kiss escalates, I slide my palm to Ruby's cheek, and to my surprise, she lets out a guttural moan like I've sucked on her clit. It's a sound so greedy and sensual, in fact, it tightens my balls and sends goosebumps erupting across every inch of my flesh.

With a loud groan that matches Ruby's, I pick her up and place her ass on the dryer. And the minute she's seated before me, her eyes at half-mast, looking like she's drunk on lust, I pull up her long gown, spread her thighs wide, and wedge myself into the newly created space.

I want to fuck her so badly, my ache is a physical pain. But there's no way I'm going to rush this. No way I'm going to disappoint her. A moment ago, Ruby called sex with Cooper "mediocre." Well, when she thinks about what I'm about to do to her, I don't want her thinking any word short of "supernatural."

With my hands exploring Ruby's cheeks, hair, and neck, I kiss her until she's panting into my lips with arousal. And when I'm certain she's ready for more, I push the fabric barely covering her right tit aside and cup the perky, smooth curve of her body in my greedy palm.

At the sensation of Ruby's small breast in my hand, my

balls tighten and my hard cock jolts. I've fantasized about this sensation so many goddamned times, my body is going haywire on me. I've fucked my fair share of women since heading off to college, but, based on the way my nerve endings are reacting to the touch of Ruby's hard, pebbled nipple between my fingertips, I might as well be a virgin now. A schoolboy who's never made it to second base.

A growl of desperation escapes me. One that's probably embarrassing. But it can't be helped. Practically wheezing, I break free of our frenzied kiss to unzip the back of Ruby's fancy dress with a shaky hand. And when my fingers reach the end of the line at Ruby's tailbone, I pull the front of her sexy dress down and ogle Ruby's newly revealed flesh: her perfect, perky tits, both of them crowned with hard, pebbled nipples that make my mouth physically water at the sight of them. I bend down and devour every inch of her breasts, and at the touch of my tongue on one of those hard, pink buds, Ruby lets out a moan of ragged arousal that makes me almost come in my pants.

When I move onto Ruby's other nipple, she props herself up with her palms flat on the dryer, throws her head back, and widens her legs like she's begging me to fuck her. Returning my mouth to hers, I brush my fingertips slowly up the length of her delicate upper thigh toward The Promised Land, quaking with excitement at every new inch traversed.

When my fingers reach soft fabric, I discover the crotch of Ruby's panties is damp and warm to my touch. Shuddering at the sensation, I take several deep breaths to keep my balls from going rogue and prematurely ending this fantasy come to life, and when I'm sure I'm under control again, I gently stroke the warm, damp fabric with hungry fingers, making her moan and shudder. Up and down, my fingers go, teasing her, making her crazy and desperate for more.

"Oh, God," Ruby croaks out. "Fuck me, Kendrick. Fuck me now."

The desperation in her voice, combined with her shocking command and my name on her lips, makes my eyelids flutter and my balls tighten yet again with the desperate urge to release. I'm drowning in pre-cum at this point. I can feel it coating my tip, dripping down my shaft, and screaming at me, forcefully, to get inside her.

But no. Fuck no.

This is all about Ruby. About making sure she doesn't regret her decision. By its very nature, a fling is about nothing but sex. Which means the sex better be out of this world amazing, or there's really no point at all. At least, from her perspective.

Again, I fight tooth and nail to get myself under control. And when I win the battle with my inner teenager, I push the moist fabric of Ruby's panties aside and slide two ravenous fingers inside the warm, wet nirvana between her legs.

As my fingers slide inside her, Ruby arches her back and groans deeply with pleasure, prompting me to grip the dryer with my free hand to keep myself from losing my legs from under me. I can't believe I'm touching Ruby's pussy. The pussy I've always fantasized about because it's owned by the only girl I've ever loved. The thought makes my cock twitch and my balls tighten again, so I banish the thought and focus on the glorious task at hand. Or rather, the pussy at hand. The magical pussy that's so fucking wet, it's making heavenly sloshing noises in response to the movements of my fingers inside her.

Now that my fingers are slick with Ruby's wetness, I get to work on her swollen clit. I swirl it around and around in languid circles at first, while continuing to kiss her lips, nip at her neck, and palm her cheek with my free hand, all the while whispering into her ear that I'm dying to fuck her.

As Ruby spirals higher and higher into pleasure, I tell her the sight of her in that dress tonight made my dick rock-hard. I tell her the way she danced and screamed while I was performing onstage, wailing her name, almost made me come in my pants. "That's why I stopped playing 'Shaynee,' mid-song," I admit breathlessly. "Because I was so turned on, I couldn't concentrate anymore."

Ruby likes that revelation. Her moans and shudders make that clear enough.

As one hand continues working her clit, I slide my other inside her to work her G-spot, and the effect is easy to surmise: she's now arrived at the bitter cusp of what's sure to be a powerful orgasm.

I lean my lips into her ear while continuing my methodical assault between her legs with both hands. "When I finally get to fuck you, I'm gonna do it from behind, so I can spank your hot little ass." It's now clear my non-existent song, and the secret fantasies Ruby imagines are contained within it, are a massive turn-on for her. So, I'm figuring the tactic will work wonders. And I'm right. In fact, I'm a genius. The second the word "spank" leaves my mouth, Ruby's intimate muscles surrounding my fingers tighten sharply, gearing up for release.

"That's it," I coo. "Let go, baby. Come for me."

"Fuck me, Kendrick," Ruby rasps out, gasping for air and gripping my bare neck.

"First, you're gonna come for me," I growl out.

"I can't . . . I can't get there," she blurts. "Fuck me. Come on."

I don't know why she's saying that when her body is so plainly telling me the opposite. Yes, every woman is a unique puzzle to unlock; I know that very well. But I've never once gotten a woman *this* soaking wet before, while her clit is *this* swollen and engorged, and her moans and pants and sounds are *this* desperate and increasingly unhinged, and then *also* felt the telltale squeeze of those intimate muscles, and then *not* made her come within minutes. As a matter of fact, based on what Ruby's body is now telling me, I'd bet every dime in my fat bank account she's going to get there in a matter of seconds.

"Oh, you're gonna get there," I coo. "Fuck yeah, you are, pretty baby. Right fucking now." I lean down and lick her nipple as my hands continue their work. And when that doesn't do the trick, I nibble on her.

That does it. She throws her head back, growls like a wild animal, digs the fingernails of one hand into my bare arm, and releases with an orgasm that feels like an undulating vise against my fingers inside her.

I'm going haywire with desire, frothing at the mouth to get my first-ever taste of Ruby, while also feeling rabid with the need to fuck her. Not able to choose my adventure, I slide the slick, Ruby-coated fingers of one hand inside my mouth, while simultaneously reaching for my zipper with my other.

It's a fatal mistake.

Even before I've unzipped my pants and freed my throbbing cock from its bondage, literally the nanosecond my tastebuds get a taste of the deliciousness that is Ruby Connolly, my eyes roll back, my balls feel like they're exploding, and my entire body convulses with an orgasm that's so powerful and unstoppable, my knees buckle.

I grip the edge of the dryer with both hands to keep myself upright as warm cum hurtles out of me and, unfortunately, all over the inside of my briefs and pants.

"Fuck me, Kendrick," Ruby gasps out, her head thrown back and her eyes closed. "Oh my god, Kendrick. I can't believe you got me there. Nobody ever has. Only Bruno. Fuck me, Kendrick. Come on."

When my pleasure subsides, Ruby's still looking like she's in heat. Clearly, she's got no idea about the mortifying thing that's just happened to me. And the last thing in the world I want to do is confess it to her.

"Kendrick, fuck me," Ruby whispers urgently. "What are you waiting for?"

I take a deep, steadying breath. "I-I can't. I'm so sorry, Ruby. I . . . I . . . can't."

Ruby opens her eyes and stares at me. But when she glances down at my crotch, understanding washes over her. "*Oh*. Did you just . . .?"

I look down, and fucking hell, there's a large, telltale wet splotch on the front of my pants. "Yeah," I admit. "I'm sorry. That's never happened to me before. Usually, I can go forever. I guess I just—"

"Don't apologize." She flashes me a sultry smile and runs her hand up my forearm. "Seriously, Kendrick, I'm nothing but honored."

I rub the back of my neck. "I don't get how this happened. I swear, it's a first for me."

"You haven't had sex in a while. Plus, this whole situation feels extremely . . . forbidden." She snickers with glee. "You got me going like never before, literally, so it's a huge compliment to know I did the same to you." When I shake my head in shame, Ruby slides her palm to my forearm and pinches me, forcing me to look at her. "Kendrick, listen to me. My entire sexual life, I've never once been able to have an orgasm with a partner without a sex toy being involved. Not once. That was a first for me. Something I've desperately wanted to happen for almost ten years now. Something I didn't think I was physically capable of doing." She smiles. "Not to mention, that was way better than any orgasm Bruno's ever given me, by a long mile. *And* on top of everything else, you got me there even faster than him."

"Seriously?"

Ruby puts her hand on her bare chest and nods. "Swear to

God. So, please, don't apologize again. If you do, I'll be forced to slap you."

I'm floored by all this new information. For all these years, I've had no idea Ruby struggled sexually like that. I mean, I've always known the girl loves herself some "me" time. She's never been shy about saying that. But whenever she's commented about preferring her dildo to the real deal, I've never understood that's the reason why.

I straighten up. "Your orgasm was insanely hot for me. The hottest thing I've ever witnessed in my life."

Ruby smiles. "Knowing you came in your pants at the sight of me coming is the hottest thing I've ever seen in *my* life, so we're even." She motions to the front of my pants. "I wish I could frame those pants and put them on my wall like a trophy."

"I'd literally have to kill you if you did that."

She giggles. "You're probably going to want to change before we head back into the party, huh?"

"Fuck the party. If we leave now, by the time we get to my house, I'll be ready to go again."

"Ooooh, count me in."

"Are you sure? I don't want to pull you away if you're not ready to leave." I grimace. "I've already done one thing prematurely tonight."

She laughs. "Yes, I'm very, very sure. And that sounded an awful lot like an apology, Kendrick."

"It was self-deprecating humor. That's a totally different thing."

"Close, though. Careful with that."

I look down at the splooge stain on my pants. "I'm supposed to return this outfit before I leave tonight."

Ruby cracks up. "You really can't leave those on the rack for some poor employee to find. Can you imagine being the person assigned to retrieve those pants in the morning and realizing what they're covered in?"

Ruby laughs at the vignette, while I can't help grimacing.

"Looks like I'm buying them now," I mutter.

"Seems like the only possible outcome." With that, she raises her arms, nonverbally asking me to help her down from the dryer, and I grab her by the waist and place her gently onto her heeled feet. From there, Ruby turns her back to me and I zip her up. But before I release her, I move her long, pink hair to the side and kiss her bare shoulder and neck.

"I love this dress on you," I whisper into her ear as my lips traverse her neck. "But I'm going to love it off you, even more."

Ruby turns around, smiling. "Is this dress the reason you got the idea to have a fling with me? If so, I'm going to name my first-born child after Laila and that stylist."

I contemplate the best, most Doberman-like answer to the question. In reality, as sexy and hot as this dress is on Ruby, it's preposterous to think it triggered tonight's display of sexual attraction to her, when, in truth, I've wanted to do every possible sexual thing to this woman's body since she slid into the chair next to mine twelve years ago.

"Bingo," I say with a wink, even though every fiber of my soul wants to confess my undying love to her. "That's one hell of a dress on you, Ruby Duby."

"Thanks. I'm supposed to return it, too. But since you're taking your fancy clothes home, I think I'll do the same. What are they gonna do? Call the cops on us?"

I chuckle. "No, but they'll most likely dock the cost from our paychecks."

"Oh. Damn."

"At least we earned those bonuses, right? That will cover it and then some."

"And then some? Try again."

"*What*? How much is that dress worth?"

"They told me sixty-five-hundred. Isn't our bonus a measly five grand?"

"Holy shit. Is it made of hundred-dollar bills or something? They said my outfit costs less than a grand."

Ruby shrugs. "Welcome to the world of women's high fashion, sweetheart. They price everything more. And don't get me started on tampons not being universally free."

I move a lock of hair out of her eyes. "Don't worry about a thing, cutie. I'll cover the cost of both our outfits. No sweat."

"I can't let you do that."

"Yes, you can. I didn't do a damned thing in that party to get that bonus. That money is blood money, as far as I'm concerned. Plus, I make more than you, remember? Let me do this, babe."

We don't talk about it much—the disparity in our earning power. But since my appearance on *Sing Your Heart Out* two seasons ago, my income jumped dramatically, thanks to all the side gigs that poured in after that. At this point, I bet I make three to four times what Ruby does. Hence, the reason she's got a tiny condo in the valley, and I was able to buy a three-bedroom, Spanish-style house in North Hollywood.

"Thank you so much," she whispers, blushing. "I really appreciate that."

"You bet." I swallow hard. "You really didn't have a clue about the hidden cameras?"

"Nope."

I shift my weight. I figured she'd say that, but still, it's good to hear one last time. "What about Cooper being at the party tonight? Were you trying to piss him off a little bit when we kissed?"

Ruby cocks her head and furrows her brow. "Cooper wasn't even in the room when we kissed."

"But he was around somewhere. Someone was definitely going to tell him about it."

"Cooper didn't even cross my mind. I forgot he existed." A vertical wrinkle appears between her eyebrows. "What's going on, Kendrick?"

My heart is thrumming. "I just wanted to confirm, one hundred percent, that kiss wasn't for show this time."

Ruby's features soften. She takes a step forward and lays a palm on my chest. "Kendrick, I promise, every single drop of lust you felt from me in that party, and in this laundry room, was the real deal."

Lust.

Welp, there it is. Confirmation, yet again, that Ruby's not feeling anything close to what I am. Yes, I feel lust for her. More so than I've felt for anyone else in my life. But my lust is tangled up with something much bigger than that. Something once-in-a-lifetime. But Ruby? It seems she's able to separate the lust she feels for me as part of our supposed "fling" from the platonic love she feels for me as her closest friend in the world. I don't know how she can do that, honestly, but I've got no choice but to accept her ability to compartmentalize and take whatever she's willing to offer. For now, anyway.

"Shit," Ruby says. "I just realized there's no way for me to get my stuff from my changing room without me being seen by everyone." She describes the path she'd need to take to her room, and I agree I've got the same problem—the route to my clothes runs right past a spot where we'll surely be seen by at least a hundred people.

"It's fine," I say. "We can come back tomorrow. For now, let's make a break for it."

"How, though? There's no safe way out."

"Where there's a will, there's a way," I mutter, striding toward a window on the far wall of the laundry room. I peek through it, and sure enough, it leads to a dark, quiet side of Reed's house—a spot where nobody is milling about and we won't be seen, if we use the window as our escape hatch.

"Okay, let's do it," Ruby says, her dark eyes sparkling. "Can we get to your car from there?"

"I assume so. Don't worry, we'll figure it out."

I grab my clothes from the chair and put them on and then get to work getting the screen off the window. It takes some doing, but I manage it, and when the necessary opening has been made, I carefully help Ruby through, taking care not to let her long dress get ripped or damaged. Thankfully, we're on the first floor of Reed's house, so her landing, as I lower her down onto her heels, is soft and easy. And finally, when Ruby's safe and sound, I heave myself through the window and join her in the cool night air.

"Identify yourselves," a deep, male voice commands from somewhere in the darkness, and Ruby and I freeze like thieves caught in the night. "Oh, it's you, KC," the deep voice says, and a second later, a large Black man emerges from the darkness.

"Oh, hey, Barry." It's the head of Reed's security, Barry Atwater. I place my hands over my crotch just in case that splooge stain is visible despite the poor lighting, but there's no need: without me needing to signal her, Ruby immediately steps in front of me to block Barry's view of my shame.

"This is Ruby, Barry. She's in the band with me. Keyboards. Ruby, Barry runs Reed's security. I'm sure you two must have crossed paths at some point."

"I'm sure we have. Hello, Ruby."

"Hello, Barry."

Barry glances toward the window. "You're sneaking out the window of Reed's laundry room?" When his gaze returns to mine, it's clear the man knows what's up. It's written all over his rugged face. I mean, he's not stupid. He knows we didn't sneak out a window at a raging party for nothing. And Ruby looks smoking hot tonight. So, surely, Barry's assuming we've got to be up to something sexual.

I gesture toward the window behind us. "Our idea of an Irish goodbye."

"Ah. I figured as much. Would you like some help with your getaway?" He asks where I'm parked, and when I tell him, he says, "Okay, I'll lead you through a locked side gate. Take that, and you can get all the way to your car without anybody seeing you."

"Thanks, Barry. You're the best. Oh, fuck. *My car keys*." I look at Ruby with wide eyes.

"They're in the room with your clothes?" she asks, wincing.

"Yeah. Oh! But I can also use an app on my phone." I address Barry. "They took our phones at the door tonight. Would you be willing to get ours for us? I'd owe you a big one."

Barry laughs, and his white teeth gleam in the night. "Sure thing, KC. I'll lead you out and then go back for them."

"You're awesome, Barry."

"Anything for you, KC. For both of you. I heard about the bonuses your band gave my security team the other day, after your tour ended. Consider this a thank you."

Ruby and I share a smile. Our band is known for our monetary generosity with our support staff and crew. We do it because we can. Because we're grateful for what we get to do for a living and want to share the joy with the people who make it possible. But it's nice to know our good deeds are coming back to us as karma now.

"Come on, guys," Barry murmurs. "Follow me."

Ruby's wearing heels and she's been drinking, so I do what I always do at times like this, without thinking twice: I bend down so she can hop onto my back and ride me, piggyback. Of course, that's exactly what Ruby does. She climbs aboard without a moment's hesitation.

But this time, as I grip Ruby's thighs and follow Barry down a random path, I don't feel the least bit disheartened that we've both slid into the usual rhythms of our friendship. On the contrary, knowing we're still *us*, despite what we just did in that laundry room, only makes me even more excited about the future we could have together. I don't want to change anything about my existing friendship with Ruby; I simply want to add sex to it. I already love the girl. I'd already die or kill for her. Move mountains for her. And now, I simply want to fuck her and eat her pussy every day of my life, too. If I could have all that with her, forevermore, I swear I'd die the happiest man who ever lived.

"You promise our fling won't ruin our friendship?" Ruby whispers into my ear, her arms wrapped around my neck. "Please, KC, swear you'll never hate me. I couldn't survive losing you as my best friend."

I squeeze her thighs. "Babe, I swear to you on all things holy, my feelings for you will be the same as they've ever been. The same as they always will be. Forever."

23
RUBY

"When we get to my house," Kendrick says, "I'm gonna make you come even harder than you did in that laundry room. Multiple times, too."

We're in his car, headed back to his house. He's driving, and I'm his passenger princess.

"There's no such thing as me coming harder than I did back there," I reply with a laugh. "And multiple times? Babe, that's never happened before, so don't set your sights on that. I appreciate the enthusiasm, though."

Kendrick looks away from the road to me. "Didn't you say I made you come harder than Bruno?"

I scoff. "So much harder, it's not even funny."

Kendrick hoots again. "Then don't underestimate me. That Kendrick Cook is a sex god, man."

I snicker. "First of all, don't refer to yourself in third person, please. It creeps me out. And second of all, don't you dare tell Bruno I said that, or he'll try to gag you to death in your sleep."

Kendrick grimaces. "Not the way I want to go out. Death by dildo."

"Did you know the French call orgasms 'little death?' *La petite mort*. So, actually, death by dildo makes perfect sense, when you think about it like that."

"Not being *gagged* to death by one, though. That's a new fear unlocked. Thanks, Ruby."

"Sure thing, babe."

Kendrick adjusts his hands on the steering wheel. "Can I ask you something, in all seriousness? If you've never had an orgasm without the assistance of a vibrator, does that mean you always use one during sex? Or do you sometimes, you know, take care of yourself afterward, or . . .?"

"Either/or," I answer honestly. "Also, there are lots of times when I just don't bother with myself." When Kendrick looks shocked, I add defensively, "Sex isn't always about orgasms, you know. Sometimes, it's about the journey, not the destination."

"Well, yeah. But if you're doing it right, isn't it about both?"

"Not always. Not for me, anyway."

He processes that. "Why don't you always bother? You know, to get yours during sex?"

"Because it's not always worth it."

"I don't understand."

"It's not always feasible to pull out a dildo, Kendrick. Also, sometimes, I don't want to take the time. Or I'm feeling embarrassed."

He looks pained. "You've got nothing to feel embarrassed about, Ruby. The guys you've been with, however ... that's another story. They should feel deeply ashamed of themselves."

I press my lips together and look out the passenger-side window of Kendrick's car—at the speckles of light rain dripping down the glass as we whiz down the freeway.

"It's not their fault," I whisper. "I don't blame them."

"Well, I do. I'd never, not in a million years, get off with you and not make sure you did, too. *Never*. So, I don't understand how any guy was okay with that for you."

It's a mind-blowing way for me to look at things. "I've never thought of it that way."

"How is that possible?"

"Kendrick, you have to understand, women get mindfucked in our society, every which way, about sex and sexuality and our role in all of it. Whether we realize it or not, we're programmed from a very young age to believe we're here to give pleasure. To be sexy for men. To be a fantasy for them. But nobody ever tells us to expect or demand equal pleasure."

"Huh."

"Add to that, I was personally raised to believe sex outside of marriage is a sin."

"You were?" He sounds shocked.

"Well, okay, or at the very least, to believe sex is only something you should do with someone you love. And *boom*. Mix that all together, and the result is me—a girl who can't seem to get there without some mechanical help."

He snickers gleefully. "Until now."

I bite my lip. "Hopefully, that wasn't a fluke."

"Oh, it wasn't a fluke. I promise you that." Kendrick pauses for a moment. "I'm pretty sure Titus had sex with a couple girls in high school, unless he lied about that."

"More than a couple."

"But wasn't he raised to think sex before marriage is a sin, too?"

"No. He's a boy. Different rules apply, babe."

"What? That's totally fucked up."

"I agree. My parents didn't mean to screw me over or give me lifelong hang-ups. They were just raising Titus and me the way they were raised, you know? And that meant being extra-protective of their sweet, innocent little daughter and her ever-so-important virginity." I roll my eyes. "I'm partly to blame, too, because I was such a people pleaser. Even if they'd tried to give Titus the same rules as they gave their sweet little daughter, he wouldn't have followed them. Titus never gave a fuck about the rules."

"You see yourself as a people pleaser? I'm shocked by that. Even in high school, I always got the impression you didn't give a fuck about rules. I mean, you were a great student and all that, but you never seemed to care about being popular, or what other kids were doing or thinking."

"I didn't give a fuck about any of that stuff. Your impression of me was accurate. But when it comes to sex, the programming a young woman gets is powerful stuff, Kendrick. I don't think you could possibly understand unless you've lived it. It messes with your head."

We're both quiet for a long moment as we process the conversation.

"You know," I venture after a while. "I bet it wasn't a coincidence I was able to come with you, and only you, for the very first time."

"Yeah, because you finally found someone with actual skills."

"No. I mean, *yes*. Of course that's true. But I mean because you're uniquely you in my life."

Kendrick turns away from the road to look at me, his face lit up. "What do you mean?"

I shrug. "I was raised to believe sex is only acceptable with someone I love. Well, I love you, right? True, I'm not in love with you in a romantic sense, but I definitely love you. So, who better to explore my sexuality with than someone I already love and trust—who's also an objective smoke show? Yes, your talented fingers were mostly responsible for that orgasm, but I have to think it helped my brain to completely let go for the first time because, subconsciously, there was no part of me that believed I was doing anything wrong or shameful."

Kendrick exhales slowly and adjusts his hands on the steering wheel again. His Adam's apple bobs. His chest heaves. "That's . . . an interesting theory. Yeah, that makes a lot of sense."

Another silence ensues—this one long enough to feel a bit awkward.

Finally, Kendrick asks softly, "Does that mean you've never loved any of your boyfriends? Or am I taking too big a leap in logic?"

My breathing hitches. I didn't realize that's what I just said, basically, because I didn't fully realize it myself. But if my theory about myself is correct, then what other conclusion is there to reach?

"I think I've *thought* I was feeling love, at times," I answer carefully. "But looking back, no, I don't think I did, because I've never fully trusted anyone I've dated. Not the way I trust you." I look at him. "Can a person really, truly love if they don't fully trust?"

Kendrick looks away from the road to meet my gaze. "No. They can't."

My heart feels lodged in my throat. Feeling tongue-tied, I look out the windshield to gather myself.

Kendrick's wipers are swiping back and forth at the light drizzle falling. And suddenly, I picture everyone on the patio at Reed's party scurrying back inside to the main party room. The thought makes me smile, for some reason.

"Thank you for telling me all this personal stuff," Kendrick says softly, drawing my gaze back to him. "It means the world to me that you trust me enough to open up like this."

"I trust you like nobody else," I whisper. "Totally and completely."

"I trust you like that, too." He shifts in his seat, and his broad chest rises and falls sharply. "I can't believe none of your boyfriends took the time to help you reach the finish line. It boggles my mind."

"It's not totally their fault. I faked it with a lot of them."

The comment draws his gaze again. "Why?"

"Sometimes, that seems like a better choice than admitting you're defective."

His beautiful features contort. "You're not defective, Ruby. Not at all."

I smile. "Yeah, I know that now, thanks to you."

He blushes, and so do I, and silence fills the cab of Kendrick's car again, broken only by the swiping sounds of his windshield wipers.

"I told one boyfriend the truth," I admit. "Remember the emo piano player I was obsessed with during my third year at Northwestern?"

"No."

"You met him twice."

"Was he a douche?"

"Very much so, as it turned out."

"Then I've probably blocked out the memory of him from sheer frustration." Kendrick looks from the road to me. "What happened when you told him the truth?"

"At first, he was into the idea of getting me there. For all of three days. But then, he said sex with me had become 'too much work,' and 'not fun, like it used to be.' And everything unraveled from there."

"Jesus Christ."

"The good news is I only dated him for about two months."

"Seems to be your outer limit."

"That's not true."

"Okay, three months. Name one relationship that's lasted longer."

I pause to think. But he's right. My relationships have always started out strong, but then they fizzle out quickly. "Okay, so I'm not good at long-term relationships. So what? I'm still in my twenties. I'm supposed to be having fun and making tons of mistakes. As I recall, your very first girlfriend is the only one you dated longer than a few months."

Kendrick exhales and practically spits out the name. "Florence."

"I despised her."

"I don't blame you. She did me dirty after my injury."

"No, I hated her from day one. Even before she dumped your ass for the crime of getting injured."

Kendrick looks shocked. "Why?"

"Because it was obvious she only wanted Kendrick the Future NFL Player, rather than my darling Kendrick, and that pissed me off."

"Wow," Kendrick says softly. "I wish you'd told me."

"Would you have listened to me?"

His chest heaves as he looks from the road to me with burning blue eyes. "If *you'd* been the one to tell me? Yeah. Absolutely."

"Oh. Really?" When he nods, I press my lips together, feeling shocked.

Another silence envelops the interior of Kendrick's car. For a long moment, I watch his windshield wipers moving back and forth, feeling electrified for reasons I can't figure out. Am I feeling this way simply because that orgasm in Reed's laundry room was so damned good? Am I feeling high from getting the "no orgasm without robotic assistance" monkey off my back? Or is there something else going on? Something even bigger than all that?

"Okay, Ruby," Kendrick says. "Here's the deal. This fling of ours? It's going to be all about you. Getting you off. Making sure you experience everything you've been denied before now."

"Kendrick, no. That's too much pressure. Let's just have fun and—"

"We will. I promise. Trust me, basically being your sex therapist will be the hottest thing imaginable for me."

"I don't want to feel pressure, though."

"You won't. Please, Ruby. Don't overthink it. Just accept that's what we're going to do, okay? Remember how you felt about helping me with my insomnia? That's how I feel about this. I want to do everything in my power to show you what your body can do. Let me do this for you. It's all I want."

He does look pretty damned excited about this idea. And I can't deny, I'm excited, too.

"Okay," I say on an exhale. "But only as long it's fun for you. And only if you promise not to make me feel pressure to perform. If I can't get there, I can't get there. It's not the end of the world."

"Pressuring you to perform is literally the opposite of what I'll do. There's no pressure on you, in the least. Your only job is to relax and have fun, and I promise I'll take care of the rest."

A ripple of excitement flashes through me. "As long as you're into it."

"I am."

"When you're not, if you feel like you're not getting enough out of it—"

"That's impossible. Ruby, I tasted your pussy on my fingers and came in my pants. I think I'll get enough out of it."

I can't help bursting into laughter. "That's a fair point."

"Glad that's settled." He exhales slowly. "This is gonna be incredible."

We've reached his house now; the rain is pouring down.

"Now, stay put, cutie," Kendrick coos as he parks his car in his driveway. "I'm gonna come around and carry you inside so your dress and shoes don't get wet and dirty."

24
RUBY

As Kendrick carries me out of the rain and into his dimly lit living room, I feel like a bride. A sexy one, thanks to my dress, but a bride, nonetheless.

He sets me down carefully onto my heels, and the scent of flowers envelops me. During my stay this past week, Kendrick replaced those first vases of tulips and added a third bouquet, a colorful spray of fragrant blooms that now sits on the nearby coffee table, making the already electrified air in Kendrick's living room feel doubly supercharged: sexy *and* romantic.

We're both slightly damp from the short trip from Kendrick's car into the house. But the rare Southern California downpour is only adding to the magical, romantic quality of the moment.

With his Adam's apple riding up and down, Kendrick looks deeply into my eyes and brushes a lock of rain-speckled hair off my face. With a slow exhale, he wordlessly slides his palm to my cheek and plants a tender kiss onto my lips.

His lips move with slow tenderness this time. Tentatively. In a way that's worlds apart from the ravenous mauling he gave me after leaping off that stage at Reed's party tonight.

And even more removed from all the voracious, desperate kisses he gave me while fingering me to an orgasm so deliciously. No, this time, as we stand in the middle of Kendrick's fragrant, dimly lit living room, the sounds of rain hitting his roof and windows all around us, we might as well be sixteen and standing underneath a porchlight after our first date.

I didn't have a boyfriend in high school. Wasn't interested in dating at all. All of Titus's friends were bone-headed jocks who didn't interest me, and those boys were the only ones who ever came around. Not that Titus would have let his friends date me, anyway. If any had tried, I'm pretty sure he would have ran them off. Besides all of them, my only male interactions at school were with my friends—guys I knew for a fact weren't interested in me like that. So, my first kiss happened at Northwestern. With Ryder. At age nineteen. Only a few weeks after my mortifying attempt to surprise Kendrick at his new college.

But that first kiss with Ryder felt nothing like this one with Kendrick. I don't know if that's because I'm not scared of what comes next with Kendrick, only excited, or if it's simply because the mind of an experienced adult processes these things differently than the mind of a virginal teenager. Or maybe it's simply because I'm kissing Kendrick. All I know is I've never swooned like this in my life. Surely, that's a good sign for what's about to happen. *Will sex with Kendrick feel sort of like a first time, too*? God, I hope so, since my first time with Ryder wasn't anything memorable. At least, it was nothing like I thought it'd be, based on what I witnessed of Kendrick going to town on Florence on his couch.

Kendrick breaks away from my lips and kisses my cheek. "Come with me, sweetheart," he whispers, grabbing my hand. "I'm gonna make you feel so fucking good."

I pause, and Kendrick immediately stops.

"You're having second thoughts? That's okay. We can cuddle or—"

"No, I want to do this. No second thoughts." It's the truth. An understatement, actually. But thinking about Ryder and the letdown of my first time, which has always been entangled in my mind with the disappointment and embarrassment I felt about my surprise trip to visit Kendrick, has planted the seed of a fantasy, just this fast. One I can't resist requesting from Kendrick, even if it's a little bit weird. Kendrick said this fling is all about me, after all. My desires and fantasies. And if I don't speak up now, this one-of-a-kind moment will be gone forever. "W-would you be willing to do a role-play with me?" I ask, my heart thumping. "Just this once. For our first time?"

Kendrick's eyebrows lift. "Anything, yes. Of course." He presses his lips together, his body language communicating he's on tenterhooks to hear my idea.

"It might be weird," I warn him. "But, since you're the guy who wrote a song called 'Spank,' I figure . . ." I trail off, feeling vulnerable. "You know what? Never mind."

"No, tell me. Please. Whatever it is, my answer is yes."

My cheeks feel hot. My heartbeat is crashing in my ears. "Could we maybe pretend I'm a virgin . . . and you're . . . my first?"

Kendrick's chest expands. "Yes," he chokes out, like he's barely able to get the word out.

"Nothing too complicated," I add quickly. "I'm not asking you to lay rose petals down or pretend I'm a serf and you're a lord."

One side of Kendrick's mouth hitches up. "I'm down to do all of that, if you want."

"No. I mean, okay, maybe later."

We both chuckle.

"But for now, for this time, you'll still be you and I'll still be me. I just mean, maybe you can take it extra slow and gentle, or however you'd do it if knew I'd never had sex before and you wanted to make it feel extra special."

His breathing is shallow. "That sounds good. I can do that, yeah."

I rub my forehead nervously. "I don't even know what this would entail, honestly, compared to what you were already planning to do, but—"

"Ruby, yes. I love the idea. It's a huge turn-on for me."

I meet his gaze. "Really?"

"Really." He smiles wickedly. "Are we our actual teenage selves, only on an alternate timeline? Or are we our present selves, but all prior sexual experiences have been wiped from our memories?"

I can't help giggling. "I'm thinking we're teenagers."

"Okay."

"But not *kids*. We're, like, nineteen going on twenty."

Kendrick bites back a smile. "I lost my virginity at nineteen, so that'll be easy for me to role-play."

"I did, too. Nineteen."

We stare at each other for a moment, the mention of our past lovers thudding like lead balloons onto the floor between us.

"Be honest with me," I say, "if this idea doesn't work for you."

"It does. Like I said, it's a turn-on. A big one." He shifts his weight. "It feels right to do it this way for our first time."

"It does, right? After this, we can swing from the chandeliers."

"Or not. Whatever works for you, when the time comes, is what will work for me. No performances required or desired, okay, Ruby? We'll take it one honest minute at a time."

"Okay," I squeak out. "Fair warning. I'm pretty sure, after this, I'll go right back to being the horny wildebeest who begged you to fuck her in Reed's laundry room."

Kendrick bursts out laughing. "You can be whatever and whoever you want to be, sweetheart. Whatever feels good to you and turns you on, whatever fantasies you have, tell me, and that's what we'll do. I want to do it all with you."

My breath comes out in a slow, stuttering stream. "Thank you."

He cocks his head. "Wait, so am I a teenage virgin, too, or just you?"

I pause to consider. "I think that would be good. But since this is a fantasy, you're a teenage virgin who somehow magically knows exactly what to do to me, just like you did in the laundry room."

Kendrick chuckles. "Okay, I'm a horn dog who's watched every how-to video he can find online."

"And your natural instincts are amazing, too." I laugh with him. "You're still you, remember? So you're a musician on this timeline, too. It makes sense you'd be good at feeling . . . a groove."

Kendrick winks. "You know what they say: drummers make the best lovers."

"Who says that?"

"Maybe it's only me."

It's not, actually. Kendrick's lucky tour fling, Tracy, said basically that same thing to her friends, once, while I was standing close enough to overhear everything. In fact, that woman didn't stop making comments, right and left, about how "amazing" and "fun" and "masterful" Kendrick was in bed. And always within earshot of me. One of those times, I vividly remember her saying, "But that's drummers for you. They know better than anyone how to keep a steady beat and lay down a dirty groove." The comment haunted me for months. Come to think of it, I'm pretty sure that comment was directly responsible for the sex dream that ended my relationship with Cooper.

"Okay, so . . ." With an exhale, Kendrick grabs my hand and kisses the top of it. "Listen, if you're not sure you're ready to do this with me, Ruby—"

"I am. Kendrick, wanting to do a role-play doesn't mean I'm not—"

"That was me starting." He winces. "Sorry. I thought we were supposed to jump right into it."

I giggle. "Oh. Yeah. That was good. Sorry."

Kendrick makes an adorable face. "Take two?"

"Yep. Go."

"Do you want to count us off or something?"

"No. Let's do it. Go."

He pauses. "Actually, I should shower before we start." He motions vaguely to his crotch, and, presumably, to the premature ejaculation that's long since dried down there. "Do you want to join me in the shower and make it part of the role-play, or wait for me in bed, or . . . ? I don't think virgins would have sex in a shower for their first time."

"Probably not."

"We could make out in there, though, while washing up, and then take things to the bed for the actual de-virginization."

I crack up at his word choice. "I agree, no sex in the shower. I don't think virgins would necessarily make out in a shower, either, but I can suspend my disbelief on that, if you can."

He waggles his eyebrows. "I definitely can."

I laugh again. This time, at the gleam in his eyes.

"Okay, let's take a shower, then, and make out as our present-day selves. No sex. And then, the role-play will start automatically, the second we get to the bed. No need to say it out loud."

"Got it. No starting gun. I dig it."

Without further ado, Kendrick grabs my hand, and we

head into his bedroom, grinning like blushing virgins at each other. But my grin isn't an act or part of a role-play. I'm feeling butterflies in my belly about this plan—about the fact that I'm going to see Kendrick Cook naked and hard, for the very first time, and he's going to make love to me, like it's my first time and his.

In the bathroom, we brush our teeth, standing shoulder to shoulder at the sink. No words exchanged. Only goofy smiles. When that task is completed, Kendrick stands before me with blazing blue eyes and wordlessly peels off his shirt, revealing the stunning torso that's been making me salivate this past week.

Visibly trembling with excitement, Kendrick turns on the shower. And while waiting for the water to heat up, he peels off the rest of his clothes, until he's standing before me fully nude with his large dick hard and straining toward his abs.

I can't get out of my dress without some assistance, so I simply stand before him, stock-still and mesmerized, staring at his beautiful, sexy body. He steps toward me, his steely dick leading the way, and comes to a stop mere inches away.

He kisses me, gently, the tip of his hard cock budging up against the fabric of my dress, and my knees physically buckle with anticipation.

Breathing hard, he turns me around and unzips me, and then, still standing behind me, he slowly pulls off my gown, planting kisses to my bare shoulders and neck as the expensive garment falls to the floor.

He turns me around to face him in my panties and kisses me again. But when I touch his hard penis and stroke him, he whispers, "I'm way too turned on for you to do that."

I shudder and release him, at which point he slowly kneels before me, links his thumbs on either side of my waistband, and pulls my panties down to the floor, as slow as molasses, planting soft kisses onto my belly and hipbone as they go.

I grip the top of Kendrick's head to keep steady, as his soft lips and gentle tongue move lower and lower on my anatomy. The closer he gets to my pulsing center, the more urgent his kisses become, the hotter his breath against my flesh. Before Kendrick's mouth reaches the folds between my legs, however, the bathroom is filled with steam, and he rises and leads me into the large shower that's plenty big for both of us.

In the shower, we wash ourselves and each other, kiss, touch, caress, and grope. And when we're both clean as a whistle, and there's nothing more to do on the functional side of things, Kendrick kneels before me again like he did outside the shower. With his palms on my ass, he pulls me into his mouth, and what follows is the best oral sex of my life.

As my groans increase in volume and desperation, Kendrick stays the course without wavering or changing things up. When it's clear something is working, he keeps at it, passionately. I grip his hair frantically as his tongue does miraculous things to my clit, and his fingers stroke a spot deep inside me, a spot that's turning me downright feral. I'm basically fucking his face by now, in a decidedly un-virginal way, as my primal instincts overwhelm me and turn me into a she-wolf in heat. And through all of it, hot water rains down onto Kendrick's broad back and sends hot steam everywhere.

Kendrick makes a guttural, tortured growl between my legs, and the sound of his desperation tightens my lower abdomen in a way that can only mean one thing. I'm about to come. In a flash, I feel like I'm waiting in suspended animation. My innermost muscles clench and ball up, and then gloriously release in rhythmic waves that make me throw my head back and babble a string of curses.

I can't believe it! What Kendrick did to me in that laundry room wasn't a fluke. The thought catapults me even further into a state of ecstasy.

Quaking, Kendrick rises from his knees, causing my hands

in his wet hair to fall to his broad shoulders. With a feral look in his eyes, he grabs my face and kisses me so passionately, it's like he's drowning and I'm his lifeline. I stroke his hard dick, simply because I'm dying for penetration at this point. Aching for it. Willing to murder for it. But when Kendrick whispers, "No," I release him like a good girl and await further instructions.

Breathing hard, Kendrick turns off the water and guides me out of the shower, and when we're both toweled off and mostly dry, he pulls me into the bedroom with urgency. Now that we've toweled off, I can plainly see his dick is dripping with his need. Obviously, he's every bit as desperate to fuck me as I am to be fucked.

With a quavering exhale, Kendrick guides me to his bed and lies me down. "Don't be scared; I'll be gentle," he chokes out. And suddenly, I remember the role-play. I'm so turned on, I don't need it anymore. Don't even remember why I asked for it now. But even so, the chance to go back in time and experience Kendrick as my first is too alluring an idea to cancel.

Rather than joining me on the bed, Kendrick heads to his nightstand and opens the top drawer. Foreplay is over. Every inch of his body telegraphs he's as desperate for penetration as I am. I watch him rolling that condom down his hard shaft, my mouth watering. My body writhing and purring with lust. My brain melting. I can't believe I'm doing this with Kendrick. That he's naked and hard for me, and I'm watching him rolling on a condom so he can fuck me. It's surreal.

When he's all covered up, Kendrick turns off the lamp and crawls on top of me. "You're so beautiful," he whispers as his skin warms mine. "You're perfect in every way, Ruby."

"So are you," I whisper back, trembling with anticipation.

"We'll take it slow," he says softly. "I want this to feel amazing for you."

I nod, quaking beneath him. Seriously, he's got a knack for

this role-play thing, because I swear, I feel so much anticipation and excitement, this might as well be my first time for real.

"Can I touch between your legs?"

"Yes."

"I'll be gentle."

My breathing is shallow. "Okay."

As the tip of his covered dick presses urgently against my thigh, he begins kissing me, more and more passionately, languidly touching my clit. Soon, I'm purring and undulating underneath him, feeling so turned on, I can't help widening my legs and jerking my pelvis in an extremely sexual manner.

"Can I put my fingers inside you?" he whispers in a shaky voice.

"Yes. Yes."

Kendrick slides his fingers in, slowly, whispering, "Does this feel good, baby?"

Baby. He's never called me that before. Not once. Cutie, babe, sweetheart. I'm used to all of it. But somehow, baby hits different. Like a bolt of lightning. "So good," I choke out in a strained, desperate voice. I'm doing a terrible job at my side of the role-play, I know, but I can't help it. I'm hanging on by a thread. I've never felt this turned on in my life.

With a low groan, Kendrick positions his cock at my entrance. "Ready?" he whispers.

I nod furiously and grip his ass, making him shudder.

"You have to say yes for me, sweetheart."

"Yes. Fuck yes. Yes, yes, yes, yes, yes."

With a shaky exhale, Kendrick slowly burrows himself inside me, and I whimper from relief and pleasure. After all the foreplay and anticipation, the bare sensation of his cock inside me is causing my eyes to roll back into my head and my toes to curl.

"Oh, God," Kendrick grits out. "You feel so good. Oh my

fucking God, Ruby." He takes a deep breath. "Are you okay? Am I hurting you?"

I grip his ass and squeeze in desperation. "Fuck the role-play. Fuck me, Kendrick. Fuck me hard."

"Oh, thank God." He begins gyrating on top of me, and within seconds, I feel like I've been sling-shotted into the blazing sun. As he fucks me senseless, he kisses me voraciously. Whispers that I feel so fucking good, it's like the pleasure is blurring his vision. He grips my hair and nips at my cheek, jawline, and ear. And all the while, he fucks me like I've never been fucked. Like he's a drug addict and I'm a line of cocaine. Until I'm so consumed with lust and pleasure, it's like my brain has melted and my body, feeling pleasure, is all that's left of me.

As Kendrick's thrusts become more and more energetic, as his body invades mine deeper and deeper and with more and more gusto, he slides one of his talented, sexy hands against my cheek. And that's it. All she wrote. At my greatest sexual fantasy coming true, my body short-circuits and every muscle in my core spasms and warps with a body-quaking release that feels more like a seizure than an orgasm.

I cry out in pleasure, bucking and jolting against Kendrick's warm skin on top of me. And as my body milks his cock inside me, Kendrick loses it with a deep roar that sends me even higher into a state of rapture.

As he comes inside me and my own pleasure spikes and fades, I clutch Kendrick's smooth ass for dear life, reveling in every sensation. And when we're both done jerking and groaning, he collapses on top of me, his breathing ragged and his skin soft, warm, and sensual against mine.

"Jesus Christ," he whispers after a long moment. He's still inside me, so I wrap my legs around him and hold on tight.

"Pretty good for your first time," I tease, sending us both into laughter.

"Pretty good for your first time, too. You really have a knack for this, babe." Chuckling, he slides off me and pulls off the condom.

"It's exciting to confirm the laundry room wasn't a fluke," I admit.

"Of course not. You're easy peasy."

Sighing happily, I stroke his arm. "I feel like a new woman. I feel high."

"Me, too. The high part. Not the new woman part."

"I'm so glad we're flinging like this. We're geniuses to do this." I giggle. "The rest of the band would crap their pants if they knew."

"Oh. So, this is a secret?"

"It has to be. How can things go back to normal afterward, if not?"

He flushes. "Yeah. I see what you mean."

I scoot close and run my finger across his abs. "Thank you so much for showing me what my body can do. I love you so much."

Fuck.

That felt weird.

But why?

I've told Kendrick that before. Lots of times. After we won a Grammy for best new artist, our whole band couldn't stop blurting "I love you guys so much!" over and over again to each other, for the rest of the night. But right after this man has fucked me into oblivion, and when we're still lying naked in bed, nose to nose, the phrase suddenly feels like it's taking on a whole new—and forbidden—meaning.

Feeling panicked, I quickly add, "You're the best friend and fling partner a girl could ever hope for."

Kendrick presses his lips together. "You, too. You're a gem of a best friend. My all-time favorite person." With that, he kisses my forehead and whispers, "Good night, cutie."

"Good night, my darling."

With a loud exhale, he closes his eyes, signaling he's checking out now, and I stroke his face and forehead for a bit while studying his beautiful face in repose.

It's a good thing Kendrick and I didn't get together when I stupidly went to surprise him that weekend. If by some chance he had said yes to me and been my first, for real, if he'd fucked me back then even half as well as he just did, then nothing would be as it is now. Kendrick and I wouldn't have lasted, because Kendrick never has long relationships, and neither do I. Also, I wasn't equipped to handle a fling back then, the way I am now. So, when things went south for us, he would have ruined me for anybody else. And then what?

Kendrick's face turns slack underneath my fingertips. His breathing is slow and rhythmic now. The handsome boy who just fucked me better than anyone else, ever, is fast asleep. And thankfully, I'm adult enough now to realize everything's worked out, exactly as it was meant to be.

25
KENDRICK

Pleasure shoots through me, sending a hair-raising torrent of electricity straight into my dick. With a soft moan, I slide my hand toward my crotch to investigate the cause of this sudden jolt of goodness and discover a bobbing head of soft hair underneath my fingertips.

My eyes flutter open as a languid smile spreads across my face. She's really here. Last night was real. And not only that, Ruby's waking me up with her voracious mouth. Dreams really do come true.

"Good morning to you, too," I growl out, my voice cracking with grogginess. "Damn. You're my kind of blushing virgin."

Ruby giggles, but the sound is muffled by the dick in her mouth. *My* dick. I can't believe it. It's literally one of my hottest fantasies come to life.

Just as my balls begin tightening in preparation for the grand finale, Ruby releases me with a loud pop of her mouth. Her face aglow, she gasps out, "You want me to keep going, or do you want me to save a horse and ride a cowboy?"

"Whichever turns you on more."

Ruby grips my hard dick and smiles wickedly. "Which option will inspire you to show me your dirty lyrics?"

"Neither. But if you stop mentioning that, I promise to make all your sexual fantasies come true."

"You're already going to do that."

She's right. I am. And nothing can stop me. Not even Ruby constantly asking me about those damned non-existent lyrics.

"Ah, well. A girl can try," she mutters, correctly interpreting my facial expression. With a sigh, she scoots across the bed to the nightstand and grabs a condom, her decision about what to do next apparently made. After handing me the packet, she leans down and pecks my lips. "Wanna know a secret?" she whispers. "You already fulfilled all my fantasies last night, anyway."

My eyebrows draw together. "Blushing virgin was your only fantasy?"

Ruby strokes my shaft. "That was an impromptu fantasy, actually. Before that moment, the only fantasy I've ever had in my life was me having an orgasm without the help of a toy."

I put my hand on hers, stopping the movement of her hand on my shaft. "If you truly intend to ride a cowboy, you'd better stop teasing his horse. Unless, of course, me coming all over your hand is another impromptu fantasy unlocked."

With a sexy little giggle, Ruby pulls her hand back, freeing me to wrap myself in the condom. When that task is done, she gleefully straddles me, hooting and yeehawing as she goes, and when her knees are firmly placed on either side of me, she leans down, kisses my cheek, and whispers into my ear. "Here's an impromptu fantasy unlocked. How about you *spank* me, while I ride you, cowboy? Can you do that for me?"

"I sure can."

"Don't be shy about it. Do it exactly the way you wrote about in those lyrics, okay? Really go for it." She positions herself at my tip. "I mean, don't hurt me. But don't hold back."

"Got it." I grip Ruby's hips and guide her down onto my shaft, and she moans as I sink deeper and deeper inside her. "Jesus Christ," I mutter, as the sensation of warm wetness squeezes every inch of me, causing electrical impulses to skate across every nerve ending connected to my dick and balls.

With my palms firmly gripping her hips, Ruby starts gyrating on top of me, making me grunt softly with every movement.

"I honestly never need to see your dirty lyrics," Ruby purrs.

"Good. Because you won't."

"The mere thought of you writing them is enough to turn me on like crazy." She moans to emphasize her point. "I can't stop imagining you lying in bed, naked and jacking off, and then having the undeniable urge to scribble all your hottest fantasies down, as fast as you could write them. God, that's so fucking hot, Kendrick. The image of you doing that is making me want to come."

That gets my attention. "I was so turned on when I wrote those words down," I grit out, figuring I'll stoke the flames of her fantasies to maximum effect. "I could barely see what I was scribbling onto the page."

"Oh, God. Yes."

"When I read it back, I couldn't believe how graphic it was. How unfiltered and raw."

"Oh, Kendrick. Tell me more."

I touch her clit, and Ruby groans and gyrates even more enthusiastically on top of me. "I read my lyrics afterward, and they made me so horny, I jerked off again."

"Oh, God. I'm so close. Wait. Again? You jerked off before *and* after writing your horny manifesto?"

"Yep. Before and after. I was on fire that night."

"So hot," Ruby grits out, throwing her head back. "Tell me more."

We're in the zone now. Moving together. Spiraling toward ecstasy.

"Did you think about anyone in particular while writing it?" she gasps out.

I don't know if it's the right answer. The wrong answer. Too big an admission. But there's only one thing I can possibly say to that, even regarding a bunch of lyrics that don't actually exist. "I thought of you, baby. Only you. Nobody else."

Ruby groans, more loudly than ever this time, and her gyrations on top of me increase in speed and intensity. I think I'm safe—she's plainly interpreting my comment as simple dirty talk and nothing more.

"Have you torn out those pages and destroyed them, or do your filthy, kinky words still exist in the world?"

"They still exist," I choke out, feeling like I'm on the cusp of losing it. "But don't bother looking for my notebook. You'll never fucking find it."

"I won't even look."

"I don't believe you."

"No, I mean it. I respect your bound—Oh, God. Kendrick. Gah."

I just now changed things up in terms of how I'm stimulating her clit. And the new tactic has plainly taken things to a new level for her.

"That's it, baby," I coo, as her movements on top of me become frenzied. "I'm never gonna show you what I wrote. And you're gonna be a good girl and accept that."

"Yes," she gasps out. "Just don't stop what you're doing, Kendrick. Don't stop."

"Baby, this house could be burning down and I wouldn't stop." I don't feel like I can call her baby unless I'm fucking her, so I'm using the word at every fucking opportunity now.

Ruby groans desperately. "I'm so close, it hurts."

And there's my cue.

Panting with excitement, I grip Ruby's gyrating ass cheek, finding my target, and then, I give her soft ass cheek a gentle spank—one that elicits a mangled, tortured whimper of excitement.

"Harder," she grits out.

I give her what she wants, and her reaction is even bigger this time, which, of course, gets me going like crazy, too.

Somehow, I manage to hang on for dear life through Ruby's excitement and keep it going for her. But I must admit I'm now hanging on by the barest of threads.

Feeling dizzy and breathless, I spank Ruby again when the scooping movements of her pelvis serve her ass cheek to me on a silver platter, while my other hand continues working her clit, and my cock remains buried deep inside her, filling her up. Moans and groans lurch out of me, and the room feels like it's spinning. And thank God, that third spank gets her across the line.

As Ruby throws her head back and comes with a keening wail, the floodgates open for me, too, and I'm catapulted into the stratosphere like I've got two rocket launchers strapped to my balls.

But even as I'm momentarily blinded by pleasure, my brain registers a startling truth. An unfortunate one, if I'm being honest. I won't survive it if Ruby doesn't catch feelings for me by the end of this supposed fling. This extended role-play. This charade.

It's undeniable to me now.

I'm a slave to this woman's body, every bit as much as I'm a slave to her heart. Her soul. Her smile. Her laugh.

Why? Because I'm deeply, madly, irrevocably, and infinitely in love with Ruby Margaret Connolly. Addicted to her. Desperate for her. God help me, I was born to love this woman. She's The One. And there's no option for me, other than making her mine, through any means necessary.

26

RUBY

A week later

"Thanks for coming to my place for the writing sesh, everyone," Kendrick says. He and our bandmates are seated in his living room, while I stand at the nearby kitchen counter, arranging a pretty charcuterie board for the festivities.

These days, whenever we get together to write music, we do it either at Savage and Laila's gorgeous place in Malibu or Kendrick's comfortable house here in North Hollywood, since those are the only two homes with full-blown recording studios in case we come up with something in record speed and want to lay down a demo. This time, since I'm staying here, Kendrick's place won out as the most convenient option.

The agenda for today's writing session is a singular one: coming up with the future mega-hit we're going to unveil during the finale of *Sing Your Heart Out* in six weeks. Luckily, that's plenty of time for us to write and record a single song.

But still, given the once-in-a-lifetime launching pad, it needs to be amazing, not merely good enough. Not to mention, we not only need to write the song, but we also need to record it, get it mixed and mastered, and rehearse it into the ground so we're foolproof and dialed in when the time comes to perform it on live TV. All things considered, I'm actually a bit stressed about the timeline.

My charcuterie board assembled, I carry it into the living room, doing my best not to hobble like a woman who's been fucked, expertly and often, over the past week. I've never had so much sex in my life, let alone sex that curled my toes so violently, they might actually be permanently deformed at this point. It's been worth it, of course. This is the best soreness of my existence, but my band doesn't need to know about that. Not when Kendrick and I have agreed that everything will go back to normal after our secret fling has run its course.

"Big ups to Savage for making it," Titus says, as I place my tray onto the coffee table and sit next to my brother. "The rest of us have had time to decompress from tour by now. I can't imagine how exhausted you must feel after shooting the show every day this week."

That's how it goes with the shooting schedule. For the judges, anyway. The first week or so involves long days that capture all the fan-favorite audition episodes, followed by the Draft Day and Guest Mentor episodes that will be shooting tomorrow.

"It was in my best interest to get out of the house today," Savage says with a chuckle. "When I left, Laila was sitting at her baby grand, obsessively writing a song like a madwoman. If I'd stuck around, I'd be dead by now for breathing or eating too loudly."

We all crack up. At one time or another, we've all been Laila—a songwriter in the zone who doesn't tolerate distractions.

"That's best part of being married to another songwriter," Savage muses. "We both understand the madness." He grins wistfully. "I can't even imagine trying to do life with someone who doesn't get what it feels like to create amazing art out of nothing."

The rest of us share a smile and encouraging comments about our friend's happy life. Savage has undergone an unbelievable transformation over the past few years, and we couldn't be happier for him.

In the midst of the back and forth, Kendrick's eyes meet mine. I flash him a secret little smile, and he returns the gesture, followed by a smolder that makes me blush and start pulsing between my legs.

I look away, not wanting our bandmates to notice him eyeball-fucking me. They still think that kiss at Reed's party was a performance for the hidden cameras we knew about, since that's what I told them in the group chat. A conscious decision to get ourselves the bonuses up for grabs. I'm determined to let them keep thinking that way.

God help me, when this fling ends, the last thing I need is for any of these people to know what we did. Titus, especially, can never know. Not because he'd be mad at either of us. Titus loves Kendrick like a brother, and I'm an adult with ownership of my own body, thank you very much. But because, honestly, I've always had a feeling Titus wishes Kendrick and I would get together one day, and I don't want to deal with his disappointment, on top of mine, when that doesn't happen.

"Wow, Ruby," Titus says, perusing the lavish offerings on my board of snacks. "This is the fanciest thing I've ever seen you make. What's gotten into you?"

I'm not offended. Everyone in the band, including my brother, knows I can't cook for shit. "Kendrick's kitchen is so pretty, it inspired me to become the next Martha Stewart."

Titus scoffs. "This is cool, but I'm pretty sure Martha

Stewart makes stuff that's more complicated than a bunch of snacks on a tray."

"Actually," Kendrick says, "I'm pretty sure Martha Stewart is the one who invented charcuterie boards."

"See?" I say to my brother. "Don't yuck my yum, dude."

"I wasn't. I just meant—"

"Don't bother. I just moved you one space higher on my kill list." I turn to Kendrick. "Thank you for defending my honor, KC. Just for that, I'm going to make you a sandwich worthy of Martha Stewart tomorrow."

"Awesome. You know how much I love me a big, fat Ruby Deluxe."

"How much longer are you staying here?" Titus asks me. "I could have sworn you were supposed to be back in your place by now."

"I was, but unforeseen problems keep popping up. Yesterday, my building manager texted me with yet another delay."

Out the corner of my eye, Savage shoots Kendrick a smile —one I'm interpreting as a show of sympathy for me being here far longer than originally planned.

"I offered to go to a hotel," I say to Savage. "But Kendrick won't hear of it."

"I like having you here," Kendrick says. "I'm having fun."

Blushing, I address the group. "It's felt like old times."

As everyone else says, yes, they remember that era, Kai asks with a snicker, "Did Kendrick swallow your face back then, too?" He's referring to the kiss from Reed's party, since the show recently released clips of it as part of their marketing blitz. Our group chat has been rife with clips and teasing about it over the past couple of days.

"No, because we weren't being paid to pretend to be a couple back then," I snipe back.

Again, Savage shoots Kendrick that same pointed smile from earlier. Only this time, the gesture makes my stomach tighten. Did Kendrick tell Savage what's going on between us, despite our agreement to keep mum about the situation?

"So, should we start the writing session now?" I ask with a clap of my palms. It's a good idea for us to get going, regardless. The damned song's not going to write itself. But I'm also feeling a strong urge to change the subject.

Everyone agrees we should get started, and Kai instructs everyone who's got notes of any kind, whether on their phones or in a journal, to share with the group. It's our usual process, taught to us by Kai himself years ago, back when he was the older, wiser music student, and the rest of us were excited little sponges.

"I've got an idea for a riff that might lead to something cool," Titus offers. He grabs his guitar that's leaning against the end of the couch and plays it, and everyone agrees it's got potential. But since Titus never supplies lyrics or melodies, that's all that happens for now. Unfortunately, though, only a long, awkward silence ensues after Titus's guitar goes silent.

"Or maybe not," Titus jokes.

"Sorry, man," Savage says with a yawn. "It was cool. I think my brain is depleted right now."

"No worries, we've got you," Titus says. He looks at Kai. "Do you have anything for us?"

Kai shrugs. "Not really. I wrote a few things in my journal during the tour, but nothing all that great. Sorry, guys. Since we got back, my brain's been pretty dead. Mostly, I've just been sleeping and smoking bowls."

Our writing sessions don't normally feel like pulling teeth. Normally, somebody has something exciting to contribute out of the gate. But then again, it's not typical for us to come together this soon after a tour—and it's certainly not normal for us to try to write a song we're going to be performing, live, for the first time, in front of millions of people on TV.

"We can't overthink it, guys," I say, my heart rate increasing. "If we focus on the massiveness of the opportunity, we'll never be able to write anything. Treat this like any other writing session. Throw in whatever ideas you've got, even embarrassing ones, because they might lead to something epic." I glance at Kendrick, letting him know I'm hoping he might relent and throw "Spank" into the mix, despite his embarrassment about it. But when he shakes his head, confirming that's not happening, I return to the group with an exhale. "Whoever's got something to share, come on, let's hear it."

With another yawn, Savage pulls out his phone and starts scrolling—presumably to find something in whatever voice memos he might have recorded to himself—while Kai and I throw our physical notebooks into the pot and then start scrolling on our phones, too.

"Where's your journal, KC?" Kai asks his brother.

"I didn't write anything in it this time," Kendrick murmurs. And nobody presses him on it, because, like Titus, it's more typical for Kendrick to contribute musical ideas, or to add to something someone else has offered.

We spend the next hour or so brainstorming, sharing tepid ideas, riffs, and melodies. But nothing hits any of us like a ton of bricks, which is what we need for an opportunity this big.

When Kai expresses frustration, Titus says, "We could always do what Reed keeps begging us for." There's no need to explain; we all know Reed wants a sequel to "Hate Sex High."

"A brazen money grab like that," Kai says, "premiered to an audience this big, would probably go straight to number one."

I take a bite from the charcuterie board. "But what would a sequel to 'Hate Sex High' even be about? Erotic asphyxiation?"

We all crack up.

"We could write a song called 'Spank,'" Savage offers, looking straight at Kendrick. "That title would grab people's attention, don't you think, KC?"

As Kai expresses interest, I launch out of my seat, shouting, "Kendrick Cook! You swore you didn't show those lyrics to anybody!"

"I didn't," Kendrick insists, shooting a death glare at Savage.

"Oh. Yeah. No, he didn't," Savage stammers. "I haven't read any of it. I just saw the title when I glanced over his shoulder once, but he slammed his notebook shut before I could read anything else."

"Same here!" I bellow, as Kai asks what the hell we're talking about. "I only got to read the title and the first line before he snatched his precious journal away from me."

"Guys, answer me," Kai insists. "You're saying *Kendrick* wrote a song called 'Spank?'"

"Lyrics, yeah," Savage confirms. "But he won't let us see them." He grins at Kendrick, who's still shooting him daggers. "All we know is whatever he wrote is hot as fuck. Filthy, to the extreme. The filthiest thing you could ever possibly imagine. And Kendrick wrote the entire thing in one sitting."

"What the fuck?" Kai says, looking flabbergasted. "That sounds like something you'd write, not Kendrick."

Savage laughs. "That's exactly what *I* said."

Kai motions to his brother. "Go get your journal, KC. Let's see this thing."

"Yeah, KC," I say with a devilish smile. "Go get your journal, KC. Let's see this thing."

"It's not in there anymore," Kendrick says, leaning back and spreading his thighs. "I ripped those pages out and threw them away."

"When?" I blurt, feeling crestfallen.

"The other night. It was trash day after that, so they're long gone now."

I gasp and clutch my chest, feeling a deep sense of loss. It was one thing for Kendrick to refuse to let me see those pages, but another thing for him to throw them away. What happened to him letting me get turned on by the very existence of those written words in this world, even if he refused to let me see them?

Kai is beside himself with frustration. "Why the fuck did you do that?" he yells. "I've told you a million times to never, ever throw anything away, because there's no such thing as a bad idea."

"This time, there was." Kendrick glares at Savage again, but he only laughs.

"Fucking hell, Kendrick," Kai says, palming his forehead. "Do you at least remember anything you wrote? I really like the title." He puts his hand up, like he's spreading letters across a marquee. "'Spank,' from the band that brought you 'Hate Sex High.'" He smirks at the group. "That title would definitely be on-brand." He's a man on a mission now, as he turns to me. "What was the first line you read? Do you remember it?"

Why, yes, I do. In fact, those words will be burned into my grey matter forever.

Lying awake, my body staging a coup/Can't have—

Unfortunately, that's all I saw, so I don't know what Kendrick thinks he can't have. Satisfaction? Relief, release, sex? What he needs, wants, deserves? It's anybody's guess.

All I know for sure is I'm not going to reveal a single word of Kendrick's private thoughts to the group. It was one thing to admit I know about the existence of those lyrics, but it'd be another thing entirely to disrespect his stated boundaries by offering up any details.

I glance at Kendrick while replying to Kai. "I don't remember any of it. Sorry. I was pretty drunk."

Kai points at Savage. "Okay, rockstar. That's your home-work assignment, then. Write up some lyrics for a song called

'Spank,' and let's see where it takes us. That should be like falling off a log for you."

"No, don't," Kendrick blurts. When everyone looks at him, he adds, "Think about it. If Savage sings a song called 'Spank' that's about all the ways he gets off on spanking an ass, everyone will assume he's singing about spanking his *wife's* ass."

Kai pulls a face. "Yeah. Obviously. So what?"

"So, that would feel forced. Like, TMI, dude. We get it. You like to bang and spank your wife. It'd feel like, you know, a money grab, and people wouldn't like it."

"What are you talking about?" Kai says with a roll of his eyes, while Savage pipes in to agree with Kendrick.

"I agree with Kendrick, too," I say. "As raunchy as 'Hate Sex High' is, it's still a love song. I know it's mostly about sex, but you can tell Savage is secretly in love with "Laila, Laila," or else why was he punching walls about her being with another guy?"

"Ruby's spot-on," Kendrick says. "A person doesn't feel jealousy about someone they don't give a shit about. Savage's emotional torture is the reason the song works."

Images of Kendrick's college girlfriend, Florence, pop into my mind, probably because that's the only time I've ever felt white-hot jealousy in my life. I was so freaking jealous of that girl, I wanted to scratch her eyes out.

"What do you know about jealousy?" Kai says to his brother. "You don't have a jealous bone in your body."

He doesn't?

True, I've never seen Kendrick exhibit jealousy in relation to one of his tour flings or girlfriends. But I've certainly seen him exhibit the emotion in relation to a few of my douchebag boyfriends. Actually, I feel like he acted a bit jealous toward Finn, too, and Finn was a sweetheart. Or maybe I'm confusing jealousy with simple protectiveness.

Savage shakes his head. "Yeah, I think it's a non-starter."

"I agree with them, for what it's worth," Titus says to Kai.

Kai looks at me. "Okay, so how about we write a response song to Cooper, then?"

"Nope," I reply without hesitation.

"Come on, Ruby," Kai says. "We could call it, 'I Wasn't Gonna Call You, Anyway, Ya Dipshit.'"

We all laugh at that, even me.

"Sorry, no. I don't want to dignify Cooper's pettiness with a song, especially one I'm going to have to play at shows for the rest of my life. I'm already sick to death of thinking about that motherfucker."

"Yeah, fuck Cooper," Kendrick says. "He's a clout chaser. Let's not help his career any more than we already have." He looks at me, his blue eyes blazing, and I must say, for a guy who supposedly doesn't have a jealous bone in his body, Kendrick looks pretty dang jealous to me.

Kai flaps his lips together. "Okay, well, are we officially out of ideas for today?"

"It kinda feels like we are," Kendrick says.

"Yeah, I'm tapped out, guys," Savage agrees.

"Let's not give up just yet," I say. "Maybe if we—"

"It's four to one, Ruby Duby," Savage says with a yawn. "The sesh is now officially over. But don't worry, maybe something we bounced around today will lead to a *spark*, later on." He looks at Kendrick like he's said something clever or funny. But if he's making a joke, I don't get it.

"Yeah, I'm sure you're right," I say. "Something we did today will definitely spark another idea. We just don't know it yet."

"Definitely." With a wink at Kendrick, Savage claps his palms to his thighs. "Got any weed, brother? Or should I go to the dispensary?"

"Yeah, I've got some," Kendrick says. "I don't have any beer, though."

Kai pops up. "I'll go get some."

"I'll order the pizzas," Titus offers, pulling out his phone. "The usual?"

Everyone confirms Titus should order the same pizzas, as always.

"What about margaritas?" Kai asks. "Should I get some mix, when I get the beer?"

Hard-liquor cocktails are the only component of our tradi-tional, post-writing-session party that's variable. Everything else remains the same: weed, pizza, cheap beer.

"I think that'd be too big a reward, since we didn't come up with anything," I say. "But, hey, maybe that's a reason to drown our sorrows."

We discuss it as a group and quickly decide drowning our sorrows is, indeed, the superior plan. And so, with that decided, Kai heads toward the front door, a man on a mission.

"You wanna come with me, baby brother?"

"Sure," Kendrick says, popping up. He strides toward his brother, but not before shooting me a look that tightens my lower abdomen—a smolder that practically screams, "I'd rather fuck you than party with these dipshits, but first things first."

"Get some munchies, too," Titus calls out to the Cook brothers. "Popcorn or chips or something."

And, suddenly, it's all I can do not to shoo everyone out so I can rip Kendrick's clothes off and let him take me to heaven, once again.

27

KENDRICK

"I thought they'd never leave," I murmur as my hungry lips traverse the length of Ruby's naked, spread thighs on my bed. I'm the perfect kind of drunk and stoned. Totally relaxed but also horny as hell—the kind of horny that makes me want to get adventurous and try something new with my little sex kitten.

"I don't think everyone realizes six weeks isn't all that long to get everything done in time," Ruby says, running her hand through my hair. "Don't forget, we not only need to write a song. It has to be *amazing*. And then, we need to—"

I look up from between her legs. "Okay, you have to stop talking now, sweetheart. You're hereby not allowed to think or talk about anything but what I'm doing to you."

"One more thing, though. I'm worried I blew it by demanding that performance slot after Cooper. I thought it was a genius move at the time, but now—"

"Babe." I crawl up to her face and lay my forearms on either side of her head, my hard dick poking her belly. "It was a genius move, and we'll come up with something amazing. It's all gonna work out."

"You think?"

"Without a doubt."

Her body softens underneath mine. "Okay. If you really think that, I'll stop stressing about it."

"I'm sure of it. When the time comes, we're gonna kill it."

Ruby puckers, and I lean down and kiss her.

"Get a condom," she whispers. "I want you inside me."

"I will, but I was thinking we'd try something new this time."

She looks at me expectantly.

"Do you trust me, Ruby?"

Ruby narrows her eyes. "That's a concerning question."

I laugh. "Come on. Do you trust me?"

"You know I do. Why are you asking me this? What's this thing you want to try?"

I grin. "A threesome." When Ruby's eyebrows ride up to her hairline, I add, "With Bruno."

Ruby swats at my shoulder and giggles. "I thought you meant for real."

I smirk. "Hell no. I'm not sharing you with anyone."

Her chest heaves underneath me.

"So, what do you think? Can I use Bruno on you?"

"I mean, sure. But kind of the whole point of all this 'sex therapy' for me is that I finally don't need him, you know? Honestly, I'm kind of enjoying—"

"I'm not talking about using him to get you off because I can't do it. I want to use him to help me do something I can't do on my own, so I can give you an orgasm that makes you not only see God, but he'll high-five you."

Ruby giggles. "You've already given me orgasms like that. Multiple times."

"Not like this, babe."

She flashes me a side-eye, her expression suggesting she's now got an inkling of where this is headed.

"DP, baby," I confirm. "Double penetration."

Ruby makes an adorable expression. One I'd caption, "You want to stick what where?"

I laugh. "Yes? No? Maybe? You have questions?"

"I've never done that before."

"I figured. Are you curious, though?"

"Would it hurt?"

"Not at all, as long as I'm gentle, which I will be. And the second you want me to stop anything, you know I will. Just say the word, and it stops."

Ruby snickers. "You mean, like, we'll agree on a safe word?"

"If you want. I was thinking we'd keep it simple and you'd just tell me to stop, but, okay, whatever floats your boat, baby."

She cackles. Clearly, she's warming to the idea.

I stroke her cheek with my thumb. "No pressure. This is your sex therapy, not mine. I don't want to talk you into anything. I want an enthusiastic yes for everything we do."

Ruby ponders that.

"Everything we do is all about you," I continue. "I'm happy and horny, as long as my body gets to touch yours in any way."

"Thank you." She puckers again, so I lean down and give her a peck. When my lips release hers, she says, "Okay, let's do it. Double-stuff me like an Oreo, baby. I trust you completely."

My breathing hitches with excitement. "You're sure?"

"Fuck yes."

Anticipation vibrates through me. "Is Bruno ready to report for duty?"

She nods. "He's charged, clean, and ready."

"And you're sure you're ready?"

"Fuck yes."

I exhale. "Okay if I handcuff your wrists and ankles, so you're completely at my mercy? I think it will add to the fun."

Ruby flushes a bright shade of crimson. But her blush doesn't come across as a sign of hesitancy. More as a sign of pure excitement. It's an assumption confirmed when she grabs my ass with gusto and says, "My darling, after seeing those cuffs in your nightstand, I thought you'd never ask."

———

Ruby's tied to my bed now, her spread limbs forming the shape of an "X."

Her nipples are hard, her skin covered in goosebumps of anticipation.

I've got my lieutenant, Bruno, at the ready, right next to a bottle of lube.

I'm so turned on, I'm panting.

I crawl between Ruby's spread legs and begin licking and lapping at her hard bud, fucking her with my fingers, worshiping every inch of her with my lips, tongue, and hands; when I spend some focused time on her most intimate nerve endings, her moans and gyrations quickly make it clear she's more than ready for her first double date.

My cock covered and hard as a rock, I slather my wingman with lube and bring it to her ass crack, at which point she shudders and moans. It's a good sign. That wasn't a sound of fear or anxiety. That was a sound of extreme arousal.

"Breathe, baby," I whisper softly. "Take a nice, deep breath for me." This thing won't fit all the way inside her. No way. Not without some slow and steady prep over time. But that doesn't matter. As long as she feels the sensation of penetration in a place that makes her feel naughty and wild, like she's doing something forbidden or taboo, that dildo in her ass, no matter how far it goes, will take her somewhere supernatural once I get inside her, too.

After guiding Ruby through three deep, slow breaths, I

slide the tip of the toy inside her, gently, provoking a moan and shudder that sends electrical impulses down my cock and into my balls.

"All good?" I choke out.

"Yes."

"I'm gonna take it a touch deeper. Yes?"

"Yes."

"Breathe for me again."

Ruby complies, and I slide the toy deeper inside her, enough to make her purr with excitement.

I put some lube on my free hand and touch her clit, and she strains against all four restraints at once.

"Still good?" I ask, as I work her clit slowly, in languid circles.

"Oh god, I think I'm gonna come like this."

"That's good. Don't hold back. Come, if you want. There's more where that came from."

Ruby whimpers and bucks again, and I stay the course, loving every minute of her obvious excitement.

"I'm gonna turn it on low now," I say softly. "Yes?"

"Yes," she chokes out. "Yes, yes."

I flip the switch, provoking a guttural groan from Ruby that makes my cock jolt in reply, and not ten seconds later, Ruby moans and releases an orgasm that makes her entire body shake and shudder against the cuffs.

Holy shit. That seemed like a good one. Bruno is doing his part beyond my wildest expectations.

"Training wheels off," I say with a smile. "You're riding like a big girl now, baby."

"Oh my god, Kendrick," she gasps out. "Do it now. Fuck me hard. Double-fuck me. Do whatever you want to me. I trust you."

Practically quaking with all the adrenaline and excitement coursing through me, I push on the vibrating dildo a touch more, ever so gently, and Ruby turns into a feral animal on me.

"More vibration? Yes?"

"Yesss," she hisses. "Give me *all* the vibration."

"Baby steps, baby." I love calling her baby. It's my favorite thing. During sex itself is the only time the word feels casual enough for a supposed fling, though, so I force myself not to slip up and use it any other time.

"I want you inside me," Ruby rasps out. "I want to feel completely filled up."

"Patience." I honestly don't know where I'm getting this shit. I've never done this before, either. But Ruby doesn't need to know that.

I continue working her clit with my thumb, round and round, while working her G-spot with my fingers inside her and keeping Bruno in place with my free hand. All I'm trying to do is get her to the bitter edge, so she comes when I fuck her. But to my thrill, she comes again. And this time, holy shit, she squirts all over my hand inside her.

"Kendrick," she gasps out. "Help me. Fuck me. Save me."

I laugh. She's sweaty. Glistening with it. Flushed, too. And it's plain to see she's no longer here, in her usual form. Her brain is off; her body is now in complete control. And by God, her body wants one thing, like her lungs need air to breathe.

I slide my fingers into my mouth to taste the liquid sweetness that squirted out of Ruby a moment ago, but when that taste of pure heaven shoves me dangerously close to the edge, I force myself to ignore my trophy for now so I won't let her down again like I did in Reed's laundry room. After taking several deep breaths to get myself under control, I push the dildo in again, if only slightly. And I'll be damned, Ruby's turned-on body receives Bruno's latest entreaty like welcoming an old friend.

The vibrating toy is now in position to stay put inside her

while I fuck her. And now that we've reached this milestone, I can't wait another second, another breath, another heartbeat.

"I'm gonna fuck you now," I gasp out, my voice strained and desperate. "Yes?"

"Yes. Fuck yes. Yes, yes, yes."

Shaking, spasming, trembling with anticipation and greed, I crawl on top of her splayed body, find my target with my fingers, and slowly sink myself inside her extra-tight wetness. Thanks to Bruno, she's throttling me as I enter her, practically strangling my dick, the deeper I get. And it feels so fucking good.

Ruby's been moaning and groaning since my tip entered her. But once I'm all the way in, and she feels the sensation of her body being completely filled up in a whole new way, her body language makes it clear she's in downright ecstasy. Euphoric. Enraptured. And that's even before I've started fucking her.

When I start moving in and out of her, carefully, while concentrating hard on *not* coming through every stroke, Ruby lets out a growl that's so unhinged and hot, so utterly wild and untethered, my aching balls tighten against my body in response, preparing to unleash their load.

"*Kendrick*," Ruby gasps out. "Kendrick. *Kendrick*." At least ten times, Ruby says my name, with each pronunciation becoming more and more ragged and frantic, until finally, she groans one final, frenzied time and comes so hard, warm fluid gushes out of her and around my cock. She came like this earlier, yes, but this time, she's a dam breaking. A rushing river carving a new path. Emotionally. Physically. Metaphorically. In every way, she's breaking free, like she's crossed into some new dimension of pleasure. Either that, or that was some amazing weed, and I'm going to buy only that particular strain for the rest of my goddamned life.

Not surprisingly, I can't hang on through her cataclysmic

orgasm. Frankly, it's a miracle I've lasted this long. As I release, my entire body jolts and flops; my vision blurs and fills with stars. I've done to myself what I promised to Ruby earlier: I've taken myself to a whole new place. One where I'm not only seeing God, I'm getting a high-five from him. No, a kiss. A medal of honor. The answers to all the mysteries of the universe.

But since all good things must come to an end, my ecstasy doesn't last forever, and neither does Ruby's. When we're both finally still and quiet, other than our ragged, fitful breathing, I pull myself and Bruno out of her, crawl between her legs, and lick and suckle every drop of sweet fluid off her while she hums and coos and rambles incoherently about how amazing that felt. How supernatural and glorious.

"You're a superhero, Kendrick," she purrs, as I move from limb to limb, untying her. "A magician. A wizard. No, a *god*."

Once she's free, I lie down next to her, chuckling at her effusiveness, and pull her to me. For a long moment, I hold her without speaking, and she nuzzles into me like a kitten kneading a blanket.

"I had no idea any of that was possible for me," she finally whispers. "Thank you, Kendrick. Thank you for taking me there and showing me what I can do. I'll never be the same again."

Neither will I, I think. But for different reasons. For me, this experience was transformative, too. But not necessarily in a good way, if this plan of mine to make Ruby fall in love with me doesn't pan out in the end. Before now, my love for her was undeniable. My lust for her, too.

But now I know a startling truth: if Ruby doesn't catch feelings for me by the end of this fling, if Ruby decides she meant every word she said about going back to normal, or, worse, if she gives a relationship with me a whirl, like she did with Cooper, and quickly decides that was a huge mistake, that we're better off as friends, I'll never recover. Never be able to enjoy sex with anyone else, ever again. Never fall in love. Never get married. Never have babies. Because she's ruined me. Without Ruby, I might as well be a eunuch.

I close my eyes, banishing my worst-case scenario thoughts. If Savage were here, he'd slap me. Well, right after high-fiving me for what I just did to Ruby. But then, yes, he'd slap me and tell me to stop spiraling and stop making failure an option. "There's only one option now," he'd say. "You're going to do whatever the fuck it takes to get her, KC. And that's that. Nothing's off-limits now. No holds barred. You're gonna go after this woman, without her realizing it, like your very life depends on it."

Ever since my football injury, I've been prone to worst-case scenario thinking. To imagining what I'd do if this or that dream doesn't come true. And Savage is always the one who shakes me out of it and keeps the dream alive. Kai, too, actually. But this time, I don't need them to shake off the ghosts of my past. This time, in the blink of an eye, I'm able to shake them off myself and get laser-focused and battle-ready.

"Kendrick?" Ruby whispers. "Are you okay?"

I swallow hard. "Yeah, I'm great. I think that melted my brain."

Ruby giggles. "Mine, too. Also, my ovaries."

I tip her face up by her chin and peck her gently. "I'm sorry your place is taking so long to get fixed. But I'm not sorry it means you're staying with me longer than originally planned. I'm having so much fun with you."

Her face lights up. "I'm having so much fun with you, too."

I love you, Ruby. I love you, I love you, I love you. The words are on the tip of my tongue. Bursting to be set free. But the plan is going too well to blow it now. So, I simply smile, kiss her again, and pull her close.

28

RUBY

"Welcome to Mentor Day!" Sunshine bellows into the camera directly in front of her, her oddly perfect veneers on full display. And, of course, the hyped-up studio audience behind the judges' table, along with all three judges and their guest mentors, applaud and cheer.

I flash a look at Laila sitting next to me that says, "I can't believe this is happening!" and she winks and beams me a huge smile in reply. This is old hat for her by now. It's her third season as a judge, and she's done all sorts of other TV appearances, too. But I'm freaking out like the newbie I am. Not to mention, I've been a fan of this show since middle school. And now I'm on it? And with three of my closest friends? It's beyond a dream come true: it's a fairytale come to life.

"After all the jockeying, negotiating, and conniving our three judges did on Draft Day," Sunshine says, "each of them has now assembled a stellar team that's ready for battle. But before the judges send them off to compete, they must coach and guide their team, with a little help from a trusted, talented advisor." Sunshine's mega-watt smile broadens. "So, let's meet the guest mentors!"

The audience cheers and applauds their effusive response.

"But before we do that," Sunshine adds, "let's watch this video package."

Laila and I exchange a snarky look. Sunshine Vaughn is a true master at drawing things out.

As the lights in the soundstage dim, I lean forward, hoping to exchange a quick look with Kendrick, but he's looking at Savage, so his head is turned—and, unfortunately, it's Cooper's gaze that meets mine. Quickly, I look at the screen, not wanting Cooper to think I've sought out his gaze, and I'm just in time to see the video begin.

We see Cooper first, his name appearing at the top of the screen as he struts around onstage, performing with his band. I peek toward Kendrick again, figuring Cooper will be too enamored with himself to be looking anywhere but the screen; and my instincts are right. Cooper's staring at the screen, while Kendrick's looking straight at me. When our eyes lock, he flashes me a look of disdain that makes me chuckle. It's like the man can read my mind.

When the audience gasps, I return to the video just in time to see Cooper being escorted out of Reed's party, followed by rapid-fire visuals of "Don't Call Me" hitting various milestones. Number one on a big chart, huge streaming numbers on the biggest platform, etc. Next, Cooper appears, smiling and winking at the camera in slow motion, dressed in the outfit he wore at the press conference, while a voice-over says, "Cooper Constantino of Alexa Play Music."

I look at Laila and we both roll our eyes and cringe. *Barf.*

Thankfully, the next image on screen is a far more pleasant one: Kendrick Cook, as he masterfully plays his drums in a packed arena. And then Kendrick looking gorgeous as he throws his head back and belly laughs at something Savage has said to him. Kendrick as he holds up one of the many awards we received after "Hate Sex High" stormed onto the scene and changed all of our lives forever. Kendrick as he strips off his shirt onstage at Reed's party and makes me scream and throw up my hands in the audience. And, finally, Kendrick wearing the clothes from the press conference, smiling in slow motion at the camera. "Kendrick Cook of Fugitive Summer," the voiceover says, and the live audience behind us goes far crazier for Kendrick's introduction than they did for Cooper's.

Laila pokes me, since I'm obviously coming up next, and I cover my eyes and peek through my fingers at the screen. To begin with, we get everything I'd expect, based on how the first two video packages went. There's footage of me playing with my band. Me acting silly with Laila. Me riding piggyback on Kendrick down a sidewalk in Europe somewhere. When was this? They must have gotten that off Fugitive Summer's social media account from years ago. Oh, jeez. In the next rapid-fire clip, I'm kissing Cooper underneath a streetlamp. Seriously? The footage is grainy and taken from a distance. Something they took off the internet, obviously, from when Cooper joined me on tour. Did I consent to them using footage of me like this?

Next up, there I am, kissing Kendrick at his birthday party in the now-viral video clip. And then mugging with Cooper into a camera in personal footage, followed by him kissing my cheek. Again, that was footage from during the tour. But Cooper definitely shot that himself on his phone, which means he must have supplied that video. Motherfucker. And finally, there I am, kissing a glistening, shirtless Kendrick in the middle of Reed's packed party, followed by Cooper being escorted out by three men dressed in black, the order of the clips making it look like those two things—me kissing Kendrick and Cooper being ushered out—happened simulta-neously.

"Such bullshit," I whisper to Laila with a scowl, since I know for a fact our mics are off.

"*Smile*," Laila whispers back through her own fake one, and I force myself to follow her lead. Laila warned me the producers would pull some kind of fuckery today, and she was right. But she also said the only thing to do is smile and not bat an eyelash, no matter what happens, and then speak up, as needed, the moment they turn on my microphone.

In conclusion, my video introduction ends the same way the other two did: I'm shown in the smoking-hot dress I wore at the press conference, beaming excitedly for the camera, blissfully unaware all prior footage would make me look like a two-timing hussy.

"Ruby Connolly of Fugitive Summer," the voiceover says. And a second later, the lights in the soundstage come back up.

"Wow, wow, wow!" Sunshine says, as the audience claps. "We've got three talented guest mentors joining us today." She side-eyes the camera. "And they bring with them a bit of drama, wouldn't you say? Oh my!" She giggles and flings her arm toward Cooper. "It's Cooper Constantino, everyone!"

The audience roars, and Cooper waves and makes prayer hands, pretending to be humble.

Banter ensues between Cooper and the host, during which I dare to peek at Kendrick again. When his eyes meet mine, he shoots me a look that says, "Don't even sweat it." And that's all I need—that tiny bit of support from Kendrick—to let that stupid video package roll off my back.

After laughing at something Cooper said, Sunshine says, "A little birdy told me you'll be performing your number one hit, 'Don't Call Me,' during the finale. Yes?"

"Yep. We can't wait."

The crowd roars its approval.

"And will you be serenading anyone in particular?" Sunshine asks. She puts up one palm vertically and points at me behind it with a comical expression on her face, while stage-whispering, "Another guest mentor, perhaps?"

The audience explodes with laughter and cheers, and Laila covertly takes my hand underneath the table and squeezes it.

"It's possible," Cooper says coyly, and the audience chuckles. But when he glances over at me, pointedly, the audience explodes, like they've been hit with a nuclear bomb.

"Fabulous. Can't wait for that." She turns to Kendrick next and smiles at the man like he's currently camped out between her legs, licking her pussy.

"Mr. Kendrick Cook," Sunshine purrs. "Welcome back to the show, you gorgeous, talented, hunk of a *shirtless* man."

The crowd erupts with catcalls, laughter, and applause. That's the culture on this show—the audience is encouraged to be boisterous and reactive. The bigger the reaction, the better.

"You've been causing quite a stir on the internet lately, sir," Sunshine continues. "What do you have to say for yourself about all that, young man?"

"I have no idea what you're talking about, Sunshine."

Again, the audience loses their shit. And just this fast, it's clear Kendrick's won the battle for the audience's heart over Cooper. Cooper might have the number-one song in the world right now—the pop-culture phenomenon everyone is talking about. But it's Kendrick Cook they'd rather sleep with, given the chance. Kendrick Cook they'd pick to be their boyfriend, over Cooper, the same way I supposedly did, based on that video package.

And you know what? I can't blame them for falling head over heels in love with him. Especially in this moment, with Cooper sitting a few seats down from Kendrick, the impulse to compare and contrast is a deeply human one—and there's truly no contest. Even when he's smiling and trying to be charming, Cooper's underbelly is coated with anger and caustic energy, while everything about Kendrick feels warm and authentic. Confident, safe, and strong. Kendrick is a warm, crackling fireplace on a snowy day, while Cooper is the hipster, edgy T-shirt with holes in it you stupidly wore outside during a blizzard because you thought the slogan on it was cool.

As she did with the first two judge-mentor pairings, Sunshine engages Savage and Kendrick in some light banter about their team's chances, and how they plan to guide them to victory. And through the exchange, both men radiate so much swagger and confidence, I'm equal parts impressed and scared by them. Truly, two mortal men shouldn't have *that* much charm. God only knows what they could do with it if they decided to use it for evil.

"Thank you, guys," Sunshine says to Savage and Kendrick, signaling she's now moving on to Laila and me. But Kendrick has another idea.

"Hey, Sunshine," he says. "Real quick. I just want to say that video package of Ruby was misleading. She never dated me during her brief, so-called relationship with Cooper. The video made it look like that, but that's not the way it happened at all. Not even close. Just thought I'd mention that, in case anyone got the wrong impression."

Laila looks down to hide her smile, but I can't hide mine. True, his comment confirmed I had a relationship with Cooper, which means I've got to be Ruby Tuesday. But at this point, that cat's completely out of the bag. No turning back. And since that's the situation now, then I'm elated Kendrick came to my defense.

"Good to know," Sunshine says brightly. But that's all she's willing to say before turning to me with a wide, sparkling smile. "Hello, Ruby! *Ruby Tuesday*?" She giggles. "We're thrilled to have you here, either way. Sorry if it's uncomfortable to be here with your ex and your boyfriend. I mean, if rumors about a certain song are to believe, it seems there's some bad blood between the three of you."

"There's no bad blood on my end," I say evenly. "And not on Kendrick's, either, I don't think."

"None here," Kendrick confirms, and the audience applauds and nods and makes it clear they think he's the better man.

I flash Kendrick a huge smile. "I think things turned out for the best. I'm nothing but happy."

"Good for you. How wonderful."

I let my eyes drift to Cooper. "You know what they say is the opposite of love? It's not hate. It's indifference. And that's what I feel about a certain very brief relationship I had once. Honestly, it's like it never even happened."

The place explodes with a cacophony of human sounds, including discernible laughter, hissing, boos, and cheers. Based on the ruckus, at least some of the audience is rooting for Cooper. Or at least, they feel sorry for his poor, jilted heart. Would they pick Kendrick, too? Hell yes. But that doesn't mean they don't want Cooper to find love, too. Also, based on that smattering of boos, at least some of them are enthusiastically villainizing me for breaking poor Cooper's heart.

Sunshine engages Laila and me in a discussion about our strategy with our team. And when that short conversation ends, we launch into some planned smack-talk with the other teams.

"Get ready to go down, *Adrian*," Laila calls out, much to everyone's delight.

"Fitzy," Savage deadpans in reply. "We're at work. We've got a job to do. Now's not the time to bark sexual orders at me, babe."

The audience roars at that, like they always do when their two favorite judges, Mr. and Mrs. Adrian Savage, grace them with one of their patented viral moments. Honestly, I'm laughing as hard as the audience. Savage and Laila make more money in one season of this show than I'll ever see in my lifetime. But they earn every penny, thanks to moments like that.

After a bit, just as the smack-talking segment feels like it's ending, Sunshine presses her finger into her ear, like she's being told something in her earpiece. "Ruby, before I let everyone go to start working with their teams, can you tell us something about the brand-new song your band, Fugitive Summer, will debut for us during the finale?"

Shit. We haven't written the song yet, so I don't know the answer to the question. Even if I did, however, I wouldn't answer it. Also, why is she asking *me* this question, when she's got the lead singer of Fugitive Summer sitting right in front of her?

"Sorry, Sunshine," I say brightly. "That's top secret. You'll have to wait and watch the performance in the finale, along with everyone else. The only thing I can tell you now is it's a brand-new song we wrote very recently, and we're performing right after Cooper and his band, so you won't want to miss it."

"Ooooh," Sunshine coos. "How exciting! And what interesting timing. I can't wait to see that." She returns to the camera in front of her. "And now, let's watch each judge–mentor duo meeting with their teams!"

"Cut!" the director yells after Sunshine has been frozen in place for several beats. "Nice work, everyone," he calls out. "Let's shoot Savage and Kendrick meeting their team first. After that, we'll take Jon and Cooper, and then Laila and Ruby." He waves to the audience. "Thank you, everyone. You're the best." He makes prayer hands and bows. "We couldn't do this without you. We love you. Now, please, listen to security's instructions as you're escorted out of the building."

29
RUBY

"I'm sorry they did that to you," Laila says. "They're such assholes."

We're in her huge dressing room, munching on box lunches while awaiting our turn to shoot the "meeting with our team" segment.

"It's fine. I knew I made a deal with the devil to get onto the show."

"Kendrick sticking up for you was swoony."

I blush. "Yeah, that was really sweet."

"Better for him to do it than you. It played better that way."

"If I'd tried to do it, they would have made me out to be a whining, complaining little bitch, and nobody would have believed me, anyway."

"Probably true." She munches on a carrot stick. "You're really okay?"

I pause to consider. "I'm better than okay, actually. I'm great. This is a dream come true, and I'm not going to let anything or anyone ruin that."

"Hear, hear." She clinks her sparkling water to mine. And

then, with a smirk, she says, "Seems like the audience is swooning hard for Kendrick. If the show is trying to pit Kendrick against Cooper, it's pretty clear who's winning that battle."

"Can you blame them? It's no contest."

Laila takes a bite of her sandwich. "You two seem closer than ever. You've had fun staying at his place, huh?"

I stare at her with narrowed eyes. I had a feeling the other day that Kendrick had told Savage about our fling, but then I got too distracted by a dildo in my ass and a dick in my vag to remember to ask about it. Well, based on the way Laila keeps trying to steer this conversation to Kendrick, I'm thinking my hunch was right: Kendrick told his best friend everything, and his best friend then turned around and told his wife.

"What did Savage tell you?" I ask.

"About what?"

"*Laila.*"

"Savage didn't tell me anything." She smiles broadly. "But you just did."

"Laila, come on."

"Okay, okay, yes, I know about you and Kendrick having a little fun while you're staying there. But don't blame Savage. I never believed that kiss at Reed's party was for the hidden cameras. I know what I saw. And so does everyone else who witnessed it. You can't fake passion like that."

My face flushes with heat, and Laila giggles.

"So, things are going well? The sex is good?"

"Good doesn't come close to covering it. It's been magical. Supernatural. *Transformative.*"

"Oh my gosh! Are you in love? Are you official?"

I exhale. "Slow down, sister. It's not like that. It's just a fling—a friends-with-benefits fling that will expire when I move back into my place."

Laila looks at me like I've got a horn growing out of my

forehead. "How is that possible? I mean, *still*? I get it to start with, but if it's going as well as you said . . ."

"We both wanted it this way. It's for the best. The only way we both felt comfortable to do this at all—"

"But *why*? Why have a fling when you two already love each other as friends?"

"That's what I'm trying to explain to you. We both realized we were curious about our physical chemistry, but not enough to let lust mess up the love we already feel for each other." Laila's silent for so long, I can't help asking, "What? Why are you reacting like this?"

Laila slowly chews on her sandwich. "No reason."

"Don't give me that. Spill, Laila."

"There's nothing to spill."

"You know something."

"I don't know anything."

"Then why do you look like you're physically biting your tongue?"

"Because I have eyeballs. Because I can plainly see what's right in front of me, unlike you. Because it's obvious to me you two aren't acting like you're in love for a show."

I'm gobsmacked by Laila's implication. But finally, I'm able to choke out, "You think Kendrick is in love with me for real?"

"You don't?"

"No. Of course, not. He . . . he's . . . he *loves* me, yes. Deeply. But he's not *in love* with me."

Laila's not buying it. It's written all over her face. "What about you? You love him deeply, but you're not in love with him?"

My chest is tight. My cheeks are burning. "That's right."

Laila leans back in her chair. "Do you like him, Ruby?"

I scoff. "You know I do. I adore him. He's my favorite person."

"Do you trust him?"

Why is she asking me these questions, when she already knows my answers? "Yes, of course, I do. Completely."

Laila's eyeballs dart right and then left, like she's exchanging looks of incredulity with non-existent people on either side of her. "Okay, so, to summarize. You love him, you like him, you trust him—*and* you feel 'supernatural, transformative' lust for him. Do I have all that right?"

I press my lips together, feeling exposed and vulnerable. When she puts it all together like that, it seems pretty easy to see I've fallen for Kendrick. Romantically. I haven't wanted to admit that to myself, but with Laila spelling things out for me, I'm suddenly finding my feelings impossible to deny.

Laila breaks the silence first. "Ruby, put all of that together, and what you've got is what the most passionate love songs are written about. Peak romantic love, not a best-friends-with-benefits fling."

I can barely breathe. "Kendrick only wants a fling, Laila. He's made that clear, and I promised that's all it'd be. I promised."

Laila looks skeptical. "Maybe his feelings have changed somewhere along the way. The same as yours."

Well, there it is. I can't deny it any longer. Shit. I've caught feelings. I'm in love with Kendrick.

"I can't mess up our friendship," I squeak out. "Laila, Kendrick's my person. My rock. I can't survive without him in my life."

"If he feels the same way, which seems pretty obvious to me, you won't have to."

My breathing catches. "You think Kendrick's caught feelings for me?"

"You honestly don't?"

"No."

Laila scoffs. "Are you blind, girl?"

"He hasn't, Laila. Trust me."

She rolls her eyes. "Just, please, tell him how you feel, Ruby. Will you do that for me? Please?"

"But what if I confess my feelings and wind up losing my best friend forever? I can't let that happen."

"What are the odds of that, though?"

"Really high! For twelve years, Kendrick wasn't interested in me, sexually. Which makes sense because I'm not his type at all. You've seen the women he dates. They all look like you. Perfect and glamorous. Also, he's the one who first insisted on a fling. He set his boundaries, and I agreed to them, so it's not like I can turn around and—"

"Listen to me, honey," Laila says. "Everything you've described about your feelings for Kendrick—love, trust, friendship, and addictive lust—is exactly what I feel for Adrian to a T. My *husband*. You've described a rare and beautiful thing here—a once-in-a-lifetime thing that's worth fighting for. Which means you have to be bold and brave and take a risk to keep it going."

My heart is racing. "I can't say it first. There's way too much at stake."

Laila palms her forehead. But before she says another word, there's a rap on the door, and Cooper of all people pops his head into the room.

"Hey, ladies," he says. "Delivery for Ruby." He holds up two box lunches. "It's a peace offering. I thought maybe we could have lunch together and talk."

I point to the lunch I'm already halfway through eating.

"Oh." He steps into the room, anyway. "Can we talk for a minute?"

"Aren't you supposed to shoot next?"

"Yeah. This won't take long."

Laila looks at me, and when I nod, she rises and murmurs, "I'll go watch Savage and Kendrick with their team."

When Laila is gone, Cooper places the lunches on a table and assumes her vacated seat.

"Hey," he says nervously.

I stare at him, letting him know I'm not interested in small talk.

"I just need to know if you slept with him while dating me," he says, his chest rising and falling sharply. "Please, Ruby. Tell me the truth."

"Why do you need to know that?"

"Because I can't sleep at night, wondering if you ever loved me. Wondering if all those sex dreams you had about him were—"

"I didn't have sex dreams about Kendrick."

"I know what I heard."

"You weren't in my head, though."

Cooper runs a hand through his hair. "How long have you wanted him? Did you only get with me to make him jealous? Was anything between us ever real?"

I exhale. "I told you I didn't want anything too serious, remember? I told you that, right up front, and you said that was great. All you wanted, too. And then you turned into an obsessive, possessive jerk on me."

"Because I was in love with you," he whisper-shouts. "Because I would have said anything to get with you. Don't you get it? I was in love with you, Ruby, heart and soul. But as I quickly found out, you were in love with someone else."

"I wasn't in love with Kendrick. You created that narrative in your head. He was my best friend. Like a brother to me."

"Apparently not, given that you're fucking him now."

He's got a point there. "Why are we doing this? Why does it matter? I never cheated on you, okay? I promise, when I said Kendrick was like a brother to me, it was true at the time. The God's truth. Yes, things changed after I said it, but that was the truth then."

Cooper scoffs. "That's not possible, Ruby."

I cross my arms over my chest. "I don't owe you any expla-nations, Cooper. I didn't do anything wrong during our rela-tionship. And I'm not doing anything wrong now. Your jealousy is making you paranoid."

Cooper takes a deep breath. "Did you ever want me? Just tell me that."

I think about that. "As a friend, I felt close to you. But once we started dating, no, I never wanted you. Not like you wanted me. I should have realized the relationship was too one-sided —doomed—much sooner than I did and cut things off. I'm sorry I hurt you."

Cooper smiles ruefully. "Hey, at least I got a hit song out of it."

I can't help smiling. "You sure did."

"Are you still pissed about the song? Word on the street is you want to string me up by my balls for it."

Before I reply, a crew member pops his head into the door. And when he sees Cooper and me in the room together, he palms his forehead. "*Fuck*. Don't let Nadine know you had this conversation, whatever it was, or she'll kill me. She told me to keep you two apart, no matter what, unless cameras were rolling."

"We won't say a word to anyone," I reply.

"Please, or I'll lose my job."

"Mum's the word," Cooper says.

"Thanks. I came here looking for you on the off-chance, Cooper, only because I've already looked everywhere else. It's time for you and Jon to meet with his team."

"I'll be right there."

"No, you need to come with me now."

Cooper doesn't move. Instead, he returns his gaze to me. "Are you still pissed?"

"Don't talk to her!" the guy says. "Come here right now!"

Even though I've got a free pass to leave Cooper hanging in suspense thanks to this PA, I can't help replying honestly. Suddenly, I realize I don't care about Cooper anymore. Or his song. Or the past. I'm only excited about the future. About my feelings for Kendrick. And nothing Cooper could possibly say or do to me, or sing about me, matters anymore.

"I'm not mad," I say, as he walks toward the door of the dressing room. "Annoyed? Yes. But I'm happy for your success and ready to move on."

Cooper pauses at the door, exhaling with relief, while the PA loses his shit that we're having this conversation off-camera. "Thanks, Ruby. I appreciate that."

"Come on, Cooper," the PA says. "Please. If you don't stop talking and come with me right now, I'm going to hit you over the head with this Coke can and drag you away."

Cooper laughs. "Okay, okay." He turns to me again, his expression earnest. "I really loved you, Ruby Tuesday. But you know what? If forced to choose, I'd honestly much rather have a hit song than you as my girlfriend, anyway."

30
KENDRICK

"How many cards, KC?" C-Bomb asks, his green eyes trained on me.

It's poker night at C-Bomb's massive beach house in Santa Monica. In addition to C-Bomb himself, the players seated at a round table in his game room are Kai and Savage, Fish and Colin from 22 Goats, and me. Behind us, there's a bar stocked with every imaginable kind of booze; half the table is smoking cigars; and the rest are smoking joints and blunts. In other words, it's a typical C-Bomb poker party.

"Three," I reply, throwing down my discards, and C-Bomb slides over some replacements with one of his tattooed, insanely talented hands.

C-Bomb's sandy hair is shaved close today, and he's wearing his beard long. He's shirtless for this poker game, which means his muscles are on full display, along with the ink that covers every inch of him, literally, other than his face. To top off his legendary-rockstar vibe, he's got a blunt hanging out of his mouth and a bottle of Jack sitting next to him on the green card table.

I've known C-Bomb for years now, and he's always been a

friend and mentor to me and our whole band. But even so, it's hard not to stare at him in awe, even now, as he sits across from me. The dude's a legend. The guy we all want to be. Minus his anger management issues, anyway. Also, if you ask Ruby, his substance abuse and addiction issues. Ruby's been vocal she thinks C-Bomb needs rehab, badly, more than anyone we know. But C-Bomb always scoffs at the idea, and he seems to be doing pretty well in life, so we leave him be. But, yeah, other than those things, the man's pretty much life goals. A towering figure to all of us at this table—a beacon of what's possible to achieve as a musician in this world.

"How many cards for you, Fish Taco?" C-Bomb asks the bass player of 22 Goats.

"Zero," Fish says with confidence.

"You sure about that, kiddo?"

"I'm sure."

C-Bomb arches an eyebrow and inhales from the blunt hanging out of his mouth. "Very interesting, Fish Taco. Can't wait to see how that pans out for ya, kid." He addresses Colin Beretta, Fish's drummer, next. "Colinoscopy? How many cards, my friend?" Those two have become particularly close lately, I've noticed, ever since Colin married C-Bomb's favorite former PA, Amy.

"Three for me," Colin replies, laying down his discards.

All discards handled, it's finally time to play the game. Betting starts, and our usual, light chatter begins.

"Why couldn't Titus make it tonight?" C-Bomb asks, after inhaling from his blunt.

"He's meeting his girlfriend's parents tonight," Kai replies.

"Sounds serious," C-Bomb mutters. "Is she cool?"

"We don't know," Kai says. "They met right before we left on tour, and she only came to visit him once. After that, they were long-distance the whole time."

"He likes her a lot, though," I interject. "He didn't seem

even tempted to break things off during the tour, even though she could only come visit him that one time."

"What about you, KC?" C-Bomb asks. "Are you dating anyone these days?"

I shake my head. "Other than my fake relationship with Ruby for the show, I'm single as ever." With Kai sitting here, and with me knowing C-Bomb's little sister is Miranda, a close friend of Ruby's, I've got no choice but to stick to the story.

"In that case, ask my sister out, would you?" C-Bomb says, as he throws some chips into the pot. "Miranda's newly single again, and I don't want her getting with another douchebag."

Kai interjects, "I'll ask her out."

"Fuck no, you won't."

Everyone cracks up at C-Bomb's clapback, even Kai.

C-Bomb adds, "I just said I don't want my sister dating another *douchebag*, remember?" As we all laugh again, C-Bomb returns to me. "Seriously, though, are you interested in her, KC? Miranda's always liked you. And if I could handpick one guy to make an honest woman out of my wild sister, it'd be you."

"Sorry, C-Bomb," Savage interjects. "KC can't date *your* sister, when he's madly in love with Titus's."

I glare at Savage with wide eyes that scream, "What the fuck, man?" But it's a pointless exercise. He's visibly drunk and stoned off his ass. Which means his filter is now gone, baby, gone.

"So, all that kissing you've been doing with Ruby on the internet has been real," C-Bomb says with a chuckle. "I figured as much, but Miranda swore it was all an act to piss off Cooper or whatever."

"It's not necessarily *real*, but it's not fake, either," Savage says incoherently. "He's madly in love, but Ruby thinks they're only having a fling."

"Wait, *what*?" Kai blurts.

"Savage. Please, shut the fuck up now."

"Ooooh, this is getting interesting," C-Bomb says. "You're flinging with your bestie, while secretly wanting more? Nice."

"Oldest trick in the book," Savage says. He raises his index finger. "But also, highly effective."

"Kendrick, what the fuck?" Kai says. "You want Ruby *for real*? Since when?"

I run a hand through my hair. "Guys, listen to me, this conversation can't leave this room, okay? Please. I'm begging you."

"Calm down," C-Bomb says with a laugh. "Savage didn't tell us anything we didn't already know. We all know you've been love with that keyboardist of yours for years now."

"I didn't know that," Kai insists.

"How is that even possible?" C-Bomb says to Kai. "He's not subtle. The kid wears his heart on his sleeve."

"How long have you been feeling this way, KC?" Kai asks, looking legitimately shocked.

"Fuck." I'm panicked. Reeling. C-Bomb's sister, Miranda, is close friends with Ruby, and everyone sitting at this table is also good friends with Titus. Oh, god. Fish's and Colin's wives are friendly with Ruby, too! And both of those women are close friends with Violet, who's one of Laila's closest friends. Fuck me. With all those connections, Savage's drunken slip of the tongue will definitely get back to Ruby, one way or another, and ruin everything for me, if I don't lock this shit down right fucking now.

"Guys, listen to me," I blurt in a panic. "This conversation seriously can't leave this room. Please. My life's happiness depends on it. This is life or death for me."

Everyone promises, looking like they're waiting with bated breath for whatever I'm going to say next. Kai, especially, looks like he's on tenterhooks.

"You can't tell anyone," I repeat. I look at C-Bomb. "Not

even your sister." I look at the other guys. "Not even your wives."

Everyone assures me they won't say a word to anyone, not even the women closest to them; and slowly but surely, I start to genuinely believe them and calm down.

"Tell me what's going on," Kai says. "How long has this been going on?"

"For me? Since day one. For Ruby, only recently. But like Savage said, Ruby thinks we're only flinging for the fun of it—and with a firm expiration date."

Kai looks flabbergasted. "So . . . When you asked her to audition for the band . . .?"

"You were right. I wanted her."

Kai's jaw drops. But apparently, he's too floored to form words.

"To be honest," Fish says, breaking the thick silence between my brother and me. "I've often wondered why you and Ruby even bothered dating other people. Your chemistry has always been so damned obvious."

I do my best to explain the history of our close friendship.

"That's why I told him, he's got to be a Doberman now," Savage says.

"Kendrick, fuck that," Fish says. "Fuck being a Doberman. You're a golden retriever, man. Through and through. Just tell her how you feel."

"I don't know, Fish," Colin says. "Amy had some diabolical tricks up her sleeve at the very beginning. You know, when I had my head up my ass. And it was only thanks to her scheming that I was able to figure out how I was feeling about her. I needed a wake-up call, you know? And I needed time. And that's what I got."

"That's exactly what Ruby needs," Savage says confidently. "A wake-up call and some time. And Kendrick's providing both." He snickers. "One bribe of her building manager at a time."

"Savage! What the fuck, man?"

Not surprisingly, everyone jumps in to ask what Savage means, at which point he gleefully tells the story of how I've bribed Ruby's building manager, *twice,* in order to keep her at my house long enough to allow our forced proximity to work its magic.

"All's fair in love and war," C-Bomb grumbles.

"That's exactly what I told him," Savage says proudly. "Sometimes, the ends justify the means."

I look at C-Bomb and Savage and suddenly realize neither man is a paragon of emotional maturity. If they both think what I'm doing is A-okay, maybe that's a surefire sign . . . it's *not*?

"Are we sure about this, guys?" Fish asks, giving voice to what I'm thinking myself.

"Well, whether what he's been doing is right or wrong," Savage says, "there's no turning back now. He's in it to win it, baby, so he might as well keep going now, till she's madly in love with him." He smiles at me. "Or she hates your guts forever for lying to her."

"*What*?" I shout. "You never said she could wind up hating me!"

"Well, I mean, it's common sense. Nobody likes to be lied to."

I thwap Savage's head, and he laughs.

"I was joking," he says, rubbing his head. "Ruby could never hate you. She thinks you walk on water."

"She could absolutely hate me, Savage. Shit. What have I done?" I lean back in my chair and rub my forehead. "I should go home and come clean to her."

"Absolutely," Fish agrees, while the rest of the table speaks over him to disagree. To say the time for that is not yet upon me. To stay the course.

"It's not like I can keep her at my place indefinitely," I say. "At some point, I'm going to have to let her leave and accept her feelings for me, whatever they are."

"Okay, but is that moment *now*?" Savage asks. "You're so close, KC. Even Laila thinks so."

"You told Laila?"

"Yeah."

"Savage."

"She's my *wife*. You knew I would. I told you that."

He's right. He did. But I can't resist teasing him about it, anyway. "You keep telling me to be a Doberman, but you've turned into as big a golden retriever as me."

"Yeah, because she's my wife now. Being a Doberman only applies when you're trying to get the girl. Once she's your wife, all bets are off and you have to be completely honest with her, always."

The entire table exchanges amused looks about how desperately in love our former fuckboy rockstar has become. Truly, Adrian Savage is one of the biggest rags-to-riches success stories in the whole world, but not for the reasons the whole world thinks. Yes, his ascendance to worldwide fame and fortune has been one for the history books, for all the obvious reasons, but even more impressive than his acquisition of money and fame, at least for me, is the way he's transformed as a person, thanks to the newfound safety, love, and connection he has with Laila.

"I swear on my life, Laila hasn't said a word to Ruby," Savage assures me. "She promised she'd keep your secret, and her word is gold, unlike mine. Actually, Laila thinks your diabolical plan is pure genius. She's fully supportive."

I feel emboldened by that. "Really?"

Savage nods. "She wants you and Ruby to get together

even more than I do, and she thinks Ruby's too clueless to get there otherwise." He snickers. "But then again, Laila is diabolical herself, so take her support with a grain of salt. Her moral compass is a little wonky."

We all laugh, along with Savage.

"Wow, if you've wanted Ruby from day one, then I really fucked you over badly, didn't I?" Kai says, leaning back in his chair. "You know, when you came home from school, and I told you that lie about what happened at Ruby's birthday party?"

I exhale. "That information definitely set me down a certain path."

Kai looks genuinely apologetic. "I'm so sorry, man."

"It's okay. Ruby didn't want me back then, anyway."

"I swear, I had no idea."

"I know. It's okay. I'm choosing to believe everything happens for a reason."

C-Bomb slides some chips into the pot. "How long do you and Ruby have to pretend to be a couple?"

I peel my gaze off my apologetic brother. "Uh, we're mostly done with that. We shot the Mentor Day episode yesterday, which was the main event for our fake relationship, but we'll need to pretend again when we shoot the finale in five weeks."

"Okay, so that's your new timeline," C-Bomb says. "Keep the fling going till then."

"For five more *weeks*?" I bellow incredulously.

Colin nods his agreement with C-Bomb. "And after that, right after the finale, do some grand gesture for her, spill your guts, and pray to God you've done enough to get her to reply with, 'I love you, too, Kendrick.'"

I scoff. "The most I could possibly pull off without having a mental breakdown is one more week. Two, tops."

C-Bomb swigs from his bottle of Jack. "You'd be surprised

what rabbits a man with no other options can pull out of his hat."

I glare at C-Bomb. I love the guy, but he's the last guy I'd turn to for romantic advice.

"He's got another option, Caleb," Fish replies to C-Bomb. "It's called *honesty*."

I lay down my cards, too wound up to concentrate on the card game any longer. "Look," I say, "there's no way Ruby would believe her place is still under repairs for that long, anyway. She's already getting suspicious about the delays."

Colin shoots me a snarky look. "I dunno, man. Flooding can cause mold. Lots and lots of mold."

"And mold notoriously takes a really long time to fix," C-Bomb offers. "It happened at my grandpa's cabin when I was kid. That shit took forever to get rid of." He winks at me. "I'm guessing she's already caught feelings for you, though. So, don't pay the building manager for five weeks up front, my brother."

Savage interjects, "Honestly, I don't see how Ruby could last another week, let alone five, without professing her undying love for this guy." He claps my shoulder. "Look at him. He's in the top three hottest guys at this table."

Everyone cracks up, including me.

"I appreciate you being my hype man, Savage," I say. "But let's get real here. I'm in the top *five*, at most."

"Now, that's plain mean," Fish says with a mock scowl, and everyone laughs at the implication. There's only six men sitting here, so he's clearly volunteering himself as the sixth guy who didn't make the cut.

"Fish, I didn't put you at six," I say.

"Who then?" he asks, motioning to the table.

"Savage, of course. Look at him. *Yeesh*."

We all bust up. Adrian Savage, more than anyone in the world, looks like he was created by AI.

With a sigh, I lean my forearm onto the card table. "Guys, I'm seriously not ready to spill my guts to Ruby yet. Soon. But not yet."

C-Bomb shrugs. "Sounds like you need to do something to keep the window of opportunity open for yourself, then."

I ponder that for a moment. "Ruby's place will be ready in two days. I mean, as far as she knows. It's been ready for a while now. So, maybe I'll try to get myself a couple more days after that?"

"Buy yourself another week," C-Bomb replies confidently. "I'd bet anything that's all it'll take."

"This is madness," Fish grumbles. "No disrespect, Caleb, but Kendrick isn't you. And he isn't Savage. He doesn't play games, like you two. Nor should he. Not with someone he loves and respects." Fish directs his earnest green gaze on me. "Go home and tell Ruby the whole truth, KC. Speak from your heart. Tell her you love her deeply, madly, and forever. Also, that you bribed her—"

"Are you insane?" Savage blurts, as Colin and C-Bomb shout something similar. "It's the waning minutes of the fourth quarter, Fish Taco! KC can't stop being a Doberman now. Not when he's almost got victory in the bag."

"I haven't been much of a Doberman lately," I admit. I look at my big brother, nonverbally seeking his direction. My whole life, I've come to Kai, more than anyone else, to get all the most important life advice. Certainly not Mr. Mercurial-and-Emotionally-Stunted Adrian Savage, though I've always loved him dearly. On the contrary, it's Savage who's always come to me for support and advice, not the other way around. So, this current state of affairs is pretty fucking bizarre and backwards.

"You need more time," Kai declares confidently. "Close the deal, KC. Get the girl."

Savage nods enthusiastically. "The plan is working, man.

Stay the course for one more week, and you'll have a future wife at the end of it. I guarantee it."

Wife. He's said the magic word. The one that flips a switch inside me and cuts off all uncertainty and equivocation.

I want to make Ruby my wife.

That much I know.

And now, suddenly, like a switch getting flipped inside me, mostly thanks to Kai's confidence about the matter, I'm now bound and determined to forge ahead and get what I want, through any means necessary.

31
RUBY

"I'm so excited you're doing this," Laila gushes into my earbuds.

I'm on the phone with her, while I frantically move around Kendrick's kitchen, trying to follow Martha Stewart's insane recipe for chicken fettuccine with pesto cream sauce. To put it mildly, I'm way, way out of my depth here.

I thought the recipe looked simple when I first read it, even for a woefully inept chef like me. That's what the top reviewer said, after all: "Simple and good." So, I figured the recipe would be right up my alley. But no. Now that I'm in the thick of it, it's clear Martha Stewart is a maniac. The woman wants me to *toast* the pine nuts for the pesto cream sauce before mixing up the ingredients? *What?* At this point, this supposedly "simple" recipe feels like I'm trying to perform Beethoven's "Hammerklavier Sonata" at my fourth-grade piano recital.

"I wouldn't get too excited," I say as I spread my measured pine nuts onto a sheet pan. "It remains to be seen if this will even be remotely edible."

"The meal itself isn't the point of this grand gesture," Laila says. "The point is that you tried. That you wanted to cook him something wonderful and homemade, because you love him. Also, that you specifically picked something you knew he'd love to eat, and you went shopping for all the ingredients yourself. That's a lot of time and effort, Ruby. That's the point." Laila makes an excited squeal. "He's going to be so surprised—and so touched."

"Yeah, well, I'm not sure if this romantic grand gesture will have quite the effect I'm going for if the chicken is rubbery, the pasta is over- or under-cooked, and the basil cream sauce tastes funny because I screwed up toasting the freaking pine nuts."

Laila snorts with laughter. "Honey, he'll love it, no matter what. I promise, he's going to swoon and spill his guts to you after one bite. No. Even before then. When he sees the candlelit table and smells the food cooking."

"If you're right about that, then let's hope his guts are filled with nothing but 'I love you, Ruby,' and not 'Sorry, Ruby, I meant it when I said I can only offer you a fling.' Or else, I'm fucked."

Laila scoffs. "Oh, Ruby. Of course he loves you."

"Tracy fell in love with him, too. Remember? And she was stupid enough to tell him so when they got back home and look what happened to her."

"You're not Tracy, Ruby. And more importantly, Tracy isn't *you*. Not even close."

I open the oven to slide the sheet pan in. "He doesn't even need to say he loves me, honestly. I'd be happy if he says he wants to continue the relationship, as it is, after I leave his place." That's the point of this grand gesture, after all: setting the stage for Kendrick to realize I've caught feelings for him, without me needing to say that out loud. Hopefully, this romantic, candlelit, homemade dinner, two nights before my scheduled departure from his place, will inspire him to at least admit he wants that—to continue our fling. Even better, if he says he's fallen in love with me.

Unfortunately, I can't say what I'm feeling first. Not when I promised Kendrick I wouldn't turn into Tracy on him. So now, I'm determined to coerce him into saying whatever he might be feeling, without him realizing I've cleverly lured him, the horse, to water and, hopefully, dunked his head into the trough and forcefully made him drink.

I press a button for the oven timer and report to Laila, "Okay, the timer's set for the pine nuts. Now what?"

"Set water to boil for the pasta."

"It's already going."

"Perfect."

"I guess it's time to cook the chicken breasts, huh?"

"Did you pound them already?"

"Almost as hard as Kendrick pounds me."

We both snicker.

Thank goodness for our conversation yesterday in her dressing room. When she told me what I'd described about my feelings for Kendrick were the same as hers for Savage—her husband, her life partner, her ride or die—a lightbulb went off in my head. I consider Savage and Laila couple goals, so when I suddenly realized what they have is what I feel with Kendrick, I felt something crack wide open inside me. And then, when Cooper came in and we had that conversation that ended in me realizing I didn't care about the past anymore, only my future—with Kendrick—that was it. I realized in that moment, without a doubt, I'm desperately in love with Kendrick Cook. Nobody and nothing else matters to me. I love him, and I have to make him love me back. Through any means necessary.

And so, after Laila and I were done shooting our scenes with her team, I pulled her aside and poured my heart out to her without holding back. At which point, Laila helped me concoct the plan for me to cook Kendrick a romantic meal while he's at C-Bomb's for a poker party and make him spill his guts to me first.

"Oh! Savage just texted he's leaving poker night," Laila reports. "Did Kendrick text you, too?"

I check my phone. "Fuck. Yes. So soon? He told me he'd be home around nine." I glance at the clock on the oven. *8:35.* And since it takes at least a half-hour to get from C-Bomb's house to here, depending on traffic, he's right on time.

Before I have a chance to say another word to Laila, another text arrives from Kendrick:

> KC: I'll pick up food for us on my way home, cutie. Tacos sound good?

I scream.

"What?" Laila gasps out. "Did you cut your finger off? Burn yourself?"

"Kendrick texted he's picking up tacos on his way home."

"Jesus, Ruby. I thought you'd maimed yourself."

"Sorry. No, I've still got all my fingers and toes, and I've somehow managed to get my chicken pieces into a hot skillet without incident."

"Never scream like that again. At least, not while you're cooking. You gave me a heart attack."

"Hang on. I need to text him back."

> Me: No need to stop for food, hot stuff. I went to the store and got some awesome sandwich fixings. I'll make us Ruby Deluxes!

KC: HUZZAH! You're a goddess! See you
soon, baby!

I gasp at the ending to Kendrick's text, but somehow, I gather myself enough to tap out a calm, normal reply.

Me: Can't wait.

To Laila, I gasp out, "Kendrick just called me baby. He's never done that before."

Laila squeals. "Did you call him baby back?"

"No! I freaked out. Fuck!"

"Text him something else and call him baby right freaking now, Ruby. Hurry."

"Hang on."

Me: Turkey or roast beef, baby?

KC: Roast beef, baby!

Me: You've got it, baby!

KC: You're a gem, baby.

"Gah! We double-triple babied each other!"

"It's in the bag, Ruby. He loves you."

"Let's not get ahead of ourselves. He might not be feeling what I am. That could have been a bit for him. A joke."

"*Ruby.*"

"Laila, I have to brace myself for heartbreak here."

She scoffs. "You're not going to get your heart broken. He's feeling exactly what you are."

She sounds so confident, I'm suddenly deeply suspicious —and cautiously optimistic. "Do you know that for a fact, or is that merely your opinion, based on observation?"

Laila pauses.

"*Laila.*"

"It's my opinion. I don't know anything for a fact. But it's so obvious to me, I don't know why you can't see it, too."

I exhale with disappointment. "Listen, I say this with love: keep your opinions to yourself, please. I really don't want to set myself up for—Fuck! I forgot to set a timer for the chicken! I have no idea how long it's been cooking. Sorry, *sautéing.*"

"Have you turned it over yet?"

"No."

"Do it now. It'll be fine."

I look at the clock and murmur. "This is so stressful." Breathing hard, I turn the chicken. "It's burned, Laila. Shit."

"Charred?"

"I don't think so. But way too dark."

"It's fine. That's called blackened chicken. It's a delicacy. Are you dressed up, nice and pretty for him?"

"No! Fuck! I was going to change, but then I ran out of time. I'm wearing sweats, and I don't have time to—"

"It's fine. I shouldn't have said anything. Is the table set?"

I exhale. "Yes. That's one thing I did right. All I have to do is light the candles."

"Perfect. Sounds like the meal will be ready at the right time. You've got this, Ruby Duby. Take a deep breath."

"The pine nuts! The timer is at zero, but I didn't hear a beep. When did it go off?"

"It doesn't matter. They're fine."

I open the oven and a plume of smoke greets me, but luckily, the pine nuts look dark brown but not burned. "They look okay. Catastrophe averted."

"Breathe, babe."

I pull the pine nuts out, finish up the chicken, and throw the pasta into my boiling water, and Laila talks me off the ledge the whole time.

"Okay, time to make the pesto," I murmur.

"Home stretch," Laila says. "You've got this."

I swipe into my recipe for guidance again and my heart sinks. "Shit, Laila. It says I need a 'food processor' for this next part, whatever that is. What does a food processor look like? What does it do?" I frantically scan Kendrick's granite kitchen counter. "I wouldn't even know one if it bit me in the ass. Does Kendrick even have one?"

"Probably not. But if he does, it's probably not out on the counter. My mother doesn't keep hers out. She just grabs it whenever she needs it. Check his cupboards."

"For what, though? What am I even looking for? Can you text me a photo of one?"

"You can use a blender, instead, for a job this small. You know what a blender looks like, right?"

"Yes! And I know for a fact Kendrick has one to make his protein shakes." I start frantically opening cabinets, but no dice. So, I drag a chair into the kitchen to check the highest shelves. "I found the blender!" I shout excitedly. "It's on a top shelf, way, way in the back, but I see it!"

"Yay!"

I get onto my tippy toes and reach as far back as I can. "What the heck?" I mutter. "How on earth is this the most convenient place to put something he uses all the time?"

"Men," Laila says with a scoff. "God knows how their brains work with all that testosterone telling them to do stupid shit."

I've got the barest of grasps on the blender's base with my fingertips, and I carefully drag it toward me, intending to catch it when it tips toward me off the shelf. But when that moment comes, catastrophe strikes: the base of the thing detaches and falls smack into my upturned face.

I scream loudly, waiting for searing pain to strike from whatever broken bone the fallen object has inflicted upon me. But to my surprise, the pain doesn't come, and whatever fell caused only a benign clunking sound when it hit the countertop beneath my upturned face.

I open my eyes and discover the blender is still completely intact and sitting on the edge of the shelf—and the thing that fell onto the countertop is a book. And not just any book. *It's Kendrick's journal.* At the realization, I scream again.

"What's happening?" Laila shouts. "Did you fall? Are you hurt?"

"No, I'm fine. I got hit by Kendrick's lyrics notebook!"

"Ruby!"

"Sorry, but this is like winning the lottery, babe."

Greedily, I get down from the chair and stare at the journal on the counter. Yes, I promised not to open it ever again, and I've kept that promise.

Until now.

Because, come on, now that it's fallen from the sky and hit me in the head, literally, how could Kendrick possibly blame me for flipping it open and finally reading "Spank"?

Okay, yes, that would be a betrayal of his confidence, technically. But a tiny one, all things considered. Especially now that he's spanked my ass, fucked my ass, and made me squirt all over his cock. I mean, come on, I'm only human, after all. And we've come a long, long way since he demanded that promise from me. Surely it's expired by now, right? Or at least become obsolete?

"I have to go," I choke out, my fingers twitching and my eyes trained on the forbidden book.

"You're sure you're okay?"

"I'm great. I just have to go now."

"My god, you're a screamer," Laila mutters with a laugh. "Lucky Kendrick."

I can't laugh at Laila's joke; I'm too wound up by the sight of that notebook sitting on the counter, screaming at me to pick it up right fucking now.

"Thank you for everything, Laila."

"Anything for you. Keep me posted!"

"I will."

After saying goodbye, I disconnect the call, grab the journal breathlessly, and furiously begin flipping its pages toward the back. In record speed, I find the entry for "Spank." And for a split second, I look up, feeling guilty. But after a short moment of sainthood, my baser instincts take over again, and I give myself permission to return to Kendrick's messy, urgent handwriting.

"Spank"

Lying awake
My body staging a coup
Can't have you, but
These embers are brewing

Can't have . . . *you*? I didn't see that coming. Who's you? Also, wait, *embers* are brewing?

My brain clacking and whirring, I look back up at the hastily written title. And suddenly, with sober eyes and the word "embers" in my pocket, it dawns on me Kendrick's rushed, slanted handwriting doesn't spell out *"Spank"* at the top of the page. *Holy crap.* It's now clear as a bell to me: that word spells out "Spark."

Spark.

Wait.

Does that mean Kendrick never wrote anything about spanking his monkey or spanking an ass? Apparently not, if the lyrics he wrote have to do with sparks and embers . . . and "Can't have . . . *you.*"

My heart hammering and my brain short-circuiting, I return to the top of the page and start reading again, from the beginning, this time with full knowledge that I'm reading lyrics for a song called "Spark," written by Kendrick Alan Cook during our tour—lyrics he lied about and adamantly wouldn't let me see, for some reason.

Spark

Lying awake
My body staging a coup
Can't have you, but
These embers are brewing

My favorite person
There is no comparison
A gem of a friendship
That's everything (but not nearly enough)

What's this riot, this mayhem,
Like a street fight inside me?
Spark to flame, flame to pyre
Ignited but fighting it

Baby, sparks are flying
I'm on fire for you

Why'd she bring him along?
Make me watch them write songs?
I've got homicidal tendencies
Hiding behind laughter and smiles

You want him, not me
And before that, my big brother
Now I'm suffocated, reeling
Awake, feeling smothered

What's this riot, this mayhem,
Like a street fight inside me?
Spark to flame, flame to pyre
Ignited but fighting it
Ooh, baby
Embers are flying inside me
Help me, help me,
Feels like I'm dying

Can't bare my soul to you
Too much to lose
You wouldn't choose me, anyway
You'd choose a dirtbag over me
Spark to flame
Flame to pyre
I'm dying inside
I'd set fire to my soul
To make you mine

I can't speak the truth to you

But baby, here's what I'd do:
Pull my head out the sand
Torpedo the band
Piss off my brother
Quit being a drummer
I'd burn at the stake for you
Burn the world down for you
Do whatever it takes,
Anything, everything
If only, if only, if only, if only
My gem of a best friend
Would love me, too

Trembling and wide-eyed, I look up from Kendrick's journal and clutch my heart. And a second later, my phone buzzes with a text from my building manager:

> Apologies, Ruby. Looks like we need one more week. Sorry for any inconvenience.

"Holy shit," I breathe out. Feeling like I'm in a daze, I turn off the burner on the stove just as Kendrick's front door opens and his happy voice sings out, "What smells so good, Ruby Duby? Hey, where are you, baby? I'm hungry for a Ruby Deluxe!"

32
KENDRICK

I'm practically skipping as I exit my car in my driveway and start walking the short distance to my front door. Maybe I'm reading into it, but when Ruby called me "baby" in those texts, I felt it in my soul. It felt like a sign—like confirmation she's going to be open to keeping our relationship going, even after she moves back home.

I swing open my front door, and my stomach instantly growls as the delicious scents hitting me. *Home cooking*. That's what it smells like in here. Did Ruby go the extra mile and order some amazing food in time for my arrival?

"What smells so damn good, Ruby Duby?" I bellow. And when I don't see any sign of her, I call out, "Hey, where are you, baby? I'm hungry for a Ruby Deluxe!"

Ruby emerges slowly from my kitchen, looking shell-shocked and pale.

"Hey," I say, unsettled and confused by her body language. But when I see my journal in her hand, I get it, instantly. *Fuck, fuck, fuck.*

"It was never called 'Spank,'" Ruby sputters. "It was always called 'Spark,' the whole time."

Fuck.

"I didn't go looking for it," Ruby says, holding up the journal. She comes to a stop in front of me, her face still pale and her eyes wide. "I wanted to make you a special meal. A Martha Stewart recipe. And I needed the blender for the pesto sauce."

I try to take a deep breath, but my lungs feel like they've shrunken down to half their capacity. It's the moment of truth I've been avoiding for weeks now. No, for twelve years. Should I deny "Spark" is about her, or is this the moment to confess every feeling I've ever had for her?

"Is it about me?" she squeaks quietly. She's visibly trembling.

Fragments and phrases flicker across my panicked brain.

Can't have you.

Gem of a friendship

You want him, not me; before that, my big brother.

I'd torpedo the band for you.

Burn at the stake for you.

Burn the world down for you.

And worst of all, *If only my gem of a best friend would love me, too.*

I feel dizzy. Trapped. There's no way out. My words on those pages aren't hard to interpret. Especially for Ruby, who knows every inch of me. There's no hiding from the truth now. No minimizing it. The time for total and complete honesty is now here, whether I was ready for it or not.

I exhale. "Yes."

"You wrote it while Cooper was on tour with me?"

I nod slowly.

"Before you found out Kai was full of shit?"

"In New York. Right after you texted me to come down for birthday drinks."

Her chest expands sharply. "You saw Cooper and me

writing songs together during the tour, and you wanted to murder him?"

I nod slowly, once again.

Ruby swallows hard. We're both standing stock-still and staring at each other.

"What parts, if any, aren't the truth?" she whispers. "What's true and what isn't, Kendrick?"

Welp, this is it. The point of no return. "It's all true," I confess. "Every word."

The admission hits Ruby like a ton of bricks. Indeed, she clutches her heart and grunts like I've shot her with an arrow. The only question is whether it's hitting her hard in a good way or a run-for-the-hills way.

Ruby takes a step forward. And then, another one. "How long before you wrote 'Spark' about me did you start feeling that way, Kendrick?"

As she stops in front of me, mere inches away, I pause an inordinately long amount of time. I feel like I'm teetering on the bitter edge of a chasm—one that can't be scaled again, once I take this leap. But what choice do I have? The truth is the truth. I love her. Madly. Deeply. Eternally. And I always have. Either Ruby feels the same way about me by now, or she doesn't. I guess I'm about to find out.

I exhale in resignation. "The second you sat next to me in chemistry class."

Ruby's lips part as her eyes widen.

"That was when I felt the initial spark, anyway," I clarify. "After that, it quickly grew into a raging, obsessive forest fire. That's why I invited you to audition for the band without knowing if you could play 'Chopsticks.' Because I wanted to spend time with you, outside of school, so I could try to make you feel the same forest fire as me. Or at least, the same spark."

"Oh, Kendrick." With a loud exhale, Ruby throws the journal onto the couch and hurls herself at me, at which point

I kiss her furiously, passionately, *desperately*, until both of us are gasping for air and murmuring all kinds of excited words into each other's lips.

Still kissing her, I stagger my way into the bedroom. And when I miraculously reach my bed without tripping, knocking over a lamp, or banging into a wall, I lay Ruby down, rip off her clothes and mine like they're on fire, and then race over to my nightstand to get myself covered up with record speed.

"It's okay," Ruby gasps out, stopping me midway through my task. "I'm on the pill. You don't need one, if you're okay with that."

She doesn't need to ask me twice.

I crawl onto the bed, my hard cock leading the way, and Ruby cups my cheeks in her palms when I reach her, pulling me in for a deep kiss.

"I love your words," she whispers into my lips. "They're the hottest thing I've ever read."

I slide my fingers into her hair as I kiss her. I've fantasized about this moment for as long as I can remember. And yet, somehow, it's even better than any fantasy.

I spread her legs and eat her pussy like a starving man. And soon, she's writhing and purring with an orgasm that sends pre-cum dripping down my cock like a river.

Panting, I crawl up the length of Ruby's body, desperate to feel myself inside her without anything between our bodies for the first time. With my hand on her cheek, and my lips on hers, I sink myself slowly inside her, as deep as I can go, prompting both of us to moan and shudder at the delicious sensation.

"You'd burn down the world for me?" Ruby grits out as I thrust energetically, in and out.

"I'd burn down every world for you, in every galaxy, in every lifetime."

Ruby moans as my gyrations pick up speed and intensity.

My heart feels like it's pounding at full capacity for the first time in my life, my nerve endings like they're teeming with electrical impulses foreign to me before now. I feel alive. Like my soul is a jigsaw puzzle and it's found its final, remaining piece. I feel complete.

"Call me baby," Ruby purrs, sinking her fingernails into my arm.

"*Baby*," I gasp out, before leaning down to kiss her deeply. I'm dying to say, "I love you, baby." But just in case it's too soon to say that, I kiss every inch of her face and neck, while thrusting with everything I've got, letting my body tell her what I'm not brave enough to put into words. "I'm on fire for you," I choke out. "I'd burn the world down for you. I'd do anything for you, baby. Anything at all."

With a keening moan, Ruby arches her back and comes underneath me, and I release inside her with my fingers lodged in her hair.

I love you, Ruby Connolly.

I love you, I love you, I love you.

After a moment, my body calms down, and I slide off her and kiss her cheek.

I hand her a tissue box, and as she cleans herself up, I lie on my side next to her, smiling broadly. "I was terrified you'd read those words and reject me."

Ruby laughs. "So, you let me believe they were for a song called 'Spank,' instead?"

I laugh. "You're the one who said it was called 'Spank.' Not me. I just didn't correct you."

"That's not true. You added fuel to that flame. Repeatedly."

I shrug. "The idea clearly turned you on, so I gave it a little fuel and let you run with it." I shake my head. "Much to my ever-increasing anxiety."

"I can only imagine how stressful that must have been, every time I brought it up."

"It was fun, too. Sometimes. But mostly stressful."

She laughs. "Why not just write a song called 'Spank' and give it to me? Problem solved."

"I tried. But you know me. I don't write lyrics the way you and Savage do. I don't even know how I wrote 'Spark,' in the first place. It came to me in a trance, and, unfortunately, it turned out that trance was a one-off."

Ruby giggles. "I'd love to read a song called 'Spank,' written by you."

"Yeah, no shit, Ruby. You've made that abundantly clear."

She laughs again. "Sorry."

"Trust me, anything I might have written to try to satisfy your curiosity would have been a major let-down for you. So, why show you something anti-climactic, you know?"

"Literally."

"That's the same joke I made to Savage."

She rolls her eyes. "You told Savage about all this?"

"I had to tell him. I was going crazy. Plus, I needed his advice about what to do."

"You needed *Savage's* advice?"

"That's how desperate I was."

We both laugh.

"So, that's what all those furtive looks at our songwriting session were all about, huh?"

I nod. "When that motherfucker brought up 'Spank' as a song idea, I seriously wanted to murder him."

"Savage could have written a song called 'Spank' for you in fifteen minutes."

"Yeah, he offered."

"*Ew.* I was joking, Kendrick."

"Don't worry, I told him no. I said that would be gross— like *him* seducing you into *my* bed."

She makes a gross-out face. "What's wrong with that man?"

I chuckle. "He was only trying to be helpful. I mean, you can't deny his version of 'Spank' would have been smoking hot and extremely effective."

"Who does he think he is? Cyrano de Bergerac?"

"Who's that?"

Giggling, Ruby explains it to me, and I have to admit it's a perfect reference.

"See, that's why you're so much better at lyrics than me. I'm a former football player who bangs on his drums for a living. But you know all these obscure literary references and shit."

Ruby bursts out laughing. "Babe, Cyrano De Bergerac isn't obscure. Modern movies steal from it all the time."

"See? I don't even know that. You're still the smartest person I know." Smiling, I run a fingertip across the curves of her breast and nipple. "I have a confession to make. The first week you were staying here, I took off my shirt a thousand times more than I ever would have if I'd been alone in a pathetic ploy to get you to notice me and think of me in a sexual way. I don't really work out shirtless."

Ruby screams with laughter. "You wanted me to notice you?"

"Desperately."

"Kendrick, I noticed you so damned much, I couldn't even look at you, or I knew a gushing river of drool would come out of my mouth and give me away. Especially when you came out in that towel. I was a goner."

"That's exactly what Savage said! He said you not catcalling me when I was in that towel was proof you wanted to fuck me."

"Wow, you've talked to Savage quite a bit about all this, huh?"

"You have no idea."

We both giggle.

"I was obsessed," I admit, tracing her belly button with my fingertip. "So, what finally did it? What lit the spark for you to finally see me as something more than a friend for the first time?"

Ruby bites her lip.

"Come on, baby. I've told you my timeline. Now, tell me yours. Was it when we kissed at my birthday party? At Reed's party? Fess up."

Ruby blushes. "It happened a little bit sooner than all that, I'd say."

A thought occurs to me. "Wait, were all Cooper's lyrics about me true?"

Ruby nods slowly. "I'm only assuming about the 'you said his name twice' thing, though. I honestly don't remember moaning out your name over and over again in my sleep like he said I did. Although, come to think of it, I'm sure he was right about that, since I was definitely having a sex dream about you."

"Holy shit. Really?"

"I denied it when he accused me. But he was right." She smiles wickedly. "I was. A really good one."

I'm blown away, dizzy with excitement. "So you never told Cooper you wanted to fuck me?"

"How could I tell him that when I didn't even realize it myself? Yes, I was having sex dreams about you, but I convinced myself they didn't mean anything. Or maybe they were just symbolic of our close bond, I don't know. I twisted myself into pretzels to explain it away."

"But Cooper could see the truth."

"Apparently so. I told him he was delusional and crazy. Because, honestly, I thought he was. But looking back, he was right to feel jealous of you."

I snort. "Poor Cooper. No wonder he wrote that song."

"Poor Cooper?"

"You gaslit him, babe."

"*What?*"

"I'm sure he was out of his head with jealousy. He could see what you couldn't, and you kept telling him he was delusional and crazy. That's textbook gaslighting."

She swats my shoulder. "Whose side are you on?"

"Yours. Always and forever." I kiss her forehead. "But you have to admit you kinda did mindfuck him."

"Not on purpose. And enough with the poor guy stuff. I didn't understand my feelings for you, Kendrick. Our friendship was complicated. And he was a total and complete dick to me."

"That's for damned sure. So, yeah, fuck him. He dated you for, what, three months and got a blockbuster song out of it— one that's going to buy him and all his bandmates condos, at least. Maybe even houses, if they get lucky and get a follow-up hit."

"Right?"

"I think Cooper would probably say getting gaslit by you was well worth it in the end."

Ruby cracks up. "He already told me that, basically."

Ruby tells me the story about her conversation with Cooper in Laila's dressing room yesterday, and we both hoot with laughter till we're crying.

"Why didn't you tell me?"

"I was freaking out. Right before Cooper came to talk to me, Laila said something that made me realize I'm in love with you, and I—" Ruby clamps her mouth shut, her eyes wide. Obviously, she didn't mean to say those three little words out loud.

I touch her cheek and smile from ear to ear, feeling like my heart is about to explode. "I'm in love with you, too. I love you, Ruby. I've always loved you."

She sighs. "I love you, too, Kendrick."

And I always will.

They're the words on the tip of my tongue. But I don't have the courage to say them. Not yet. Baby steps.

We embrace and kiss, and after a bit, Ruby breaks away and says, "I have a confession to make, too." She bites the inside of her cheek. "The spark didn't happen for me instantly, like it did for you. But only because you were a football player, and I thought those were totally gross."

I laugh.

"But when you went off to school, I missed you so much, it felt like a physical ache was wracking my body. Like I was missing a limb. I dreamed about you every night, Kendrick. At first, we'd be playing music together or watching a movie in my dreams. But then, I was kissing you. And then . . ." She blushes. "I was losing my virginity to you."

My breathing catches. "Oh my god, Ruby."

"I realized I wanted that in real life. Not only in my dreams. I wanted you to be my first."

"Why didn't you tell me this back then?" I'm beside myself. I sit up in the bed, my legs bent and my mind racing. "I would have dropped everything to come to you, Ruby! Do you have any idea how many girls I turned down in high school, specifically because I wanted you to be my first? Because I was in love with you, and only you? Because being with you for my first time was my biggest fantasy? I was totally obsessed with the idea."

Ruby runs both palms down her face. When she emerges, she's red-faced and panting. "I didn't tell you—not over the phone, anyway—because I decided to surprise you at school on your nineteenth birthday and ask you to take my virginity in person."

My jaw drops. "Why didn't you go through with it? I would have said yes."

"I did go through with it. I took the train and made it all the way to your doorstep."

"What?"

"But then, I saw something through your front window that made me turn around and hop the next train home."

"You were there? What did you see?"

Ruby presses her lips together. "You and Florence. Having sex on a couch. I saw you without meaning to do it through a tiny gap in your blinds."

I palm my forehead. "No. *No.*"

"I turned around and went home and never told another living soul about what happened and the stupid thing I did."

"Oh my fucking God, Ruby. It wasn't stupid. *I wanted you.* Only you. You're the only one I've ever truly wanted, baby. Fuck me. If only I'd known."

Ruby snorts. "I appreciate the sentiment, but it sure looked like you were enjoying your couch time with Florence quite a bit."

"Because I couldn't have you! I settled for her, the same way I've settled for every fucking woman since. All because I couldn't have you." I can't help returning her wicked smile. "Okay, yes, okay. I was nineteen and horny and putting my dick inside a pretty girl, probably for one of the first times, given the timing, so, yes, I'm sure I thought it didn't completely suck at the time."

We both guffaw. And in this moment, I couldn't love Ruby more.

"But I swear to God, if I'd known you wanted me back, I would have waited for you for the rest of my life. I would have hopped a train the second I found out." I run a hand through my hair. "I would have *killed* for us to be each other's first, Ruby." I pause, my heart pounding in my ears. "Your first was Ryder, right?" We've never talked about it, but based on timing, that's got to be the guy, the lucky bastard.

Ruby nods and winces. "I wished he was you the whole time."

"I wished Florence was you, too. I've wished every woman I've ever been with was you." I'm quaking with adrenaline. Also, with grief over what might have been. "That's why I came in my pants at Reed's party. Because I'd been dreaming about tasting your pussy for twelve long years, and my inner teenager couldn't handle it finally coming true." I exhale and gather my courage to say something on the tip of my tongue. "If you'd been my first, Ruby, you would have been my last. My only."

Her eyes prick with tears. "Oh, Kendrick. Mine, too."

My heart bursting, I kiss her again.

"I have another confession to make," I say, breaking contact with her lips. "Your place has been move-in ready for weeks now. Sorry about that."

"What?"

I tell her what I've done—the bribes I've paid to her building manager—and Ruby looks shocked. Flabbergasted to the extreme.

"How much did you pay him?"

I tell her the outrageous number, and to my relief, Ruby throws her head back and belly laughs from the tips of her toes.

"You're psychotic," she says, still laughing. "I'm so turned on."

I laugh with her, basking in an ocean of relief and love for her. "It was Savage's deranged idea. I can't take full credit for it."

"Of course, that was Adrian Savage's brainchild. I should have known."

"I'm the one who executed on it, though," I say defensively. "So, I think I should still get most of the credit. Enough for you to feel turned on by me and only me."

"Oh, I do, baby. Most definitely." She strokes my face and grins. "Is there anything else you need to confess? Any other insane lies that need to be untangled now, before we officially start this thing and promise total honesty going forward, or is every dastardly secret of yours out in the open?"

I twist my mouth. "Hmm."

"Oh boy," she says. "Lay it on me, baby. Now's the time."

"I actually passed out cold during the flight from New York to Vancouver. I slept like a baby, as a matter of fact."

Ruby chortles. "Why did you lie about something as stupid as that?"

"Because you said you'd take a nap with me *if* I didn't get any sleep on the plane!"

"Kendrick!"

"I would have said anything to get to lie down with you in an actual bed, Ruby. Also, in my defense, I was still sleep deprived when I woke up. I had a lot of catching up to do. So, it was only a tiny lie."

Ruby giggles. "Anything else, you psychopath?"

"That journal in my nightstand? It was a decoy, babe. My old journal from last year."

"Kendrick Cook."

I can't help grinning proudly at my chess playing. "I knew you'd snoop around to find my journal the second I left you alone—"

"I didn't!"

"So I left something for you to find and get turned on about."

"I swear, I didn't snoop. Like I told you, I was looking for a place to put my bag of nighttime stuff."

"Liar."

"Oh, *you're* calling *me* a liar—after all the lies you've now admitted to telling to get me into your bed?"

I snicker. "Good point. Not only to get you into my bed,

though. I've always wanted more than that." I touch her hair. "So much more."

"Oh, Kendrick."

I gasp. "I just thought of another lie. Those handcuffs in my nightstand? I bought them specifically for you to find, along with the decoy journal. That huge bottle of lube, too. I didn't already own any of that stuff. It was all a set-up, designed to feed into your frenzy over 'Spank.'"

Ruby pulls a face. "You didn't already own lube?"

"That's your takeaway from everything I just said? No, I'd run out. And I've never once owned a bottle of lube that goddamned big in my life. Who needs a bottle *that* big?"

"I mean, it's definitely come in handy."

We both snicker, remembering all the dirty, filthy, naughty —and oh-so fun—things we've been doing together since she first rolled her little suitcase into my house weeks ago.

"More lies," she demands. "I want all of them, big or small."

I contemplate for a moment. "I don't buy my mother flowers whenever she comes to visit. I've never once done that, actually, and I have zero idea about the name of her favorite flower."

Ruby bats her eyelashes. "You mean you got handcuffs, lube, *and* tulips, especially for lil ol' me? How romantic."

"I was trying to seduce you with all that stuff, babe. Not romance you. And failing badly."

"I'm here, aren't I? Seems to me it was mission accomplished."

We share another giddy smile.

"More lies," Ruby commands, tapping an insistent fingertip against my bare chest. "I want every last one."

I pause to consider, feeling physically high with happiness. Drugged, like I've got an IV pumping happy juice into my veins. "When we had that threesome with Bruno, that was my first time doing that. I pretended to be an expert, but I was honestly bluffing. Flying blind."

Ruby laughs uproariously. "Oh my god, babe. You were incredible at that."

"You enjoyed that, huh?"

"If I didn't already love you, that would have done the trick. Come here."

I scoot to her and we lie nose to nose with her arm draped over me and mine doing the same to her.

Sliding her fingers into the back of my hair, she looks into my eyes and says, "I love you so fucking much, Kendrick Alan Cook. And to be clear, I don't mean like a brother."

I smile so big, my cheeks hurt. "I love you, too, Ruby Duby Doo Connolly. And definitely *not* as a bestie."

"Definitely not." She narrows her eyes. "You don't remember my middle name?"

"Of course I do. Margaret. I remember every damned thing you've ever told me, Ruby Margaret Connolly." As she swoons, I blurt, "Move in with me, baby. Sell your place; rent it—I don't care, as long as we live together and keep going, exactly like this."

Forever.

That's the word I want to add to the end of that plaintive speech, but I lost my nerve at the last second.

Ruby nuzzles her nose against mine. "Baby, I thought you'd never ask."

"So, that's a yes?"

"It's a fuck yes."

I'm dizzy with excitement, love, and relief. "I love you so much, Ruby Connolly."

She replies with the best words known to mankind. Or, at least, to me. "Kendrick Cook, my darling, I love you, too."

33
KENDRICK

"If anyone wants something more than these snacks," Laila says to the group—Ruby, Kai, Titus, and me—as we get settled in her and Savage's expansive living room, "there's a Mexican place down the road that delivers."

We're at her and Savage's gorgeous, beachside home on a Malibu cliffside for another all-hands-on-deck writing sesh—this time with Laila contributing her talents to the cause. We don't normally invite outside co-writers into our process, even our only honorary band member, but desperate times call for desperate measures.

"I could go for a burrito," Titus murmurs, patting his flat stomach.

"There's plenty of snacks right here, T," Ruby says to her brother, motioning to the impressive spread on the coffee table. "We'll get an actual meal later as a reward for writing a kickass masterpiece."

"But I didn't eat breakfast," Titus says with a pout.

"Deal with it," Ruby snaps. "Whenever you eat a full meal at the beginning of a writing sesh, you fall into a food coma, and we need you, and everyone here, working at maximum capacity."

"I don't know why you're so stressed," Titus says with a yawn. "We've still got plenty of time. It's only one song, dude."

"Yeah, but it has to be *amazing*. And don't forget, we also have to record and rehearse it into the ground. All our calendars are getting so busy with side gigs these days, so finding time when the five of us can get together—the *six* of us, sorry" —she motions to Laila— "is going to get more and more difficult."

With a grin, I pipe in to say, "Since our guest mentor episode aired, Ruby's calendar has filled up like crazy with songwriting sessions. Some of them with legit heavy hitters."

Everyone expresses excitement for Ruby, and when I prompt her to elaborate, she lists off the artists she'll be working with soon with a wide smile and sparkling eyes.

"Reed predicted this exact thing would happen as a domino effect to Cooper's song," I say. "I guess The Prick really does have some kind of a crystal ball, huh?"

"That's giving Cooper way too much credit," Laila says. "Yes, Cooper's song helped get things rolling, but Ruby's the one who did this for herself. She's the one had the genius idea to kiss you at your birthday party, and she's the one who noticed someone recording. Ruby's also the one who's co-written some of the most kickass songs in the world for Fugitive Summer, and she's the one who expertly plays them live for tens of thousands of people around the world."

"I get it. No, you're totally right. Sorry."

"Also," Laila continues, "Ruby's the one who negotiated the performance slot term in her contract."

"So true," I concede. "I shouldn't have said that."

"And then," Laila continues. "As if all that wasn't enough, Ruby went on to shine like a thousand suns during the press conference and Guest Mentor episode. So, please, let's not let Cooper's stupid song about some mystery girl named 'Ruby Tuesday' eclipse everything she's done to seize the day and make hay while the sun just so happened to be shining down on her, simply because Cooper lifted the shade on a nearby window. Okay?" She looks around sternly at the group for emphasis.

Every man in the room mumbles, "Okay," since we're now feeling like she's talking to all of us, not just me. And after that one-word response, we all press our lips together, feeling appropriately shamed and stupid.

"Good. Thank you."

Ruby laughs. "Thank you, Laila." She's laughing through tears. Clearly, Laila's speech meant a whole lot to her. "Thank you not only for those amazing words," Ruby clarifies. "But also, for going to bat for me as your mentor this season. I'll never be able to repay you for what you've done for me." She looks at me and blushes. "Personally and professionally."

"No repayment necessary, babe. I asked for you because you're incredibly talented, and a great friend, and I wanted the whole world to see what I've known about you for a long time."

"Laila's absolutely right," I say, feeling like it's safe for me to speak again. "You've earned everything coming to you. I didn't mean to imply otherwise, baby."

"*Baby*?" Titus says, his eyebrow cocked.

"Reed's point wasn't necessarily wrong, though," Ruby says, not addressing her brother's question. "Cooper's song was the first domino to fall. Don't you dare tell Reed I said that, though. On principle, it annoys me no end how that man always thinks he's right about every fucking thing."

"Ain't that the truth," I mutter.

"Hello?" Titus says. "You called Ruby baby, KC." He looks at me with narrowed eyes. "I've never heard you call her that before. Cutie, sweetheart, babe, Ruby Duby. But *baby*? That's a new one."

Grinning mischievously, I look at Ruby for permission to break our fantastic news, and she returns my smile and nods.

Ever since we spilled our guts and opened our hearts to each other last week, we've been dying to tell our bandmates everything, but we've both wanted to do it in person and while we're all together. Well, this sure feels like the perfect moment.

"Great catch, T," I say with a wink. "I called Ruby baby, because she's finally my baby." My grin widens. "We're officially together, guys. As a couple."

As everyone whoops, cheers, and claps, Ruby adds, "We're officially living together at Kendrick's place. I've already got a renter for my place." She gazes at me adoringly. "We're endgame, guys. We both know it."

The group instinctively gets up and huddles in the middle of the living room for hugs and congratulations.

"I told Ruby the truth about everything," I tell Savage during our hug. "Even the building manager. She laughed about all my lying and scheming. She wasn't mad at me at all."

"What lying and scheming?" Titus interjects.

Shit. Ruby's protective brother is standing behind me, much closer than I realized.

Reluctantly, I fill him in on the gist of the story, since he wasn't at C-Bomb's poker party; and to my relief, Titus seems every bit as amused about everything as his sister.

"You two already knew about all this?" Titus asks, motioning between Savage and Laila. Apparently, he's surmised as much from their not-at-all-shocked body language.

"KC came to me for advice," Savage says proudly. "And I helped him tap into his inner Doberman to get what he wanted."

"And surprise, surprise," I add sarcastically, "he then babbled everything we'd talked about to his wife."

"She's my *wife*," Savage mutters, like he had no choice in the matter.

"Adrian knows there's no point in him keeping anything from me," Laila says with a waggle of her eyebrows. "I've got a few foolproof ways of getting information out of him."

Everyone laughs.

Everyone but Kai, I can't help noticing.

"Hey, Ruby," my brother says. "I've already apologized to Kendrick for fucking everything up for you two. But let me apologize to you, too. I really fucked up, and I'm so, so sorry."

"It's okay, Kai," Ruby says. "I think Kendrick and I both feel like everything happened, exactly as it was supposed to."

"I just want you to know I couldn't be happier for you two or sorrier for what I did."

Ruby and I wrap Kai in a warm, forgiving hug, and my big brother is visibly holding back tears by the time we release him.

When that side conversation is done, everyone sits again, this time with Ruby and me sitting together and holding hands, and the rest of the group chatting enthusiastically about our happy news.

"Honestly, I've wanted you two to get together since high school," Titus confesses. He flashes Kai a snarky look. "When I found out she had a crush on you, I thought, 'Wrong Cook brother, Ruby, ya dumbass!'"

We all burst into happy laughter.

"Trust me, if I could rewind the clock, I would," Ruby says, squeezing my hand. "But in my defense, I did try to right that horrendous wrong pretty early on. Unfortunately, it didn't go as planned." She tells the group the story of her coming to surprise me at school, and everyone reacts with gasps and pained body language, the same way I did when Ruby told me.

On and on, we talk about everything with our best friends. Our found family. And every time I lock eyes with any of them, whether it's Savage, Kai, Titus, or Laila, their smiles and body language tell me they couldn't be more thrilled for Ruby and me. For our whole band. Because at the end of the day, our happiness is theirs. Our love, theirs to share. The truth is, we all want what's best for every person in this room, in whatever form that takes.

After a while, Ruby looks at her watch and gasps. "Shit. Guys, we really need to get to work. Let's write a hit song."

"Actually, sorry, before we do that," Savage says. He looks at Laila, and she beams a smile at him that he apparently perceives as permission. "As long as we're sharing good news with the band, Laila and I have some we've been waiting to share in person with all of you." He looks at Laila again, looking like a kid on Christmas. "Tell 'em, Fitzy."

Laila's practically bursting with excitement. "I'm pregnant," she shouts. "Four months along!"

The room erupts with congratulations and cheers. And in short order, we're all up again and group-hugging with Savage and Laila this time.

When it's my turn to hug Savage, I squeeze him tight and tell him I'm thrilled for him. "I must admit," I say, "I'm surprised to see how happy you are about this news." As long as I've known this boy, he's always said he's got no interest in becoming a father, thanks to his own difficult childhood. At age twelve, his amazing grandma, Mimi, saved him from the hell of his early life in Phoenix by moving him to live with her in Chicago. But before that, to put it mildly, those first twelve years of Savage's unhappy, neglected, and abused life left more than a mark on the poor guy.

"I'm surprised, too," Savage admits. He looks at Laila across the room. "But Laila makes everything fun for me. I want to do everything there is to do in life, now that I've got her. Every damned thing."

I look across the room to where he's gazing, to where Ruby and Laila are chatting happily, and it's just in time to witness Ruby doing a little happy dance while laughing with Laila. "I know what you mean, my brother. When you find the right person, it changes everything."

Savage follows my gaze. "Can you imagine yourself having babies with her one day?"

"Hell yeah."

He returns to me with a beaming smile on his face. "Does that mean you're planning to pop the question, or are you two just gonna live together and—"

"Hell yeah, I'm gonna propose to her. As soon as possible."

He gasps. "Holy shit, KC. Congrats."

"Not so loud, dude." I look around to make sure nobody's lurking too close to overhear. "I just need to get the—" I covertly point to my ring finger, and Savage's face lights up.

"If you ask her during the finale," Savage whispers, "I know for a fact Nadine would buy you the—" He points to his ring finger. "That's what she offered to do for me during our first season. I turned her down, but you wouldn't have to do that."

I remember that from when it happened. Savage said he didn't want to propose on TV. He wanted to do it in private. Plus, he didn't want anyone paying for his future wife's engagement ring. He wanted to spend his own damned money on that.

"The idea wasn't for me," Savage continues, cutting through my wandering thoughts. "But that doesn't mean you can't go that route, if you want to get her a big, fat you-know-what for free."

Savage makes a whole lot more money than I do, thanks to the show and all the side gigs that have flowed from it, and I greatly appreciate him being non-judgmental about the disparity in our financial situations. Compared to the world at large, I'm a baller, thanks to the success of our band and my various sponsorships and endorsement deals. But the fact remains, Savage's bank account dwarfs mine. Hence, his sprawling, beachside home in Malibu that didn't cause him a moment's pain to buy with cash vs. the modest, three-bedroom home I stretched to buy in North Hollywood with a mortgage.

"I'd want to buy the thing myself, just like you did," I say. "And I wouldn't want to do it on the show. Maybe at a party, with all her friends around. I think she'd really like that. Oh! Her birthday's coming up in a couple weeks. I could do it then."

Savage contemplates that. "Her birthday is Titus's, too, though. Maybe you shouldn't mix all that together."

I pull a face. "Adrian Savage, are you becoming *wise* on me? What the fuck?"

He chuckles. "Hey, a broken clock's right twice a day."

I peek over at Ruby again. She's still happily immersed in animated discussion with Laila, who's now showing her what appears to be a sonogram photo. "I must admit," I whisper, "now that I've got the idea, I want to do it as soon as possible. I can force myself to wait till after the finale, so Nadine can't get her grubby little paws all over it. But that's as long as I'm willing to wait."

"Nadine would absolutely find a way to use it in the show. I'm sure she'd make Cooper look like the ultimate victim."

I roll my eyes. "Talk about lying and scheming. Nadine's next level."

Savage agrees. "Hey, what about doing it at a birthday party for me? The finale will air on my birthday. Did you see that?"

"No, I missed that."

"Laila could throw me a party here that night, right after we shoot the live taping. We could all come straight here from the soundstage, and you could do it that very night."

Excitement rockets through me. "Holy shit, Savage. Yes. You're sure you wouldn't mind sharing your birthday with Ruby and me like that?"

"It'd be the best birthday present you could ever give me."

I hug him and pat his back. "Thanks for everything, man. Not just about Ruby. For my life. For making me who I am today. I wouldn't be standing here without you. Maybe not here at all." Savage's expression tells me he knows what I mean. When I got injured in college and it became clear my football dreams were done and dusted, my will to keep going and care about pretty much anything was touch and go for a while.

"I owe you the same debt," Savage whispers. "When I first came to live with Mimi, I would have run away if it weren't for you and Kai living down the hall and making me feel cool. But especially you."

"You *were* cool. I'm sure you popped out of the womb cool." I grin at his reaction. "I love you, brother."

"I love you, too. Can you believe this is how our lives have turned out?"

I shake my head and laugh. "No, sir. I cannot."

"Okay, guys," Ruby calls out, clapping her hands. "Unless anyone else has some major life news to share, we need to get started with the writing sesh now. I'm honestly starting to freak out."

"*Really?*" Titus deadpans. "I hadn't noticed."

We resume our seats and start looking through our notes, in whatever form. But before we get too far into the process, Titus says, "Actually, as long as we're sharing life updates—"

"Titus!"

"This will be quick, Ruby. Calm your tits." He returns to

the group. "I broke up with Stephanie. That's not a major life thing, but still."

"What happened?" Kai asks. "You were just meeting her parents a week ago. And you were a monk for her through the entire tour."

Titus shrugs. "When I met her parents, everything went downhill from there. They didn't approve of their precious daughter dating a musician with 'so many horrible tattoos,' even a successful one, and I didn't approve of me dating someone who gave more of a shit about her parents' opinion of me than her own."

I flash Titus an encouraging look, and he nods at me in reply. Thanks to Ruby, I already knew about Titus's breakup coming here today, and, like Ruby, I couldn't be more supportive of his decision. Ruby and I both liked Stephanie when we met her, briefly, during the tour; but like Ruby told her brother during a recent phone call, Titus deserves a woman who appreciates him for him. A woman who's willing to fight for him, tooth and nail, every bit as much as he's willing to fight for her.

"Okay, that's enough about that," Titus murmurs. He picks up his guitar, the same as he did during our first attempt at writing this damned song, and offers up the first idea of the day: a killer guitar riff—one that makes all of us visibly perk up.

We all say basically the same thing: it's fucking awesome, cool, and super-catchy. Something we can build on as a group. And just like that, a familiar kind of energy courses through us —one that was noticeably lacking from our prior, tepid writing session at my house.

At Kai's request, Titus plays his riff again, and then again and again, on a running loop, so we can all start vibing with it and formulating ideas about how to build on it.

A few loops in, Kai starts playing a bassline that perfectly complements Titus's riff. In fact, it makes the damned thing pop and sizzle in a whole new way.

"Oooooooh, that's sick," Savage says, perking up. "Give me a beat, KC. I've got an idea."

I grab my laptop and find a looped beat at the right tempo —one I'll surely replace or at least supplement with live drums, when the time comes, if this seed of an idea ever blooms into an actual Fugitive Summer song.

Not surprisingly, my contribution takes Titus's and Kai's playing to a whole new level. Because that's what beats do. They make everything musical sound better. Sicker. Cooler. And after feeling the groove for a minute, Savage strums his guitar in a way that fills out the existing sounds, which then prompts Laila to excitedly slide behind her baby grand in the corner and start adding some tasty chords.

Not to be outdone, Ruby starts adding some riffs and accents on the mini-keyboard in her lap. But even better than that, she starts humming some melodic gibberish as our topline—and, suddenly, it feels like we're barreling toward an actual song here. A great one, in fact.

We all agree we're cooking with gas now as our jam session gains momentum and Ruby's vocal melodies start to solidify and take hold.

"So, what's this song about?" Savage asks, as everyone continues jamming. Ruby's melodies are a slam dunk. But since she's singing gibberish, rather than actual words, it's now time for us to decide the direction we want to go with the lyrics, so we can fill in the syllables with something that makes sense. But that, in turn, hinges on the emotional vibe of this budding song.

"I'm getting anger," Titus says, still playing his riff on a loop.

"More like *angst*," Ruby supplies.

The whole room agrees with Ruby. Yes. *Angst*. That's it.

"Sexual frustration?" Savage asks, and everyone laughs, because of course that's Savage's take on the vibe. But also, yeah, he's kind of right. That's definitely in there, too.

"'Why the fuck can't I get what I want?'" Kai offers. "That's the vibe I'm getting. 'I want this so badly, and I can't have it. Why, why, *why*?'"

"Love it," Laila says. "I feel that, too."

As everyone agrees with Laila, Ruby gasps loudly and stops playing. "Kendrick, can I speak to you for a sec? Privately, on the balcony?"

Without waiting for a reply, she slides her mini-keyboard off her lap and pops up, and off she goes, like a woman possessed.

Outside, I close the sliding door behind us. It's early afternoon, and the sun is glimmering off the nearby ocean. A gentle breeze is rustling our hair. It's a relaxing scene, but Ruby looks far from relaxed. In fact, she looks amped up in a way I've seen many, many times before. The muse is calling to her. There's no doubt about it.

"What's up, baby?"

"I didn't want to say this in front everyone," she says, practically bouncing up and down. "But when I was singing that melody, the only words I could hear in my head were *yours*."

I tilt my head, not understanding.

"From 'Spark!'" she shouts.

"What? No, Ruby."

"You have to admit those lyrics would fit perfectly with the vibe of this song. At least, as a starting point."

I shift my weight. We've never used my words as the starting point for a whole-ass song before. We've used snippets of my ideas, here and there, but nothing like this. And we've certainly never used words I'd written privately, while in a weird trance, while secretly losing my mind with jealousy and yearning for the girl I've loved for twelve years, a girl who happens to be one of my bandmates who'd have to play this song, live, for God knows how many years to come. "Wouldn't you feel embarrassed to have my words out there in the world?"

"*Embarrassed*? No. I'd be proud."

"But it's obvious the whole thing is about you. Also, wouldn't it be weird for Savage to sing *my* words about *you*?"

Ruby looks wholly unbothered. "Savage sings all our words, all the time. And some of them were my honest, vulnerable thoughts at one point. Honestly, it's always a source of pride for me to see him re-interpreting my most honest feelings and making them his own. He's so good at it." She's got a point. Savage always sings them so convincingly, it's like he wrote the damned words himself.

Ruby takes my hand. "I don't want you feeling pressured. This is your decision, completely. But don't make your decision based on protecting me. I'd feel nothing but electrified if the world heard your words about me."

"Electrified?" The description is a huge surprise to me. "Why?"

"Kendrick, nobody's ever written a song about me before. It's the coolest, swooniest thing that's ever happened to me."

I press my lips together. Seems like she's conveniently forgetting Cooper's song. Not to mention, she's dated several musicians. Not a single one of those dickheads wrote a song about her? I find that hard to believe.

"Cooper's song doesn't count," Ruby says, reading my mind. "That was a diss track. I meant nobody's ever written a *love* song about me. Yours was a first, baby. A beautiful first, and I can't deny I'd be elated for the world to hear it."

"What I wrote is outdated. The song I'd write for you now would be nothing like that. I was tortured when I wrote it."

"I know. It was delicious." When I look unsure, she adds, "Most songs become outdated after they're written. Sometimes right away, because the very act of putting one's feelings into the world makes them obsolete. That doesn't make the song any less worthy of being put out into the world, does it?"

She makes another valid point. "So, you're saying you want the world to know how badly I wanted you, huh? That's what this boils down to, right?"

Ruby bites back a smile. "Is that bad of me? Am I a monster, once again?"

I laugh and hug her. "No, not at all. It's pretty hot that's what you want, honestly." I kiss her forehead. "Bonus points, some of my lyrics could be interpreted as a reference to Cooper, which is exactly what the label wants and what the world will be expecting from us, so it would be a smart move, from a business standpoint."

"Good point. I didn't think of that, but the lyrics hint at him just enough to make the internet go feral over dissecting them." Ruby smirks. "And you know what happens when people go feral over dissecting lyrics, don't you?"

I wink. "The song becomes a smash hit, baby."

"Amen to that."

We high-five and laugh.

"Okay, cutie. Your wish is my command. Let's do it."

Ruby squeals and thanks me.

"The only problem is, I didn't bring my journal with me today, and I don't have any of that stuff memorized."

"I do. Every word."

I smile. "Of course you do."

Ruby snickers. "Not that it matters, since I also took photos of those two pages."

"Ruby!"

"Not to do anything bad with them. Only because I love your words so much, I wanted to be able to read them, again and again, anytime."

"Why do you need to read them, if you've got them memorized?"

Ruby tilts her head up for a kiss. "Your frenzied handwriting is a huge turn-on for me."

Laughing, I lean down and kiss her. "How are you so cute? It's like a superpower." I exhale. "Okay, come back inside, baby, so you can tell everyone about 'Spark' and then text them the photos."

I turn around and bend down, and without needing to be told what I'm intending, Ruby hops aboard my back with a whoop, even though the ride back into the house will be extremely short. With one hand around my neck and the other swirling in the air like a cowgirl, Ruby bellows, "Come on, baby! Let's spin your gorgeous words into a goddamned hit song!"

34
RUBY

"Who will take home the crown tonight?" Sunshine Vaughn booms into the camera in front of her. "Will it be Chase or Roe? That's what we're here to find out!"

We're almost midway through the live taping of the bloated finale episode, and Sunshine hasn't stopped shamelessly stretching things out between every chat segment and musical performance.

True to form, Sunshine adds, "But first, let's watch this video about the long and winding road our two talented finalists have traveled to become the last contestants standing."

The lights in the studio dim, and the video begins on the greenroom monitor we're all watching on, at which point, all of us exchange eyerolls.

All members of Fugitive Summer are sitting in here in this greenroom, other than Savage. Our swaggy front man is currently awaiting his imminent performance with his wife in the wings somewhere, while the rest of us were told to wait here for our cue to perform "Spark," later in show, immediately after Cooper's band performs "Don't Call Me."

Where is Cooper now? I have no idea. After our initial chat segment with Sunshine to kick off the show, he was ushered away in the opposite direction from Kendrick and me, and I haven't seen him since.

"Excuse me," Kendrick says to a PA standing by the door of the greenroom. "Savage and Laila are performing next, right?"

The PA nods. "Right after this video ends."

Kendrick flashes me a pointed look. One that says, "Let's make a break for it, baby," and I nod to convey my readiness to execute our plan. Yes, we're supposed to stay here to await our band's performance, but Kendrick and I both feel too excited about what Savage and Laila are about to do to witness it on a teeny monitor in a greenroom. Instead, we both want to witness our best friends making their once-in-a-lifetime announcement, live and in the flesh, from the wings.

"Excuse me again," Kendrick says to the same PA. "Could you please find me some Tums or something like that? My stomach feels a bit funny. Nerves, I guess."

"Oh dear. Of course. I'll be right back with that." And off she goes, like an innocent lamb to slaughter.

"We'll be right back, fellas," Kendrick drawls to Titus and Kai, as he pulls me off the couch by my hand. "We're gonna watch Savage and Laila's performance from the wings."

"Godspeed," Kai says with a yawn, as Titus grunts in reply while scrolling on his phone.

Those two only know that Savage and Laila are performing a duet of Laila's hit song, "Savage Love," for the first time, ever. Which, apparently, they both think is a cool enough first to inspire our prison break.

Our hands joined, Kendrick and I sneak out of the green-room and down a short hallway toward the stage. And just as we get settled into a perfect, covert spot with a clear view of the performance area, Sunshine Vaughn enthusiastically flings her arm to the side and bellows, "It's Savage and Laila, everyone, performing a duet of Laila's hit song, 'Savage Love,' for the very first time! Happy birthday, Mr. Savage!"

As the studio audience applauds and cheers, a spotlight illuminates Savage and Laila on the other side of the stage from Sunshine, but close enough to our hiding spot that we can see every micro-facial expression of the pair. Laila's seated at a baby grand in a flowing ballgown, her blonde hair magnificently piled atop her head, and Savage is standing next to Laila's piano with his acoustic guitar, and both husband and wife are gazing at each other lovingly.

"Happy birthday, baby," Laila coos into her microphone, right before he launches into singing the first, familiar verse of her hit song:

One for the money
Two for the show
Three cuz you're so good givin' Os
Oooooooooooh

Four for the cameras
Five for the fame
No catchin' feelings, only a game
Oooooooooooh

But then six came along when we had our first kiss
Six made me swoon, yell out "I call dibs!"
Six watched you sleep, whispered, "I want this."
Six held you tight in a white-knuckled grip
Oooooooooooh

. . .

And now I've got a savage love for you
I've lost count of all the ways you've made me a slave to you
There's no doubt my love is here to stay; I'm addicted to you
I've got a savage love for you, infinite and everlasting

Six hit the road, now it's long gone
Seven came along, now you're second to none
Ooooooooooh

Cameras are off and our love remains
*Eight, nine, and ten, **let's have a baby***

Kendrick and I look excitedly at each other. Our friends told us they were planning to announce their pregnancy in some way during their performance, but they wouldn't tell us exactly how. Well, there it was. That last line was supposed to be "Eight, nine, and ten, *our love never fades.*" And based on the over-the-top reaction of the audience, every person in this soundstage is well aware of the lyric change and its obvious implication.

With huge smiles on their faces, Savage and Laila continue with their song:

Fake became real and want became need
Can't live without you, I need you to breathe
You're swimming in my bloodstream, enmeshed in my heart
I dream about you, in pain when we part
Ooooooooooh

. . .

And now I've got a savage love for you
I've lost count of all the ways you've made me a slave to you
There's no doubt my love is here to stay; I'm addicted to you
I've got a savage love for you
Infinite and everlasting

Take my heart, take my soul,
Take my blood, bones, and flesh
Take the air from my lungs, every pound, every inch
Take it all, every ounce, I give everything
Savage love, **let's have a baby**

They did it again! And this time, the crowd is going even more crazy than before, right along with Kendrick and me.

When the song reaches its last note, Laila gleefully slides off her piano bench and rises to accept her husband's offered hug and kiss. But before she falls into Savage's waiting arms, Laila pointedly presses her flowing gown tightly against her growing midsection, revealing the lovely baby bump that's recently sprouted there—and all of it with a mischievous look on her beautiful face that says, "Gosh, what do we have here?"

Of course, the crowd goes wild and crazy in reaction. So much so, I'm surprised their unhinged energy isn't physically blowing the roof off the place.

Laila's exciting pregnancy reveal completed, she accepts Savage's giddy embrace and kiss. The pair waves to their adoring live audience, and then to the cameras trained on them, and their spotlight slowly fades to black.

"Congratulations, Mr. and Mrs. Savage!" Sunshine sings out, sounding genuinely delighted. "Happy birthday to Mr. Savage, indeed! My goodness!" She fans herself. "That was a surprise to me, too, folks. How wonderful!" Laughing, she beams at the camera. "Let's take a quick commercial break, so we can scream and cry with our besties about this amazing news. And when we come back, Jon Stapleton will be here to perform one of his greatest country hits with ten of your favorite contestants from the season!"

"There you are," an annoyed voice whisper-shouts. It's the PA Kendrick duped earlier, standing next to us with a roll of antacids in her hand and a giant "fuck you, Kendrick" on her face. Scowling dramatically, she pushes a button on her head-set. "Yeah, I found them. I'll take them back there now." She holds up the roll of antacids. "I'm assuming you don't actually need these?"

"Nope. Not at all. Sorry."

The PA rolls her eyes. "Follow me, please."

"It was all Ruby's idea," Kendrick jokes, making me swat his arm and giggle, and the PA turns around and hushes us.

"Sorry," we whisper at the same time. But when our eyes meet, we crack up again, which only pisses off the PA even more. I can't say I blame the woman. From what the director told us in rehearsal earlier today, these live tapings are a stressful juggling act for the crew, since they're shot precisely as the show will air, with no opportunity for edits or re-dos. Which means, in theory, everyone needs to follow instructions to a T—and at least stay put in greenrooms, when told to do that. But oh well. I don't regret what Kendrick and I did for second. It would have been a crying shame for us to miss out. Fuck the show.

We return to our holding cell, where we're surprised to discover Titus and Kai aren't alone in the room any longer, as before. Now, they've been joined in waiting by none other than Cooper and his two bandmates from Alexa Play Music. Indeed, Titus and Kai seem to be in the midst of a calm conversation with all of them—the kind they used to have when APM opened for us a few years ago.

"They made us wait in here," Cooper blurts at his first sight of Kendrick striding into the room. "Don't come at me, bro."

Cooper's bandmates get up and greet us warmly, while Cooper hangs back in his seat.

Suddenly, Kendrick's words from a while back pop into my head: *You gaslit the poor guy!* And, suddenly, I can't shake them. I didn't mean to do that to Cooper. But I did. Just like Kendrick said.

I release Kendrick's hand and head over to Cooper.

"Can we talk for a minute? Maybe over there?"

I gesture toward a large snack table in the corner, and Cooper looks wary.

"They're gonna come get my band any minute now for our performance."

"This will only take a minute, Coop."

This time, Cooper looks at Kendrick, like he's trying to gauge if saying yes will get him punched.

"Don't worry about him," I say. "He's the one who said the thing that made me want to apologize to you."

That gets Cooper's undivided attention. "*Apologize?*" He blinks rapidly, like he can't fully process my words. "To me? For what?"

"Come talk to me in private and find out."

"Is this a trick?"

Rolling my eyes, I call over to Kendrick. "I'm gonna talk to Cooper in the corner over there. Will that elicit any kind of reaction from you, babe?"

"None whatsoever." With that, Kendrick blandly returns to his conversation with Cooper's bass player, Scottie.

"Okay," Cooper mutters. With an exhale, he gets up and

follows me into the corner I've gestured to, and when we get to our destination, I get right to the point.

"Kendrick made me realize," I take a deep breath, "I gaslit you, Cooper. It wasn't intentional, and I certainly didn't realize that's what I was doing at the time. But looking back, Kendrick is right: that's what I did, and I'm sorry about that."

Cooper looks stunned. "You gaslit me about what?"

I explain what I mean, wrapping up with, "So, you weren't as paranoid and delusional as I kept insisting. Yes, you were paranoid about me cheating. I didn't do that, I swear. But looking back, I had feelings for Kendrick that I wasn't even consciously aware of while I was dating you. I gave you plenty of reasons to feel insecure and jealous about my friendship with Kendrick, even though I kept telling you that was crazy talk. That he was like a brother to me. I'm sorry you went through that, thanks to my cluelessness about my own feelings. I didn't mean to do it to you, but, obviously, I did, and I'm sorry."

"I . . . Wow." Cooper scratches his arm, looking dazed and surprised. "Thank you for saying all that, Ruby."

"You deserve to know the truth. You're the villain in this story, to be clear." I smile. "But maybe you're not quite as big a villain as I made you out to be in my head."

He chuckles. "Thanks. That means a lot. Back at you." He presses his lips together. "So, does that mean we're now letting bygones be bygones?"

I shrug. "Sure. You're an artist. You should be allowed to express yourself honestly in your art." I narrow my eyes. "Would I have preferred you didn't use my actual name in your lyrics, you little prick? Yes. But such is life. Such is art."

Cooper laughs. "Yeah, well, I would have preferred my girlfriend didn't moan another guy's name while sleeping next to me in bed, so . . ."

"I've apologized, Cooper. Let's not beat a dead horse here, or I might feel compelled to retract everything I've said."

Miraculously, we're both able to share a smile about the whole thing. Cooper's smile looks rueful to me. Tinged with sadness, unlike mine. But you know what? I'll take it. I glance over at Kendrick across the room. Not surprisingly, he's watching Cooper and me intently. Which means his blasé, nonchalant reaction from earlier was an act, God bless him. I flash him a thumbs-up, and my boyfriend winks and goes back to his conversation.

"Is Kendrick furious he's in the song?" Cooper whispers. "Do I need to avoid him for the rest of my life, or maybe bring bodyguards with me whenever we're going to be at the same place?"

"Nah, you're good. My man's a lover, not a fighter."

"My man," he mutters. "No need to rub it in, Ruby."

"I just meant we're both ready to move on. You'll be fine."

Cooper cocks his head. "So, I can stop worrying the song you're about to debut tonight is gonna trash me?"

During rehearsal earlier today, we didn't perform "Spark" at our soundcheck. We performed "Hate Sex High," specifically to keep the live debut of our new single under wraps.

"I didn't say that," I say coyly. "You'll just have to wait to find out, like everyone else."

A PA pokes his head into the room and calls out, "APM! You're up. Come with me."

"Break a leg," I murmur. Cooper tosses me a snarky look as he walks away, like he's wondering if I'm wishing him luck or being literal.

It's a little bit of both, if I'm being honest. Yes, I've apologized. And, yes, I'm now putting him soundly in my rearview mirror. But I can't deny a part of me hopes Cooper will forget his lyrics or sing off-key during his imminent performance . . . or even better, fall and break a leg. Or at least sprain an ankle or toe or otherwise suffer some indignity or slight injury as one final, karmic consequence for him so frequently being a total and complete dick.

[To listen to Savage and Laila's duet of "Savage Love" go here - https://laurenrowebooks.com/pages/spark-savage-baby]

35
RUBY

"Put your hands together for Fugitive Summer!" Sunshine shouts with gusto.

The lights go up. The little red lights on all the cameras pointed at us turn on. And off the five of us go, like we've done many times before in rehearsal, only this time for the live studio audience, and it's plain to see we're all thoroughly pumped about it.

Indeed, as the band rocks out, and Savage does his thing out front, giving voice to Kendrick's words about me, I can't stop making giddy, joyful eye contact with the writer of those lyrics. My man. My boyfriend. My love. I'm officially a muse, bitches! A part of musical history now. And lucky for me, I'll get to relive this feeling every single time Fugitive Summer performs this song, forevermore.

Thank goodness, our performance is going off without a hitch, the same way Cooper's performance did before ours (unfortunately). Not only that, but the audience is also thoroughly into it, which only energizes us all the more. In fact, I think it's fair to say we're now performing this song better than we did in any rehearsal.

When we reach the final bars, as we're just about to hit the outro, Kendrick does something we've never rehearsed. Something that's not on the recorded track and not in the plan for tonight. After banging out his final drumbeats, he leans into his mic and snarls out, "Hey, dickhead, you're the last person she'd call, anyway. Don't call *you*? Don't call *her*, you whiny little bitch, or you'll have to answer to me."

As the audience roars its approval of Kendrick's unexpected smackdown, there's a commotion behind the cameras. Surely, the director and whoever else are frantically trying to figure out how to deal with this unexpected gift they've been given during the next segment. Most likely, they're also trying to figure out how to quickly bleep out Kendrick's bad language during the slight delay imposed on live broadcasts.

Laughing and barely holding it together behind my keyboard, I meet Kendrick's gaze and raise my hand to my mouth to blow him a giddy, euphoric kiss, but before I complete my gesture, the lights go out and we're consumed by blinding darkness.

Several PAs arrive to escort us off the stage, and we're led to a new holding area in the wings—a spot where we're told to wait for a few minutes before storming the stage after the winner's name is imminently announced.

When we reach our waiting spot—the second we come to a stop there, in fact—I throw myself into Kendrick's waiting arms and devour his lips with an enthusiastic, adrenaline-fueled kiss that practically knocks him over.

"You're not pissed at me for that?" he whispers against my lips.

"Pissed? That was *amazing*! Swoony. Hot!"

Kendrick laughs. "You said you didn't want to dignify Cooper's song with a response."

I snort. "I didn't and I still don't. But my *boyfriend* doing it for me because he simply couldn't help himself—because he's a protective, sexy hottie who doesn't let anyone disrespect his woman? Baby, I've never wanted to give you a blowjob more than right now!"

A shocked PA shushes me, and I cover my mouth with my palm and squeal with laughter behind it, while Kendrick hoots and kisses my forehead with glee.

When we break apart, our other bandmates give Kendrick high-fives, kudos, and hugs, with everyone agreeing he's a king for that unexpected smackdown. And a moment after that, guess who arrives but Reed, dressed like a billion bucks, with Nadine at his side.

Both of them congratulate us on our "killer" performance, and, thankfully, nobody chastises Kendrick for his impromptu speech at the end.

On the contrary, Reed lays his hand on Kendrick's shoulder and says, "Thanks to that stunt—"

"And Ruby's face when he did it!" Nadine whisper-shouts excitedly.

"Thanks to all that," Reed continues.

"We got you in close-up, Ruby!" Nadine whisper-shouts again.

Reed laughs. "Thanks to all that, 'Spark' will be sitting at number one all over the world by the time we get to Savage's birthday party."

We all laugh and high-five; and as we're doing that, Cooper appears out of nowhere, trailed by a frantic PA. "Cooper, get back here," the PA hisses. "I'm so sorry, Nadine. I tried."

"I thought we buried the hatchet," Cooper stage-whispers at me. "You apologized to me, privately, but then you let Kendrick do that to me in front of the whole world?"

"Ruby had nothing to do with it," Kendrick says, sliding

his arm protectively around my shoulders. "So, slow your roll." He smiles like a shark. "I'm an artist, dude. I felt inspired in the moment, so I went with it. You know all about that, right, Cooper? When the muse strikes, artists like us have to follow her lead—and to hell with whoever might get their feelings hurt as a result."

36
KENDRICK

Music is thumping.

All the party people surrounding me in Savage's massive, stylish living room are laughing, dancing, moving and grooving. Mostly, we're celebrating Savage's twenty-eight trips around the sun. Secondarily, we're drinking to our kickass performance of "Spark" earlier tonight. Just as The Prick predicted, by the time we arrived at Savage's house from Burbank, our new song was sitting at number one on all major streaming platforms, and early indicators suggest it'll debut in at least the Top 10 on the most important charts. Probably much higher than that.

We've got a lot to celebrate tonight already. But, hopefully, before the night is through, Ruby and I will add another reason to the long list. The best one. Our engagement.

"Hey, you two," Reed says to Ruby and me, and he approaches with his gorgeous wife, Georgina, by his side. I'm in the midst of mixing cocktails for Ruby and me at a stocked bar, so I offer to play bartender for them, too, and they accept.

As I make the drinks, Reed says, "I heard the big news. Congrats. It's about time."

I freeze. Fuck. Is Reed referring to the fact that Ruby and I are living together now? Or did Mr. Loose Lips Whenever He's Drunk Adrian Savage blab to Reed about my plans, and Reed, who's just arrived at the party, mistakenly thinks the big question has already been popped?

"What big news?" Georgina asks.

"These two kids finally figured out they're made for each other," Reed replies. "They're shacking up. True?"

"True!" Ruby confirms happily.

"Glad to hear it. I like it when good people find each other."

Ruby and I look at each other, like, "What's happening?" Reed isn't normally one to say nice things like that. Seems like he's on his best behavior in front of his wife.

"Oh, Ruby, speaking of big news," Reed says. "I've got another co-writing session for you, if you're interested." He tells Ruby the name of the artist who's interested in writing with her, and Ruby loses her shit. I'm not surprised. The solo artist requesting her is as big as they come.

"*Are you serious*?" Ruby screams, her palms on her cheeks. "Of course, I'm interested. I'm elated."

"They saw you on the show," Reed says. "Which you got hired for, by the way, because I didn't pull Cooper's song."

And the Reed we know is back.

Reed's tone dripping with snark, he adds, "Who knew things would work out so damned well for you? Hmm. Was it a defamation lawsuit you threatened to slap me with, or am I misremembering that detail, Ruby Tuesday?"

Ruby fakes a yawn. "I have no idea what you're talking about, Mr. Rivers. That stupid song has never bothered me in the slightest."

We all crack up at her comedic delivery—nobody more so than Reed himself.

"Aw, come on, Ruby Tuesday," Reed says. "Give credit

where it's due. Things have worked out exactly like I said. Even better. At least admit Cooper's song was a blessing in disguise."

Ruby stares at Reed, unyielding, her face a perfect portrait of snark, and soon, he gets the message: she's not willing to backtrack on a single thing she's ever said to him.

"Stubborn Ruby," Reed murmurs with a chuckle. "Okay, I'll check back with you again in a year or so, after you've had a massive hit song for a huge artist—a writing gig you wouldn't have gotten if not for *Sing Your Heart Out*, which you wouldn't have gotten if not for Cooper's song—and we'll try this again."

"That sounds like a plan, Reed," Ruby says, her tone sardonic. "Yes, let's reconvene on this matter when that happens, so I can give you the exact same response as this time."

Shaking his head at Ruby's adorableness, Reed says to me, "Is she stubborn like this with you, too?"

"Even more so. It's awesome."

Reed winks. "Thanks for the cocktails, bartender. I seriously couldn't be happier for you two kids."

"Thanks, Reed."

The Man with the Midas Touch, as he's known in the industry, slides his arm around his wife's shoulders. "We're going to mix and mingle now. Have fun, you two. I told Owen to start a group chat, letting us know all the numbers coming in on 'Spark' throughout the night." With that, he heads off with his wife, while Ruby and I head off in the other direction into another corner of the packed party, at which point the birthday boy converges on me, looking like he's having the time of his life.

"Hey, KC!" Savage shouts. "Are you two ready to be victimized by some *Birthday Truth or Dare*?"

The question sounds routine, but Savage is actually

speaking in code to me: asking if I'm ready to proceed with my plan to pop the question to Ruby now.

I inhale deeply to calm my suddenly jangly nerves. "Yeah, sure. I think so."

"You think so, or you're sure?"

I take another deep inhale. "I'm sure. Let's do it." I lean into Ruby's ear, since the party is loud, and Savage is standing next to me. "Savage wants to play *Birthday Truth or Dare*. Will you help me gather the band?"

"I'm on it!" she chirps.

We divvy up the names and head off in opposite directions. And a few minutes later, all the members of Fugitive Summer, plus Laila, are standing at the ready in front of Savage the Birthday Boy, per tradition, waiting to perform whatever stupid and/or infantile and/or humiliating birthday dare he's going to dole out. At least, that's what Ruby thinks we're doing. Titus and Kai, too. The rest of us are in on the plan.

"Okay, everyone," Savage says to the group, his dark eyes gleaming. "There's no Truth option tonight. Only Dare. I don't give a shit about whatever secrets you might be keeping from me or each other."

While everyone chuckles around me, I reflexively lay my palm over the ring box in my pocket. As Savage and I have discussed, he's going to dole out my dare last, because that's what I said I wanted. But now, suddenly, I'm wondering if I might pass out from anticipation while waiting through everyone else's turns.

"Kai," Savage says with confidence. "Your dare is to perform your choice of the following." Savage counts off the options on his fingers. "An original poem, song, or interpretative dance for the entire party's entertainment and/or amusement."

Kai doesn't hesitate. "Interpretative dance." His pick

wouldn't be a surprise to anyone who knows him. My big brother can't sing for shit, and he's way too drunk to compose a coherent sentence, let alone an actual poem.

"Excellent." After rubbing his palms together like Dr. Evil, Savage hops up onto Laila's piano bench and waves his arms at the noisy, distracted crowd. "Attention, please!" he booms, and after a moment, everyone turns to face him. "Can someone turn off the music for me?" He pauses till the loud music vanishes. "Thanks. As some of you know, my bandmates and I have a long, rich tradition of playing *Birthday Truth or Dare* on all of our birthdays. As tonight's birthday king/czar/god, I've selected Kai to kick things off, because he's so drunk, he probably won't be standing by the end of the game."

Everyone laughs.

"With that said, please, enjoy Kai Cook performing an interpretative dance for your amusement." As everyone cheers, Savage addresses his wife standing on the other side of her fancy piano. "Fitzy, would you do the honor of accompanying Kai's dance?"

Laila snorts. "With pleasure, my love."

Savage steps to the end of the piano bench so Laila can sit next to his feet and play her instrument, and everyone clears a large circle of space for the dance we're about to witness from Kai.

"Now, what should Kai *interpret* in his dance?" Savage asks the crowd, beckoning to them to throw out ideas. "Come on now, don't be shy. Shout out your ideas."

Several people call out their suggestions, but it's Reed's idea—"woodland creatures"—that makes Savage light up and point exuberantly at him. "Yes! Woodland creatures, it is! Laila?"

After stretching out her fingers dramatically, Laila shakes out her hair like she's starring in a shampoo commercial, and with those two bits of preparation out of the way, the maestro lays her talented fingers on her keys and launches into a joyful, uplifting sonata that inspires Kai to flit around the makeshift dance floor like a woodland creature, much to everyone's belly-laughing delight.

When Kai's dancing is done and Savage has ruled his dare officially satisfied, the birthday boy turns to his next victim, Titus, and offers him the same three choices. And like Kai before him, Ruby's brother chooses to entertain the party with another interpretative dance.

"What should Titus interpret for us?" Savage bellows to the crowd from his perch on Laila's piano bench.

Suggestions pour in. But this time, it's C-Bomb who offers the winning idea that gets Savage's juices flowing: "A man with explosive diarrhea who's desperately looking for a bathroom in a long hallway, but all the doors are locked."

As everyone guffaws at the suggestion, Laila launches into a classical piece on her gorgeous piano—a frantic, foreboding tune that perfectly fits Titus's over-the-top, frenzied dance movements. To put it mildly, Titus's performance is a huge hit. Even bigger than Kai's.

"Fitzy?" Savage asks his wife sitting at his feet. "Do you want to do a dare, baby?"

"Yes, but not here, my love. Dare me tonight, when we're all alone, and I promise I'll do *anything* you want, Birthday Boy."

The party whoops at that, and Savage plays up the moment for a long beat, making everyone laugh and cheer even louder. Finally, however, the birthday boy returns to the task at hand by selecting his next victim down the line: *Ruby*. The woman who's got no idea she's about to become my fiancée. My future wife. God willing, anyway.

"Ruby Duby," Savage says solemnly, leveling her with every ounce of his world-famous charisma. "Would you like to perform an original poem, song, or interpretative dance for the party?"

"A song."

The crowd cheers.

"That is, if Laila is okay with me borrowing her beautiful piano for a few minutes?"

"Please, do."

As the rowdy crowd titters and claps, Savage and Laila both vacate the piano bench, and Ruby gets herself situated. Like Laila before her, Ruby stretches out her fingers like a virtuoso preparing to play at Carnegie Hall, and a moment later, Ruby begins playing a dramatic, foreboding introduction that could easily be something from *Phantom of the Opera*.

The crowd is transfixed, holding their collective breath in anticipation of whatever lyrics Ruby's going to pair with this dramatic instrumentation. But when Ruby knows she's got everyone here in the palm of her hand, she pauses in her playing, ever so briefly, with her head slung back and her eyes closed, before lifting her head, hunching over, and launching into a two-chord, up-and-down banger that's straight out of a circus.

Everyone guffaws at the sudden shift in tone, and a moment later, Ruby sings, "Savage sang *Laila*, tried to sell it as la-la. We all knew the truth, though, our rockstar was a gone-ah. And now, a soon-to-be daddaaa!"

The crowd cheers.

"Ooooh, nothing makes me gladda, than a fuckboy breaking freeeeeeeee! And finding the soulmate that makes him so happyyyyyyyy!"

Again, the party cheers, while Savage and Laila snuggle and laugh their asses off.

Ruby continues singing, "Oh, Mister Savage, do you know the old adage? Happy wife, happy life. Happy man, happy band. We're all so happy for you, Adri-an. So happy, I can't make a joke about that. Now, to your future kiddo: Oh, the places you'll go! And wherever that is, always know, you'll have your Auntie Ruby in tow to love you like her oooooooown!" Ruby plays a chord and lets the sound reverberate for a beat through the room—long enough to signal the ending to her masterpiece and elicit hoots and applause. But just as the applause starts in earnest, Ruby belts out her final line with enthusiasm, drawing out every syllable for emphasis: "Happy birthday, Savage!" Finally, with her song officially completed, she throws back her head dramatically and plays a rumble on the piano, while the crowd applauds loudly and raucously.

As the crowd continues expressing its approval, Ruby gets up from the piano bench and takes a demure bow, before accepting a hug from both Savage and Laila.

But when our hosts are done loving up on my future wife, I pull her to me and gush about how awesome that was, almost forgetting . . .

"Okay, KC," Savage says. "You're up."

That.

Shit.

Fuck.

The moment I've been waiting for has finally arrived, and I'm equal parts ecstatic and terrified.

"Original poem, song, or interpretative dance?" Savage asks.

My heart feels lodged in my throat. "Poem."

Next to me, Ruby cheers, along with the rest of the party. And it's easy to surmise she, and everyone else, are excited to witness Savage's third option being selected for the first time in his silly game.

My heart stampeding, I climb to standing on the piano bench vacated by Ruby, and Laila, who knows what's coming next, helps me out by pulling her to a spot that's a few feet away from me in perfect view of everyone.

"Savage," I bellow. "Happy twenty-eighth birthday, my brother. In your honor, I will be performing an original poem, written by me—a dramatic and erotic poem that's going to take your breath away with its honesty, vulnerability, humanity, and pure filthiness."

"I'd expect nothing less from such a wordsmith," Savage says, making everyone chuckle.

I hang my head down and clasp my hands in front of my crotch for a long moment. And when I finally raise my head, I lock eyes with Ruby and announce, "Behold, this poem called . . . '*Spank.*'"

Predictably, Ruby loses it, along with our other bandmates and Laila, all of whom know the backstory behind the joke. Everyone else at the party is laughing, too. Just as hard as Ruby, actually. But, obviously, they're all busting up, simply because the title of my piece is a titillating word that's not at all what they expected, given my dramatic wind-up.

In a sudden fit of nerves, I brush my fingertips against my pocket, yet again ensuring I can feel the outline of the ring box there. When I do, I clear my throat and will the words to come out of my mouth, as I've practiced them, again and again. But, suddenly, I feel tongue-tied. Obviously, my excitement in this one-of-a-kind moment is getting the best of me.

"Well, don't keep us in suspense," Ruby calls out playfully. "I feel like I've waited half my life to hear this freaking poem!"

Everyone in the room bursts out laughing with her, but nobody more so than the handful of people with a full understanding of Ruby's joke.

"You can't rush a masterpiece," Savage says. "Take your time, KC."

He's right. You definitely can't rush a masterpiece. *Or a marriage proposal.*

"Spank, spank, spank!" C-Bomb begins chanting, and the mantra catches on like wildfire, until, soon, the whole place is energetically demanding my recitation like a mob going after a hunchback in a Disney movie.

"Okay, okay," I yell, waving my hands to quiet everyone down. "The bard is ready to perform now. I just needed a second to gather my thoughts."

"Quiet down, you animals!" Savage booms, and the crowd dutifully pipes down.

I return my gaze to Ruby's sparkling eyes, and she unknowingly calms me down. "'Spank,'" I manage to say. "A dramatic, erotic poem by Kendrick Cook." After brushing my fingertips against the ring box one last time for good measure, I finally begin in earnest, "There once was a man from the South Side."

A tidal wave of laughter and cheers slams into me—one that would surely drown out my voice, if I tried to continue speaking. Obviously, a classic limerick set-up for my "dramatic and erotic" masterpiece isn't what anyone expected.

I wait for the noise to die down before starting again. And when the volume in the party simmers down enough for me to hear myself think, I start reciting the poem from the top, once again, this time determined not to stop till I've reached the end:

> *"There once was a man from the South Side*
> *Who fell in love with a gem at first sight."*

Ruby makes an "aw" face that sends butterflies into my belly, and I flash her a broad, beaming smile in return. Emboldened, I continue:

. . .

"He couldn't have her, he thought
So he spanked his monkey raw
And bided his time till he got her."

The crowd roars its approval, apparently thinking my limerick called "Spank" is now over. But, baby, I'm just getting started.

"Once he got her, oh my
How the spanking intensified!
But not with his monkey
With her backside."

Ruby giggles and blushes. But there's no mistaking the fact that she's now looking at me with the same kind of energy she had at Reed's party, when I unexpectedly wailed her name instead of Shaynee's, during my performance of Red Card Riot's famous song. Again, I wait for the noise to die down a bit. And when it does, I forge ahead, determined to make Ruby my fiancée:

"Oh, how he spanked his ruby-red gem,
Till she screamed his name and came undone!
Till she turned his life upside down
Making him happier than a simple best friend
Until, lo, to a birthday bash he went
With a ring in his pocket and a prayer, heaven sent
That the question he'd devised to ask her tonight
Sweet Ruby would answer, "Yes, KC . . . I'll be . . . your bride."

. . .

Ruby gasps at the final words out of my mouth, while the crowd around her explodes like a nuclear bomb. But a moment later, as if on cue, everyone stops screaming, all at once, in order to give me the floor for what's obviously coming next.

I step off the piano bench slowly, feeling like every breath in this room is being held around me, the same as my own. With my heart thumping in my ears, and my skin tingling, I pull out the ring box from my pocket with a shaking hand and walk toward Ruby, who's now standing alone after being deserted by Laila.

When I reach my future wife, she's shaking and wide-eyed.

Slowly, I sink to my knee before her, eliciting titters and muted squeals all around me. And when I'm in the traditional pose, I flip open the ring box and raise the sparkling diamond Laila helped me pick out, making Ruby gasp and burst into tears.

"Ruby Margaret Connolly, I love you, baby. I always have, and I always will. I don't want to live a single day without you by my side, and I can't wait to call you my wife. Please, baby, will you *please* marry me?"

"Yes!" Ruby shrieks, throwing her palms to her rosy, tear-streaked cheeks.

With a huge smile, I rise, pull her to me, and kiss her deeply. And by the time I get the ring onto her correct finger, we're being mobbed by our bandmates and closest friends.

"That poem was amazing!" Ruby shrieks, as we hug and kiss gleefully. "Kendrick, oh my god, baby, this ring is insane! Gorgeous!"

"Laila helped me pick it out."

"She gave you excellent advice. I would have picked this out myself, if I'd been there." Squealing, Ruby throws her arms around my neck and peppers my face with kisses. "I loved your proposal so much!"

"Good, because I love you. So fucking much."

"And you thought you couldn't write a poem called 'Spank.' *Ha*!"

A few feet away, Savage yells to nobody in particular to crank up the music again. And God bless whoever's manning the tunes—they put on "Spark." Why not? It's about Ruby, after all. And this right here is quite the surprise happily-ever-after for the tortured poet who wrote those words with no idea of the joy they'd bring him one day soon.

"I love you so much, my love," Ruby yells above the music. "I can't wait to marry you."

"I love you, too, baby. And *not* like a sister, to be clear."

Ruby snorts. "God, I hope not."

We both laugh as music, love, and joy swirl around us.

"I can't wait to marry you," I shout, simply because it feels so good to say it. I take her hand and kiss the new ring on her finger. The symbol of the life we're going to build together. "I love you so much, Ruby Connolly! And, baby, I always will."

If you're interested in hearing the musical accompaniment to each dare and song during Savage's Birthday Party, go here - https://laurenrowebooks.com/pages/spark-chapter-36

EPILOGUE
RUBY

Five years later

"This is . . . unexpected," Kendrick says, as he looks around C-Bomb's bumping, family-friendly Fourth of July party on the shore of his lake house in Prairie Springs, Montana, of all places.

"I wouldn't have imagined Caleb's life turning out like this in a million guesses," I reply in a murmur.

"A billion," Kendrick replies.

"A trillion. Did Aubrey give him a lobotomy?"

"We stay here," our two-year-old son, Kyrie, who's standing next to Kendrick, murmurs, right before smashing his sweet little face into his daddy's muscular thigh.

"Yep, we'll stay here till you're ready," Kendrick coos to him. "We'll hang back and get a lay of the land, okay? We've got you, cutie. Take your time."

We've just stepped foot into Mr. and Mrs. Caleb and Aubrey Baumgarten's outdoor, lakeside summer bash that's mostly taking place behind C-Bomb's beautiful, rustic home on Lake Lucille. And as per our custom when introducing our shy, easily over-stimulated two-year-old to new places and people, we're letting him acclimate for a minute before entering the fray.

Frankly, I'm glad for the chance to get my bearings, too, Kyrie notwithstanding. This party is incredible. Right out of a movie. And genuinely shocking, because it's *C-Bomb's* happy, family party—a visual representation of where Caleb Baumgarten has unexpectedly landed in his life, thanks to his saint of a wife, Aubrey, and their beautiful preschooler, Raine.

Truly, I couldn't be happier for Caleb and the way he's taken control of his sobriety to become the man he is today. Aubrey helped him get here, no doubt about that. In fact, that incredible woman saved Caleb's life—literally, if you ask me. But still, nobody could do it for him. He had to want it. To fight for it. And to his credit, that's exactly what he did.

As I look around the loud, happy, chaotic party at all the familiar faces, it's plain to see nobody's noticed our arrival yet. If they had, we'd surely be mobbed by now, since half the people here are our closest friends. If not for the guest list, I doubt we would have made the trip—frankly because, no offense, but why would we fly to Prairie Springs, Montana for a lakeside Fourth of July party, when we could conveniently party at our friends' beachside house in our hometown? Especially with my morning sickness lately, traveling feels like a very big deal. Now that we're here, however, I can easily see the trip was well worth it.

Although, come to think of it, Savage and Laila are here, too, so I guess we would have needed another beachside house to party at in my hypothetical scenario. Indeed, it was Savage and Laila who invited us to fly with them on their private jet, along with their sassy, almost-five-year-old,

Valentina. So, it was a no-brainer for us to join them—even to Prairie Springs, Montana.

"Looks like we're the last ones to arrive," Kendrick murmurs, scanning all the familiar faces whooping it up in the summer sun.

"Sorry about that." We're late because of me. Because the little girl in my belly demanded an epic barf-o-rama in her honor, much like pagan gods might demand a nice smattering of goat blood, right before we were supposed to leave our room at the tiny hotel in town. After that, I had to lie down and nibble on crackers for a bit before I felt human enough to face the sunshine, let alone a loud party filled with all my favorite people.

"No need to apologize for cooking our baby, baby. You know that."

Kyrie gasps and points. "Look!" he shouts. "My fwends!"

We follow his gesture and discover three kids Kyrie knows and loves, hunkered down and playing with sand toys together right at the edge of the lake: Valentina, who dotes on our boy like a big sister; three-year-old, Winston "Wi-Fi" Fishberger, Fish and Ally's sweet little cutie, and Rocco Beretta, Colin and Amy's four-year-old Mack truck of a boy.

"See? I told you there'd be lots of friends and fun stuff for you to do here, buddy," Kendrick says. "Looks like they're having lots and lots of fun."

"And there are lots of other new friends around here for you to meet, too," I add. Not that Kyrie cares about that. Our son doesn't love meeting new people, for some reason. He does fine, once he's gotten comfortable. Once he's acclimated. But he's the kid who sits to the side at birthday parties, feeling shy, while everyone else screams out their demands to the balloon animal clown without hesitation. The kid who's too scared to ask if he can have a piece of candy from the bowl after he sat through his entire haircut crying his eyes out because the lady looked him in the eyes.

"Can I play with dem?" Kyrie asks, his cherubic face upturned excitedly toward his daddy and his blue eyes wide with excitement.

"Absolutely."

"As long as you're wearing sunscreen," I quickly add.

"I already slathered him liked a greased pig at the hotel," Kendrick says.

"Okay, but you still need to wait, Ky. I want you to wear a hat, too. It's bright out here." As Kyrie dances from foot to foot with eagerness and impatience—that's new—I fish around in the large bag on my shoulder for his bright blue bucket hat with a dinosaur on it—the one that matches our son's gorgeous blue eyes. Lucky boy, Kyrie inherited Kendrick's everything, basically, in the DNA lottery. In fact, the second that kid popped out of me and the nurse laid him onto my sobbing chest, I could instantly surmise the person Kendrick and I had created from scratch together, supposedly, bore zero resemblance to me. On the contrary, even from minute one, I knew our baby was Kendrick's cookie cutter. His mini-me. Which is why, in my hospital room a minute later, I suggested we carry on the Cook family tradition of giving boys a name that starts with K, rather than the one we'd originally picked out.

Thankfully, Kendrick loved the name idea. Apparently, there's some famous basketball player named Kyrie. Who knew? Not me. I'd only heard the name in connection with a Canadian singer-songwriter. But, whatever, Kendrick was sold on it, and so was I, so our baby officially became Kyrie Adrian Cook.

I find the hat and place it onto Kyrie's blonde head. His hair is platinum blonde for now, just like Kendrick's was at his age. "Now, listen," I say to my son, who's looking up at me like

I walk on water. "You're not allowed to take that hat off, no matter what, okay?"

"Okay, Mommy. I go now?"

"Not yet. You're also not allowed to step a single toe into that water without Mommy or Daddy being there to say yes and hold your hand, okay? Not even a toe, Ky."

"But I can put in dis *lake shoe*?" Kyrie asks innocently. He lifts up one of his tiny feet, clad in a bright green rubber shoe, and Kendrick and I both burst out laughing at his adorableness.

Thank goodness for those "lake shoes," or who knows how today might have gone for all of us. Also, for the "beach shoes" that came before them to lead the way—the ones that had to be replaced right before we made this trip. If we hadn't figured out Kyrie's sensory tantrums and shrieks of "no!" and "icky!," every time we went to the beach at Savage and Laila's house were caused by our boy freaking out over the sensation of sand between his tiny toes, we might not have made this trip today out of sheer embarrassment.

All's well that ends well, though. Once we figured it all out and got our sensory king his first pair of "beach shoes" for our next day with Uncle Savage, Auntie Laila, and Valentina, the kid spent half the day blissfully making sandcastles with his honorary big sister, while the rest of us sat nearby in beach chairs, chatting happily. Apparently, it's only Kyrie's toes and soles that react badly to sand. The rest of his body parts don't mind getting a granular massage. In fact, after that first successful visit with those "beach shoes" on his feet, Kyrie ended the happy, exhausting day covered in sand—everywhere except his mercifully protected feet.

"No, buddy," Kendrick explains, laughing at our son's misunderstanding. "You can't put anything into the lake at all. Not even your lake shoes. But don't worry, Mommy and I will be sitting right there, right next to you with all our friends, so if you want to go into the lake, one of us will be there to take you."

"That would be Daddy," I murmur. "He'll be the one to take you."

Kendrick laughs. "It would be my pleasure."

"Good, because you're definitely taking him."

Laughing, Kendrick gestures to a large group sitting in beach chairs next to where the boys and Valentina are blissfully playing in the sand: Savage and Laila, Fish and Ally, Colin and Amy, Violet and Dax, Miranda and whoever she's currently dating. They never last, so we don't bother getting to know them too well. And on and on.

I scan and locate Kai and Titus nearby, too, talking in another group that includes Aloha Carmichael and her adorable husband, Zander.

Kendrick nudges my arm. "Aloha's here."

"I just noticed that. I didn't know she was coming."

Kendrick grins. "Maybe you two will get some inspiration while you're here for your next big hit. A country tune called 'Under the Big Montana Sky,' perhaps?"

I laugh—partly because writing a country song isn't on the menu for me, for one thing. Especially not for a popstar like Aloha Carmichael. But mostly because I can't believe this is my life. Being married to the love of my life and having the cutest little boy with him, with a baby girl on the way, is enough good fortune for ten lifetimes. But professionally speaking, I've also hit the jackpot these past five years; in fact, I've never felt happier or more fulfilled in my career.

Fugitive Summer is still going as strong as ever, though our touring schedule has morphed and slowed down quite a bit since our early days. Once Valentina, and then Kyrie, came along, we all put the kids first. We're a family, after all. And we all love those two like our own.

In addition to all the fun stuff I still get to do with Fugitive Summer, however, my songwriting career has really taken off over the past few years. Especially since Aloha invited me to write with her about four years ago. It happened right after Kendrick and I got back from our honeymoon, and I practically crapped my pants when her personal text landed on my phone. The woman's been my idol since middle school, since the days when I'd watch her Disney show, *It's Aloha!*, so, honestly, her invitation to write with her felt even bigger to me than my own band's Grammy win.

Thankfully, the song I wound up creating with Aloha became one of her biggest hits, ever. Almost as big as "Pretty Girl," which, let's face it, is impossible to beat. It's a once-in-a-generation song. And after that, Aloha and I continued writing together several more times, always to fantastic success—and even better, we became close friends along the way.

Sure, I would have probably become friends with Aloha regardless, since she's close friends with all my close friends. But I think, if it hadn't been for our writing sessions together, I would have always been "Laila's close friend, Ruby" to her. Rather than "*my* close friend, Ruby," as I've become.

"Okay, okay, you can go now," Kendrick says, laughing, after Kyrie begs to be let loose. And off our boy goes, straight to his favorite three people, where he practically dives onto the sand next to them, gleefully shrieking his hellos.

"That's new," I say excitedly. "I've never seen him run away so confidently like that."

"Or so quickly, after arriving in a new place."

"Progress."

"I'd say so."

We share a smile. Thankfully, Kendrick's parenting style is the same as mine. We both want Kyrie to learn to be independent, of course. We both want him to stretch himself, whenever he can. But we also both agree the kid is *two*. Which means we're going to envelop him in safety and soft landings, every which way we can.

"KC!" C-Bomb booms from his shallow spot in the lake, where his tiny daughter is swimming circles around him, and a whole bunch of people turn their heads and notice us standing on the fringes of the party. Apparently, Kyrie's mad dash to his friends attracted attention. And since Kyrie looks exactly like a miniature version of his daddy, that made everyone start looking around for the kid's larger, much beloved doppelganger.

"C-Bomb, hey!" Kendrick replies, waving to our host.

"Hi, Caleb!" I join in. "This is quite the party! Wow!"

Kendrick takes my hand, and we stride toward the shore, as C-Bomb scoops up his little waterlogged daughter and begins trudging out of the lake, accompanied by Reed, his trajectory suggesting he's planning to meet us at our friend group.

As I walk with Kendrick, I can't help peeking at Reed. I already knew C-Bomb is sporting eye-popping tattoos and muscles. So, his physique in a bathing suit wasn't a surprise to me. But I don't get to see the Big Boss in a bathing suit very often. In fact, I'm not sure I've ever seen him this way. And I must admit, it's now clear to me why Georgina puts up with at least some of Reed's shit. He's a striking figure over there. A truly gorgeous man. Plus, he keeps getting nicer and nicer with each passing year of his marriage. At this rate, he might even be one-tenth as nice as my husband as early as next year.

We reach our friend group and receive exuberant hugs and greetings from everyone, with all of them commenting excitedly about my baby bump, how much Kyrie's grown, and how fit and happy Kendrick looks, and on and on. All the usual stuff, when it's been too long since we've all gotten together, all at once. And of course, we return all the exuberant compliments and good vibes.

C-Bomb and Reed reach the group, sans the former's little daughter, Raine. Apparently, C-Bomb dropped her off to play in the sand with the other kids, including Kyrie, before heading to our group to chat.

After a moment, we're joined by Aubrey and Georgina, and exuberant conversation ensues, punctuated by frequent belly laughter and boisterous storytelling.

Another group comes over to mingle, one that includes Miranda and Aloha, and we launch into yet another round of happy hellos, conversation, and catching up.

Someone asks Caleb his plans for his beautiful lake house. Apparently, he's trying to decide if he should expand his existing home or perhaps buy the place next door and expand his empire that way. As Caleb discusses the two possibilities, Reed sidles up to me with a grin on his face and nudges my shoulder.

"Hey, Ruby Duby. How's it going? It's great to see you and the fam looking so well." He already greeted me, briefly, a moment ago, when everyone else did. But this is our first chance to chat, one-on-one.

"You, too."

"Congrats on that." He points to my belly.

I pat my baby bump. "Thanks. This one makes me barf up a lung at least twice a day, but other than that, I couldn't be happier."

Reed's gaze lingers on my belly a beat too long. And that's when I remember something Miranda recently told me about him and Georgina.

Nobody talks about it to Reed's face, simply because it feels too awkward to do that with someone who's not prone to opening up about his personal life and feelings, to put it mildly—but we all know, thanks to the grapevine, that Mr. and Mrs. Rivers have been trying for a baby for a few years now. Indeed, from what Miranda told me, Reed and Georgina have recently decided to go the IVF route.

God willing, that will do the trick for them, because I know Georgina, especially, has baby fever. Of course, if that doesn't work, I'm sure Reed will do whatever it takes to give his wife the baby she's yearning for. That's a perk of having money in situations such as these: a person can explore every conceivable option. But even if they get where they want to go in the end, I want the smoothest, easiest road for them both, because, truthfully, I like them so much, I consider them family, whether they realize it or not. It's hard to believe I feel that way about Reed sometimes, given how I used to join in on calling him "The Prick" at every turn. Still do, sometimes. Just for yucks. But I don't think Reed is a prick anymore, but, rather, a softie who's covered himself in about a hundred layers of armor.

"So, are you finally ready to do it now?" Reed asks with a smirk.

I look at him funny. "Do what?"

"Admit me not pulling Cooper's song—"

"This again?"

"—was a blessing in disguise."

"Give it a rest, Reed."

"Admit it. That song was the best thing that's ever happened to you."

I burst out laughing, and Reed joins me. In fact, he laughs so damned hard, he gets tears in his eyes to match mine.

I haven't thought about Cooper Constantino in years. I mean, yes, whenever his song comes on while I'm at the grocery store or in a bank or whatever, he pops into my mind, briefly. That can't be helped. But it's like remembering a movie or a silly story someone once told me. A memory that's not even my own. That's how removed I feel from Cooper's song, at this point; how removed I feel from the woman who wailed and screamed about being called Ruby Tuesday in a pop-punk song that would soon become known as a one-hit wonder, when all APM's next offerings fell flat and quickly disappeared. Looking back, I truly can't believe I let the whole fiasco bother me in the slightest.

"What's so funny?" Kendrick asks, coming to a stop next to me.

"Once again, Reed is insisting I admit Cooper's song is the best thing that's ever happened to me. A blessing in disguise."

To my surprise, Kendrick doesn't laugh like Reed and I did a moment ago. On the contrary, my husband simply shrugs and says, "I'd say so. Fuck yeah, it is."

I'm shocked. He said that like it was the most obvious thing in the world.

But before either Reed or I can react to Kendrick's nonchalance, he adds, "Frankly, I thank Cooper Constantino every day of my life for calling me the brother she wanted to fuck. God knows where I'd be today if he hadn't gotten the ball rolling for us like that."

For *us*.

He means for him and me.

As in, our marriage.

Our life together.

I gasp and instinctively clutch my baby bump, having an epiphany.

I've never looked at things that way. I've always thought about Reed's "blessing in disguise" comment in terms of my professional aspirations and opportunities. Me getting onto *Sing Your Heart Out*, for example. Which then propelled sales of our next single and put me in mind when a whole bunch of artists sat down to write their next hit song.

But Kendrick's absolutely right. If it wasn't for Cooper's song, and specifically, the lyrics about him forcing some long-overdue honesty between us, would I be standing here now with Kendrick Cook as my husband and Kyrie Cook happily making mud pies in the sand with that gaggle of little ones over there? Would Kendrick's daughter be growing inside me—her name as yet unknown—making me lose the contents of my stomach every single day for a very worthy cause?

It's impossible to know for sure what might have happened if Cooper's lyrics hadn't come along to force the issue, but I'm guessing without his revelations forcefully pushing us together and making me do the unthinkable— kissing Kendrick at his birthday party five years ago—none of the other dominoes likely would have fallen thereafter.

When I emerge from my spiraling thoughts, I discover Reed leveling me with dark, amused eyes. "So?" he asks. "Got anything to say to me, now that Kendrick's clearly on my side?"

"You're relentless, Reed."

"You have no idea, Ruby."

We share a smile.

"You know what?" I say. "Yeah, I do have something to say to you."

"Oh boy," he says, gearing up for whatever tongue-lashing he thinks is coming.

"Thank you, Reed. You were right. You not pulling that song was the best thing that's ever happened in my life, and I couldn't be more grateful for that decision of yours, even though you did it to benefit you and your greed, and nothing else, and you really didn't give two shits about me at the time. Thank you, Reed. I'm eternally grateful."

He bursts out laughing. "That was you being grateful?"

"Take what I'm willing to give you. I assure you, this moment won't come around again."

Reed belly laughs, and I giggle with him. It feels like a huge achievement, making him laugh hard like this. It's hard to make him smile, let alone guffaw. And I'm savoring the moment.

"Thank you for finally acknowledging my brilliance," Reed says, wiping his eyes.

"It's only right." I take Kendrick's hand and lean my cheek against his broad shoulder. "Credit where credit is due, right?"

Despite my snarkiness, Reed looks genuinely touched as he gazes at Kendrick and me.

"I'm really happy things have worked out so well for you two," he says softly. "I don't like a whole lot of people. But I've always liked you both."

Kendrick and I chuckle.

"Thanks, Reed," Kendrick says. "I must admit, you've grown on me."

"Enough to stop calling me The Prick?"

Kendrick gasps.

"You thought I didn't know you all call me that?" Reed says, his eyebrow arched. "Kids, I know *everything*. Never, ever forget that."

We all laugh together this time, although I'm not entirely sure if Reed is kidding.

"For what it's worth, we haven't called you that in years," Kendrick says.

"I have. Maybe about a month ago," I say. "But before then, it'd been a really long time."

Reed clutches his heart. "I'm so touched. I guess Georgina's still working her magic on me, huh?"

"She's definitely had a good influence on you," I agree.

"Speaking of my wife," Reed says, looking around. "Where'd she go?"

I point over his broad shoulder. "She's over there."

Reed turns and follows the trajectory of my gesture to where Georgina is chatting with a trio of women: Violet, Miranda, and Laila. "Ah. Thanks, Ruby Duby."

With a wink, Reed leaves. And when I'm alone with my husband, I pull him into a hug and peck his lips.

"I never thought about Cooper's song, in terms of it leading to you and me. To our life together. But it kind of did."

"Not kind of. It's a direct line. I should probably send that dude a car or something to thank him."

"Okay, Mr. Drunk with Happiness, let's not get too crazy here. He got paid plenty well for his stupid song. He doesn't need anything else from us."

Kendrick cracks up and nuzzles my nose. "I'm really glad we decided to come here. I'm already having a blast."

"Me, too." I look over at Kyrie in the sand a few yards away, where he's hard at work on a sandcastle with Valentina. "My gosh, look at him. He's a happy, busy little bee."

"He's in the zone in record speed." Kendrick returns to me and grins. "I don't only thank Cooper every day for giving me this life with you, by the way. I thank my lucky stars, too. The universe. God. My father in heaven. And, yes, Reed, for putting out that song, so I could hear it and start mustering the courage to go after what I'd wanted since age sixteen." He smiles. "Anyone and everyone with even the slightest role in making this dream-come-true life with you possible for me, I owe them everything."

"Aw, baby." My eyes prick with tears. My husband says swoonworthy stuff all the time. He's a true romantic by nature, unlike me. But that little speech was particularly romantic and moving. In fact, it hit me like an arrow from Cupid, shot straight into my heart. "You only have yourself to thank, baby," I reply, touching the scruff on his cheek. "*You* made this possible, Kendrick, because you're the beautiful person you are." I smirk. "Also, because you bribed my building manager."

Kendrick hoots with laughter at that, and I giggle along

with him. But after a bit, my laughter subsides and emotion overtakes me.

"Seriously, though, love. You're the reason we're here today. Not me. And definitely not Cooper or Reed. We're here because you always kept that spark lit inside you, no matter what. Because you could envision this happily ever after for us, all along. Thank you for always being able to see this as our future. For never, ever giving up on me. On us."

"How could I give up on you? You're my all-time favorite person. My gem."

We share a goofy smile. He's referencing a line from "Spark." But it's as true today, for both of us, as it was when Kendrick wrote the words in that frenzied, urgent hand all those years ago in a hotel room, while his brother fucked a groupie against their shared wall.

I think that's been the most important ingredient to our incredible marriage, actually: the fact that we've always been best friends first—each other's all-time favorite person. Oh, and we *also* love to fuck each other's brains out.

"I love you so much," I whisper.

"I love you, too. So, so much." Kendrick presses his forehead to mine, one palm placed on my cheek and the other resting on my baby bump. "And I always will."

THE END

If you want to watch and/or read bonus material from *Spark* and the world of River Records, check out the River Records tab of Lauren's website (www.LaurenRoweBooks.com).

. . .

To read Savage and Laila's spicy, swoony, enemies-to-lovers romance, check out *The Hate Love Duet*, a bundle containing their two individual books, featuring loads of banter, spice, swoon, and original music.

To read about Caleb "C-Bomb" Baumgarten and his soul-mate, Aubrey Capshaw, the woman who made love, sobriety, fatherhood, and Caleb's annual Fourth of July party in the small town of Prairie Springs, Montana possible, check out **Finding Home**.

To read the spicy, addicting story of the man, the myth, the legend, Reed Rivers, and the aspiring journalist, Georgina Ricci, who brought him to his alpha knees, check out their three books, all bundled together into one as *The Reed Rivers Trilogy*.

And finally, you can find information about Fish's and Colin's love stories, *Smitten* and *Swoon*, respectively, along with a suggested reading order and tons of bonus material, on Lauren's website.

Happy reading!

There's no correct order for any of these books. Read whichever one is calling to you first!

And thank you for reading and reviewing *Spark*!

When aspiring singer-songwriter, Alessandra, meets Fish, the funny, adorable bass player of 22 Goats, sparks fly between the awkward pair. Fish tells Alessandra he's a "Goat called Fish who's hung like a bull. But not really. I'm actually really average." And Alessandra tells Fish, "There's nothing like a girl's first love." Alessandra thinks she's talking about a song when she makes her comment to Fish— the first song she'd ever heard by 22 Goats, in fact. As she'll later find out, though, her "first love" was actually Fish. The Goat called Fish who, after that night, vowed to do anything to win her heart. SMITTEN is a standalone romance in the world of River Records.

Swoon

When Colin Beretta, the drummer of 22 Goats, is a groomsman at the wedding of his childhood best friend, Logan, he discovers Logan's kid sister, Amy, is all grown up. Colin tries to resist his attraction to Amy, but after a drunken kiss at the wedding reception, that's easier said than done. Swoon is a standalone romance in the world of River Records.

Finding Home

When the "bad boy" drummer of Red Card Riot is forced to become a father to his toddler after tragedy strikes, he hires his young daughter's only remaining lifeline, Aubrey, as his live-in nanny and sobriety coach in her small town. He's determined not to give in to his white-hot attraction to Aubrey. There's only a month before the custody hearing that will decide his fate as a father, and he needs Aubrey to testify on his behalf. Well, you know what they say about best laid plans, right? FINDING HOME is a standalone romance in the world of River Records.

The Josh & Kat Trilogy

It's a war of wills between stubborn and sexy Josh Faraday and Kat Morgan. A fight to the bed. Arrogant, wealthy playboy Josh is used to getting what he wants. And what he wants is Kat Morgan. The three books of the trilogy have been bundled, or you can read the individual books in order:

Infatuation

Revelation

Consummation

The Club Trilogy

When wealthy playboy Jonas Faraday receives an anonymous note from Sarah Cruz, a law student working part-time processing online applications for an exclusive club, he becomes obsessed with hunting her down and giving her the satisfaction she claims has always eluded her. The books of the trilogy have been bundled, or you can read the individual books in order:

The Club: Obsession

The Club: Reclamation

The Club: Redemption

The fourth book, *The Club: Culmination (A Full-Length Epilogue Novel)*, is a full-length epilogue with incredible heart-stopping twists and turns and feels. Read the fourth book after finishing The Club Trilogy or, if you prefer, after reading The Josh and Kat Trilogy, since this book includes glimpses of Josh and Kat's future, too.

Hacker in Love

When world-class hacker Peter "Henn" Hennessey meets Hannah Milliken, he moves heaven and earth, including doing some questionable things, to win his dream girl over. *Hacker in Love* is a steamy, funny, heart-pounding, *standalone* contemporary romance with feels, laughs, spice, and swoons that crosses over into the worlds of River Records, the Morgan Brothers, The Club, and Josh and Kat.

Lauren's Standalone Romantic Comedies: "Meet Me At Captain's" series

Who's Your Daddy?

When thirty-year-old patent attorney, Maximillian Vaughn, meets a sassy, charismatic older woman in a bar, he invites her back to his place for one night of no-strings fun. It's all Max can offer, given his busy career; and luckily, it's all Marnie wants, too. But when Marnie discovers a shocking connection between her and Max, things take a hilarious and unexpected turn that changes both of their lives forever.

Textual Relations

When Grayson McKnight unknowingly gets a fake number from a woman in a bar, he winds up embroiled in a sexy text exchange with the actual owner of the number—a confident, sensual older woman who knows exactly who she is . . . and what she wants.

My Neighbor's Secret

When Charlotte gets into her new dilapidated condo to start fixing it up for resale, she finds out the infuriating stranger who's thoroughly messed up her life is her new next-door neighbor. Also, that he's got a big secret.

Misadventures Standalones (unrelated standalones not within the above universe):

- *Misadventures on the Night Shift* –A hotel night shift clerk encounters her teenage fantasy: rock star Lucas Ford. And combustion ensues.

- *Misadventures of a College Girl*—A spunky, virginal theater major meets a cocky football player at her first college party . . . and absolutely nothing goes according to plan for either of them.

- *Misadventures on the Rebound*—A spunky woman on the rebound meets a hot, mysterious stranger in a bar on her way to her five-year high school reunion in Las Vegas and what follows is a misadventure neither of them ever imagined.

The Secret Note: A Spicy Standalone Novella with HEA

He's a hot Aussie. I'm a girl who isn't shy about getting what she wants. The problem? Ben is my little brother's best friend. An exchange student who's heading back Down Under any day now. But I can't help myself. He's too hot to resist.

Lauren's Dark Comedy/Psych Thriller Standalone

Countdown to Killing Kurtis

A young woman with big dreams and skeletons in her closet decides her porno-king husband must die in exactly a year. This is not a traditional romance, but it will most definitely keep you turning the pages and saying "WTF?" If you're looking for something a bit outside the box, with twists and turns, suspense, and dark humor, this is the book for you.

PLAYLIST FOR SPARK

"Hate Sex High" — Fugitive Summer

"Don't Call Me"— Alexa Play Music

"Savage Love"— Laila Fitzgerald (performed in duet with Adrian Savage here)

"Spark"— Fugitive Summer

All songs written and created by Lauren Rowe. Copyright Lauren Rowe 2025.

A NOTE FROM LAUREN ROWE ABOUT THE MUSIC IN *SPARK*:

None of the bands/artists in *Spark* actually exist in the real world. There's no existing band out there, for instance, that pretended to be Fugitive Summer or APM, for the purposes of this story. Similarly, there's no existing songs that were plucked from reality to use in this book. On the contrary, all the talented musicians and vocalists featured in the music for *Spark* were hand-picked, hired, and assembled by me, specifically to give life to the music and characters in my head. As I've done with other books in the River Records universe, I worked hard to bring the music to life for you with the help of some very talented people, with the hope that the music would add to your reading pleasure and enjoyment.

You might have noticed there's no song for "Spark." We'll all have to use our imaginations for that. I'm so sorry. I tried. I really did. But in the end, I couldn't come up with something that was good enough. Something that truly sounded like a smash hit song by Fugitive Summer. And so, since I'm a romance author and not really a band of 20-something hit makers, I decided to leave it alone and write this note to you, instead. I figured no song is better than a crappy one in this context.

If the music that did make it into this book isn't to your liking, or not what you pictured or expected, I hope it won't diminish your enjoyment of the story. It's meant to be a bonus for you: a little cherry on top of a fun, romantic sundae. But the sundae is, and always will be, the books themselves. Also, if you're kindly hoping to find the musicians who helped me create the music for *Spark*, so you can listen to some of their other work in the real world, they've all requested to be presented with pseudonyms for this project. Otherwise, I promise I'd be screaming their names and social media handles from the highest rooftops.

Thank you so much for reading *Spark* and any of my other books. I'm eternally grateful to you! If you enjoyed the book, I'd be grateful for a review. Thank you again!

BOOKS BY LAUREN ROWE

Look for Lauren's Football and Feels series coming from Kensington Publishing in 2026, beginning with *Chasing the Ring*. Until then, check out the rest of Lauren's catalog in any order:

The Morgan Brothers

Read these standalones in any order, but chronological reading order is below:

Hero

The love story of heroic firefighter, Colby Morgan and single mom/widow, Lydia Decker. When catastrophe strikes Colby on the job, will his physical therapist Lydia save him . . . or will he save her?

Captain

The insta-love-to-enemies-to-scorching-hot-lovers romance of tattooed, pierced sex god, Ryan Morgan, and the exciting woman he'd search the world over to find again . . . and then, move heaven and earth to claim.

Ball Peen Hammer

A steamy, hilarious, friends-to-lovers romantic comedy road-trip romp about cocky- as-hell male stripper with a heart of gold, Keane Morgan, and the sassy, smart young documentarian who shows him "quiet moments of magic" while unexpectedly bringing him to his knees.

Mister Bodyguard

The Morgans' beloved honorary brother, Zander Shaw, meets his match in the feisty pop star, Aloha, he's been assigned to protect on tour.

ROCKSTAR

When the youngest Morgan brother, Dax Morgan, meets a mysterious woman who rocks his world, he must decide if pursuing her is worth risking it all. Be sure to check out Dax's original songs from ROCKSTAR, written and produced by Lauren at the River Records tab at www.LaurenRoweBooks.com.

The Reed Rivers Trilogy

Reed Rivers meets his match in the most unlikely of women—aspiring journalist and spitfire, Georgina Ricci. She's much younger than the women Reed normally pursues, but he can't resist her fiery personality, ambition, and drop-dead gorgeous looks. But in this game of cat and mouse, who's chasing whom? The books have been bundled together or read the individual books in order:

Bad Liar

Beautiful Liar

Beloved Liar

Also, be sure to check out the spoiler-free bonus content at the River Records tab of Lauren's website: www.LaurenRoweBooks.com

The Hate Love Duet

Rockstar Savage of Fugitive Summer and popstar Laila Fitzgerald are stuck together on tour. She hates his guts. And he *really* likes it. The two books of this duet have been bundled together, or read the individual books in order:

Falling Out of Hate with You

Falling Into Love with You

Spark

When Ruby drunkenly kisses her longtime best friend and bandmate from Fugitive Summer, Kendrick, in order to piss off her ex, the forbidden spark Kendrick's been working hard to snuff out for over a decade bursts into a raging pyre. Kendrick can't stop obsessing about The Kiss That Changed Everything and yearning for another one . . . and hopefully, far more than that. SPARK is a standalone romance in the world of River Records.

Smitten

ABOUT THE AUTHOR

Lauren Rowe writes spicy, swoony, open-door romances that will make you laugh out loud, fan yourself, and, most importantly, feel something, as her characters barrel ahead toward their happily-ever-after.

Lauren lives in San Diego, California with her family and dogs, where she loves hanging out with her family and besties, cooking, walking her dogs, working out, singing with her wedding band, and thinking up imaginary people who always feel real to her, like family, by the time she writes "The End," once again.

To check out some spoiler-free bonus material from the world of Fugitive Summer and River Records, check out the River Records tab at Lauren's website: www.LaurenRowe-Books.com.